TRANSFORMERS
ROBOTS IN DISGUISE
A NEW MISSION

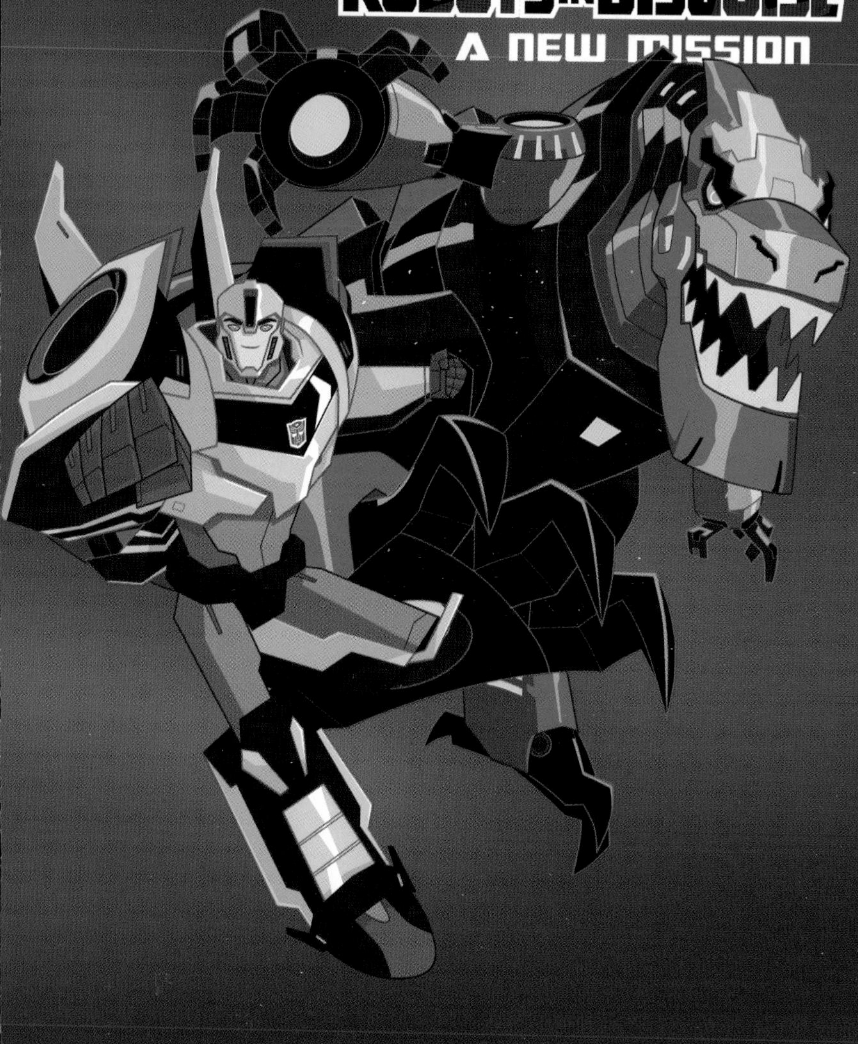

For international rights, please contact
licensing@idwpublishing.com

Special thanks to Mikiel Houser, Ed Lane, and
Michael Kelly for their invaluable assistance.

ISBN: 978-1-63140-501-3
19 18 17 16   1 2 3 4

www.IDWPUBLISHING.com

IDW® Licensed By:

Ted Adams, CEO & Publisher
Greg Goldstein, President & COO
Robbie Robbins, EVP/Sr. Graphic Artist
Chris Ryall, Chief Creative Officer/Editor-in-Chief
Matthew Ruzicka, CPA, Chief Financial Officer
Dirk Wood, VP of Marketing
Lorelei Bunjes, VP of Digital Services
Jeff Webber, VP of Licensing, Digital and Subsidiary Rights
Jerry Bennington, VP of New Product Development

WRITTEN BY
ADAM BEECHEN & DUANE CAPIZZI

ADAPTATION BY
JUSTIN EISINGER

EDITS BY
ALONZO SIMON

PUBLISHED BY
TED ADAMS

LETTERING AND DESIGN BY
GILBERTO LAZCANO

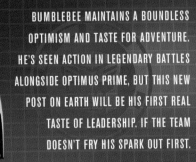

BUMBLEBEE MAINTAINS A BOUNDLESS OPTIMISM AND TASTE FOR ADVENTURE. HE'S SEEN ACTION IN LEGENDARY BATTLES ALONGSIDE OPTIMUS PRIME, BUT THIS NEW POST ON EARTH WILL BE HIS FIRST REAL TASTE OF LEADERSHIP. IF THE TEAM DOESN'T FRY HIS SPARK OUT FIRST.

BUMBLEBEE

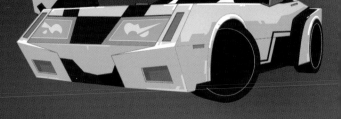

FIXIT IS EQUAL PARTS MECHANIC/I.T./MASCOT, AND ARCHIVIST OF THE "MOST WANTED" DOSSIERS—HE WAS THE PILOT OF THE CYBERTRONIAN PRISON SHIP, THE *ALCHEMOR*, THAT CRASH LANDED ON EARTH, AND IS THUS INTIMATE WITH ITS FORMER INHABITANTS, THEIR CRIMES AND ATTRIBUTES. HE'S A VERITABLE "SWISS ARMY KNIFE" OF MECHANIC'S TOOLS.

FIXIT

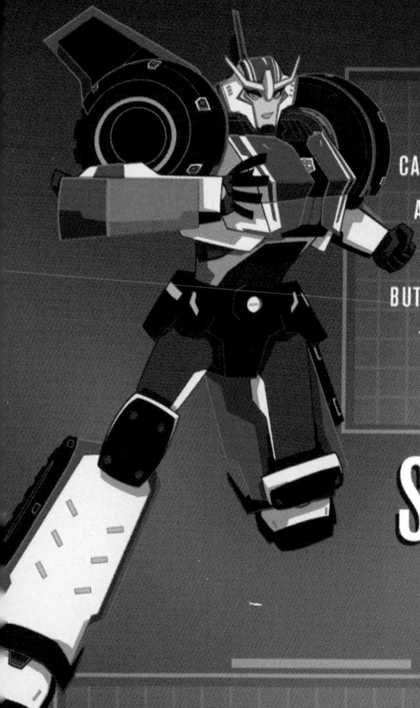

STRONGARM IS STAUNCHLY DEDICATED TO HER CAREER IN LAW ENFORCEMENT AND CAN'T IMAGINE A WORLD WHERE EVERYONE DOESN'T FOLLOW THE "LETTER" OF THE LAW (I.E., THE RULES). BUT TO STAY ON 'BEE'S SUPREME TEAM SHE'LL HAVE TO LEARN TO BEND A LITTLE MORE BECAUSE NOT EVERYTHING IS SO EASY AND CUT-AND-DRY.

STRONGARM

A STREET-SMART, FAST-THINKING REBELLIOUS 'BOT, SIDESWIPE IS A LONER—BUT WHEN PUSH COMES TO SHOVE, HE HEEDS THE CALL TO ACTION. SIDESWIPE IS COOL UNDER PRESSURE AND HE'S QUICK WITH HIS WORDS AND HANDS. HE'S ALL ABOUT GETTING THE DROP ON HIS OPPONENT—AND LOOKING COOL DOING IT.

SIDESWIPE

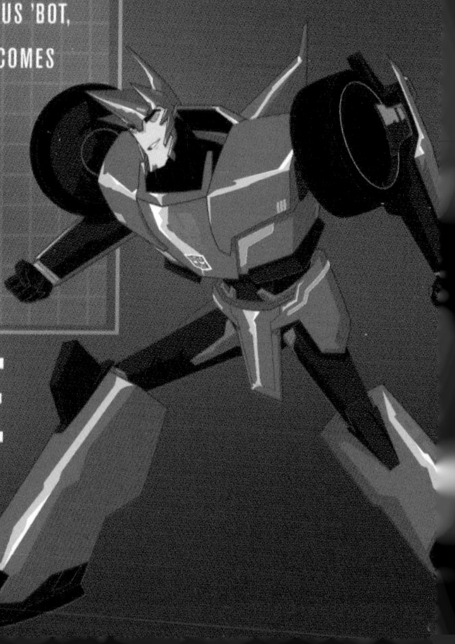

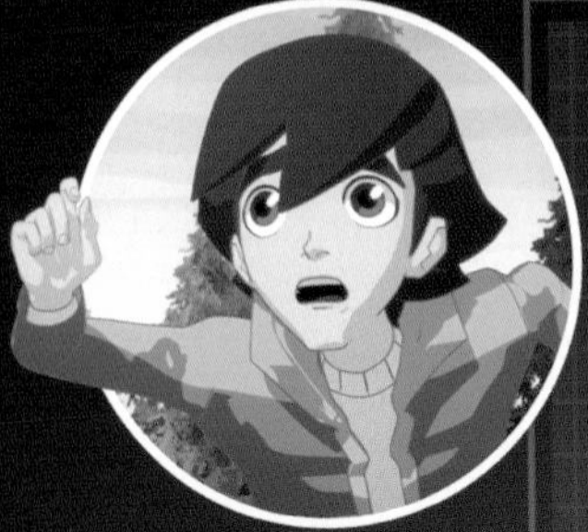

RUSSELL CLAY IS DENNY'S SON, AND HE'S NOT ALWAYS WILD ABOUT HANGING OUT WITH HIS ECCENTRIC DAD ON HIS JUNKYARD LOT. BUT WHILE HANGING WITH DAD BRINGS ON A FEW AWKWARD GROANS, HE'S ABOUT TO DISCOVER A NEW CALLING WHEN TEAM 'BEE GETS TO TOWN.

RUSTY

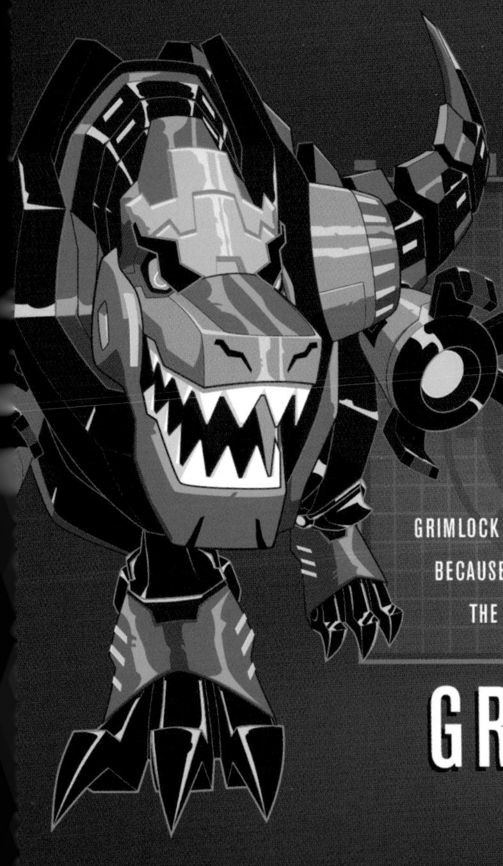

A PROVERBIAL "NEANDERTHAL" WITH A HUGE HEART, GRIMLOCK IS A DINOBOT THAT FIGHTS HARD AND PLAYS HARD. UNJUSTLY IMPRISONED EONS AGO FOR HIS LOOKS AND NOT HIS DEEDS, GRIMLOCK JOINS UP WITH TEAM 'BEE SIMPLY BECAUSE HE DIDN'T WANT TO MISS OUT ON THE "FUN" OF A MONSTER BEAT DOWN!

GRIMLOCK

DENNY CLAY IS RUSSEL'S DAD, AND OWNER OF THE LARGE JUNKYARD OUTSIDE OF CROWN CITY. A RELENTLESS TINKERER AND COLLECTOR, DENNY'S HORDE KEEPS GROWING ALONGSIDE HIS *ASPIRATIONAL* PLANS FOR THE JUNKYARD... AND RUSSELL!

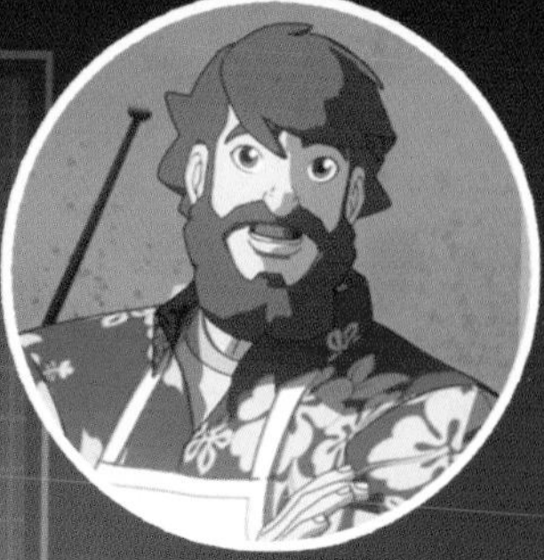

DENNY

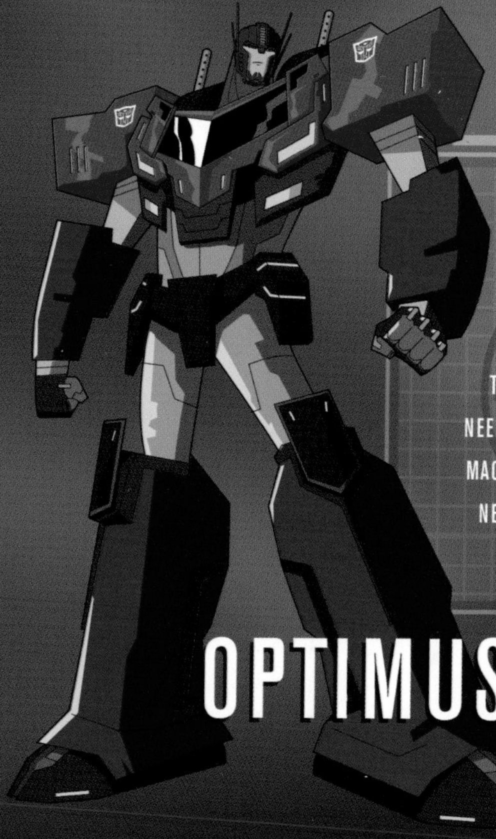

OPTIMUS PRIME IS... SOMEWHERE. WITH OPTIMUS' WHEREABOUTS UNKNOWN, BUMBLEBEE MUST LEARN TO BE TEAM LEADER. HIS NEW RECRUITS NEED TO FUNCTION AS A WELL-OILED MACHINE AND OPTIMUS PRIME WILL NEED TO FULFILL HIS DESTINY AND ACHIEVE THE NEXT STEP IN HIS

OPTIMUS PRIME

TRANSFORMERS
ROBOTS IN DISGUISE
A NEW MISSION

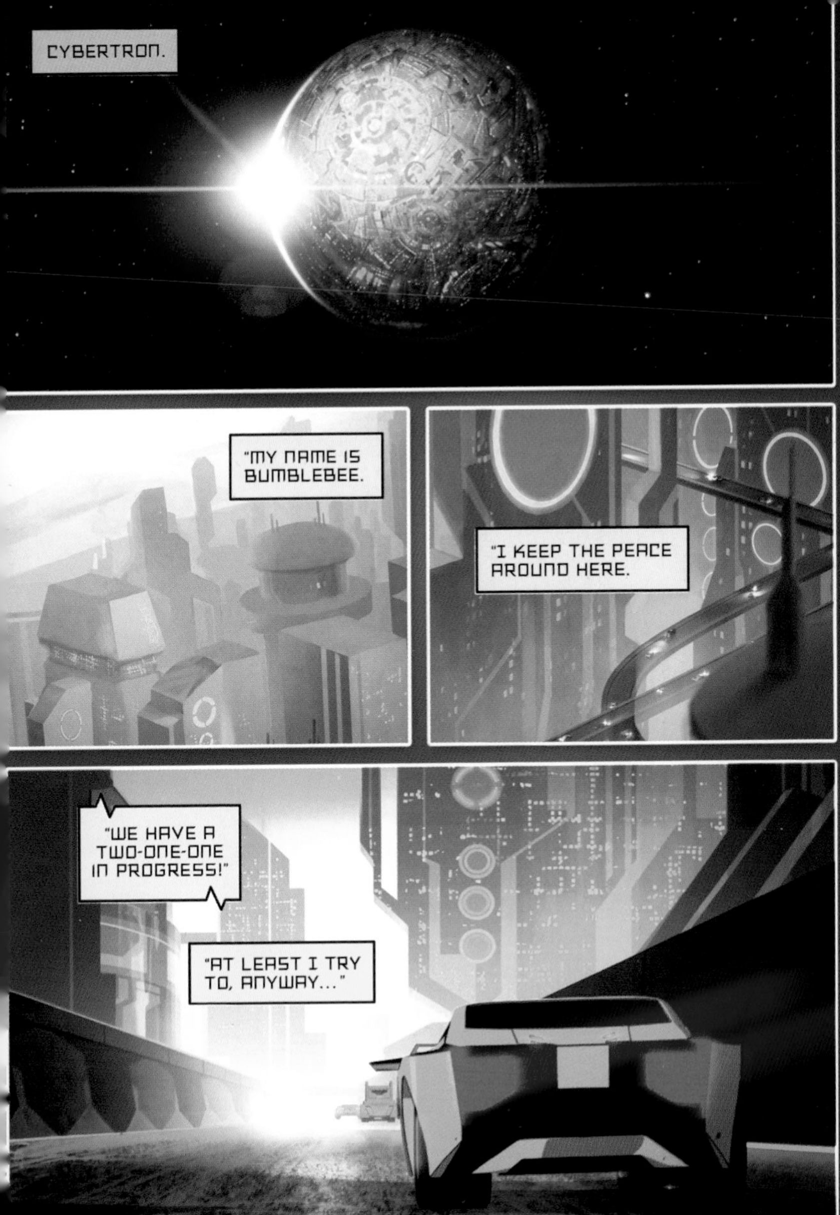
CYBERTRON.
"MY NAME IS BUMBLEBEE.
"I KEEP THE PEACE AROUND HERE.
"WE HAVE A TWO-ONE-ONE IN PROGRESS!"
"AT LEAST I TRY TO, ANYWAY..."

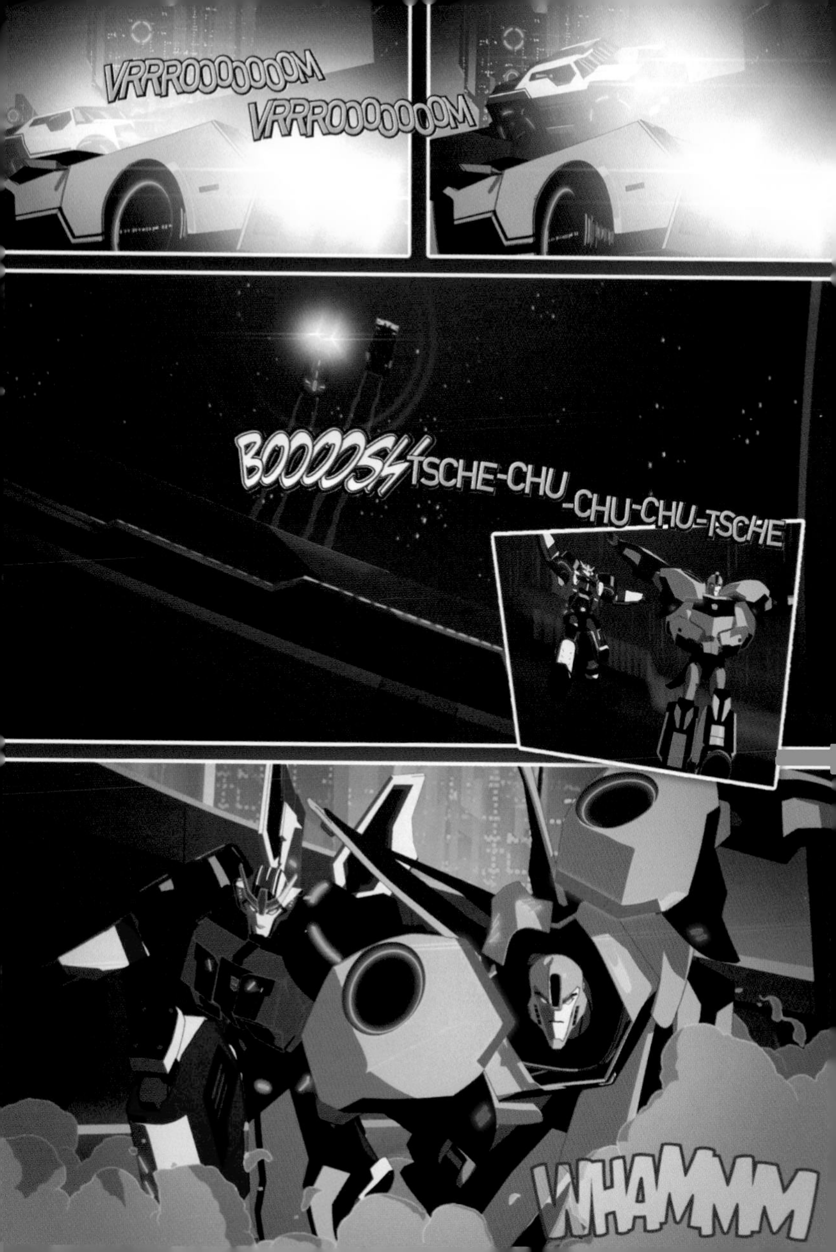
VRRROOOOOOOM
VRRROOOOOOOOM
BOOOOOSH
TSCHE-CHU-CHU-CHU-TSCHE
WHAMMM

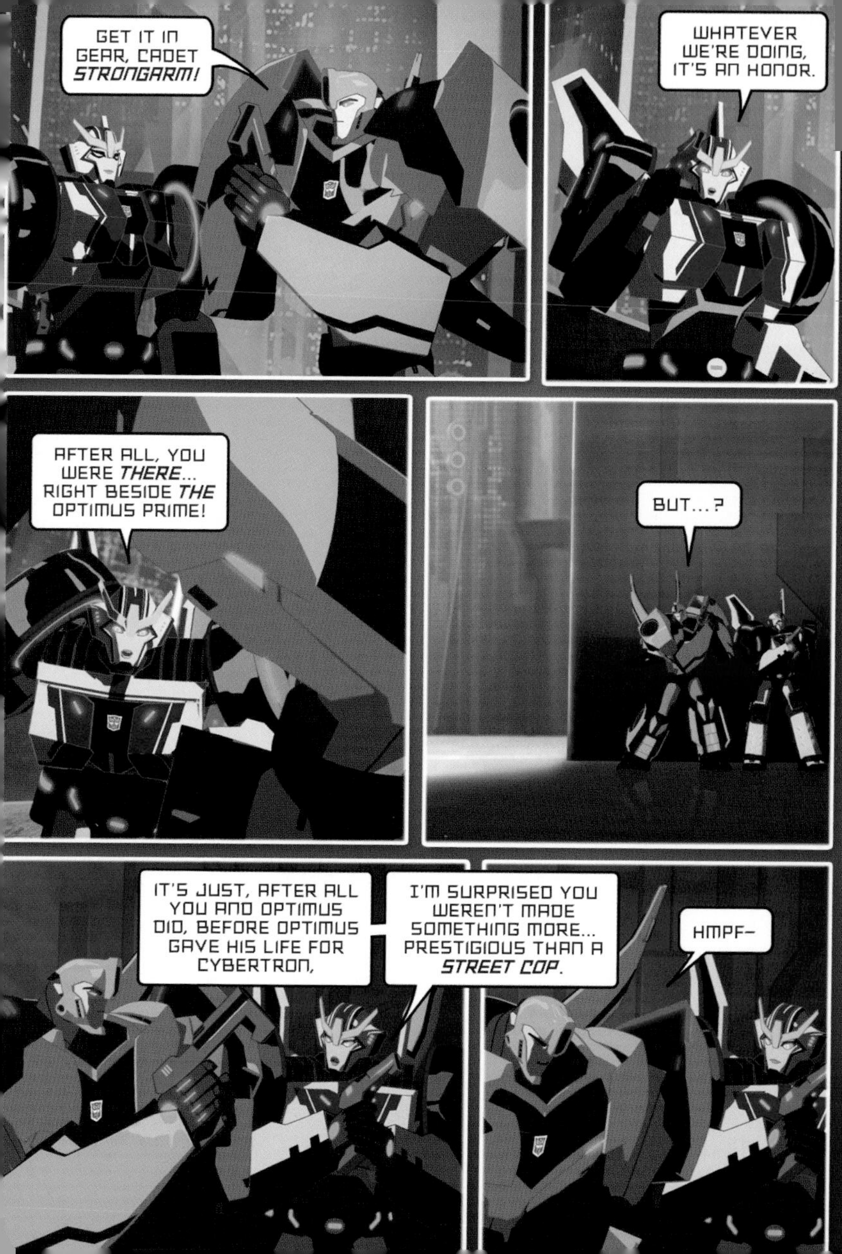
GET IT IN GEAR, CADET *STRONGARM!*
WHATEVER WE'RE DOING, IT'S AN HONOR.
AFTER ALL, YOU WERE *THERE*... RIGHT BESIDE *THE* OPTIMUS PRIME!
BUT...?
IT'S JUST, AFTER ALL YOU AND OPTIMUS DID, BEFORE OPTIMUS GAVE HIS LIFE FOR CYBERTRON,
I'M SURPRISED YOU WEREN'T MADE SOMETHING MORE... PRESTIGIOUS THAN A *STREET COP*.
HMPF–

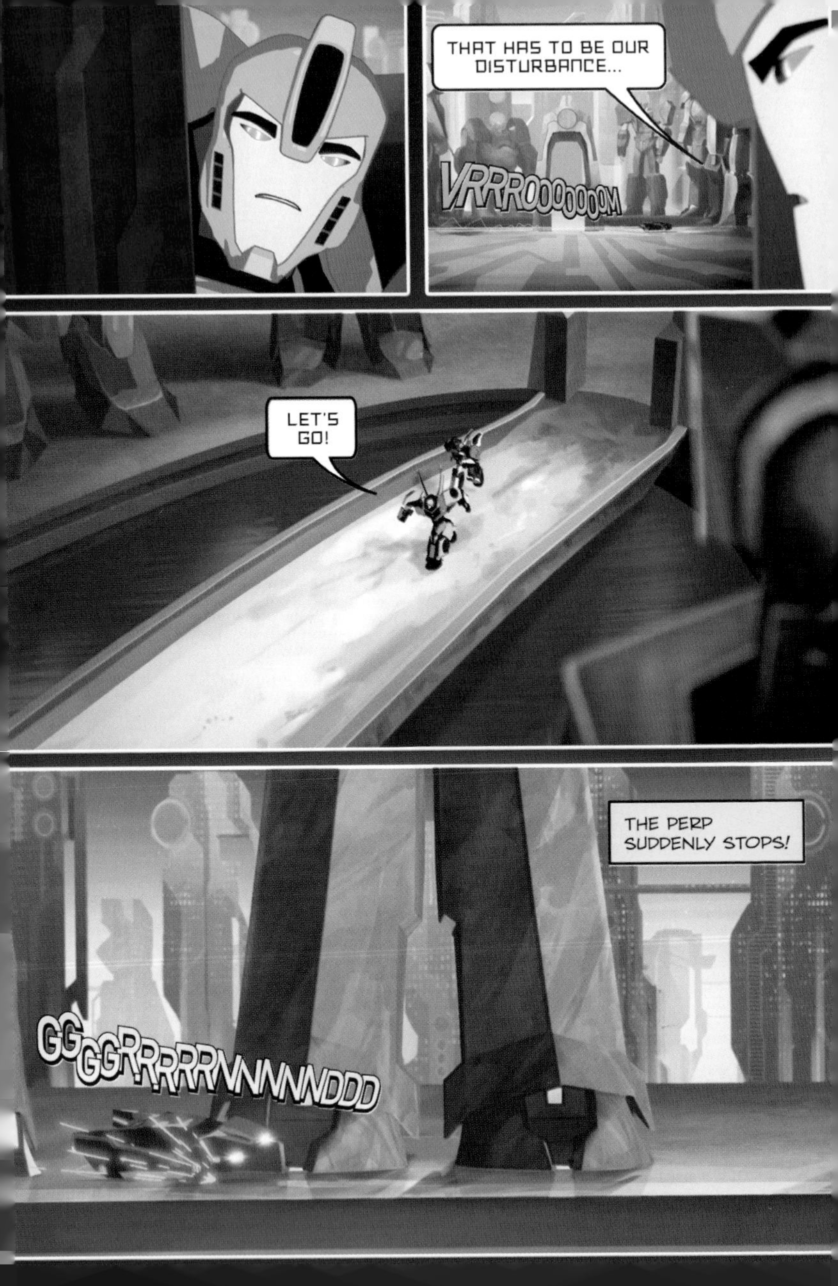
THAT HAS TO BE OUR DISTURBANCE...
VRRROOOOOOOM
LET'S GO!
THE PERP SUDDENLY STOPS!
GGGGRRRRRNNNNNDDD

VRRROOOOOOOM

GGGGRRRRRNNNNDDDDDD

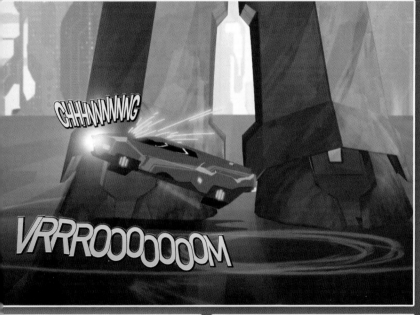

CHHNNNNNG

VRRROOOOOOOM

IN FRONT OF THE *OPTIMUS* STATUE!

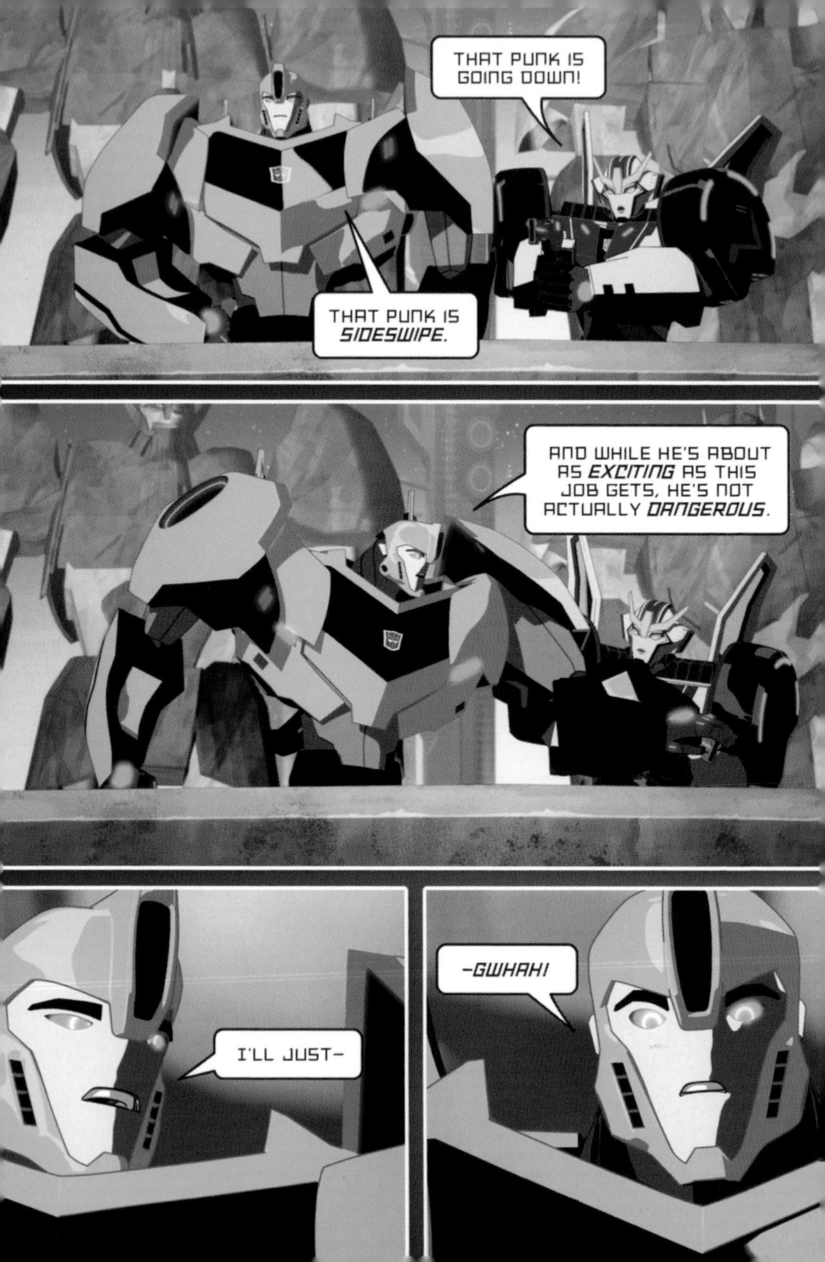
THAT PUNK IS GOING DOWN!
THAT PUNK IS *SIDESWIPE*.
AND WHILE HE'S ABOUT AS *EXCITING* AS THIS JOB GETS, HE'S NOT ACTUALLY *DANGEROUS*.
I'LL JUST–
–GWHAH!

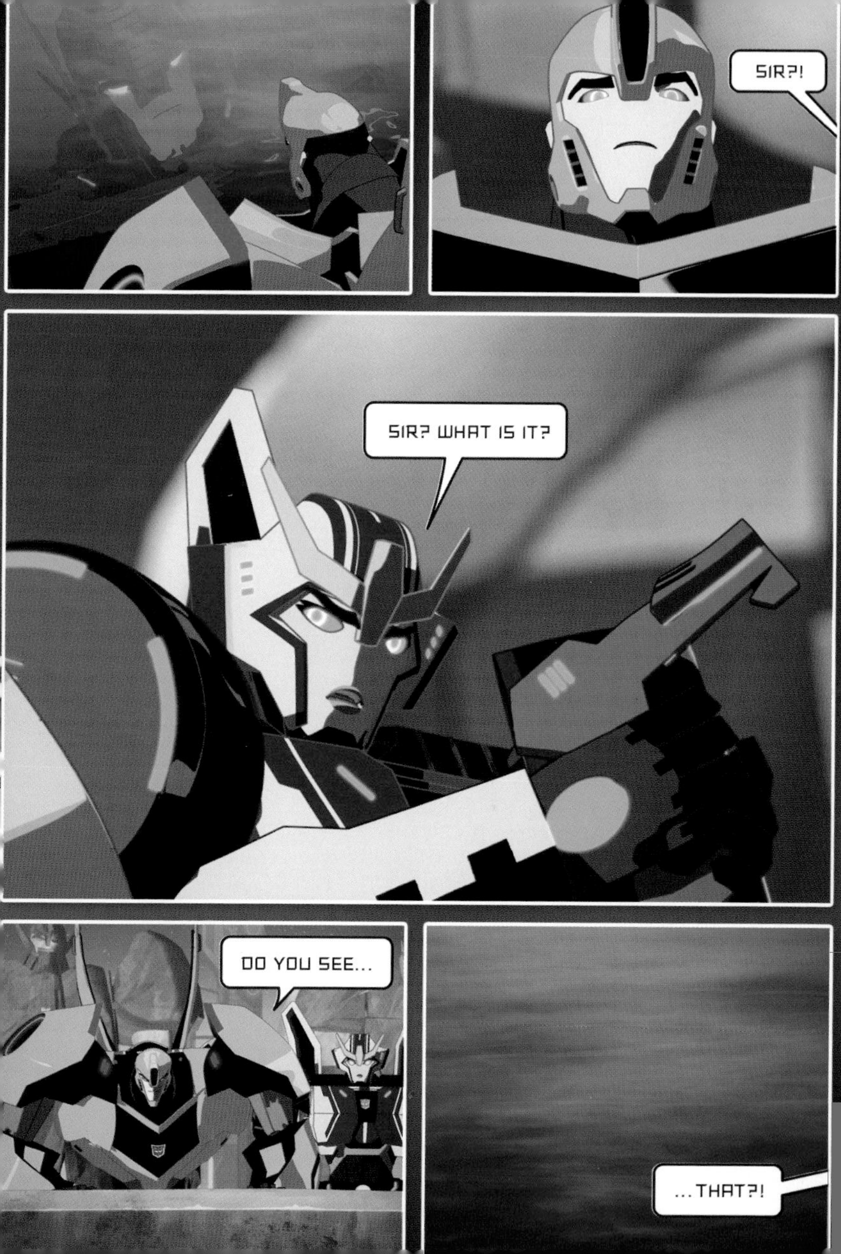
SIR?!
SIR? WHAT IS IT?
DO YOU SEE...
...THAT?!

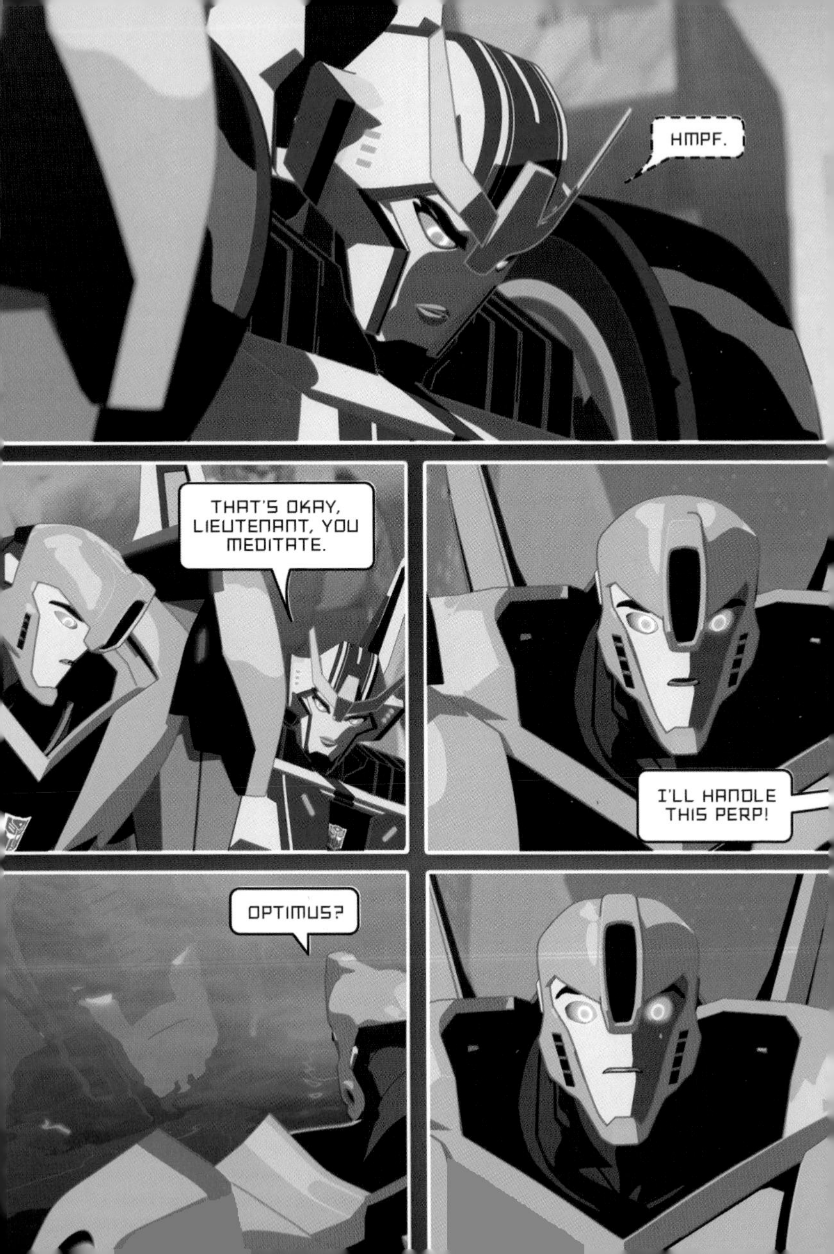
HMPF.
THAT'S OKAY, LIEUTENANT, YOU MEDITATE.
I'LL HANDLE THIS PERP!
OPTIMUS?

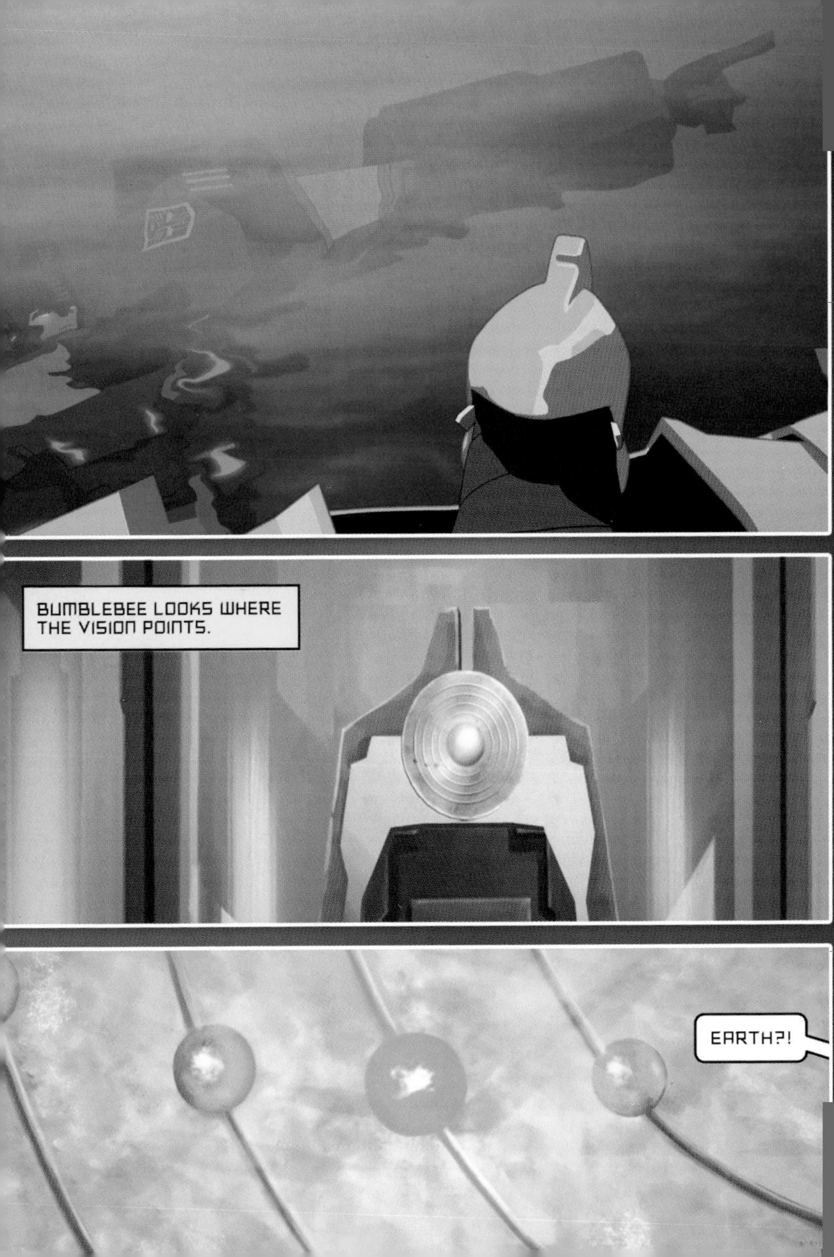
BUMBLEBEE LOOKS WHERE THE VISION POINTS.
EARTH?!

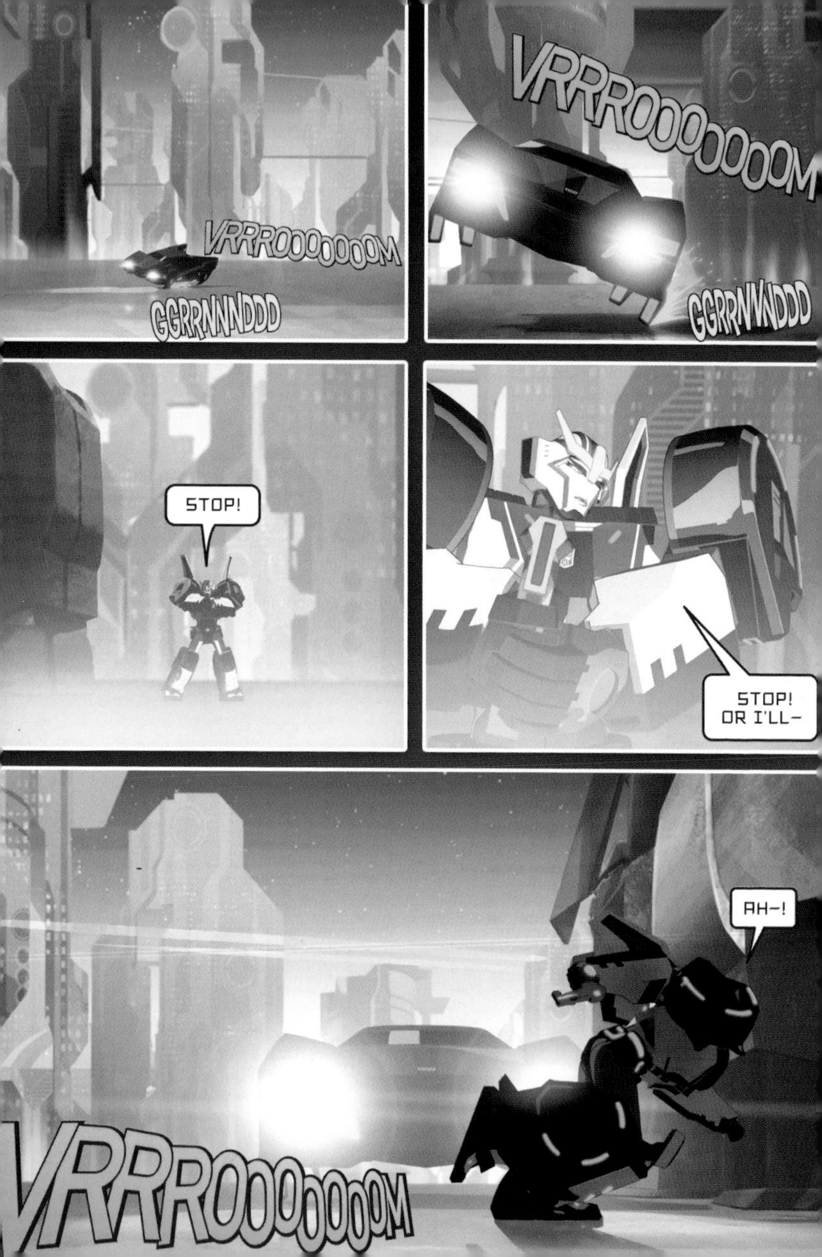
VRRROOOOOOOM
GGRRNNNDDD
VRRROOOOOOOOM
GGRRNNNDDD
STOP!
STOP! OR I'LL–
AH–!
VRRROOOOOOOM

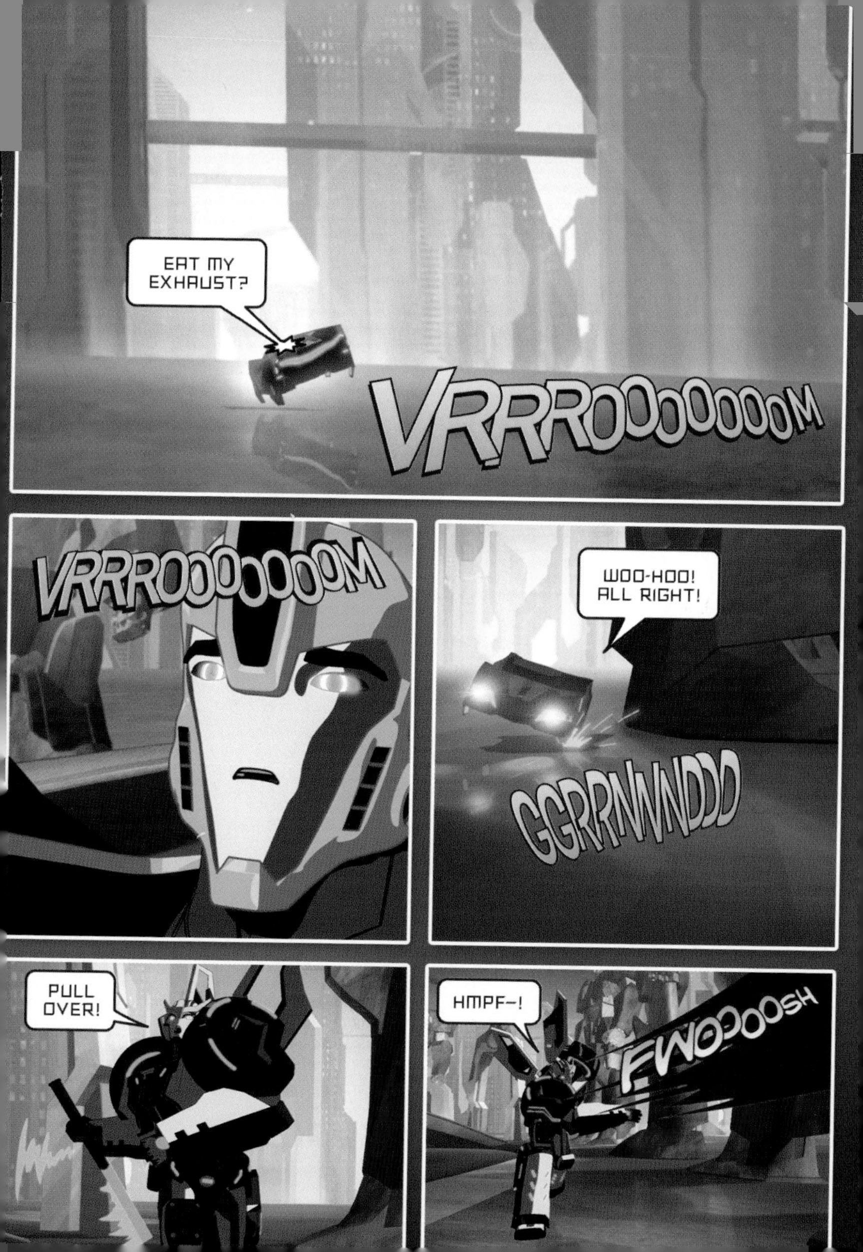
EAT MY EXHAUST?
VRRROOOOOOOOM
VRRROOOOOOOOM
WOO-HOO! ALL RIGHT!
GGRRNNNDDD
PULL OVER!
HMPF--!
FWOOOOOSH

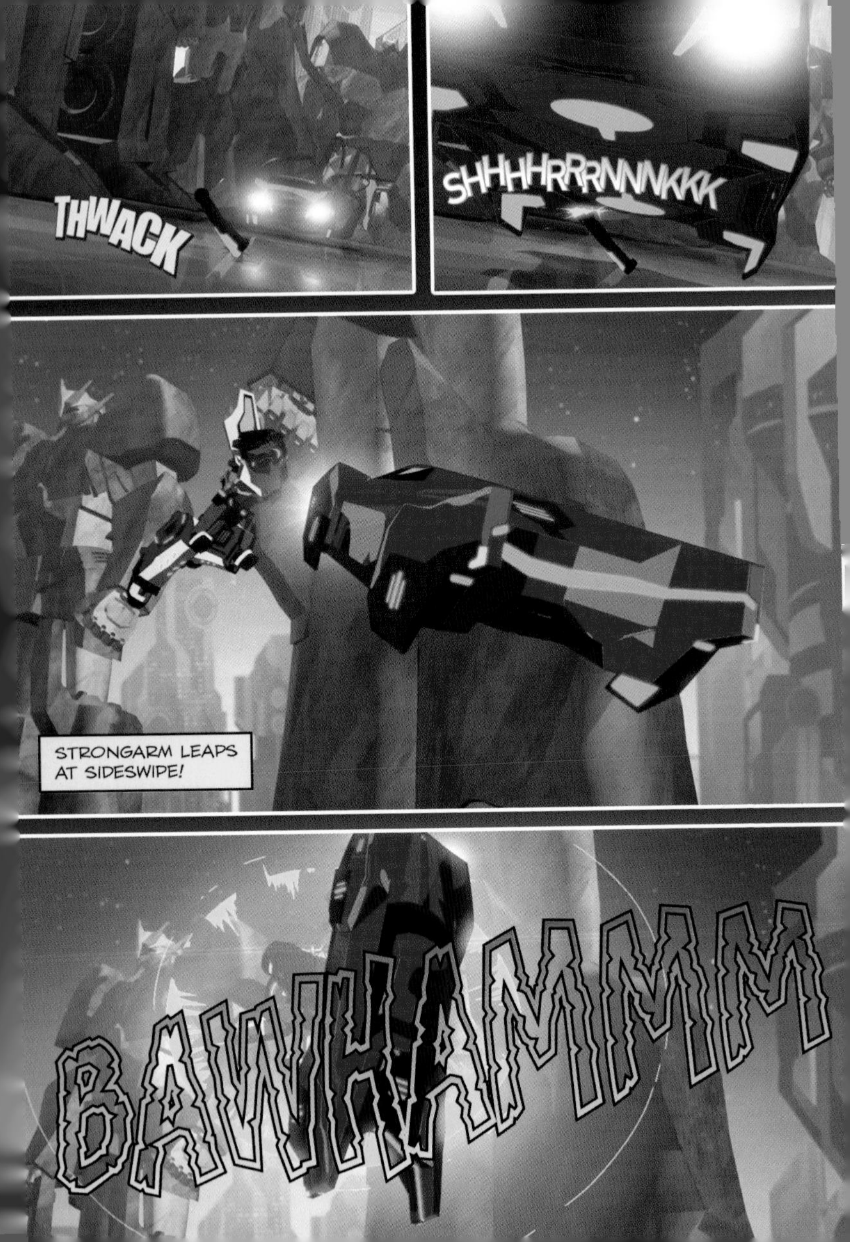
THWACK
SHHHHRRRNNNKKK
STRONGARM LEAPS AT SIDESWIPE!
BAWHAMMM

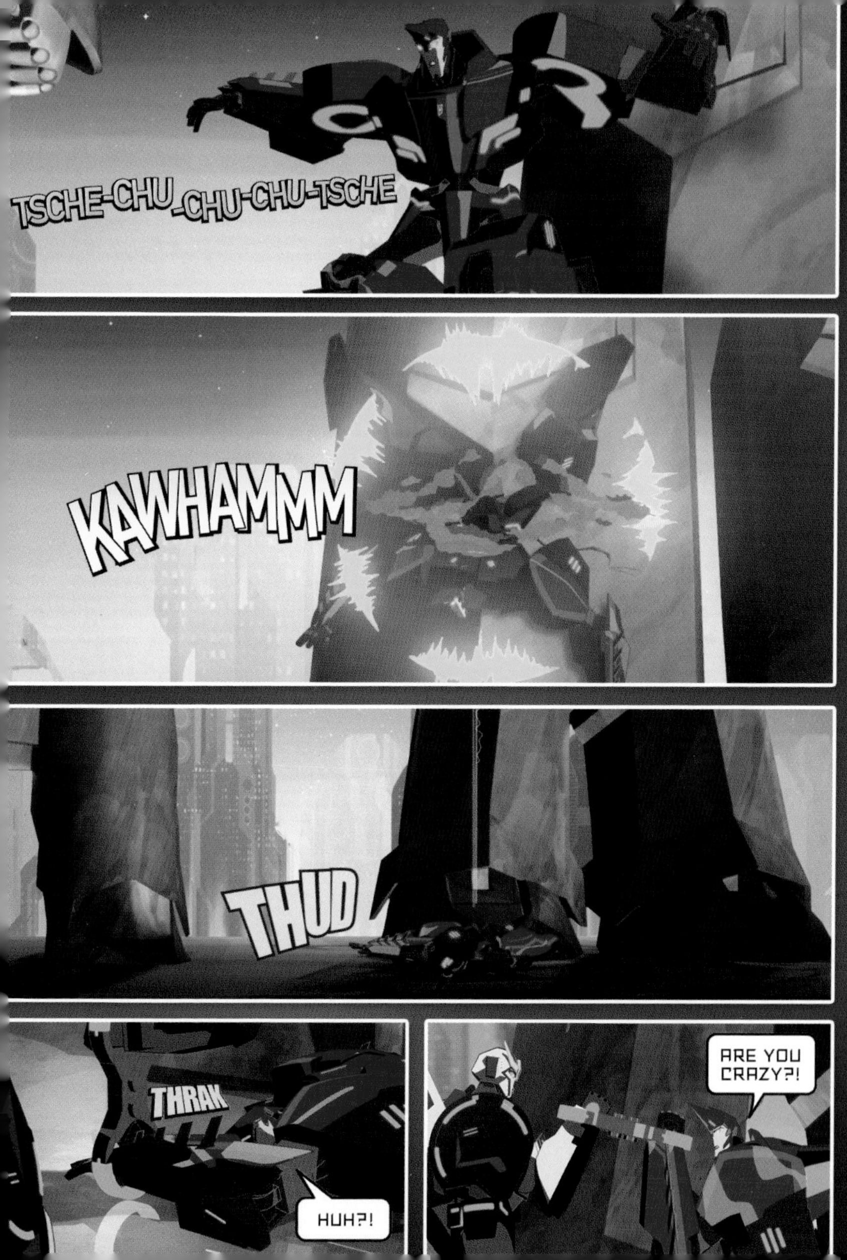
TSCHE-CHU-CHU-CHU-TSCHE
KAWHAMMM
THUD
THRAK
HUH?!
ARE YOU CRAZY?!

RUMMMMMBLE

THE OPTIMUS PRIME STATUE!

RUMMMMMMBLE

NO!

RUMMMMMMBLE

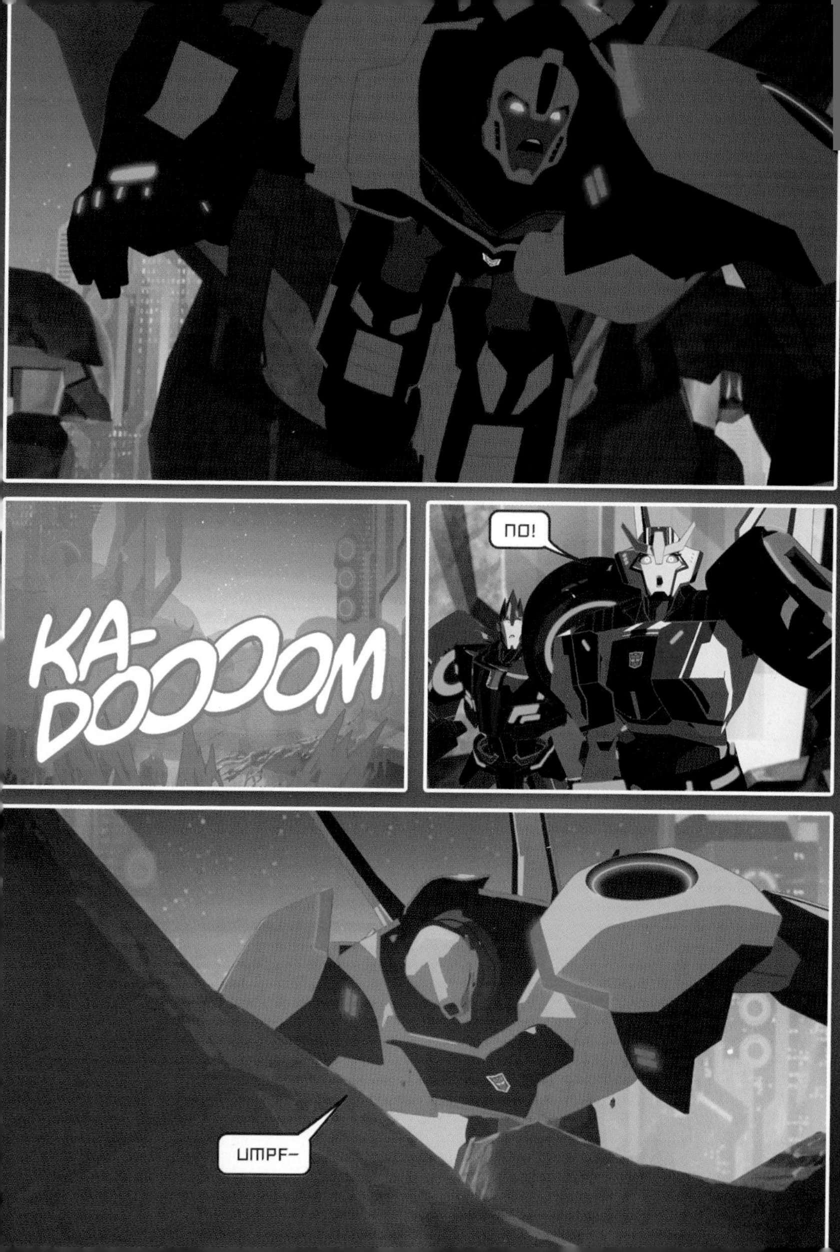
KA-DOOOOOM
NO!
UMPF–

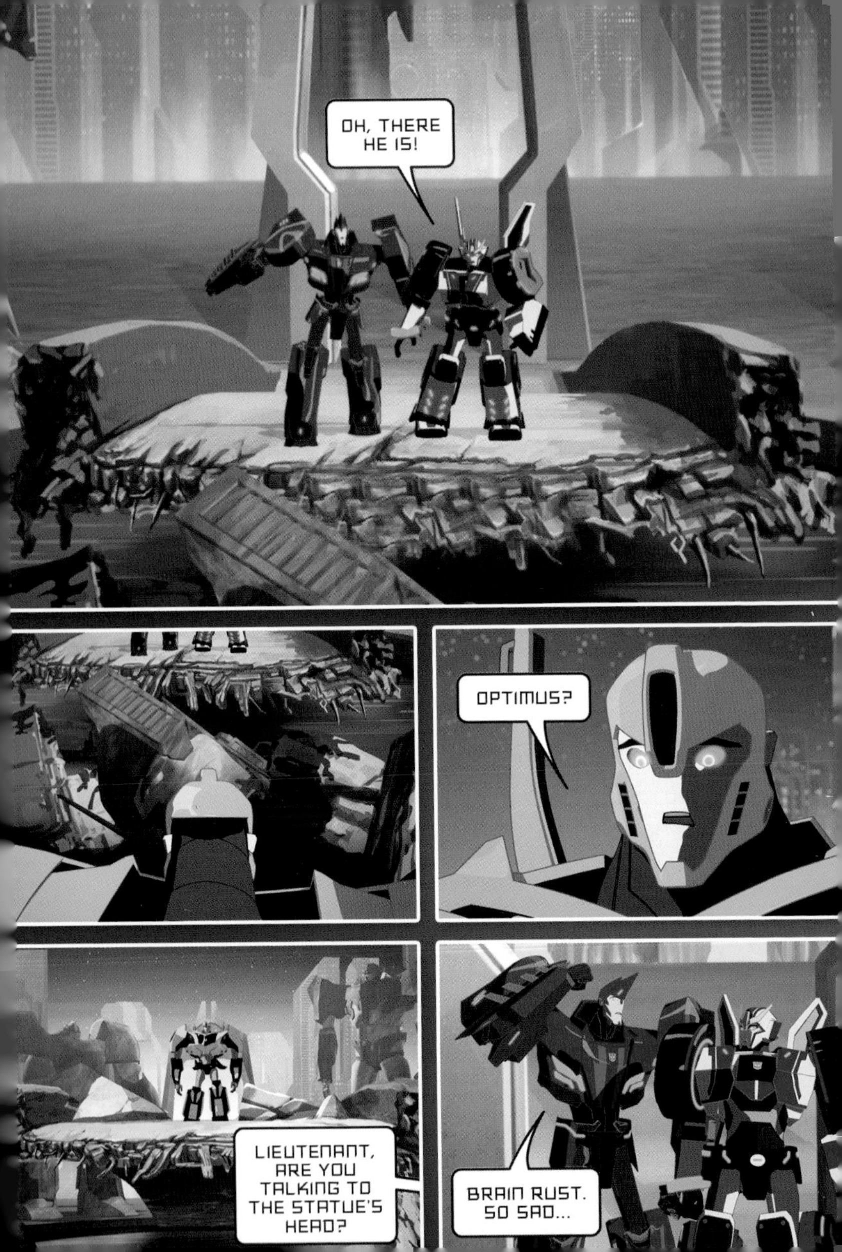
OH, THERE HE IS!
OPTIMUS?
LIEUTENANT, ARE YOU TALKING TO THE STATUE'S HEAD?
BRAIN RUST. SO SAD...

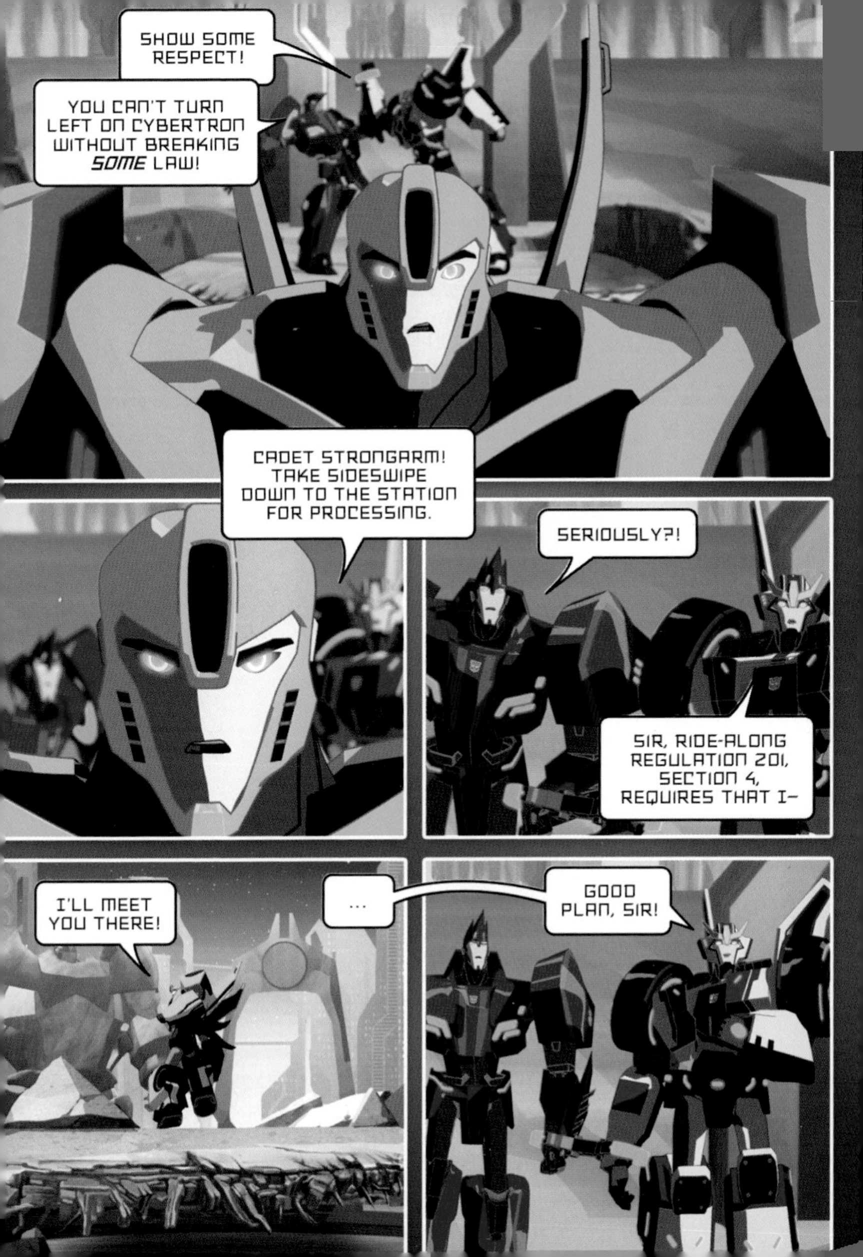
SHOW SOME RESPECT!
YOU CAN'T TURN LEFT ON CYBERTRON WITHOUT BREAKING *SOME* LAW!
CADET STRONGARM! TAKE SIDESWIPE DOWN TO THE STATION FOR PROCESSING.
SERIOUSLY?!
SIR, RIDE-ALONG REGULATION 201, SECTION 4, REQUIRES THAT I—
I'LL MEET YOU THERE!
...
GOOD PLAN, SIR!

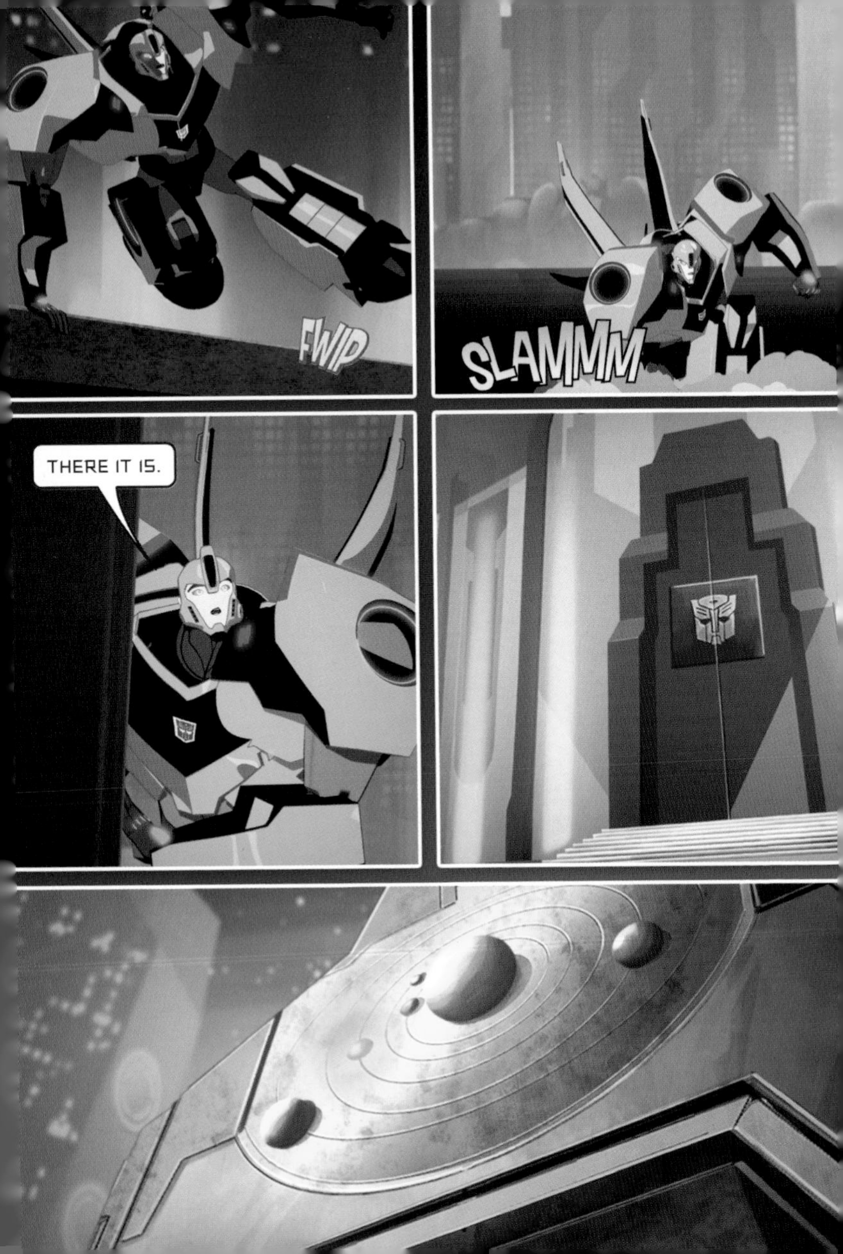
FWIP
SLAMMM
THERE IT IS.

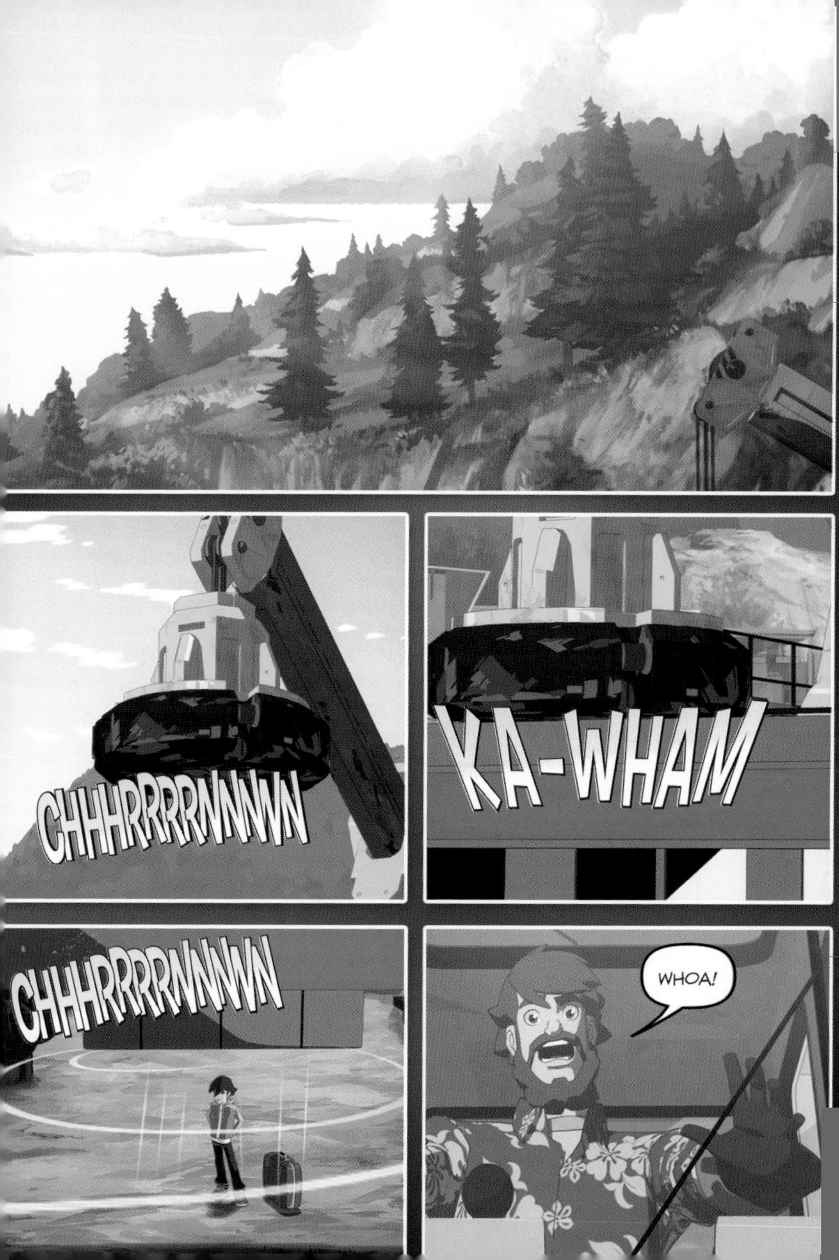
CHHHRRRRNNNNN
KA-WHAM
CHHHRRRRNNNNN
WHOA!

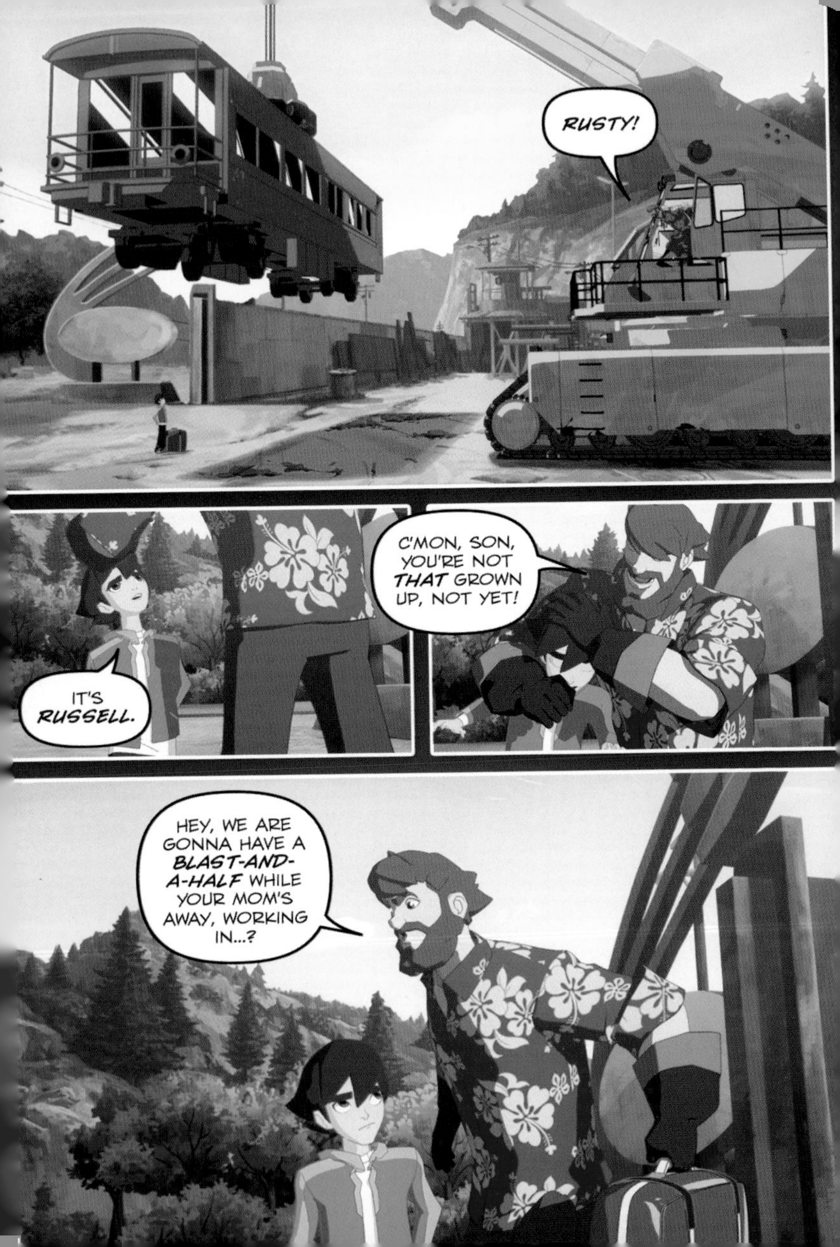
RUSTY!
IT'S RUSSELL.
C'MON, SON, YOU'RE NOT THAT GROWN UP, NOT YET!
HEY, WE ARE GONNA HAVE A BLAST-AND-A-HALF WHILE YOUR MOM'S AWAY, WORKING IN...?

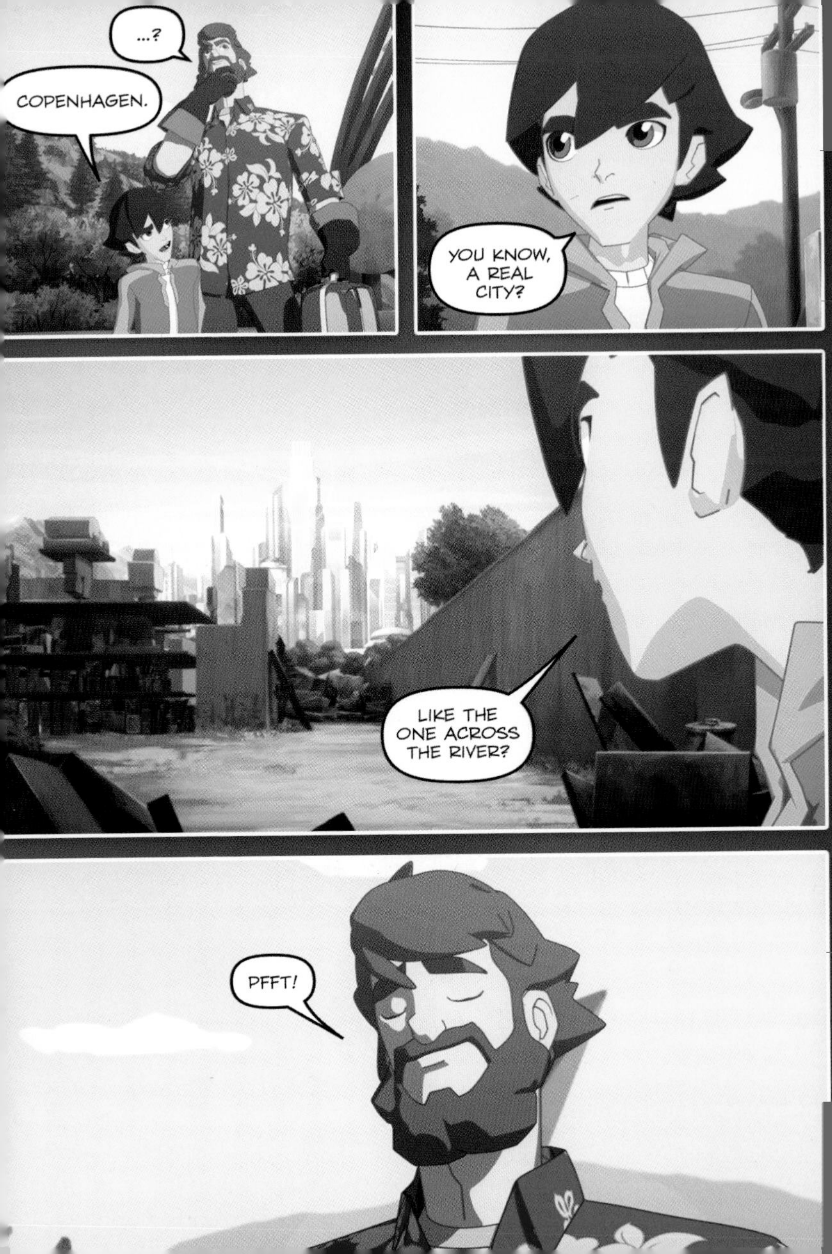
...?
COPENHAGEN.
YOU KNOW, A REAL CITY?
LIKE THE ONE ACROSS THE RIVER?
PFFT!

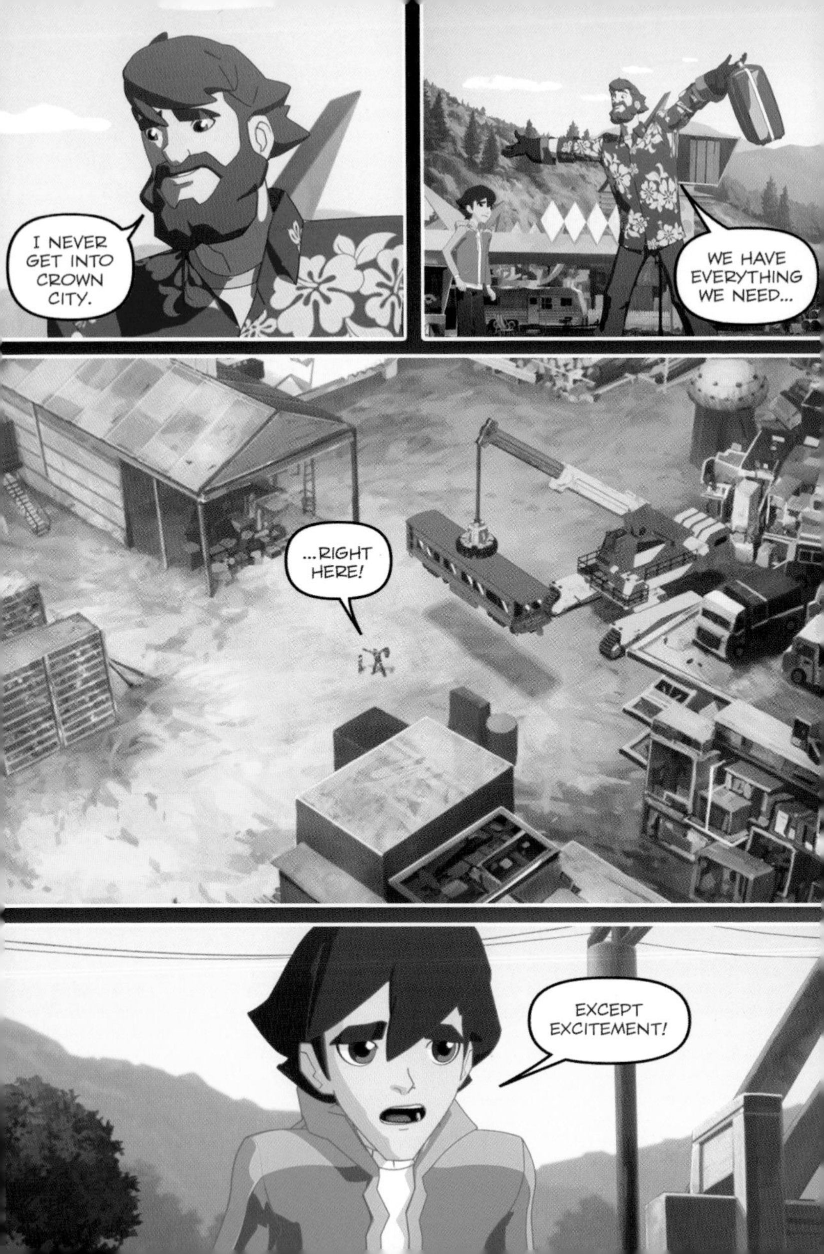
I NEVER GET INTO CROWN CITY.
WE HAVE EVERYTHING WE NEED...
...RIGHT HERE!
EXCEPT EXCITEMENT!

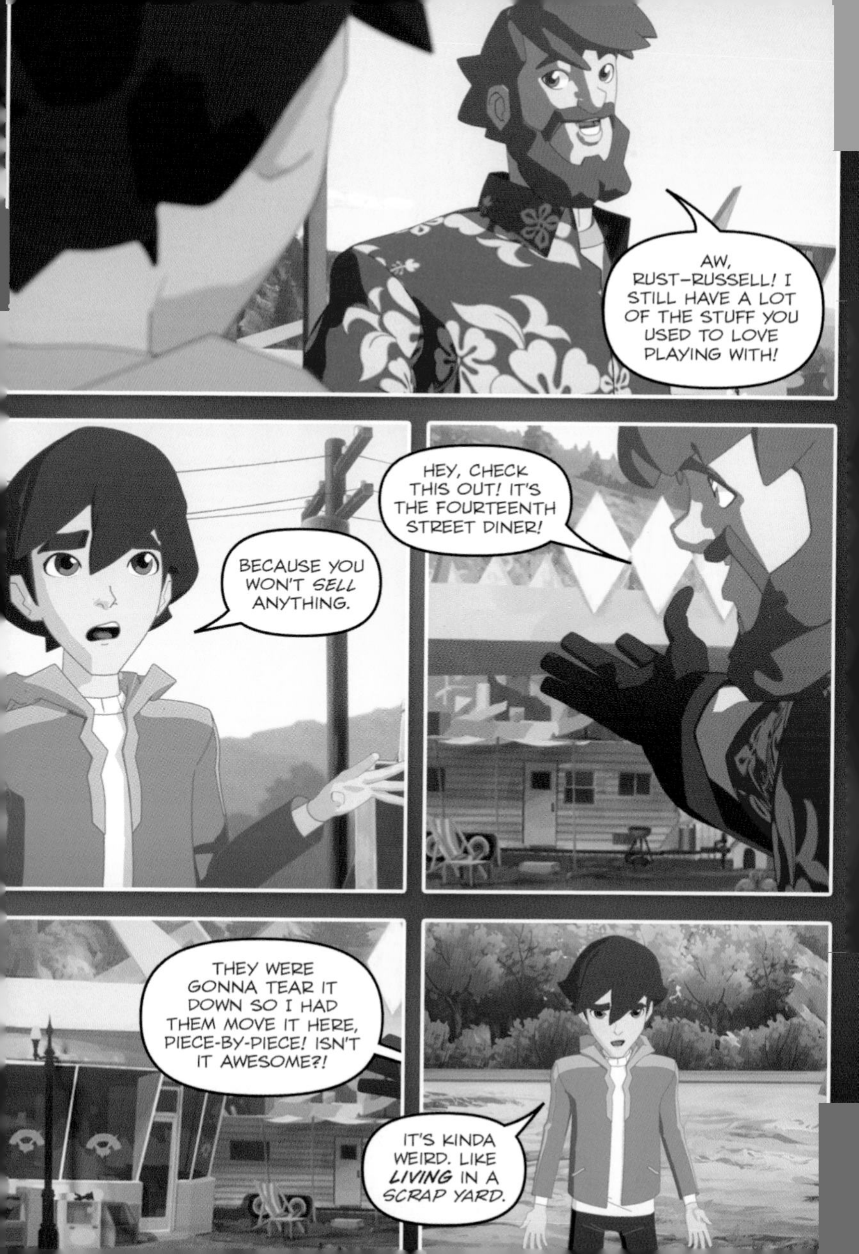
AW, RUST-RUSSELL! I STILL HAVE A LOT OF THE STUFF YOU USED TO LOVE PLAYING WITH!
BECAUSE YOU WON'T *SELL* ANYTHING.
HEY, CHECK THIS OUT! IT'S THE FOURTEENTH STREET DINER!
THEY WERE GONNA TEAR IT DOWN SO I HAD THEM MOVE IT HERE, PIECE-BY-PIECE! ISN'T IT AWESOME?!
IT'S KINDA WEIRD. LIKE ***LIVING*** IN A *SCRAP YARD.*

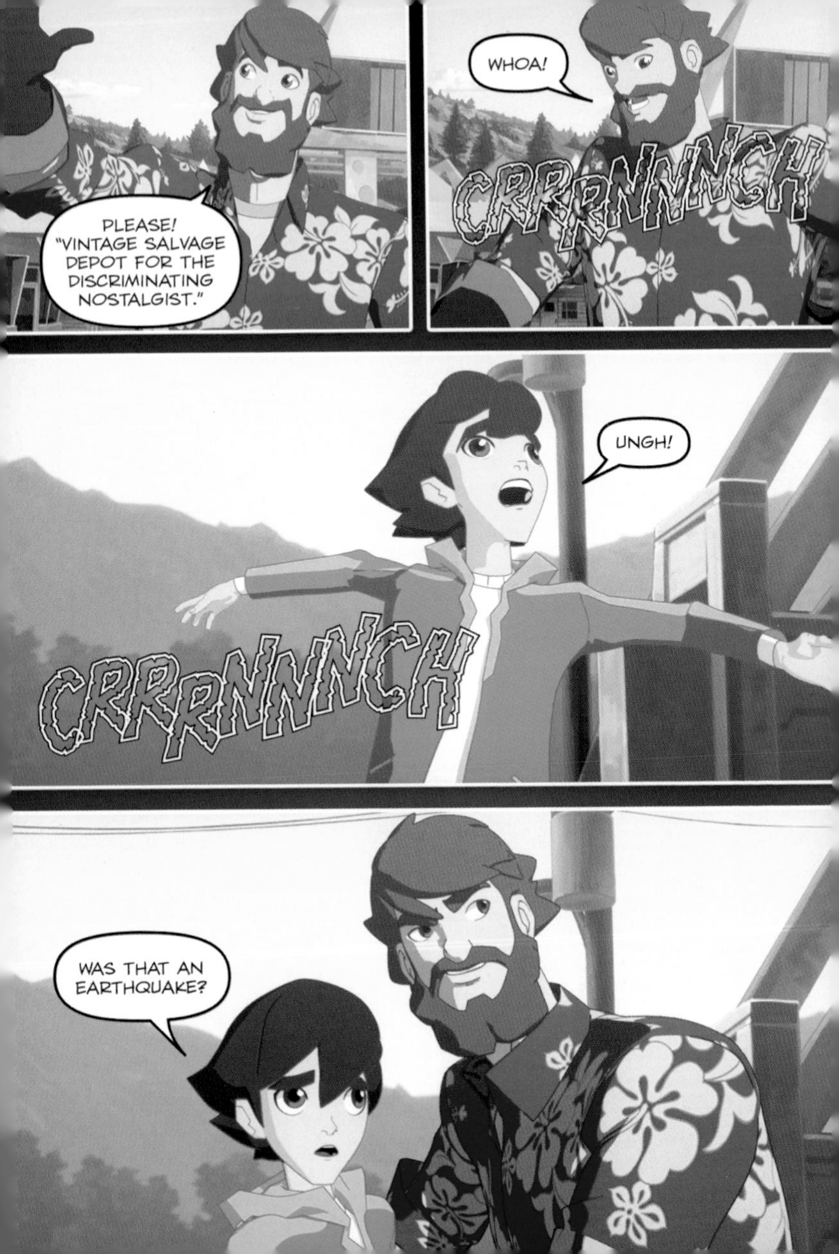
PLEASE! "VINTAGE SALVAGE DEPOT FOR THE DISCRIMINATING NOSTALGIST."
WHOA!
CRRRNNNCH
UNGH!
CRRRNNNCH
WAS THAT AN EARTHQUAKE?

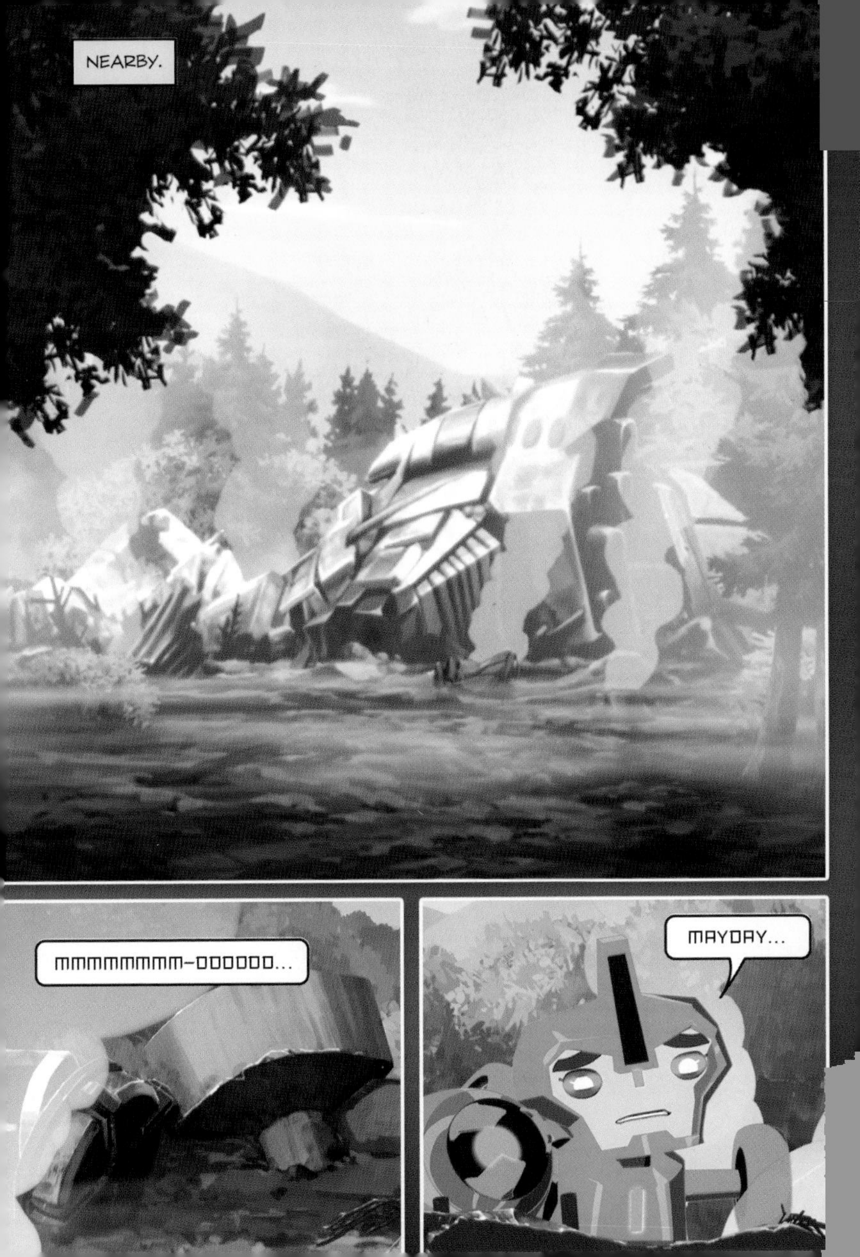
NEARBY.
MMMMMMMM-OOOOOO...
MAYDAY...

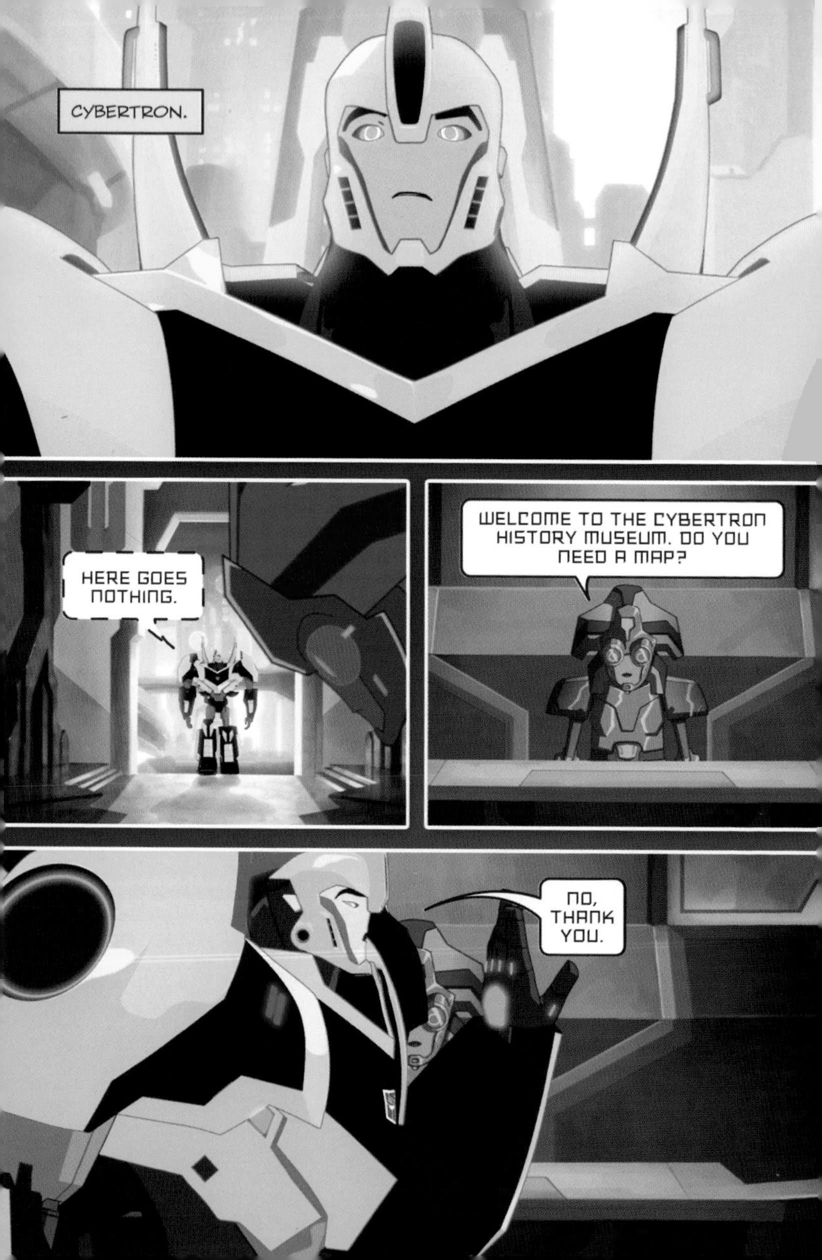
CYBERTRON.
HERE GOES NOTHING.
WELCOME TO THE CYBERTRON HISTORY MUSEUM. DO YOU NEED A MAP?
NO, THANK YOU.

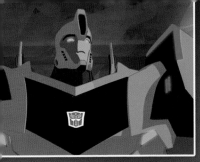

DEEEEEP

BAWHOOOOSH

WHAT—?

A SPACEBRIDGE?!

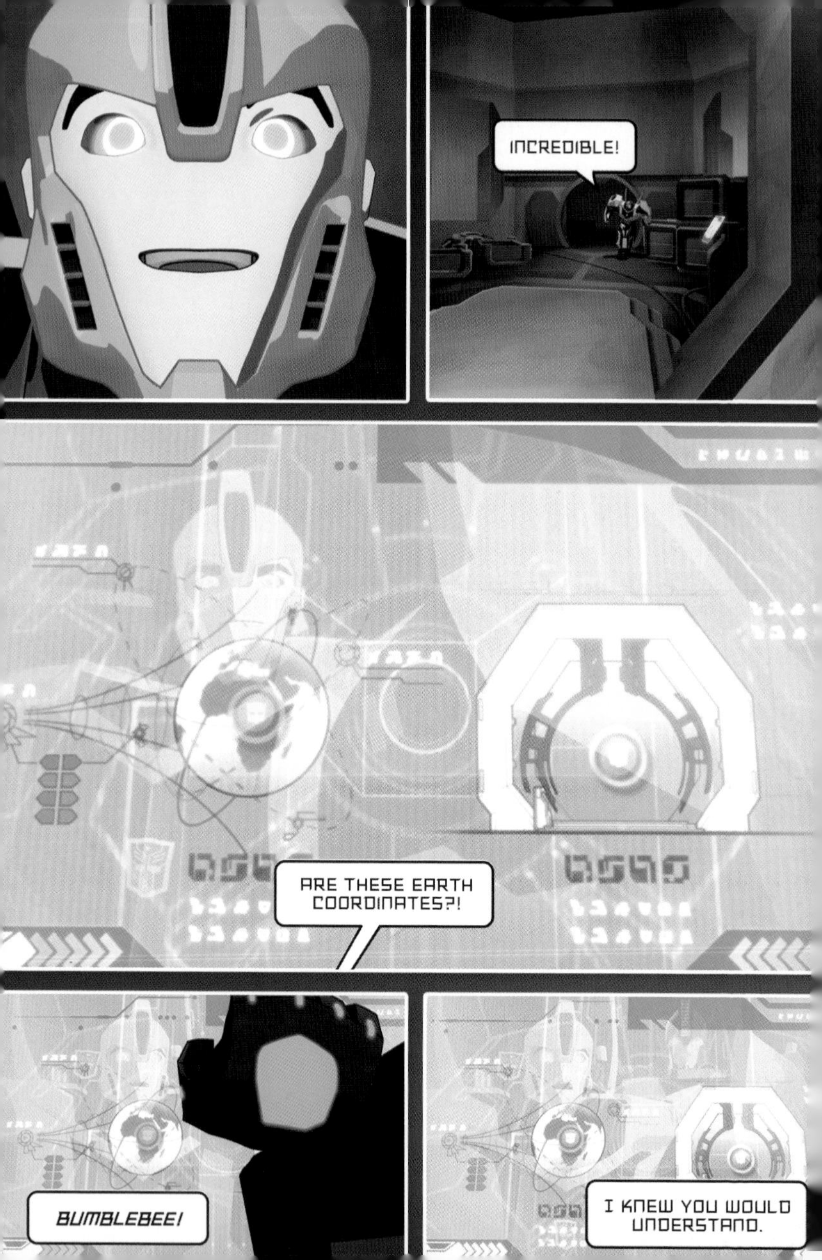
INCREDIBLE!
ARE THESE EARTH COORDINATES?!
BUMBLEBEE!
I KNEW YOU WOULD UNDERSTAND.

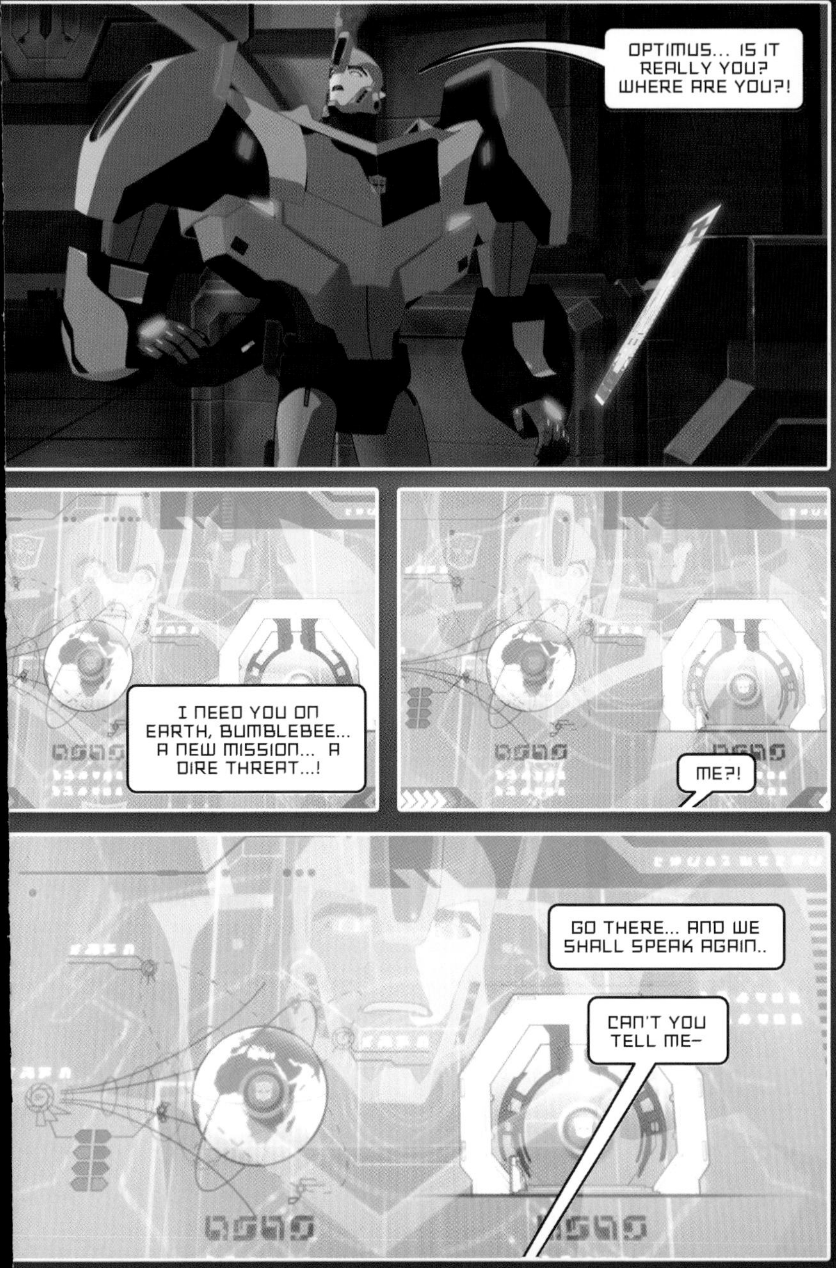
OPTIMUS... IS IT REALLY YOU? WHERE ARE YOU?!
I NEED YOU ON EARTH, BUMBLEBEE... A NEW MISSION... A DIRE THREAT...!
ME?!
GO THERE... AND WE SHALL SPEAK AGAIN..
CAN'T YOU TELL ME–

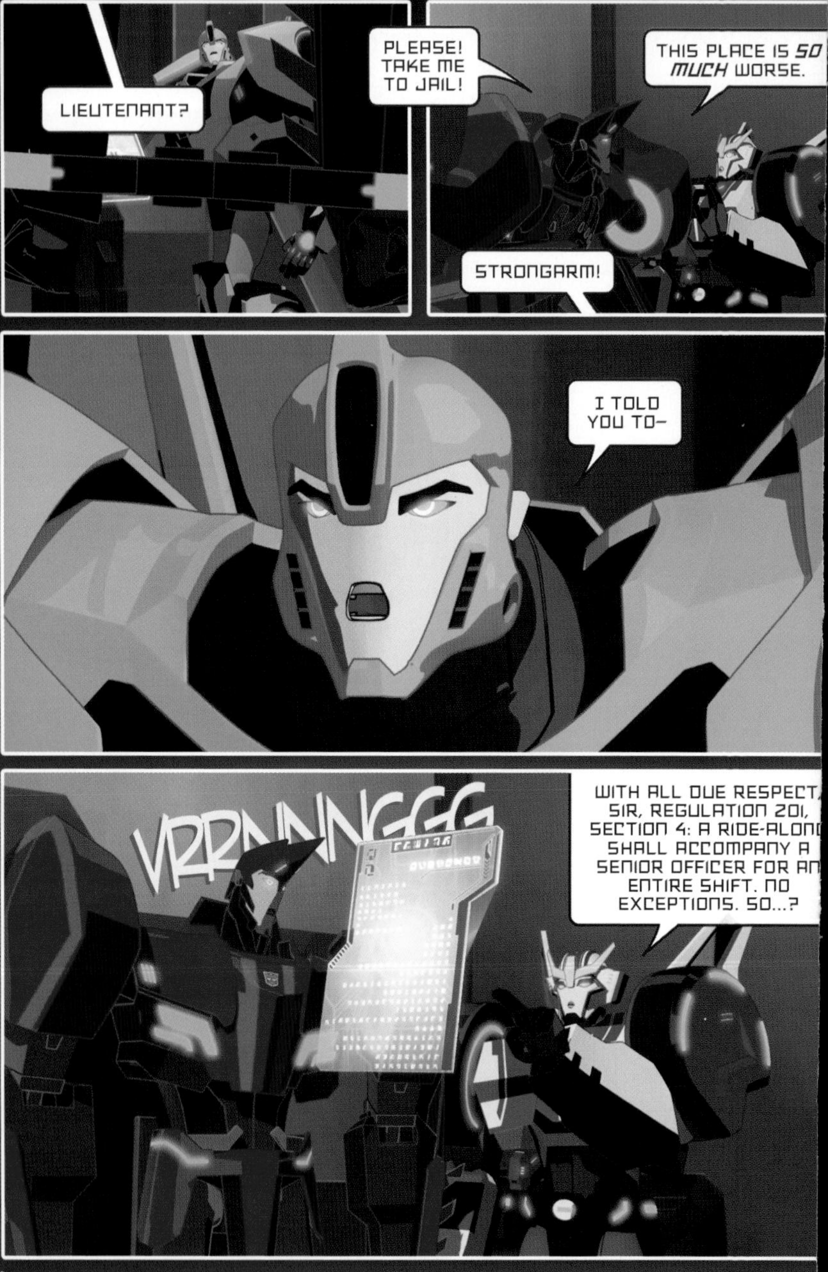

LIEUTENANT?
PLEASE! TAKE ME TO JAIL!
THIS PLACE IS *SO MUCH* WORSE.
STRONGARM!
I TOLD YOU TO—
VRRNNNGGG
WITH ALL DUE RESPECT, SIR, REGULATION 201, SECTION 4: A RIDE-ALONG SHALL ACCOMPANY A SENIOR OFFICER FOR AN ENTIRE SHIFT. NO EXCEPTIONS. SO...?

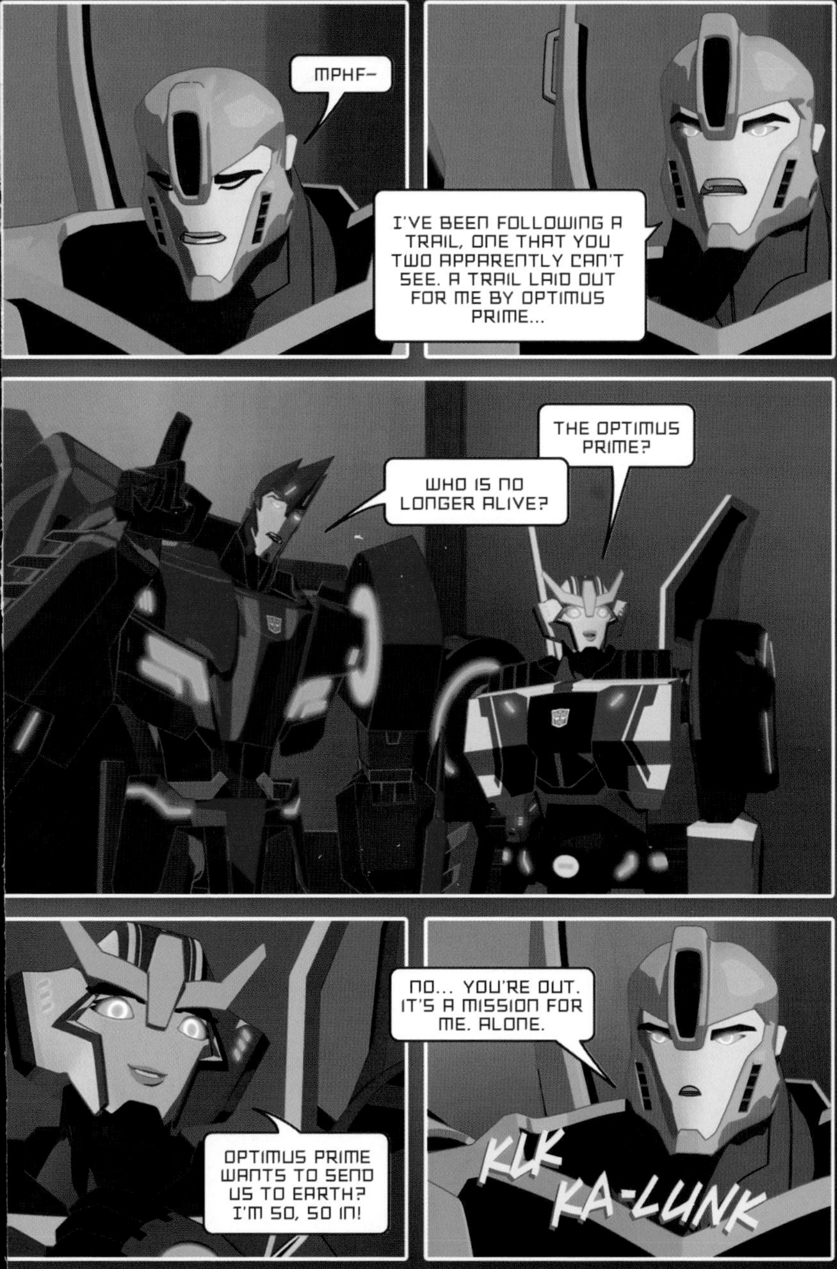
MPHF–
I'VE BEEN FOLLOWING A TRAIL, ONE THAT YOU TWO APPARENTLY CAN'T SEE. A TRAIL LAID OUT FOR ME BY OPTIMUS PRIME...
THE OPTIMUS PRIME?
WHO IS NO LONGER ALIVE?
OPTIMUS PRIME WANTS TO SEND US TO EARTH? I'M SO, SO IN!
NO... YOU'RE OUT. IT'S A MISSION FOR ME. ALONE.
KLK
KA-LUNK

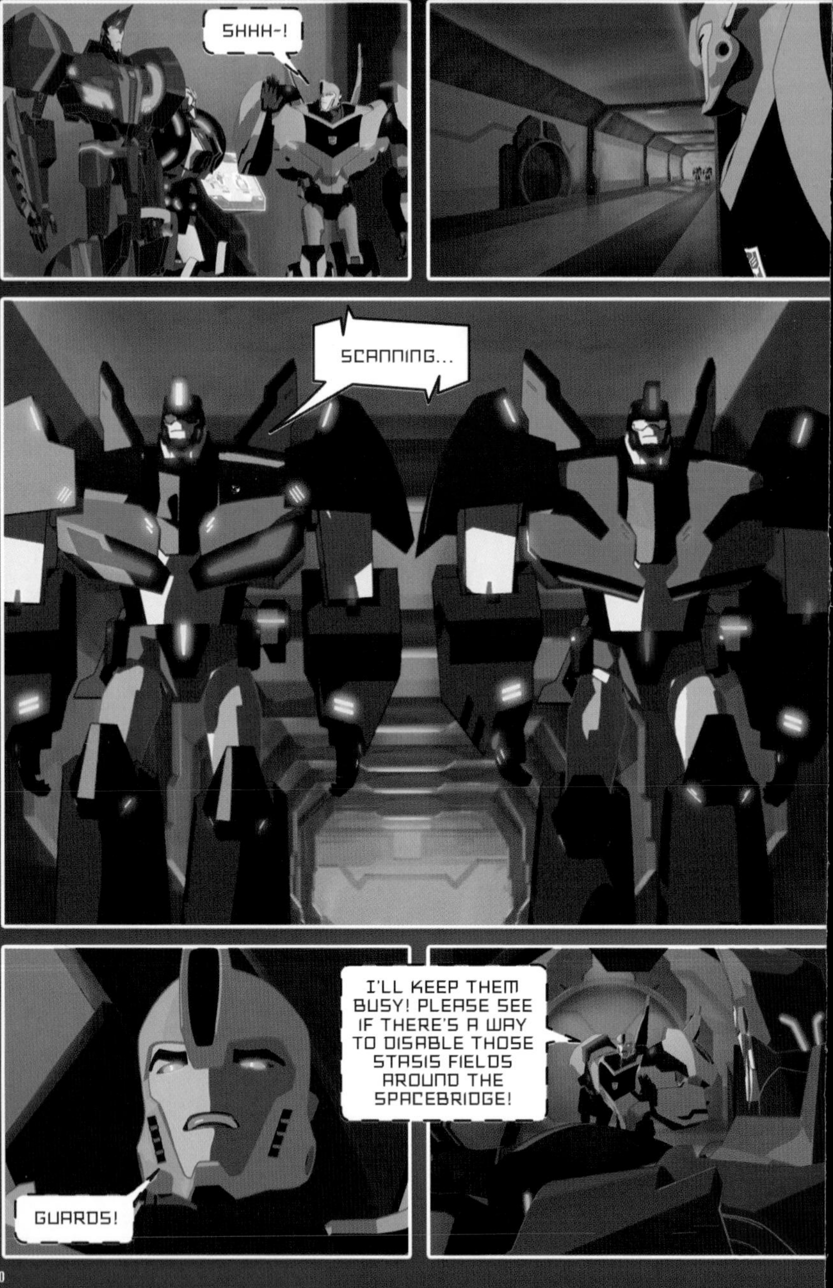
SHHH-!
SCANNING...
GUARDS!
I'LL KEEP THEM BUSY! PLEASE SEE IF THERE'S A WAY TO DISABLE THOSE STASIS FIELDS AROUND THE SPACEBRIDGE!

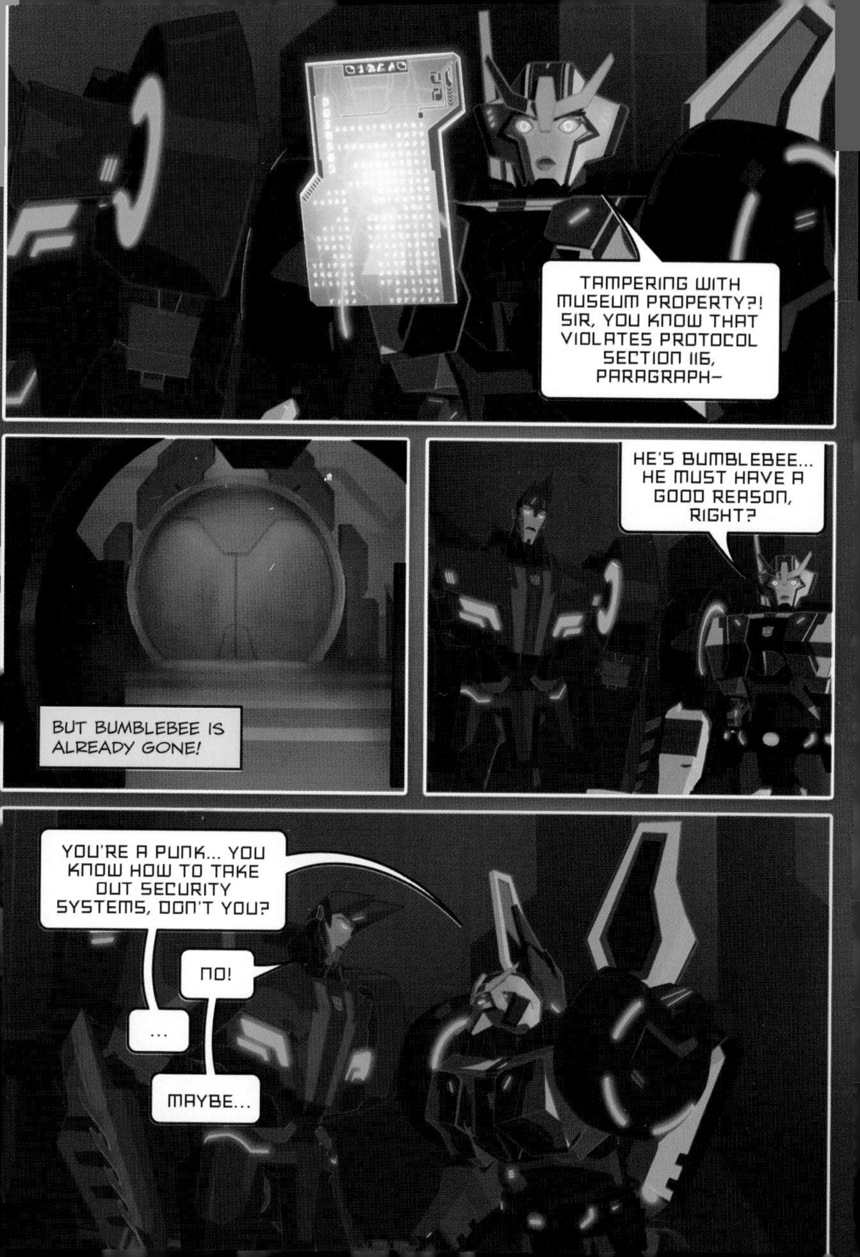
TAMPERING WITH MUSEUM PROPERTY?! SIR, YOU KNOW THAT VIOLATES PROTOCOL SECTION 116, PARAGRAPH–
BUT BUMBLEBEE IS ALREADY GONE!
HE'S BUMBLEBEE... HE MUST HAVE A GOOD REASON, RIGHT?
YOU'RE A PUNK... YOU KNOW HOW TO TAKE OUT SECURITY SYSTEMS, DON'T YOU?
NO!
...
MAYBE...

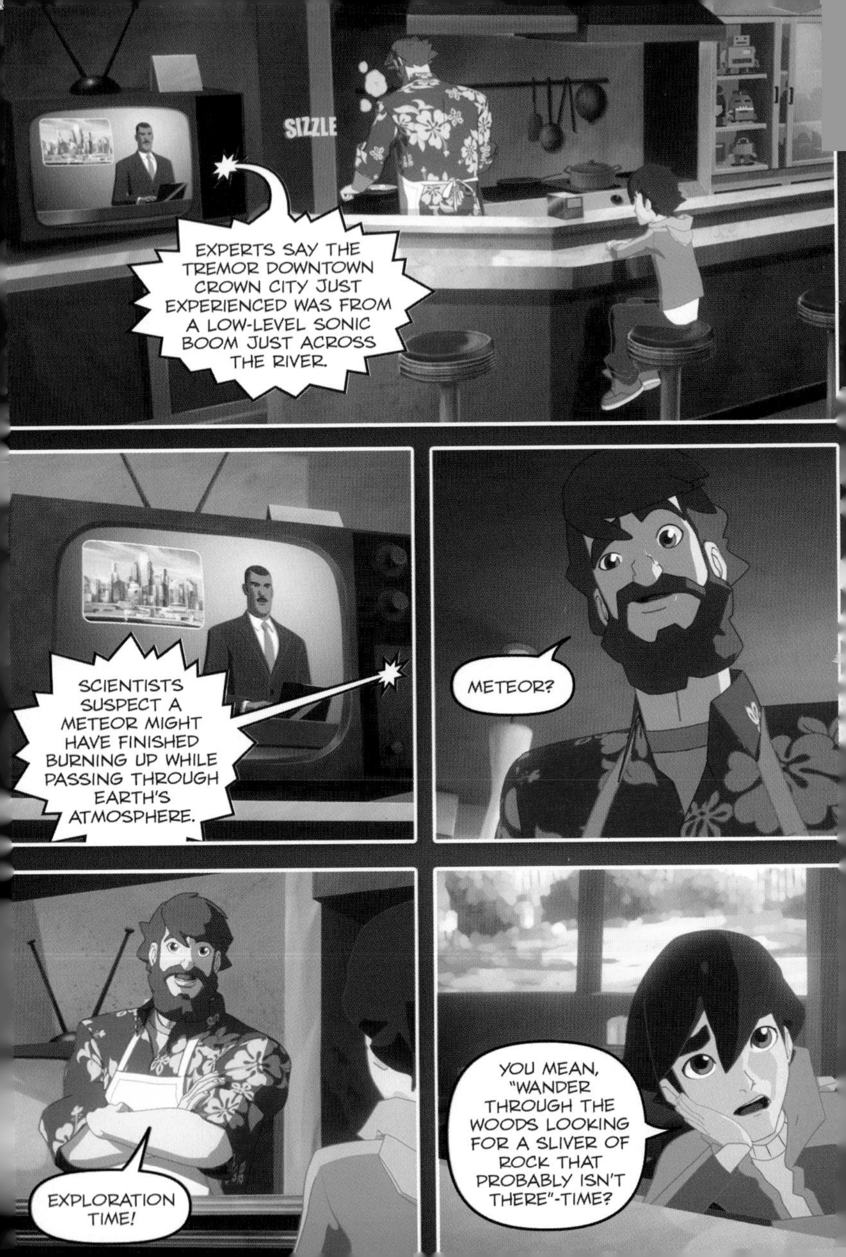
SIZZLE
EXPERTS SAY THE TREMOR DOWNTOWN CROWN CITY JUST EXPERIENCED WAS FROM A LOW-LEVEL SONIC BOOM JUST ACROSS THE RIVER.
SCIENTISTS SUSPECT A METEOR MIGHT HAVE FINISHED BURNING UP WHILE PASSING THROUGH EARTH'S ATMOSPHERE.
METEOR?
EXPLORATION TIME!
YOU MEAN, "WANDER THROUGH THE WOODS LOOKING FOR A SLIVER OF ROCK THAT PROBABLY ISN'T THERE"-TIME?

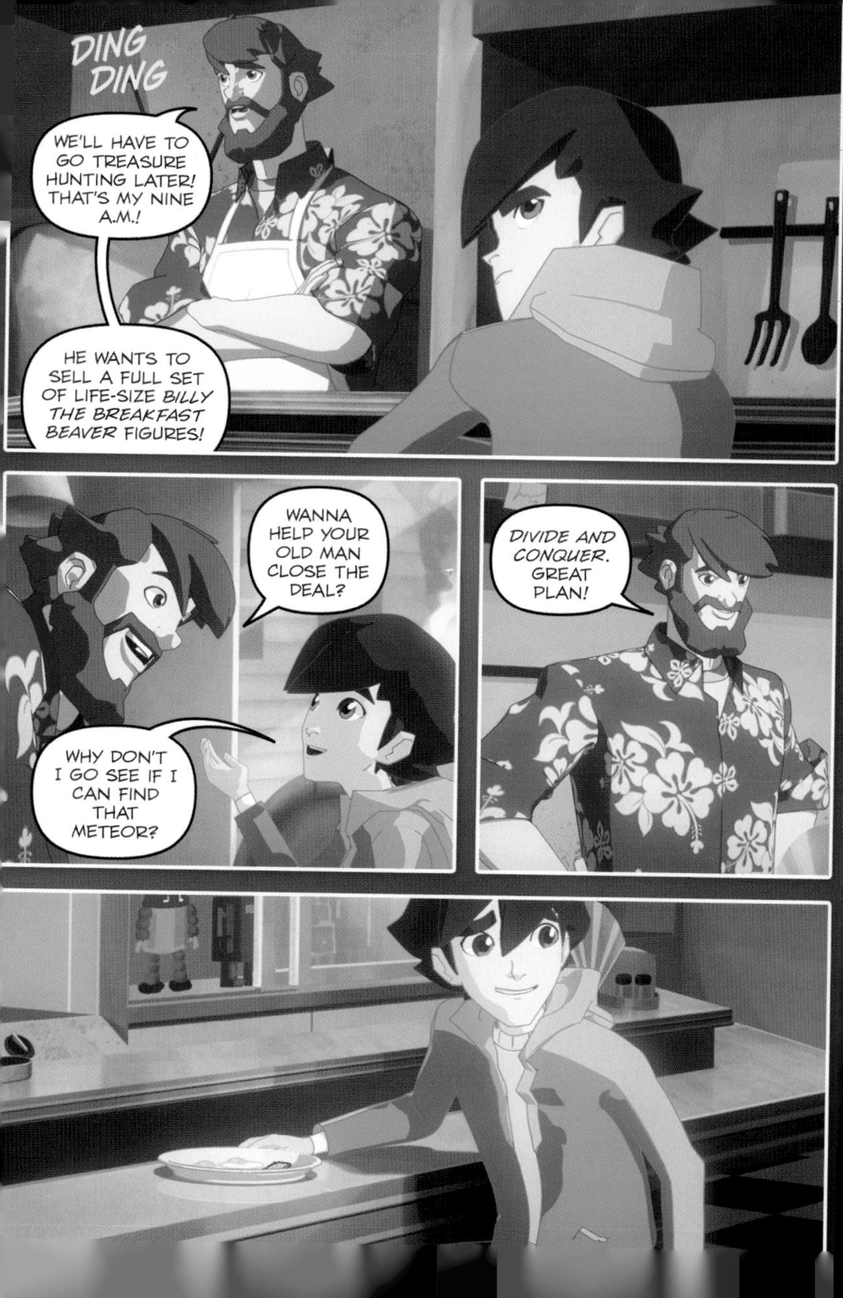
DING DING
WE'LL HAVE TO GO TREASURE HUNTING LATER! THAT'S MY NINE A.M.!
HE WANTS TO SELL A FULL SET OF LIFE-SIZE *BILLY THE BREAKFAST BEAVER* FIGURES!
WANNA HELP YOUR OLD MAN CLOSE THE DEAL?
WHY DON'T I GO SEE IF I CAN FIND THAT METEOR?
DIVIDE AND CONQUER. GREAT PLAN!

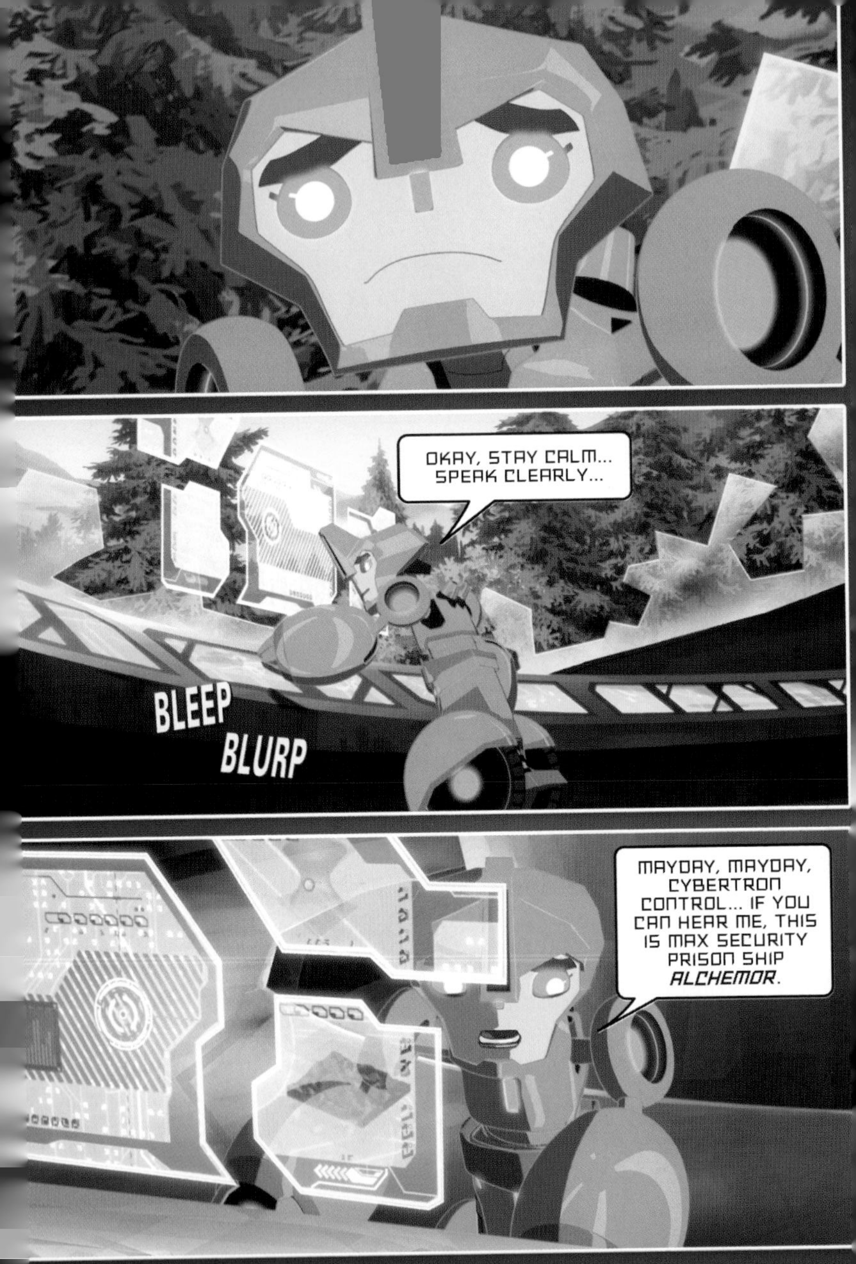
OKAY, STAY CALM... SPEAK CLEARLY...
BLEEP
BLURP
MAYDAY, MAYDAY, CYBERTRON CONTROL... IF YOU CAN HEAR ME, THIS IS MAX SECURITY PRISON SHIP *ALCHEMOR*.

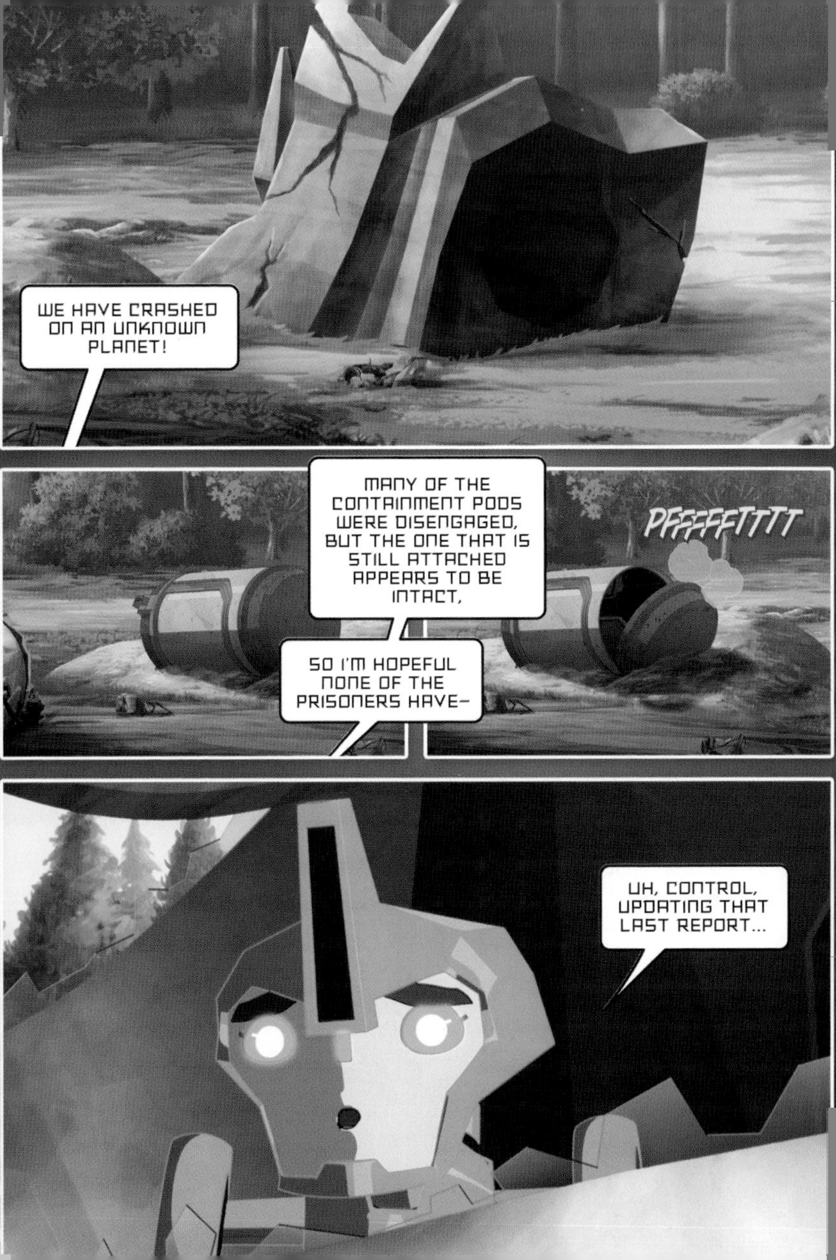
WE HAVE CRASHED ON AN UNKNOWN PLANET!
MANY OF THE CONTAINMENT PODS WERE DISENGAGED, BUT THE ONE THAT IS STILL ATTACHED APPEARS TO BE INTACT,
SO I'M HOPEFUL NONE OF THE PRISONERS HAVE–
PFFFFFTTTTT
UH, CONTROL, UPDATING THAT LAST REPORT...

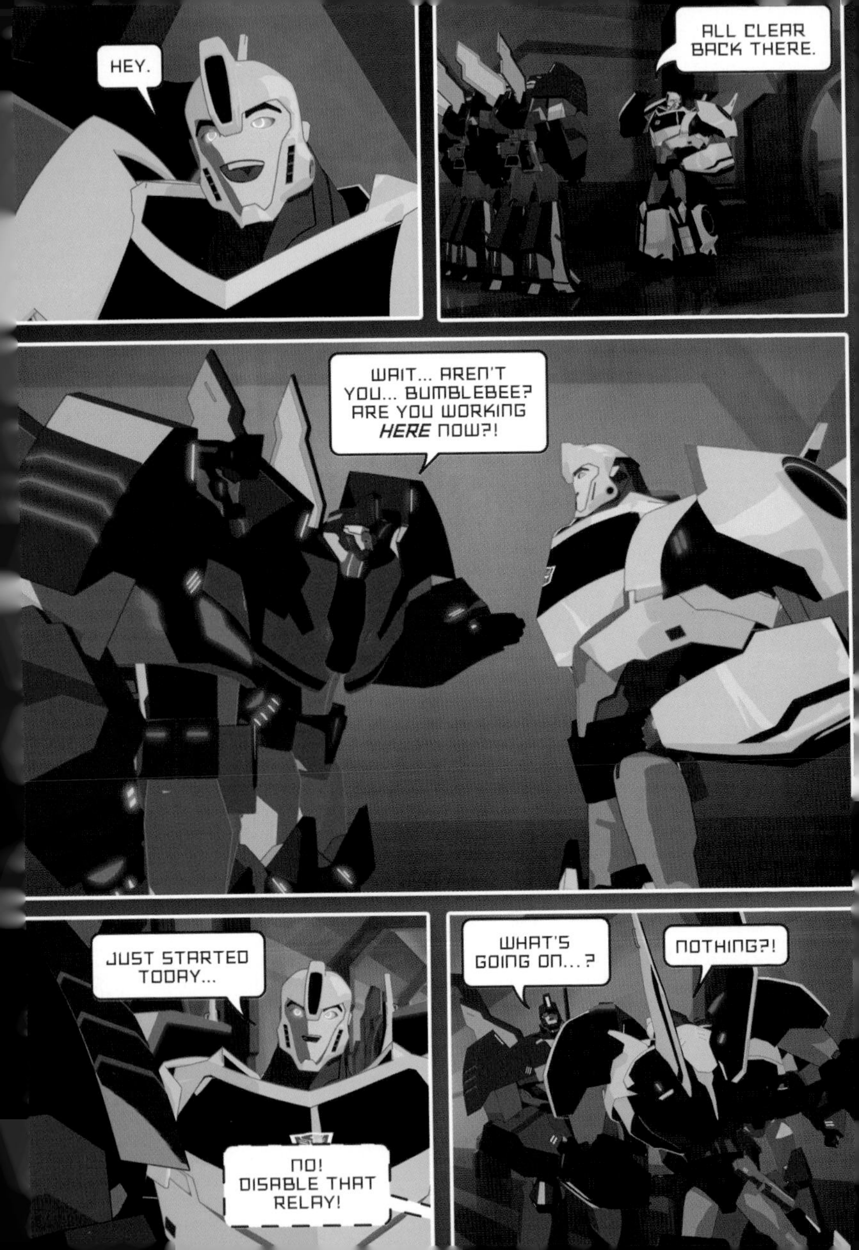
HEY.
ALL CLEAR BACK THERE.
WAIT... AREN'T YOU... BUMBLEBEE? ARE YOU WORKING *HERE* NOW?!
JUST STARTED TODAY...
NO! DISABLE THAT RELAY!
WHAT'S GOING ON...?
NOTHING?!

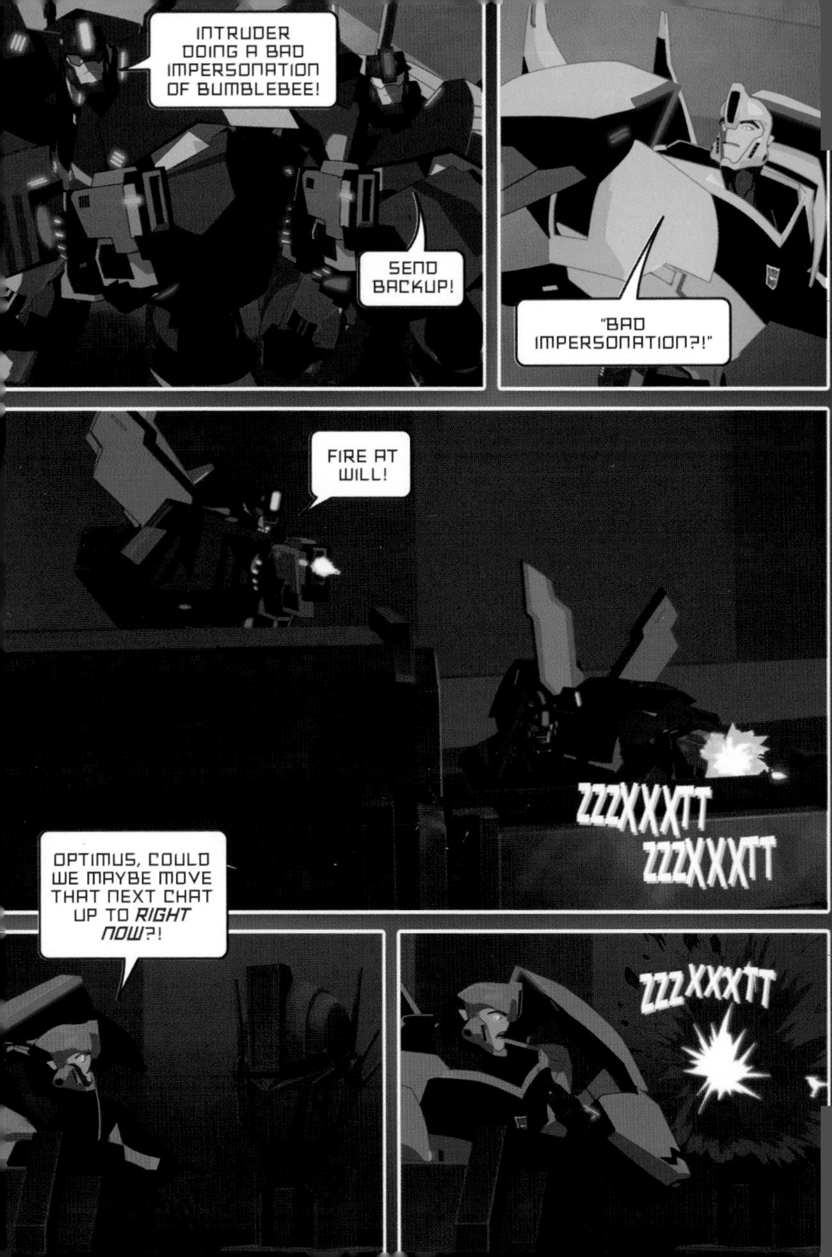

INTRUDER DOING A BAD IMPERSONATION OF BUMBLEBEE!
SEND BACKUP!
"BAD IMPERSONATION?!"
FIRE AT WILL!
ZZZXXXTT
ZZZXXXTT
OPTIMUS, COULD WE MAYBE MOVE THAT NEXT CHAT UP TO *RIGHT NOW*?!
ZZZXXXTT

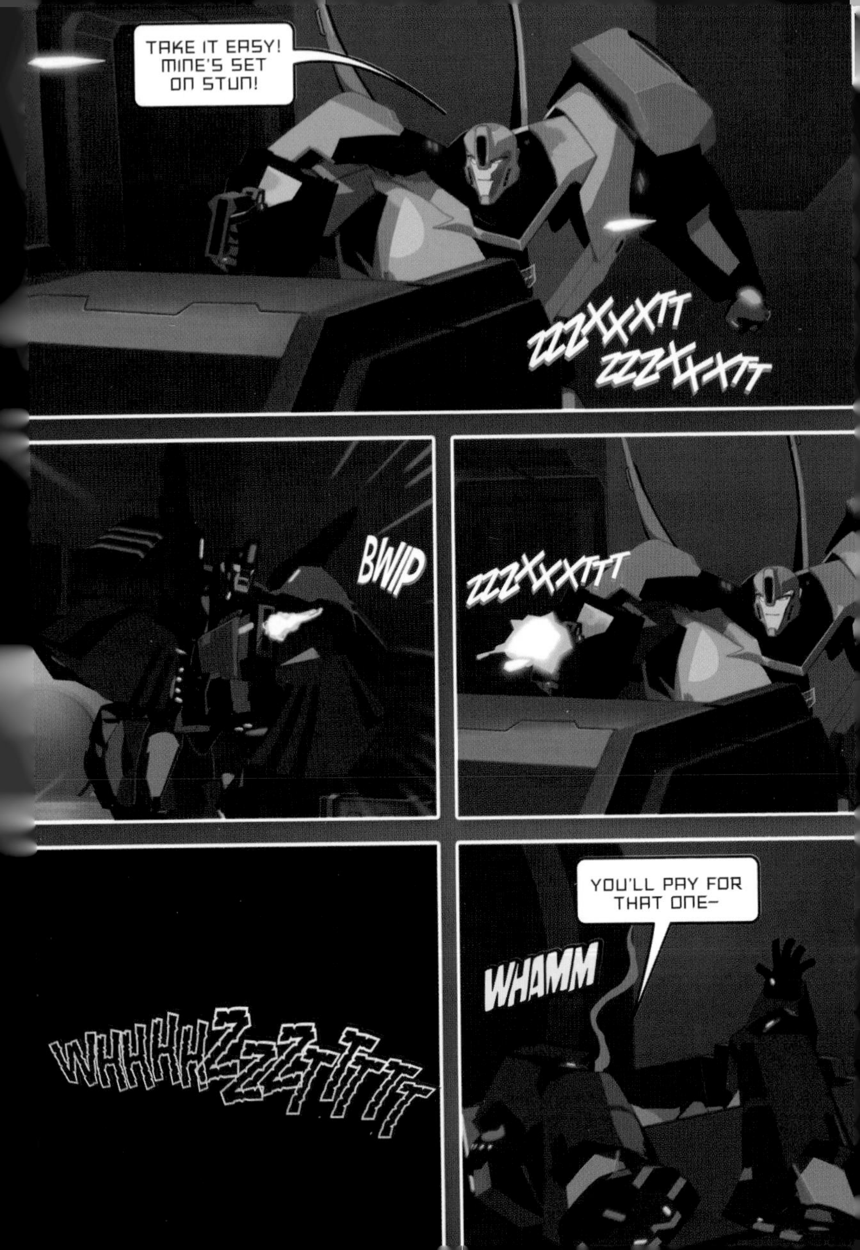
TAKE IT EASY! MINE'S SET ON STUN!
ZZZXXXTT
ZZZXXXTT
BWIP
ZZZXXXTTT
WHHHHZZZTTTTT
WHAMM
YOU'LL PAY FOR THAT ONE–

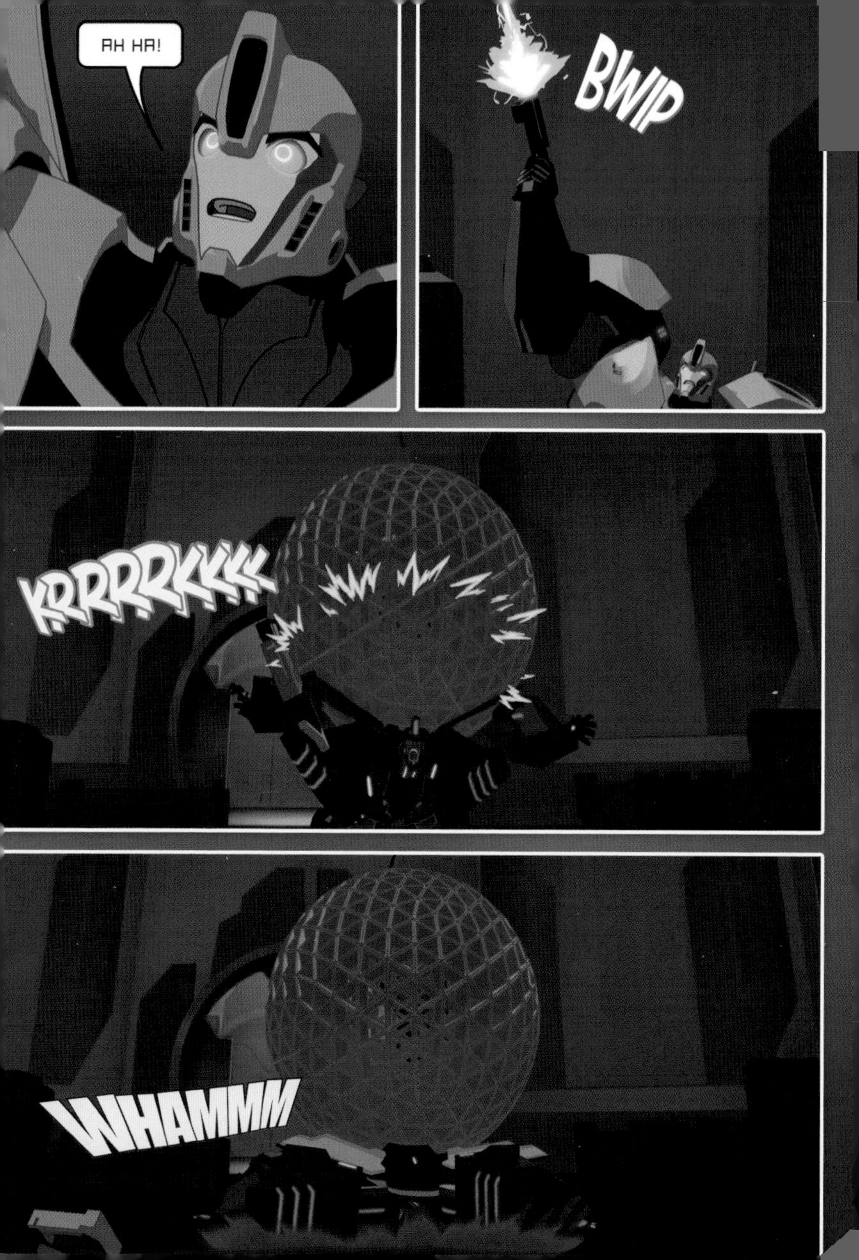
AH HA!
BWIP
KRRRRKKKK
WHAMMM

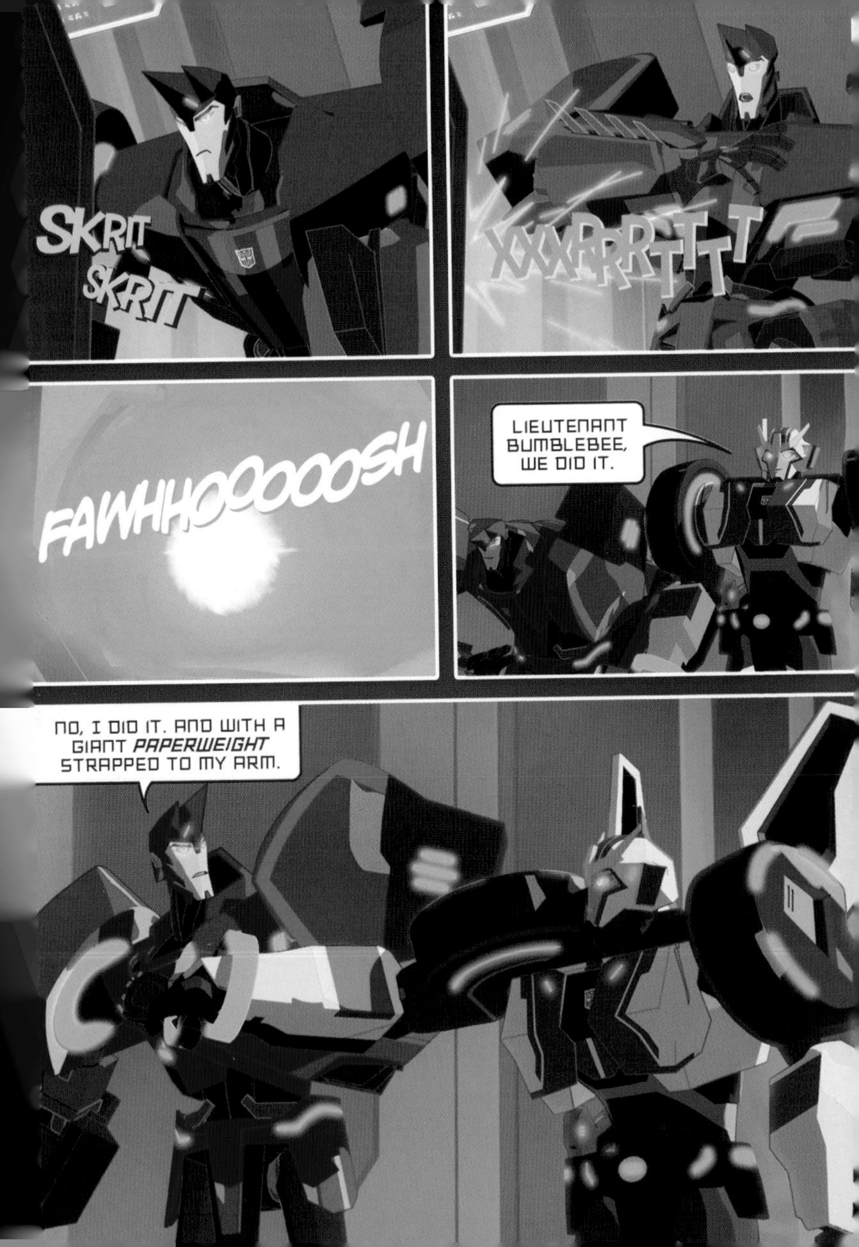
SKRIT
SKRIT
XXXRRRTTTT
FAWHHOOOOOOSH
LIEUTENANT BUMBLEBEE, WE DID IT.
NO, I DID IT. AND WITH A GIANT *PAPERWEIGHT* STRAPPED TO MY ARM.

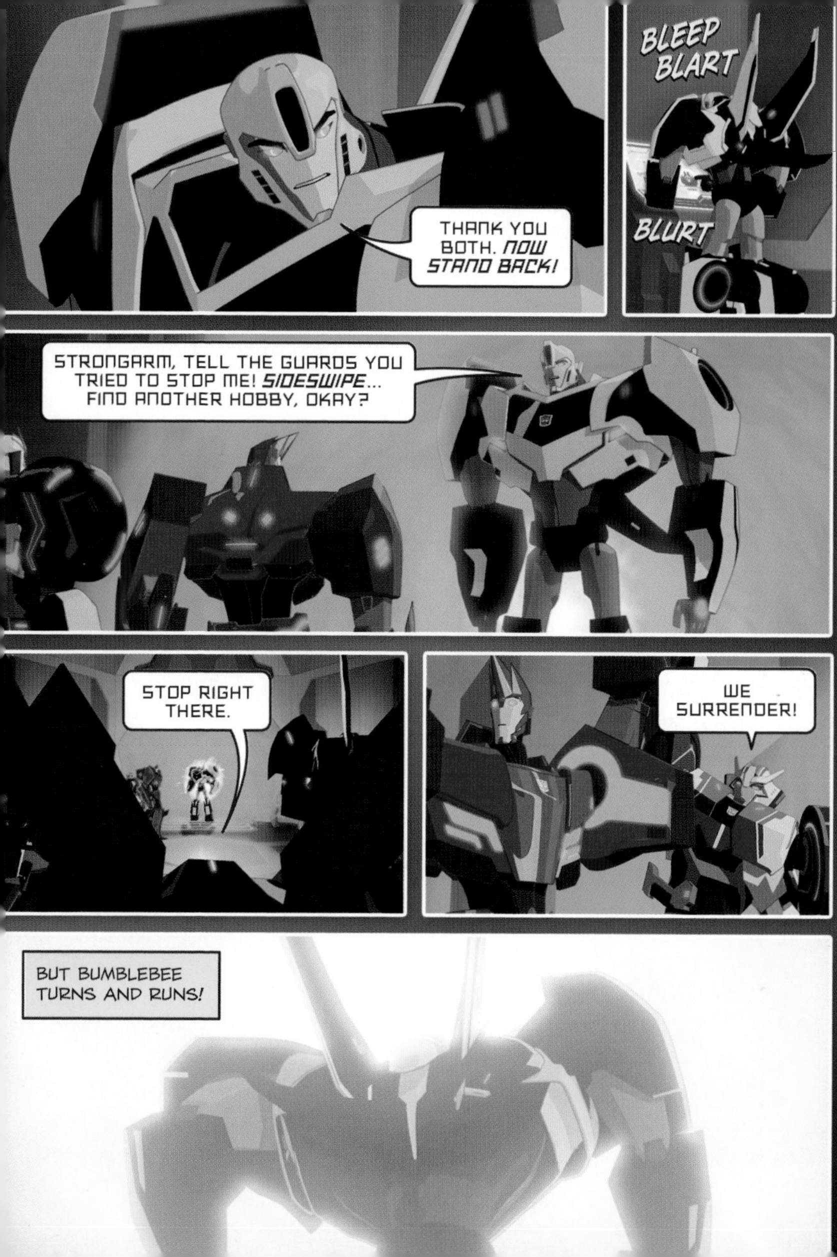
THANK YOU BOTH. NOW STAND BACK!
BLEEP BLART
BLURT
STRONGARM, TELL THE GUARDS YOU TRIED TO STOP ME! SIDESWIPE... FIND ANOTHER HOBBY, OKAY?
STOP RIGHT THERE.
WE SURRENDER!
BUT BUMBLEBEE TURNS AND RUNS!

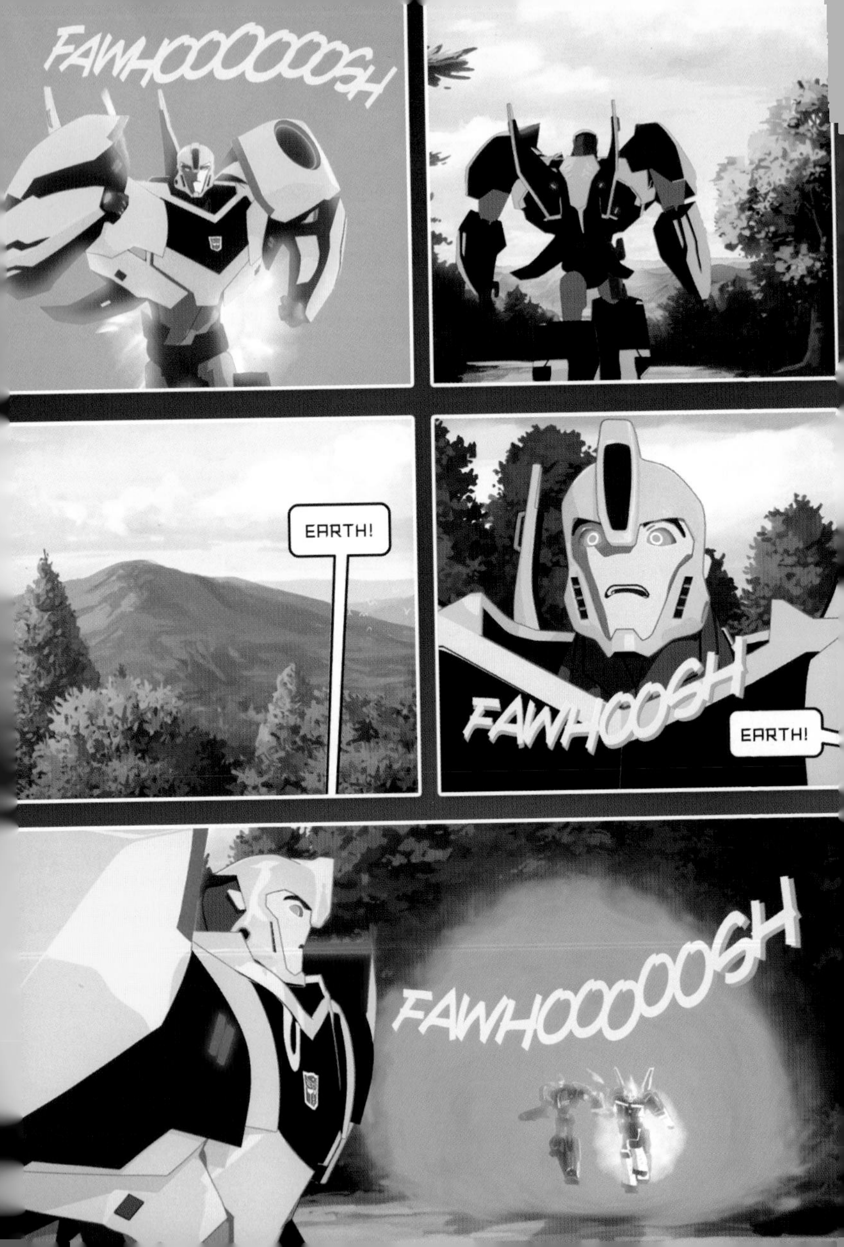
FAWHOOOOOOOSH
EARTH!
FAWHOOSH
EARTH!
FAWHOOOOOOSH

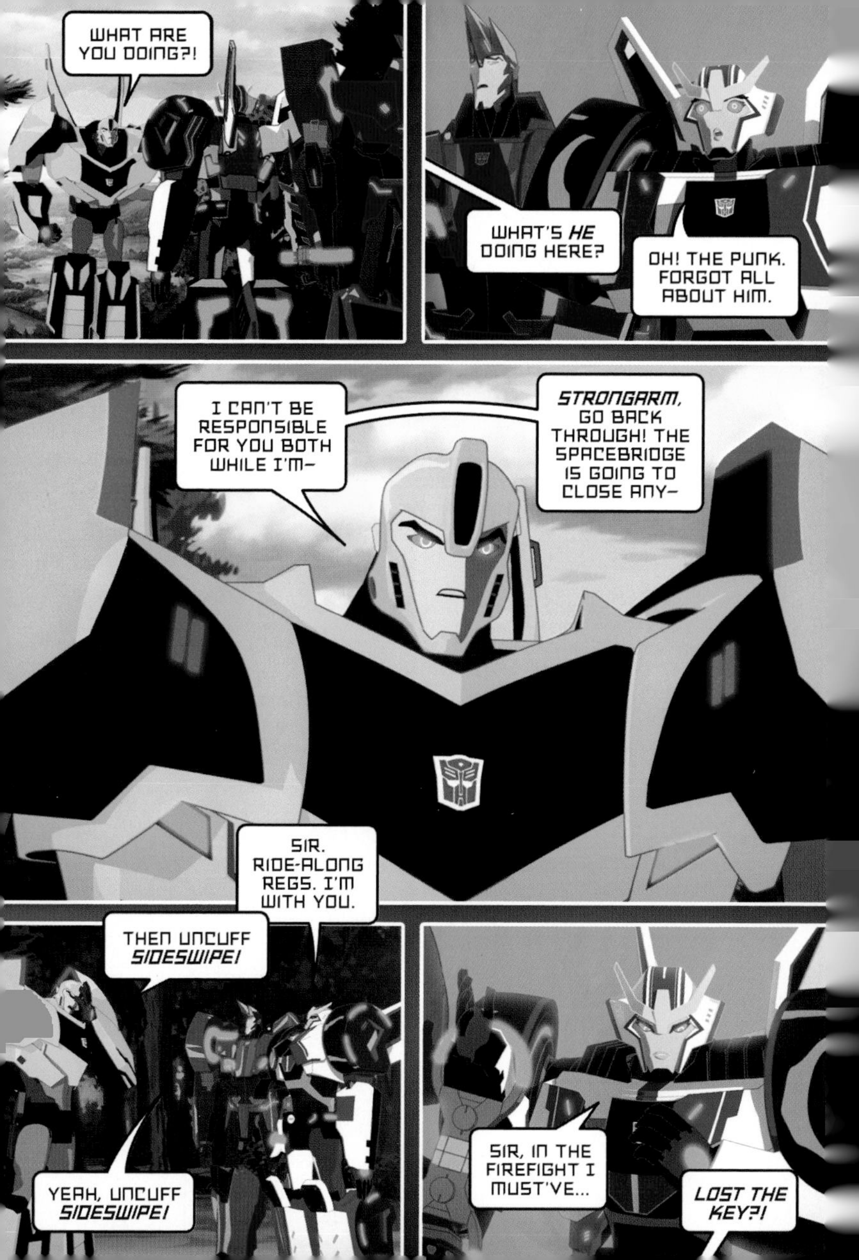
WHAT ARE YOU DOING?!
WHAT'S *HE* DOING HERE?
OH! THE PUNK. FORGOT ALL ABOUT HIM.
I CAN'T BE RESPONSIBLE FOR YOU BOTH WHILE I'M–
STRONGARM, GO BACK THROUGH! THE SPACEBRIDGE IS GOING TO CLOSE ANY–
SIR. RIDE-ALONG REGS. I'M WITH YOU.
THEN UNCUFF *SIDESWIPE!*
YEAH, UNCUFF *SIDESWIPE!*
SIR, IN THE FIREFIGHT I MUST'VE...
LOST THE KEY?!

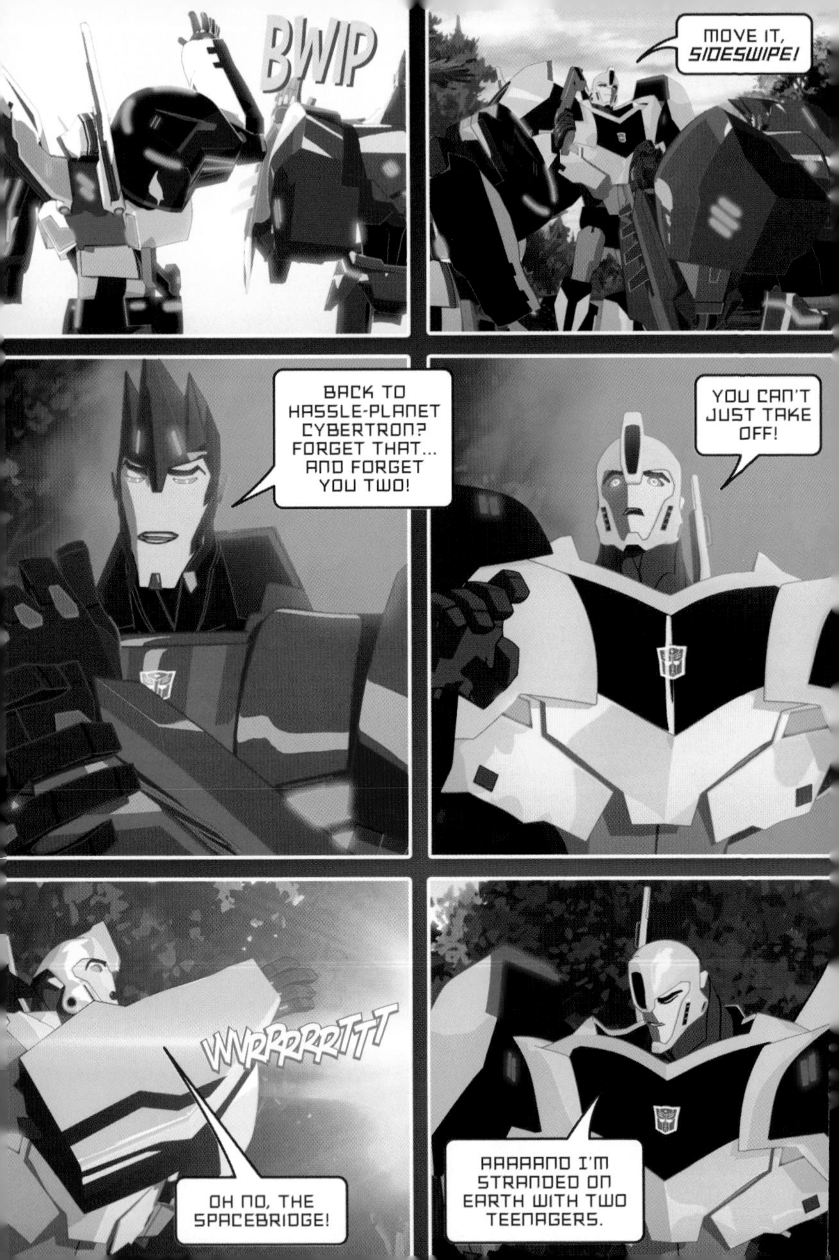
BWIP
MOVE IT, SIDESWIPE!
BACK TO HASSLE-PLANET CYBERTRON? FORGET THAT... AND FORGET YOU TWO!
YOU CAN'T JUST TAKE OFF!
WVRRRRRTTT
OH NO, THE SPACEBRIDGE!
AAAAAND I'M STRANDED ON EARTH WITH TWO TEENAGERS.

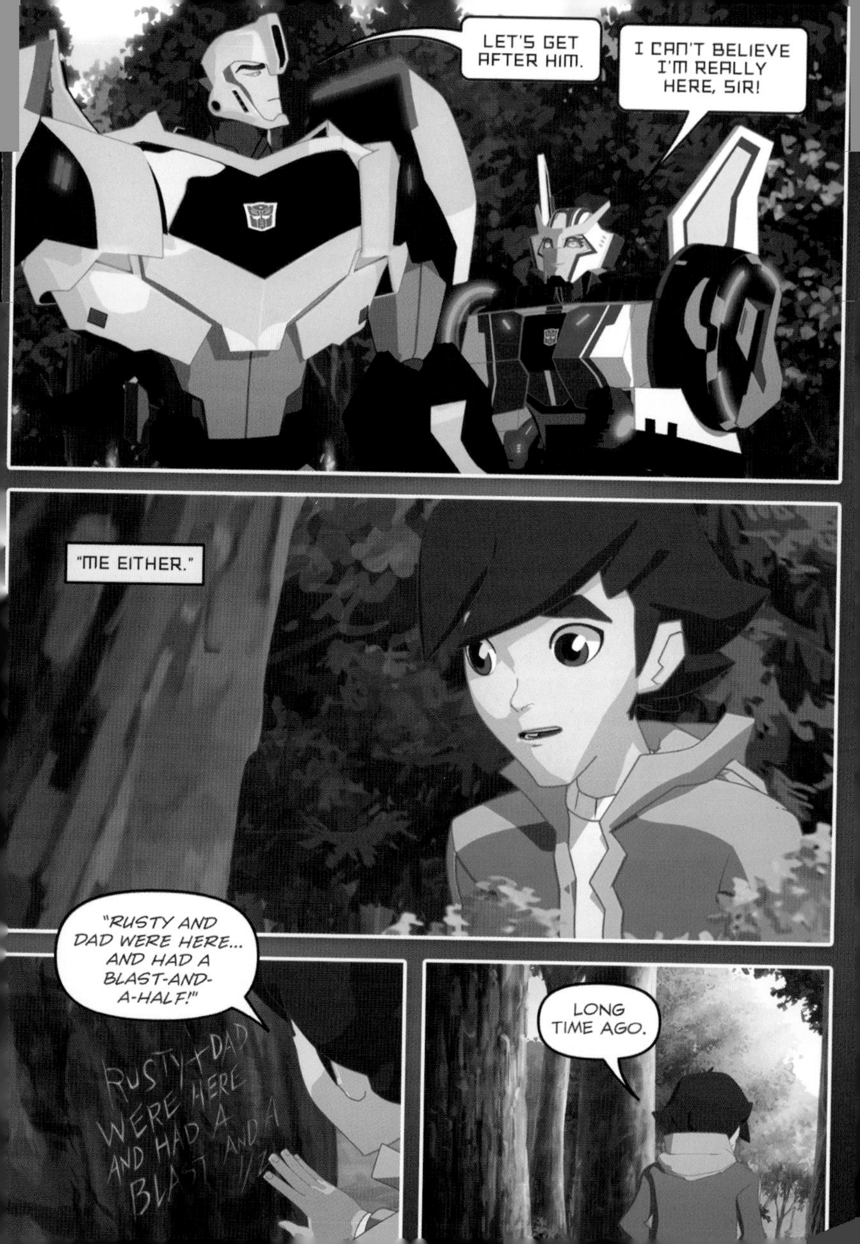
LET'S GET AFTER HIM.
I CAN'T BELIEVE I'M REALLY HERE, SIR!
"ME EITHER."
"RUSTY AND DAD WERE HERE... AND HAD A BLAST-AND-A-HALF!"
RUSTY + DAD WERE HERE AND HAD A BLAST AND A 1/2
LONG TIME AGO.

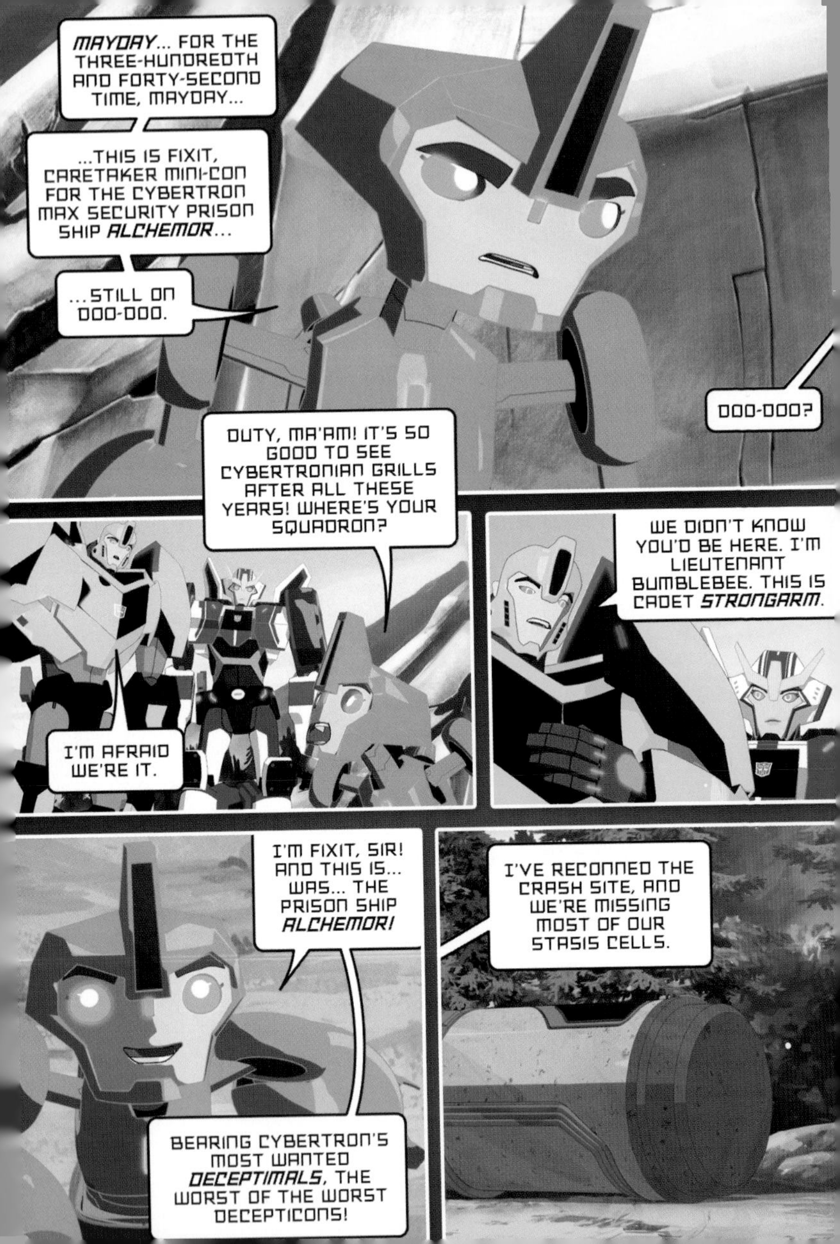
MAYDAY... FOR THE THREE-HUNDREDTH AND FORTY-SECOND TIME, MAYDAY...
...THIS IS FIXIT, CARETAKER MINI-CON FOR THE CYBERTRON MAX SECURITY PRISON SHIP ALCHEMOR...
...STILL ON DOO-DOO.
DOO-DOO?
DUTY, MA'AM! IT'S SO GOOD TO SEE CYBERTRONIAN GRILLS AFTER ALL THESE YEARS! WHERE'S YOUR SQUADRON?
I'M AFRAID WE'RE IT.
WE DIDN'T KNOW YOU'D BE HERE. I'M LIEUTENANT BUMBLEBEE. THIS IS CADET STRONGARM.
I'M FIXIT, SIR! AND THIS IS... WAS... THE PRISON SHIP ALCHEMOR!
BEARING CYBERTRON'S MOST WANTED DECEPTIMALS, THE WORST OF THE WORST DECEPTICONS!
I'VE RECONNED THE CRASH SITE, AND WE'RE MISSING MOST OF OUR STASIS CELLS.

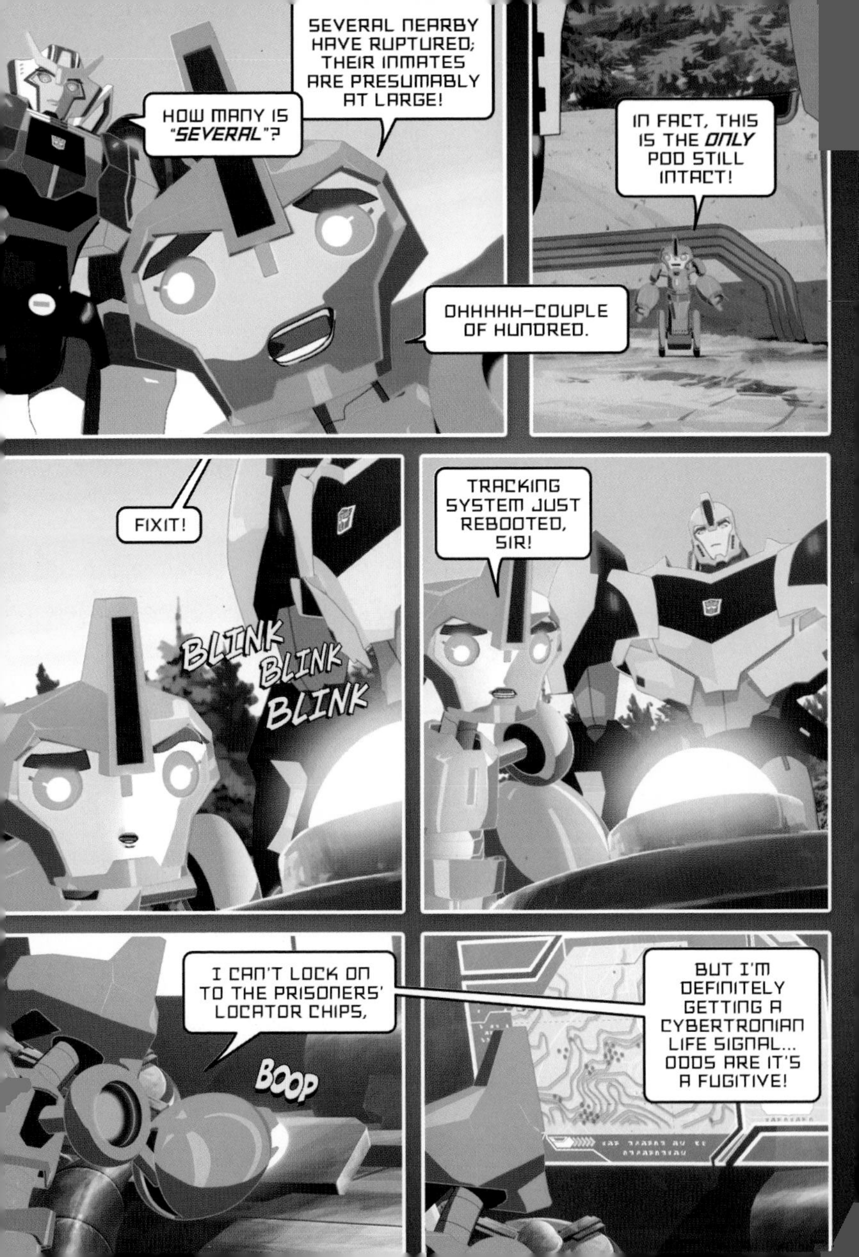
HOW MANY IS "SEVERAL"?
SEVERAL NEARBY HAVE RUPTURED; THEIR INMATES ARE PRESUMABLY AT LARGE!
OHHHHH—COUPLE OF HUNDRED.
IN FACT, THIS IS THE ONLY POD STILL INTACT!
FIXIT!
BLINK
BLINK
BLINK
TRACKING SYSTEM JUST REBOOTED, SIR!
I CAN'T LOCK ON TO THE PRISONERS' LOCATOR CHIPS,
BOOP
BUT I'M DEFINITELY GETTING A CYBERTRONIAN LIFE SIGNAL... ODDS ARE IT'S A FUGITIVE!

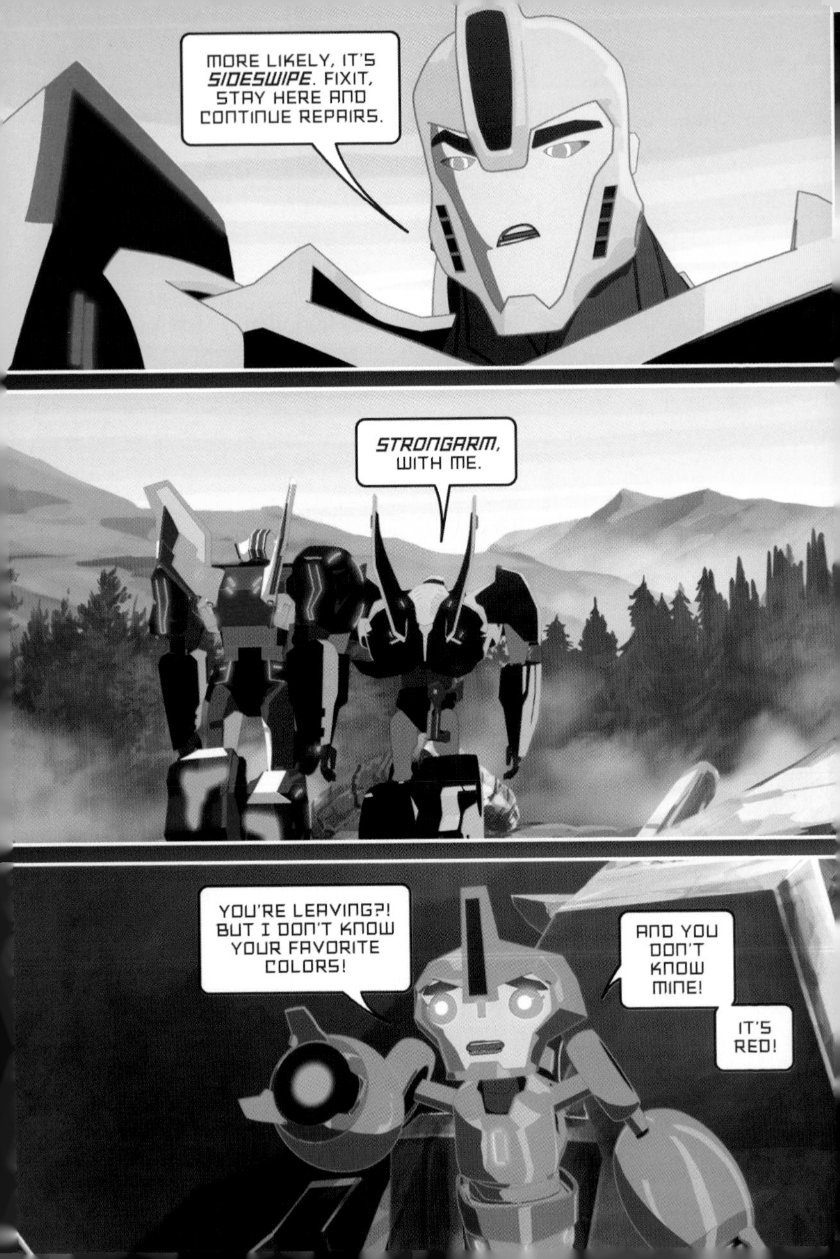
MORE LIKELY, IT'S *SIDESWIPE*. FIXIT, STAY HERE AND CONTINUE REPAIRS.
STRONGARM, WITH ME.
YOU'RE LEAVING?! BUT I DON'T KNOW YOUR FAVORITE COLORS!
AND YOU DON'T KNOW MINE!
IT'S RED!

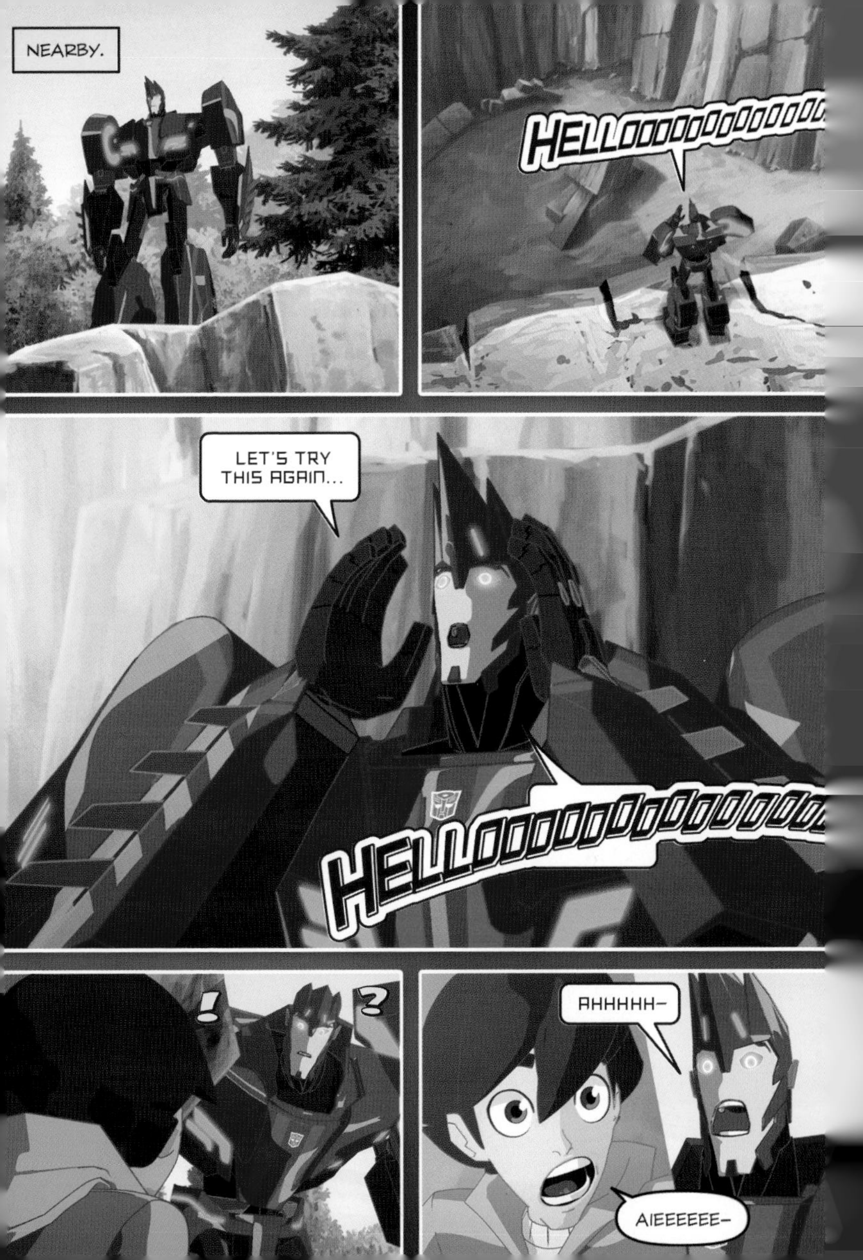
NEARBY.
HELLOOOOOOOOOOOO
LET'S TRY THIS AGAIN...
HELLOOOOOOOOOOOOOOOO
!
?
AHHHHH-
AIEEEEEE-

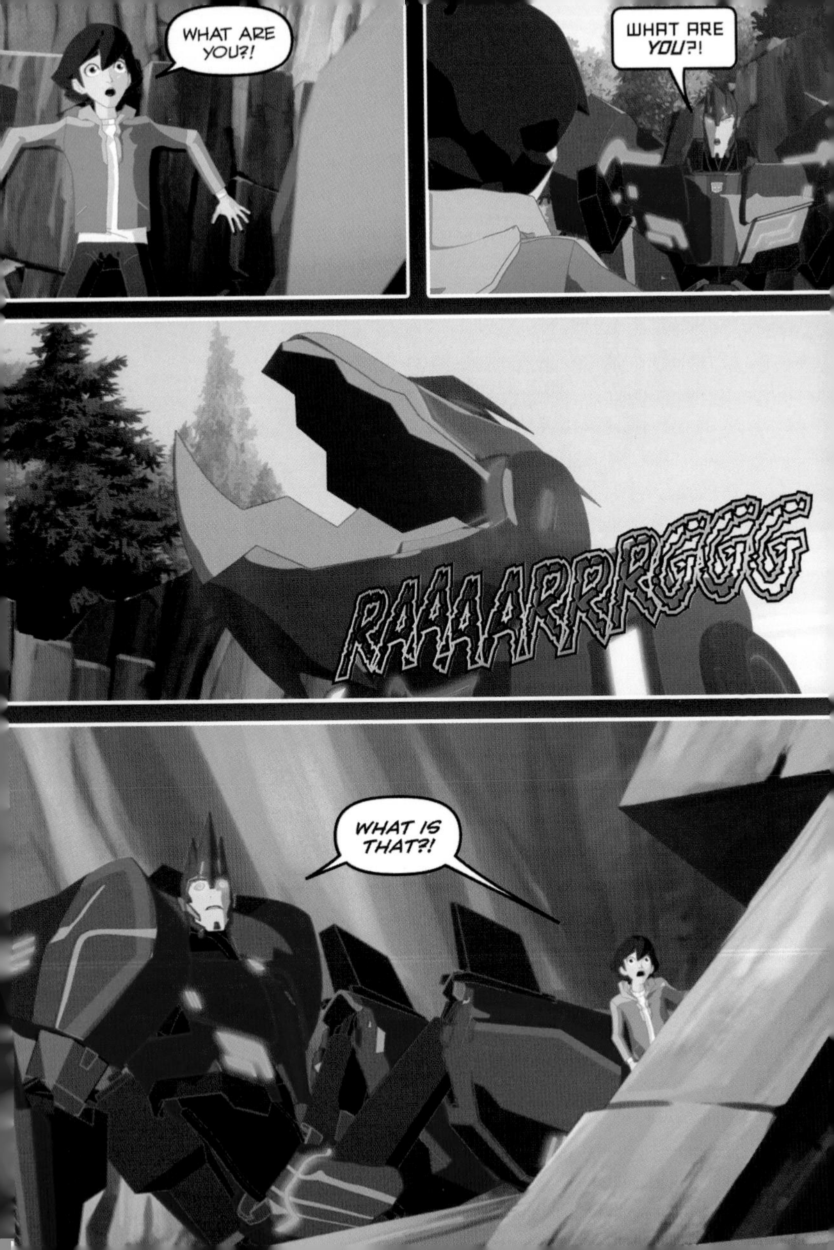
WHAT ARE YOU?!
WHAT ARE *YOU*?!
RAAAARRRGGG
WHAT IS THAT?!

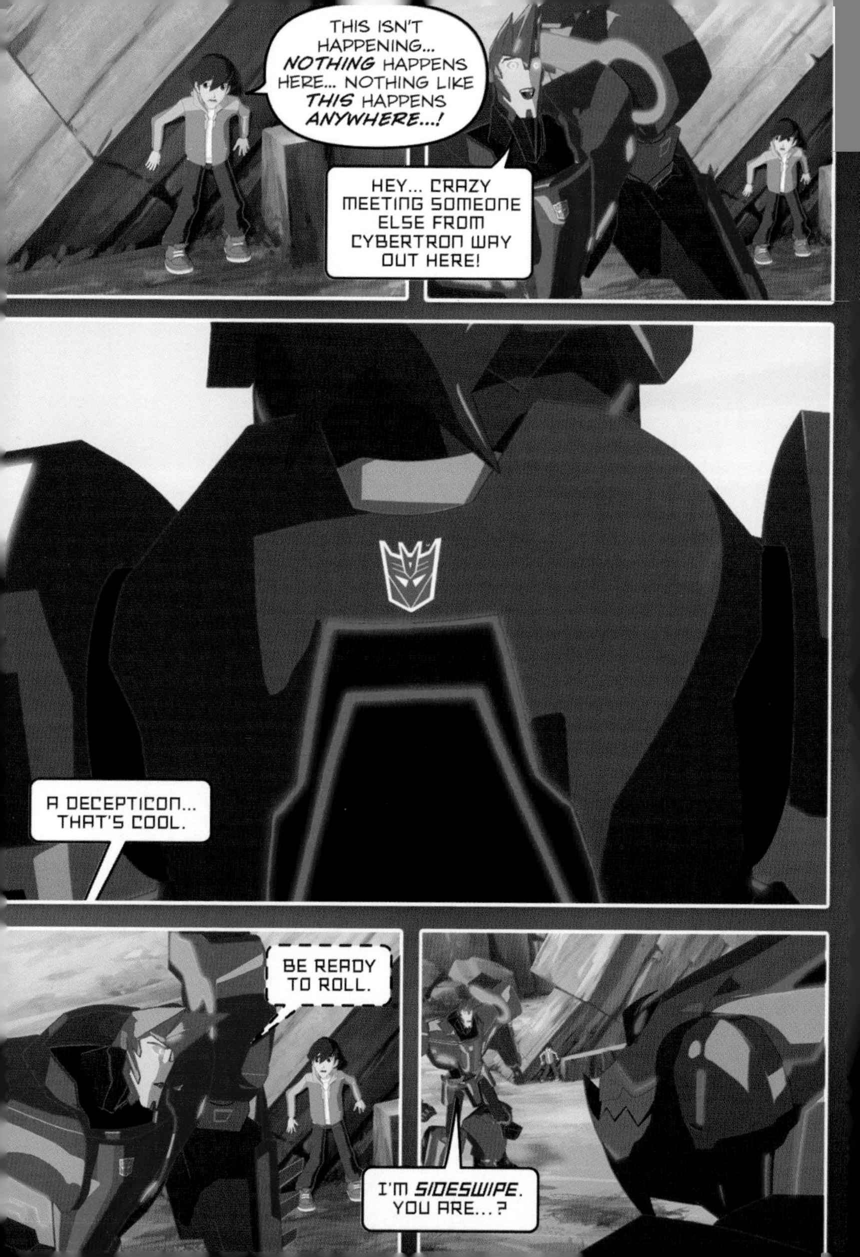
THIS ISN'T HAPPENING... *NOTHING* HAPPENS HERE... NOTHING LIKE *THIS* HAPPENS *ANYWHERE*...!
HEY... CRAZY MEETING SOMEONE ELSE FROM CYBERTRON WAY OUT HERE!
A DECEPTICON... THAT'S COOL.
BE READY TO ROLL.
I'M *SIDESWIPE*. YOU ARE...?

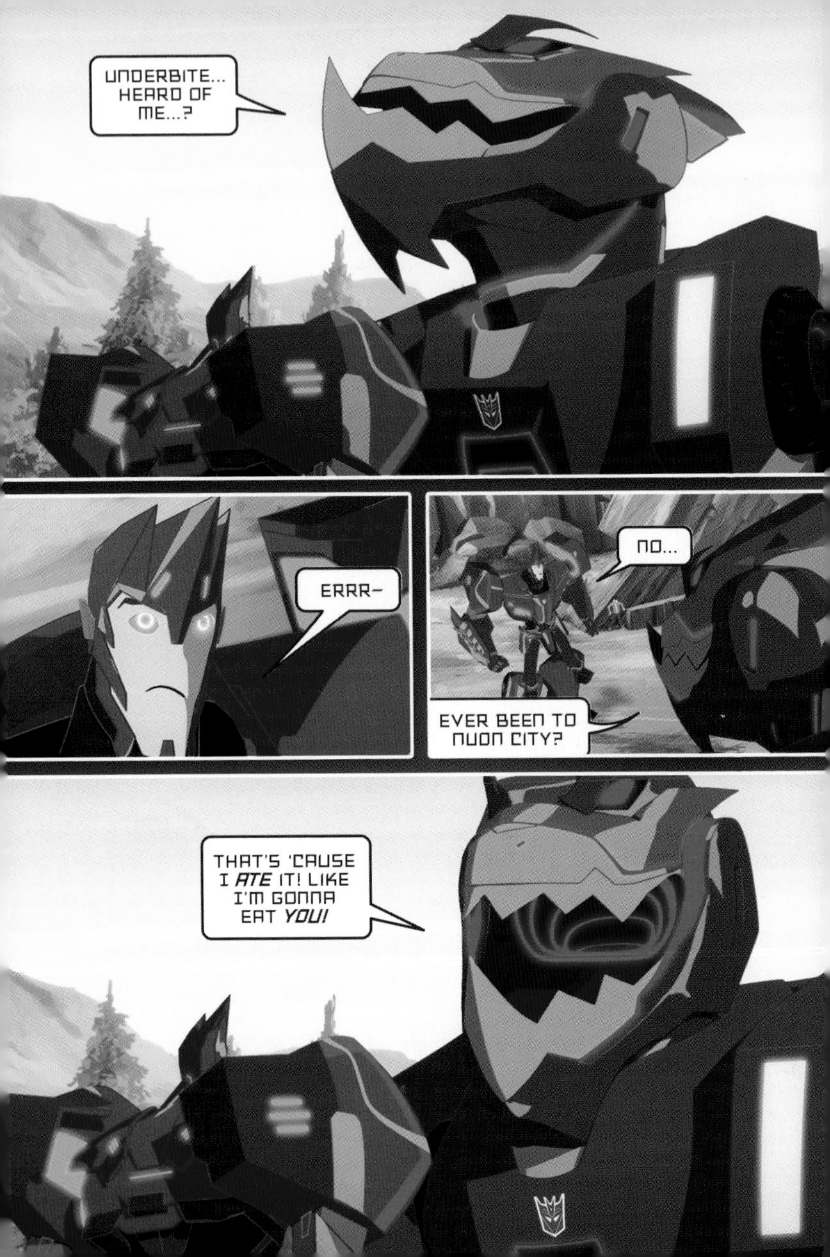
UNDERBITE... HEARD OF ME...?
ERRR–
NO...
EVER BEEN TO NUON CITY?
THAT'S 'CAUSE I *ATE* IT! LIKE I'M GONNA EAT *YOU!*

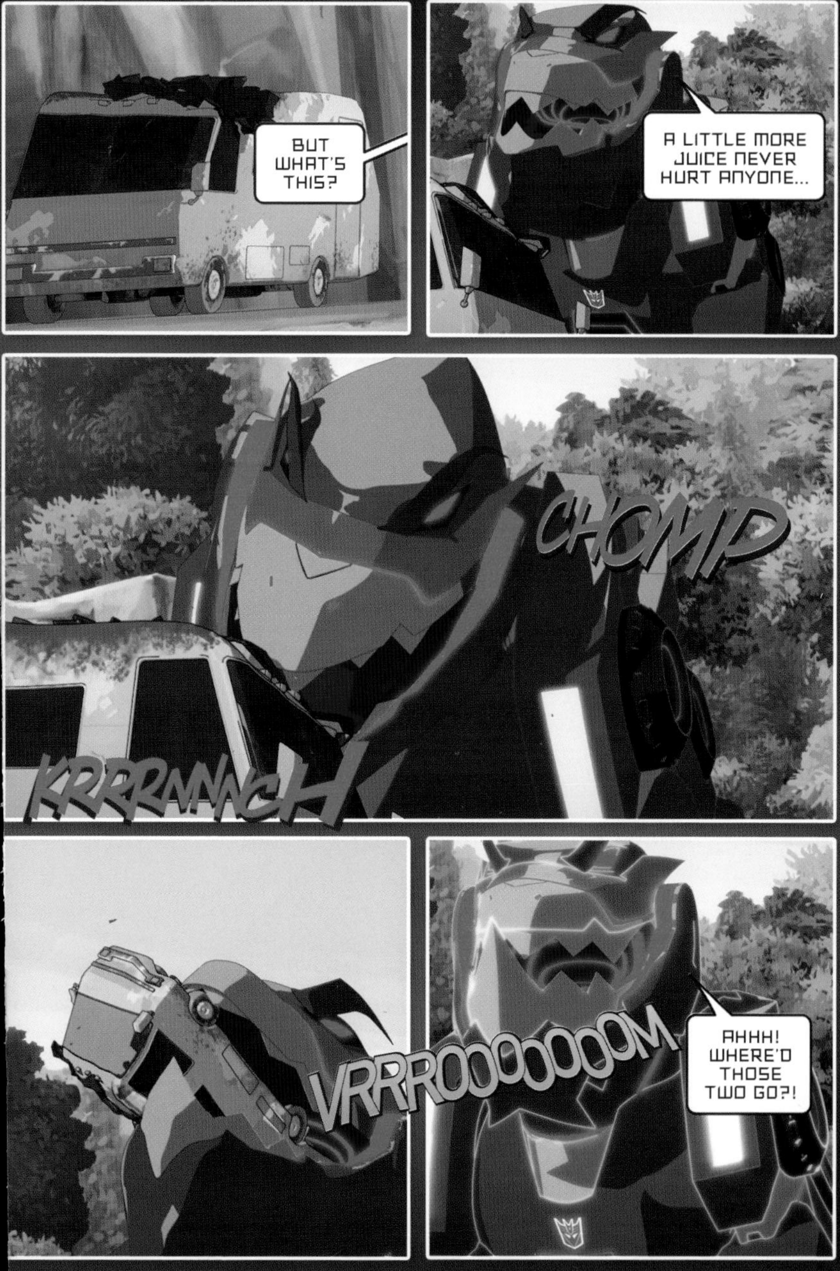

BUT WHAT'S THIS?
A LITTLE MORE JUICE NEVER HURT ANYONE...
CHOMP
KRRRNNNCH
VRRROOOOOOOOM
AHHH! WHERE'D THOSE TWO GO?!

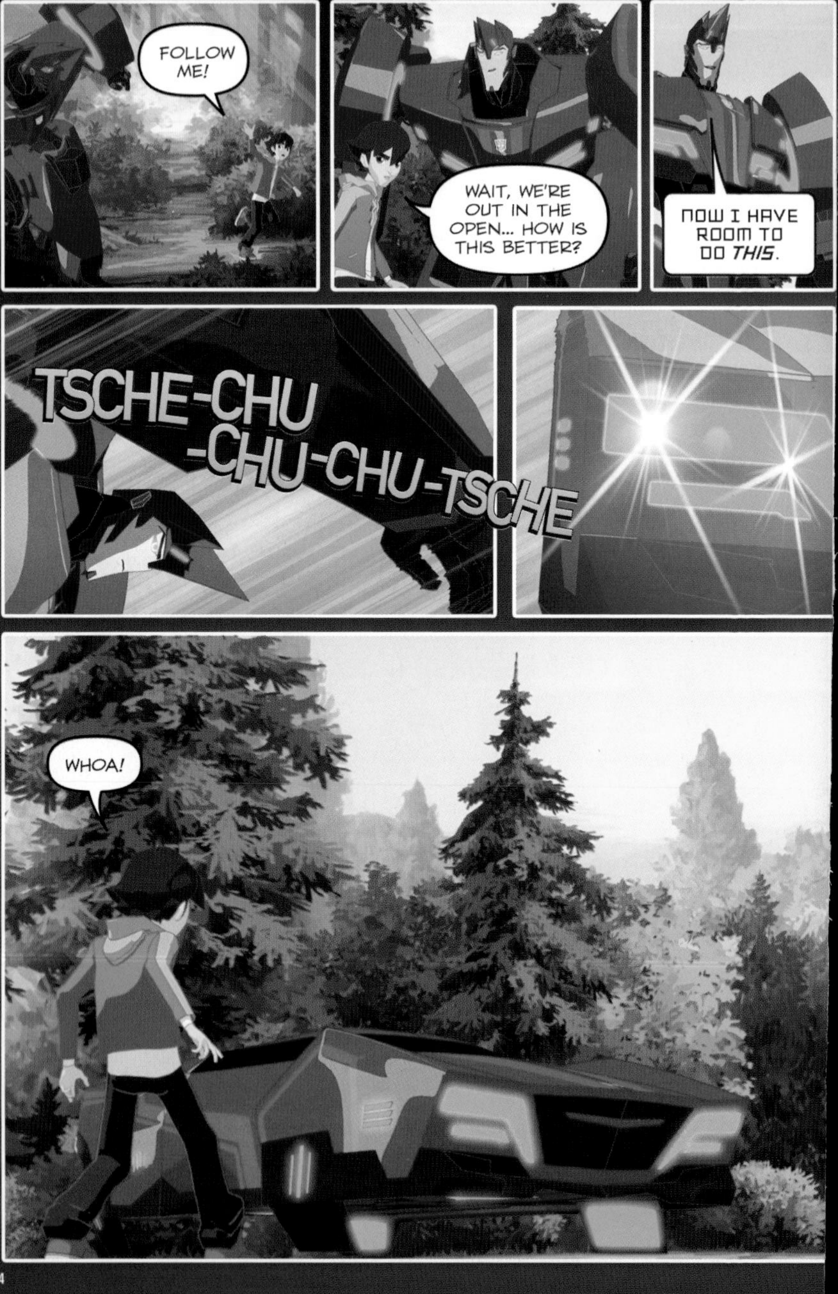
FOLLOW ME!
WAIT, WE'RE OUT IN THE OPEN... HOW IS THIS BETTER?
NOW I HAVE ROOM TO DO *THIS*.
TSCHE-CHU -CHU-CHU-TSCHE
WHOA!

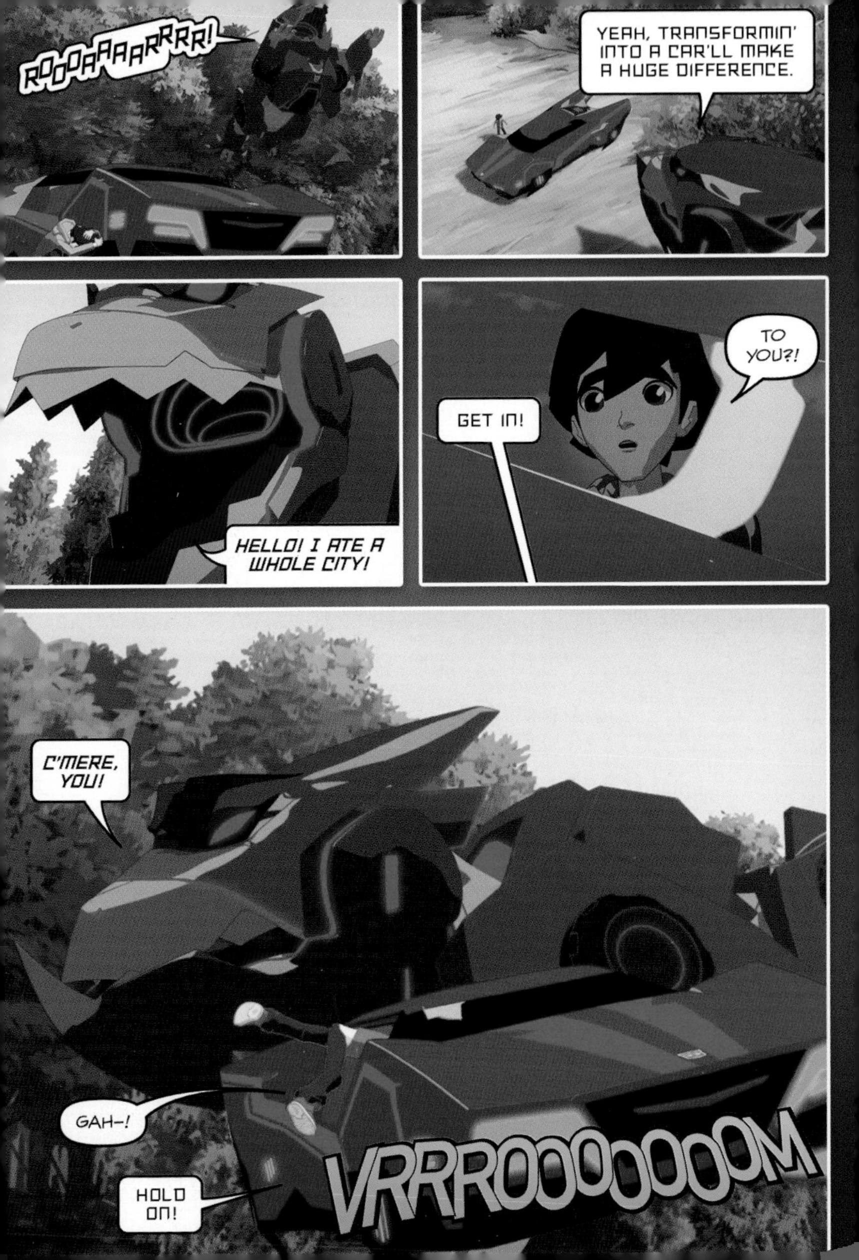
ROOOAAAARRRR!
YEAH, TRANSFORMIN' INTO A CAR'LL MAKE A HUGE DIFFERENCE.
HELLO! I ATE A WHOLE CITY!
GET IN!
TO YOU?!
C'MERE, YOU!
GAH-!
HOLD ON!
VRRROOOOOOOOM

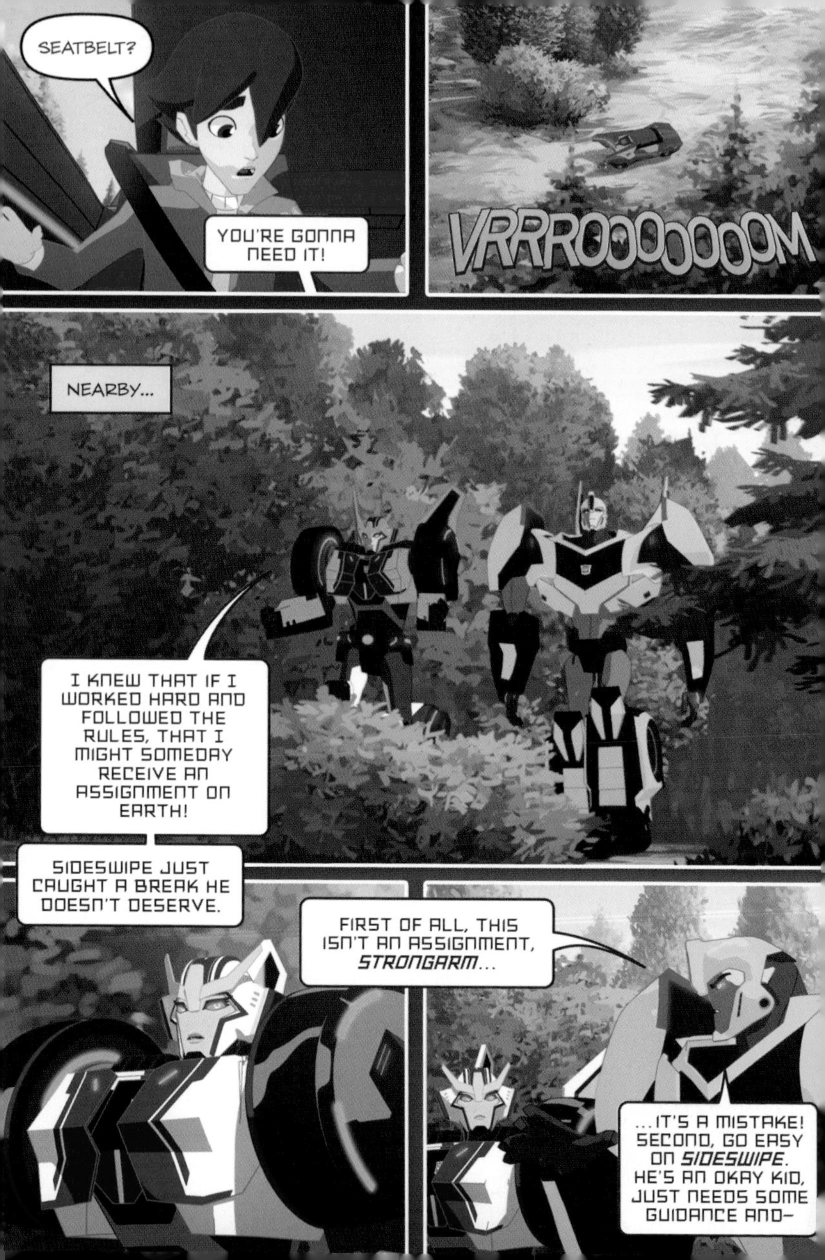
SEATBELT?
YOU'RE GONNA NEED IT!
VRRROOOOOOOOM
NEARBY...
I KNEW THAT IF I WORKED HARD AND FOLLOWED THE RULES, THAT I MIGHT SOMEDAY RECEIVE AN ASSIGNMENT ON EARTH!
SIDESWIPE JUST CAUGHT A BREAK HE DOESN'T DESERVE.
FIRST OF ALL, THIS ISN'T AN ASSIGNMENT, *STRONGARM*...
...IT'S A MISTAKE! SECOND, GO EASY ON *SIDESWIPE*. HE'S AN OKAY KID, JUST NEEDS SOME GUIDANCE AND–

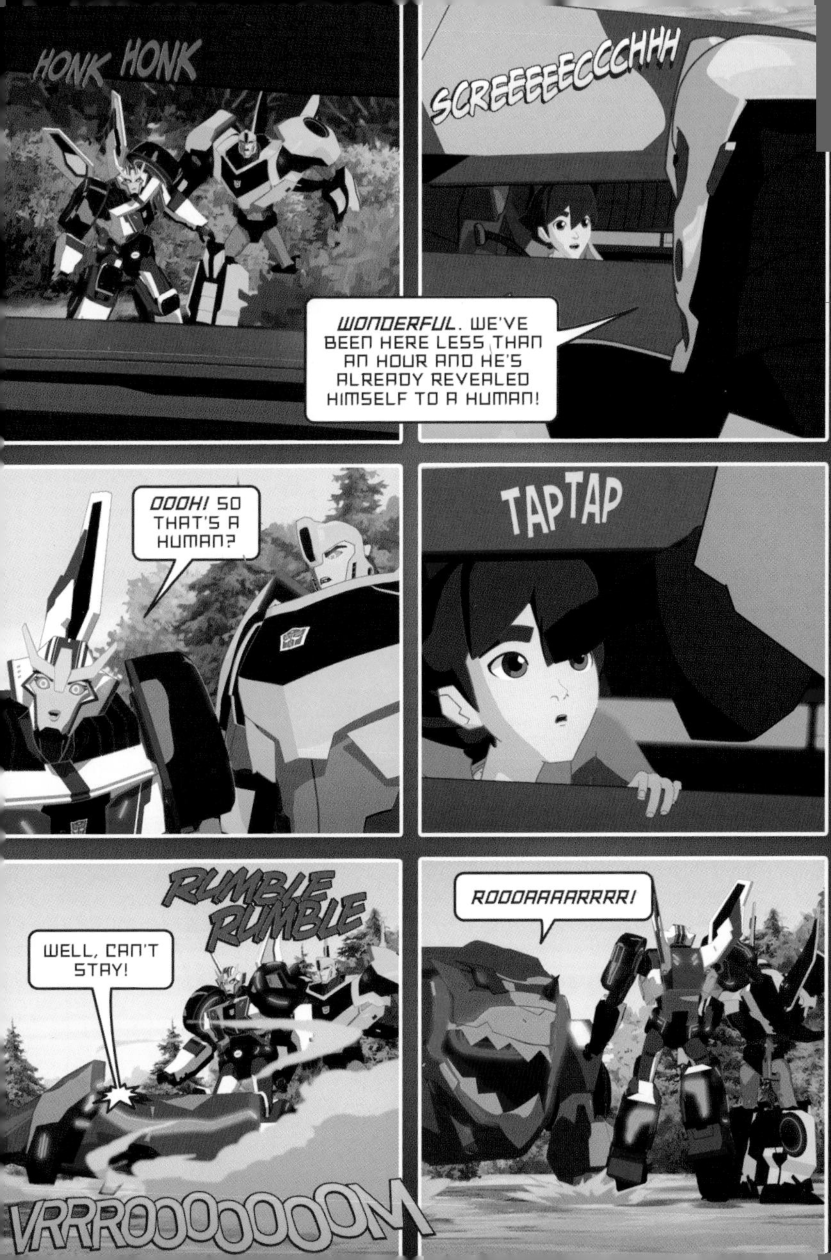
HONK HONK
SCREEEEEECCCHHH
WONDERFUL. WE'VE BEEN HERE LESS THAN AN HOUR AND HE'S ALREADY REVEALED HIMSELF TO A HUMAN!
OOOH! SO THAT'S A HUMAN?
TAPTAP
RUMBLE RUMBLE
WELL, CAN'T STAY!
VRRROOOOOOOOM
ROOOAAAARRRRR!

I KNOW WHAT YOU'RE THINKING.

"IS THAT TALL, DARK AND HANDSOME 'CON *REALLY UNDERBITE, DEVOURER OF NUON CITY?*"

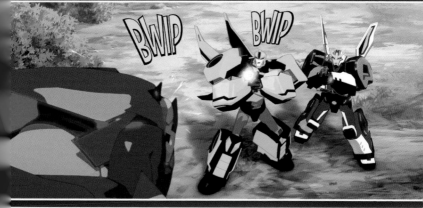

BWIP

BWIP

NO ONE RECOGNIZES ME?

RUN!

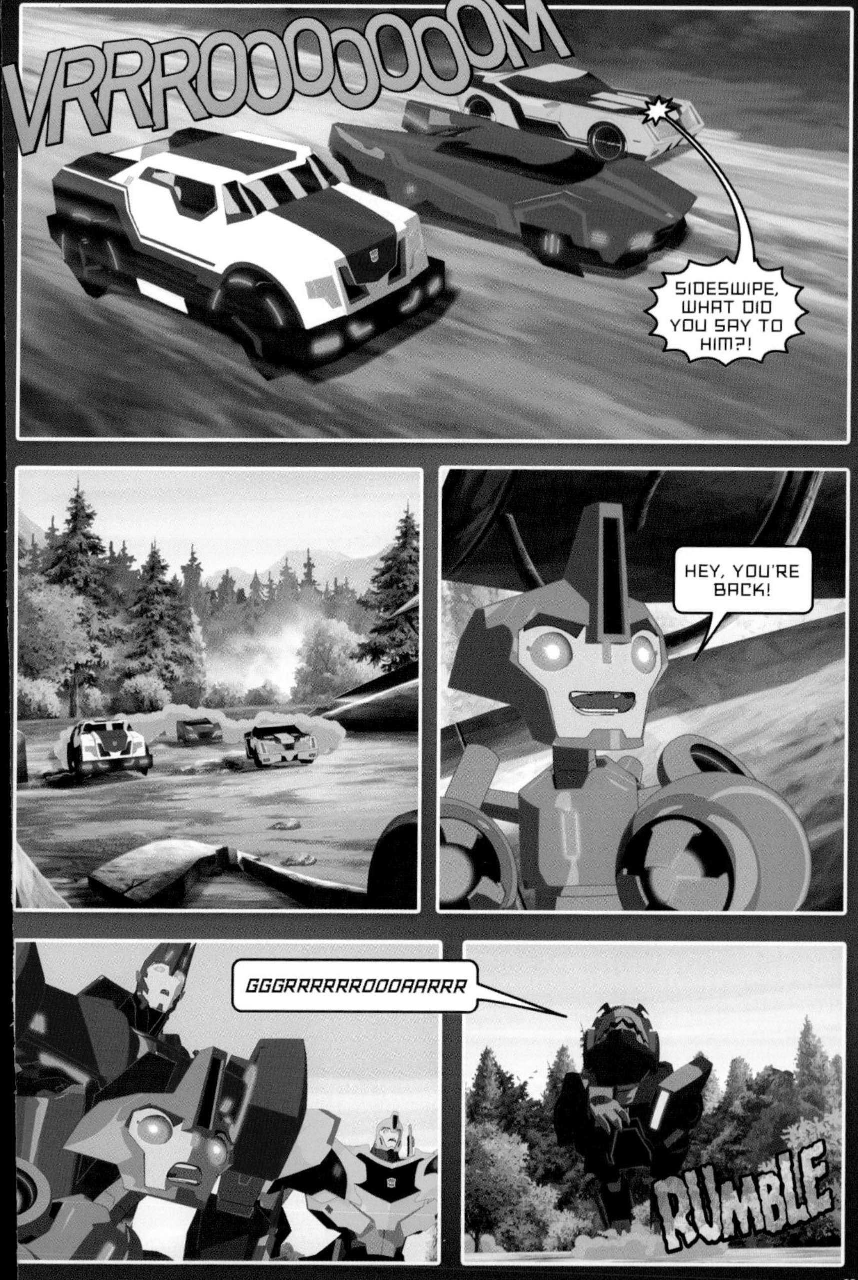
VRRROOOOOOOOM
SIDESWIPE, WHAT DID YOU SAY TO HIM?!
HEY, YOU'RE BACK!
GGGRRRRRRROOOAARRR
RUMBLE

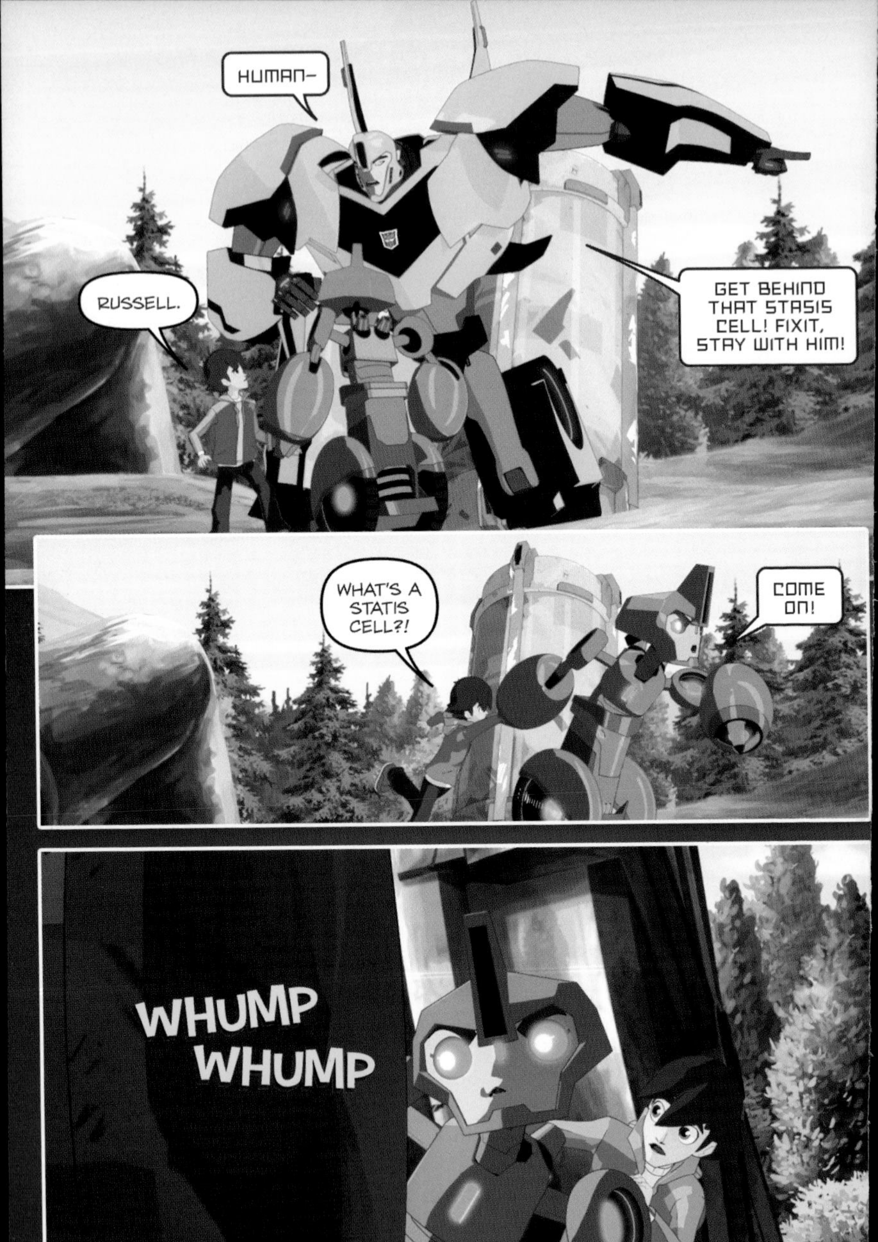
HUMAN–
RUSSELL.
GET BEHIND THAT STASIS CELL! FIXIT, STAY WITH HIM!
WHAT'S A STATIS CELL?!
COME ON!
WHUMP WHUMP

BRAKK

GWARRGGG!

I HEAR FIGHTING! WHO'S FIGHTING?!

I WANT TO FIGHT!

BACK IN YOUR CELL!

KRRRRRRTTT

OWWWWW-!

WUMP

GGGRRRRAAAADDDDR

LOOK OUT!

STRONGARM, SIDESWIPE... FAN OUT!

SWAKKK

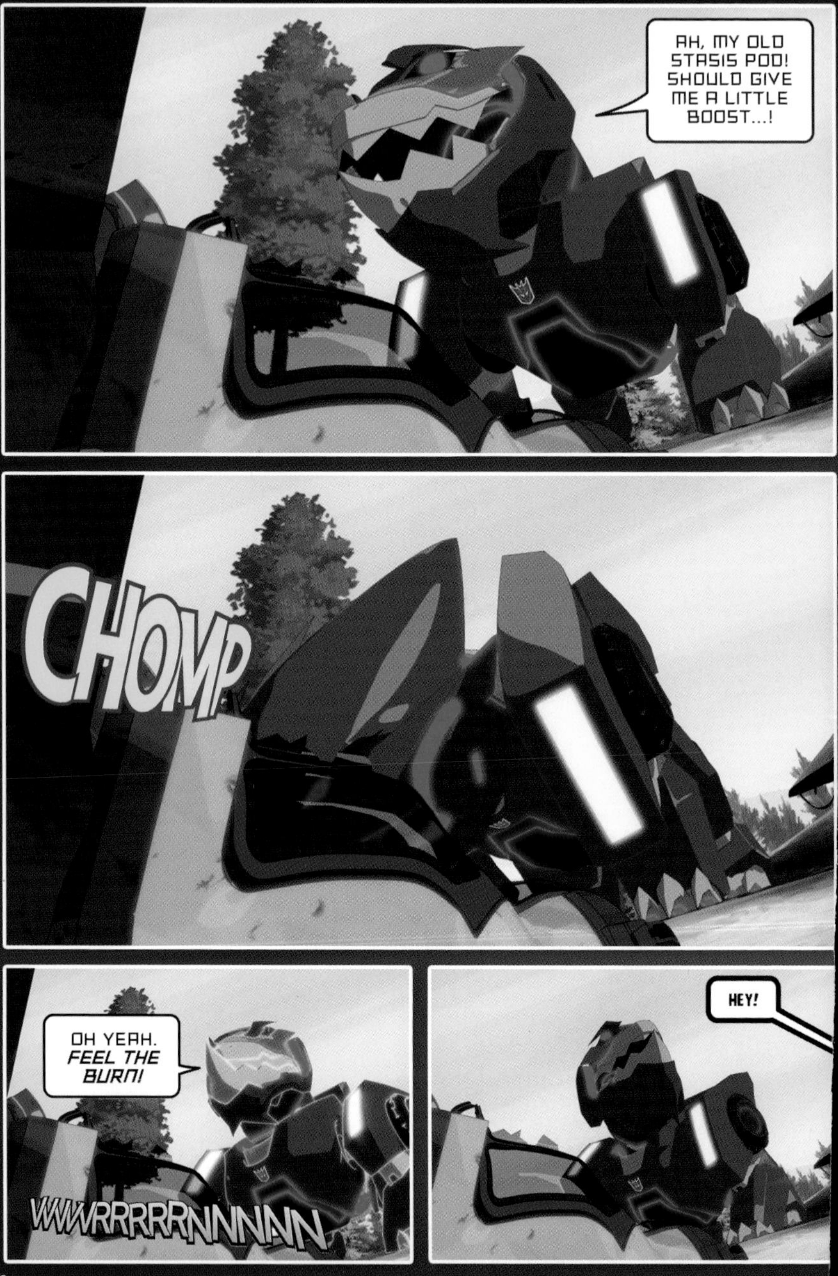
AH, MY OLD STASIS POD! SHOULD GIVE ME A LITTLE BOOST...!
CHOMP
OH YEAH. *FEEL THE BURN!*
WWWRRRRRNNNANN
HEY!

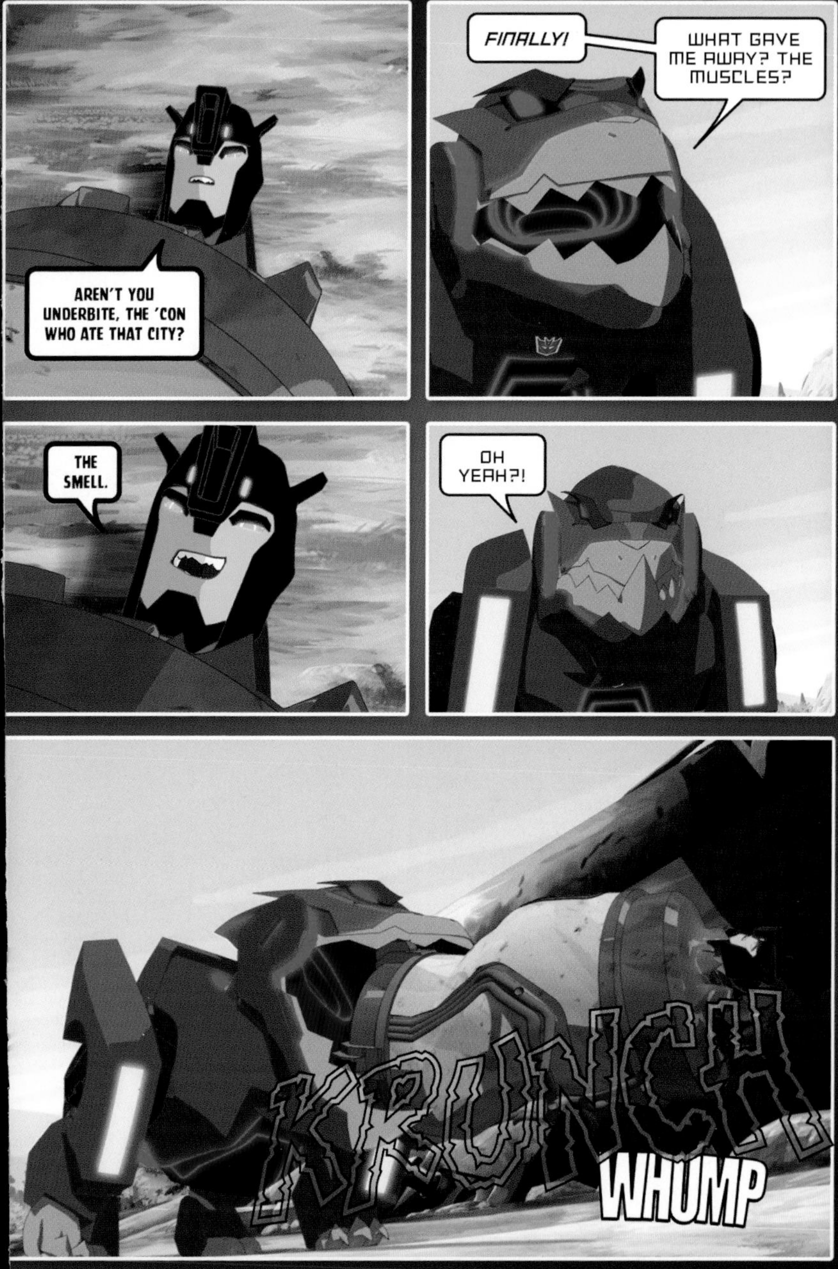

AREN'T YOU UNDERBITE, THE 'CON WHO ATE THAT CITY?
FINALLY!
WHAT GAVE ME AWAY? THE MUSCLES?
THE SMELL.
OH YEAH?!
KRUNCH
WHUMP

HOW'S *THAT* SMELL, YOU LITTLE—

EH? WHERE'D HE GO?

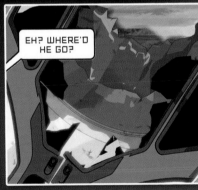

HUH? WELL, WELL...

LOOKS LIKE I'M HEADED FOR HUGENESS.

UNDERBITE HEADS OFF IN SEARCH OF FUEL.

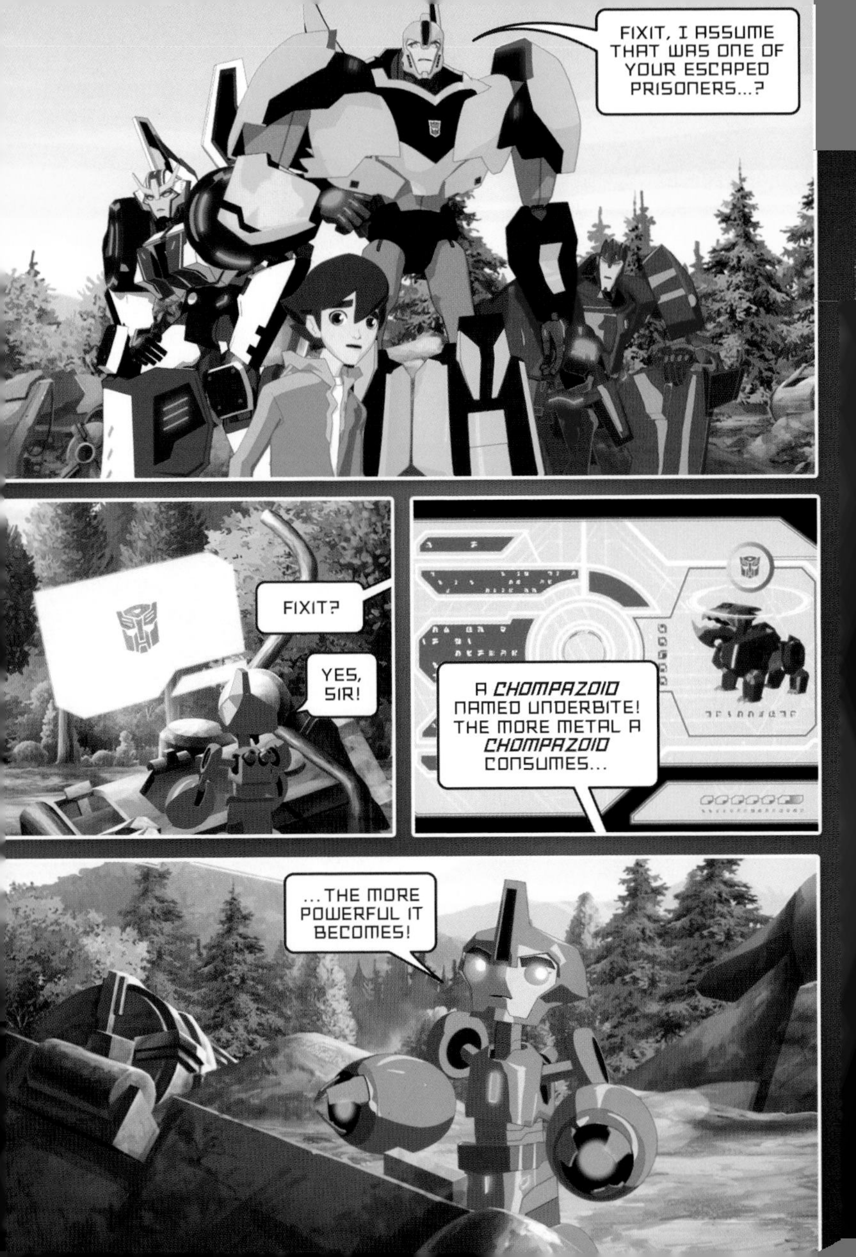
FIXIT, I ASSUME THAT WAS ONE OF YOUR ESCAPED PRISONERS...?
FIXIT?
YES, SIR!
A *CHOMPAZOID* NAMED UNDERBITE! THE MORE METAL A *CHOMPAZOID* CONSUMES...
...THE MORE POWERFUL IT BECOMES!

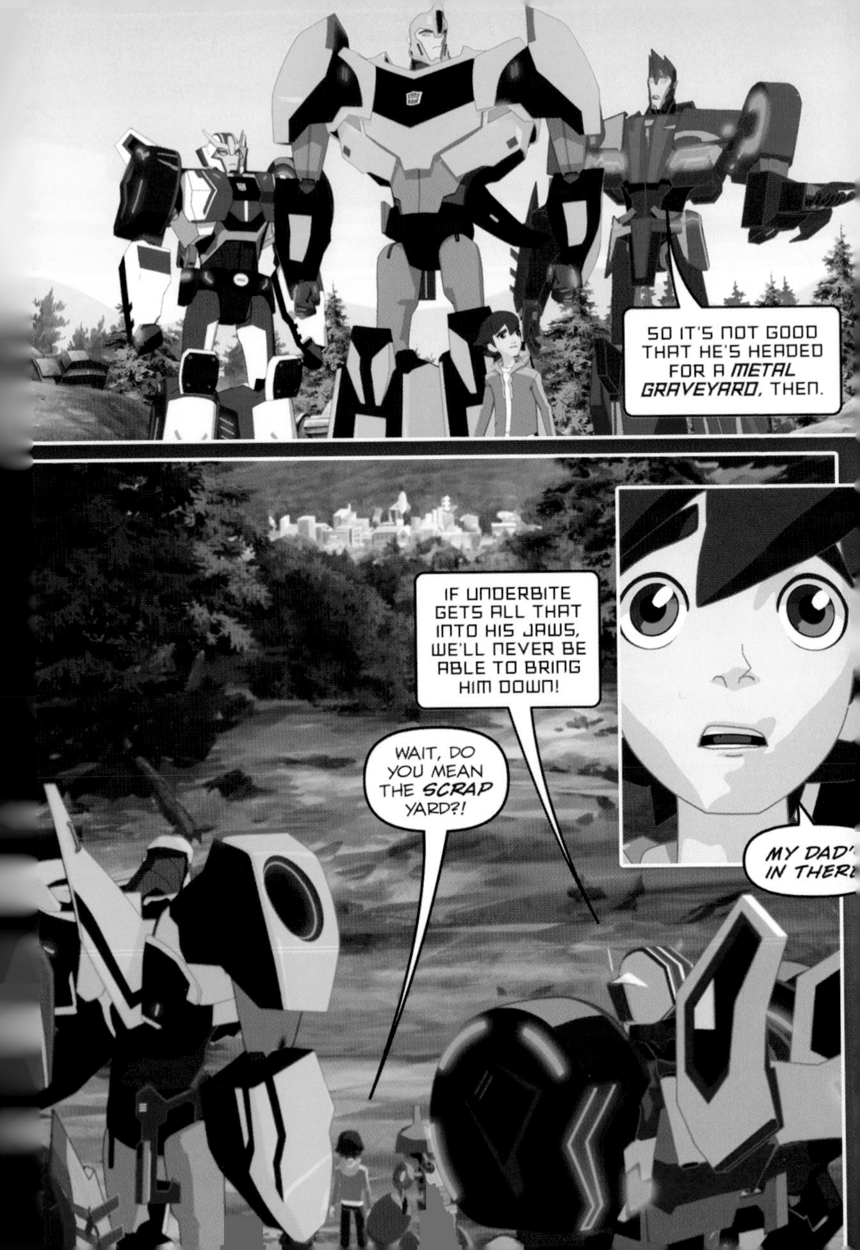
SO IT'S NOT GOOD THAT HE'S HEADED FOR A *METAL GRAVEYARD*, THEN.
IF UNDERBITE GETS ALL THAT INTO HIS JAWS, WE'LL NEVER BE ABLE TO BRING HIM DOWN!
WAIT, DO YOU MEAN THE *SCRAP* YARD?!

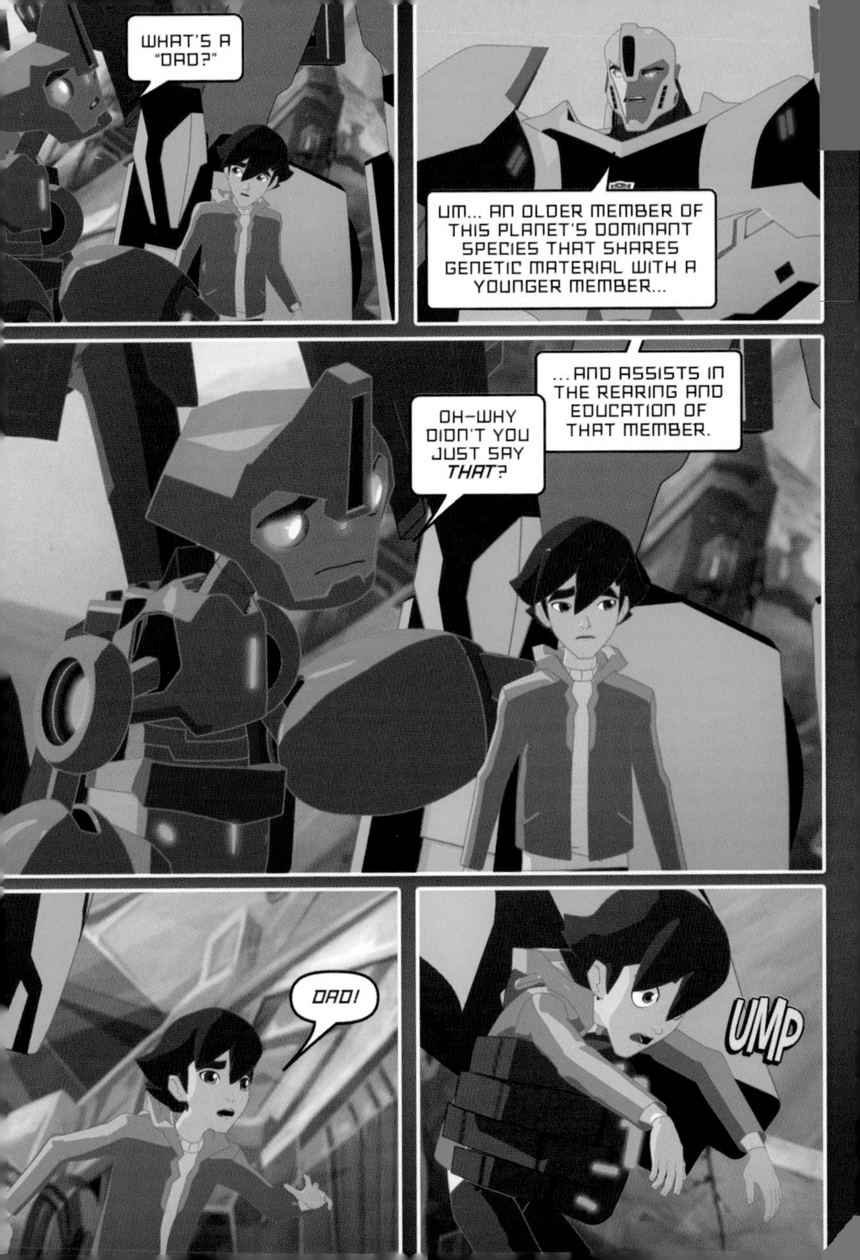
WHAT'S A "DAD?"
UM... AN OLDER MEMBER OF THIS PLANET'S DOMINANT SPECIES THAT SHARES GENETIC MATERIAL WITH A YOUNGER MEMBER...
...AND ASSISTS IN THE REARING AND EDUCATION OF THAT MEMBER.
OH—WHY DIDN'T YOU JUST SAY THAT?
DAD!
UMP

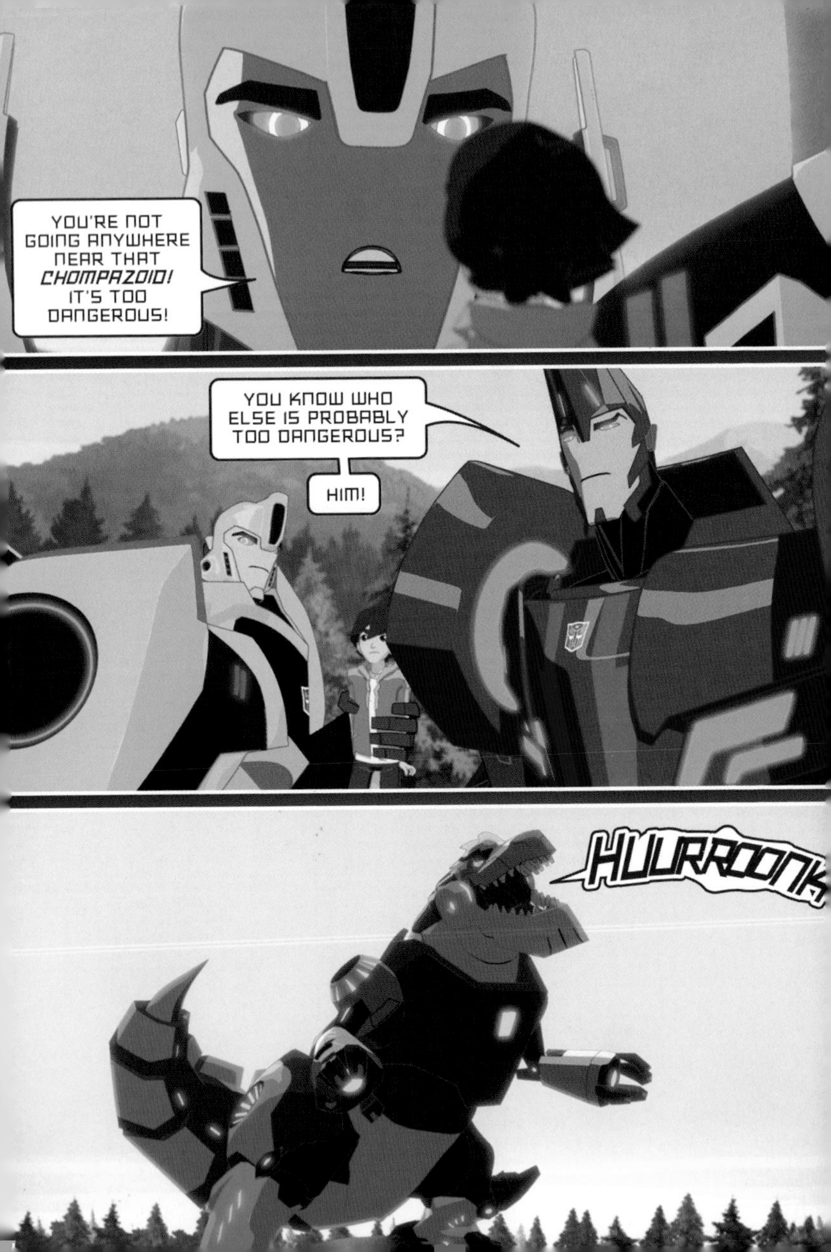
YOU'RE NOT GOING ANYWHERE NEAR THAT *CHOMPAZOID!* IT'S TOO DANGEROUS!
YOU KNOW WHO ELSE IS PROBABLY TOO DANGEROUS?
HIM!
HUURROONK

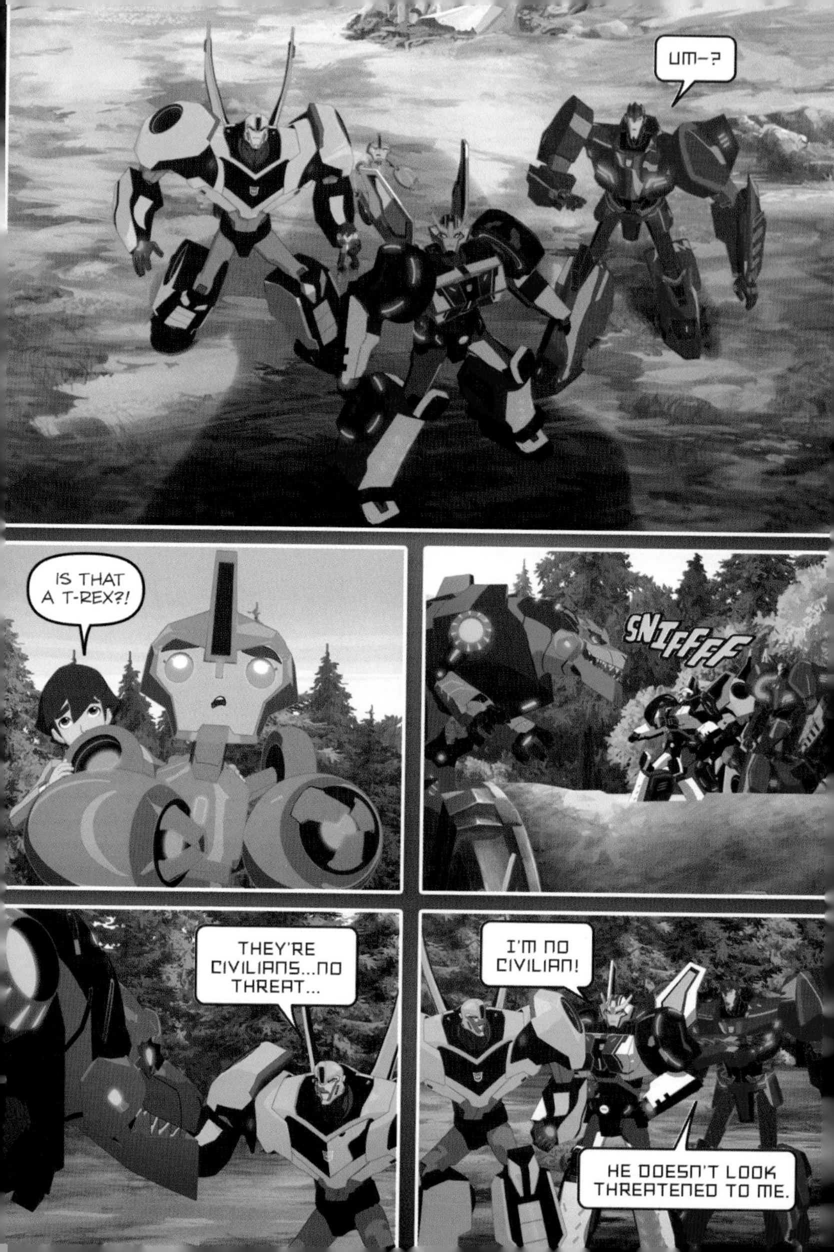
UM-?
IS THAT A T-REX?!
SNIFFFFF
THEY'RE CIVILIANS...NO THREAT...
I'M NO CIVILIAN!
HE DOESN'T LOOK THREATENED TO ME.

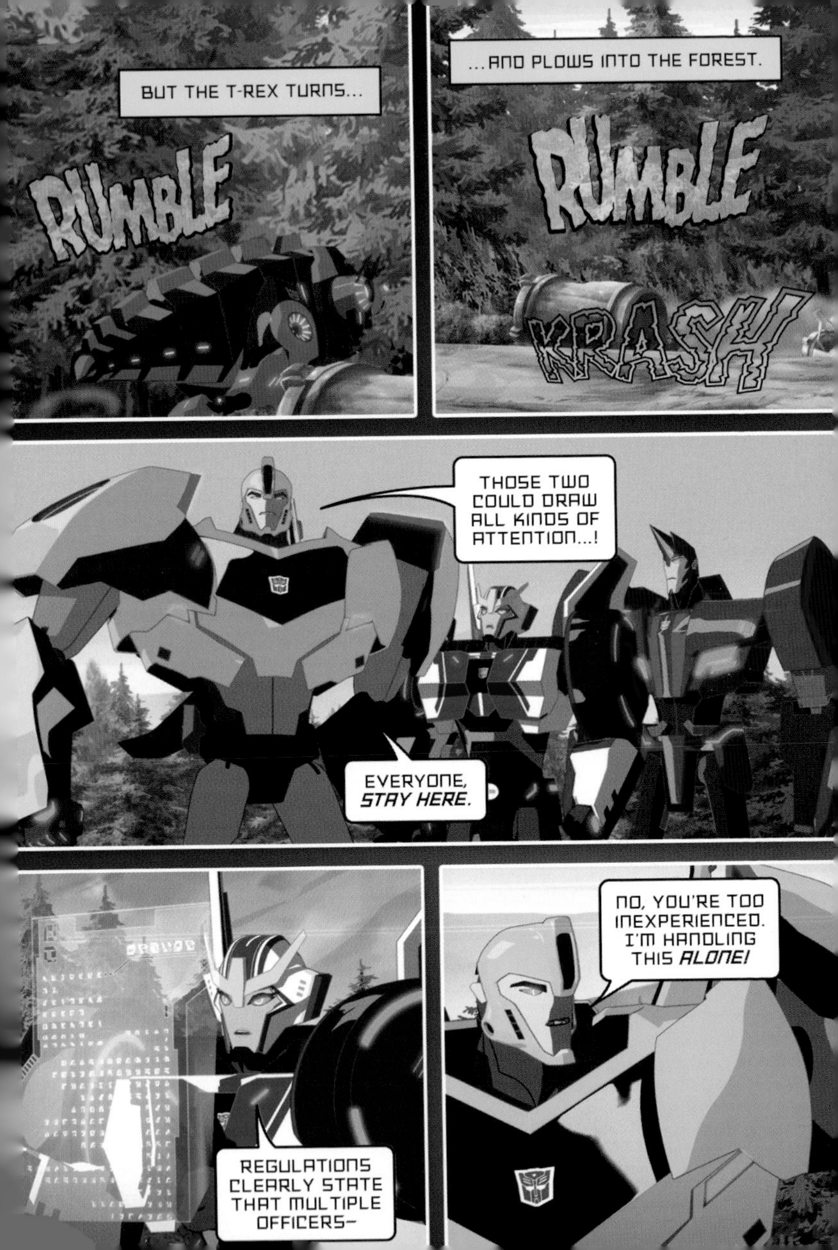
BUT THE T-REX TURNS...
RUMBLE
...AND PLOWS INTO THE FOREST.
RUMBLE
KRASH
THOSE TWO COULD DRAW ALL KINDS OF ATTENTION...!
EVERYONE, *STAY HERE*.
REGULATIONS CLEARLY STATE THAT MULTIPLE OFFICERS—
NO, YOU'RE TOO INEXPERIENCED. I'M HANDLING THIS *ALONE!*

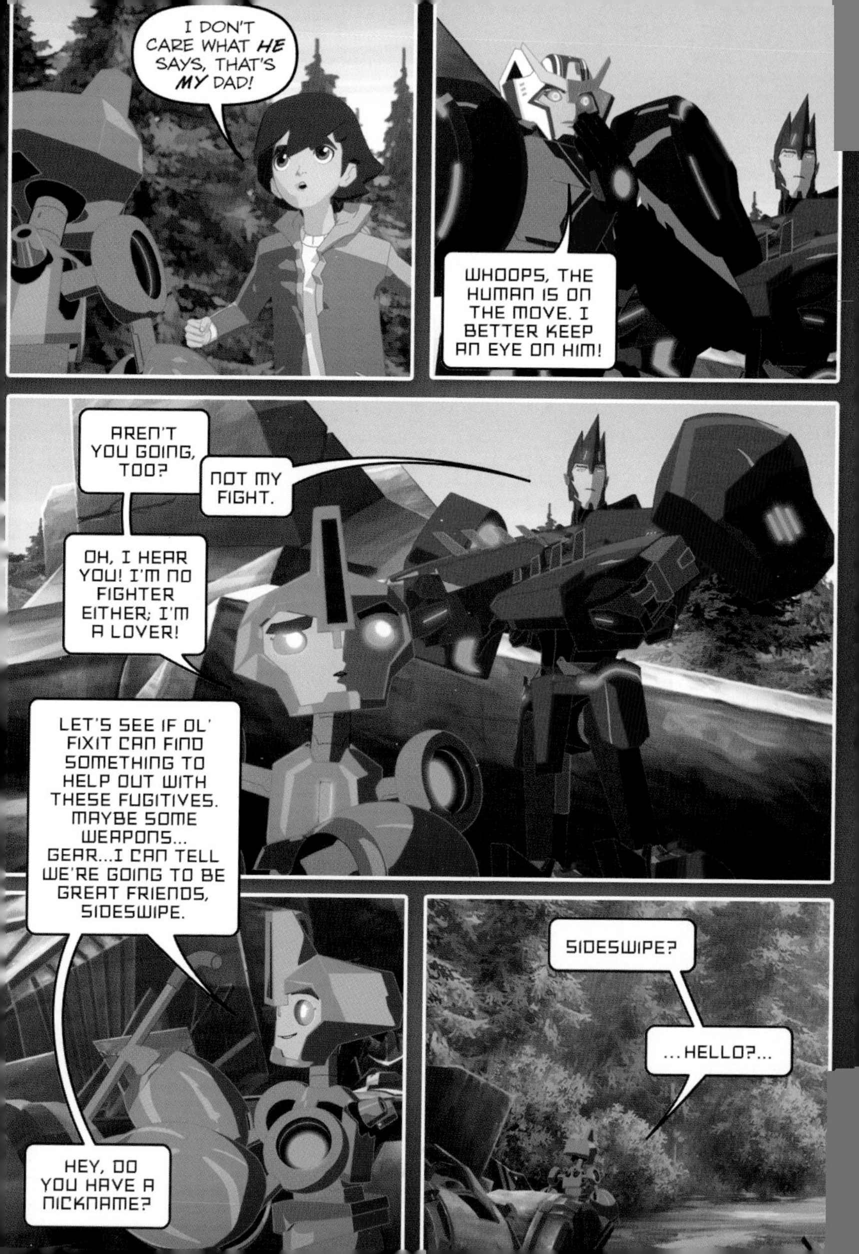
I DON'T CARE WHAT *HE* SAYS, THAT'S *MY* DAD!
WHOOPS, THE HUMAN IS ON THE MOVE. I BETTER KEEP AN EYE ON HIM!
AREN'T YOU GOING, TOO?
NOT MY FIGHT.
OH, I HEAR YOU! I'M NO FIGHTER EITHER; I'M A LOVER!
LET'S SEE IF OL' FIXIT CAN FIND SOMETHING TO HELP OUT WITH THESE FUGITIVES. MAYBE SOME WEAPONS... GEAR...I CAN TELL WE'RE GOING TO BE GREAT FRIENDS, SIDESWIPE.
HEY, DO YOU HAVE A NICKNAME?
SIDESWIPE?
...HELLO?...

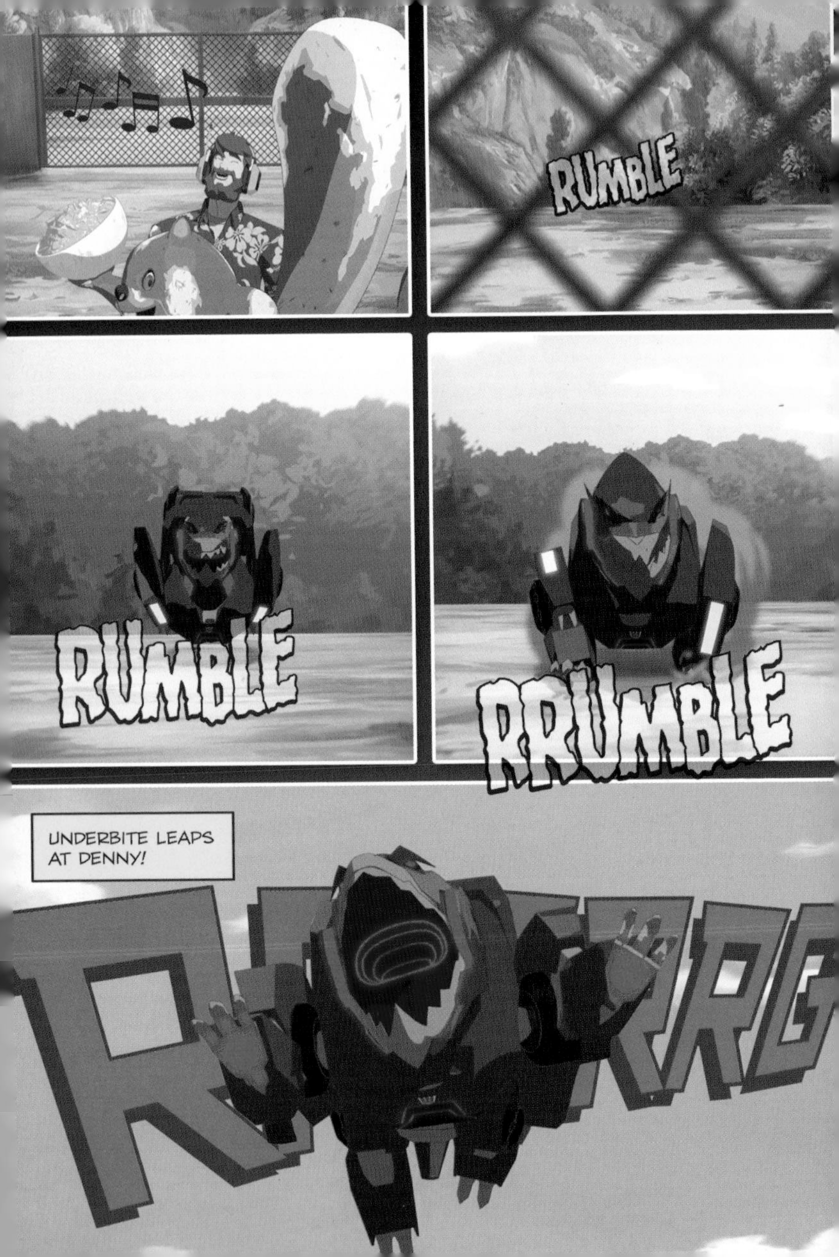
RUMBLE
RUMBLE
RRUMBLE
UNDERBITE LEAPS AT DENNY!

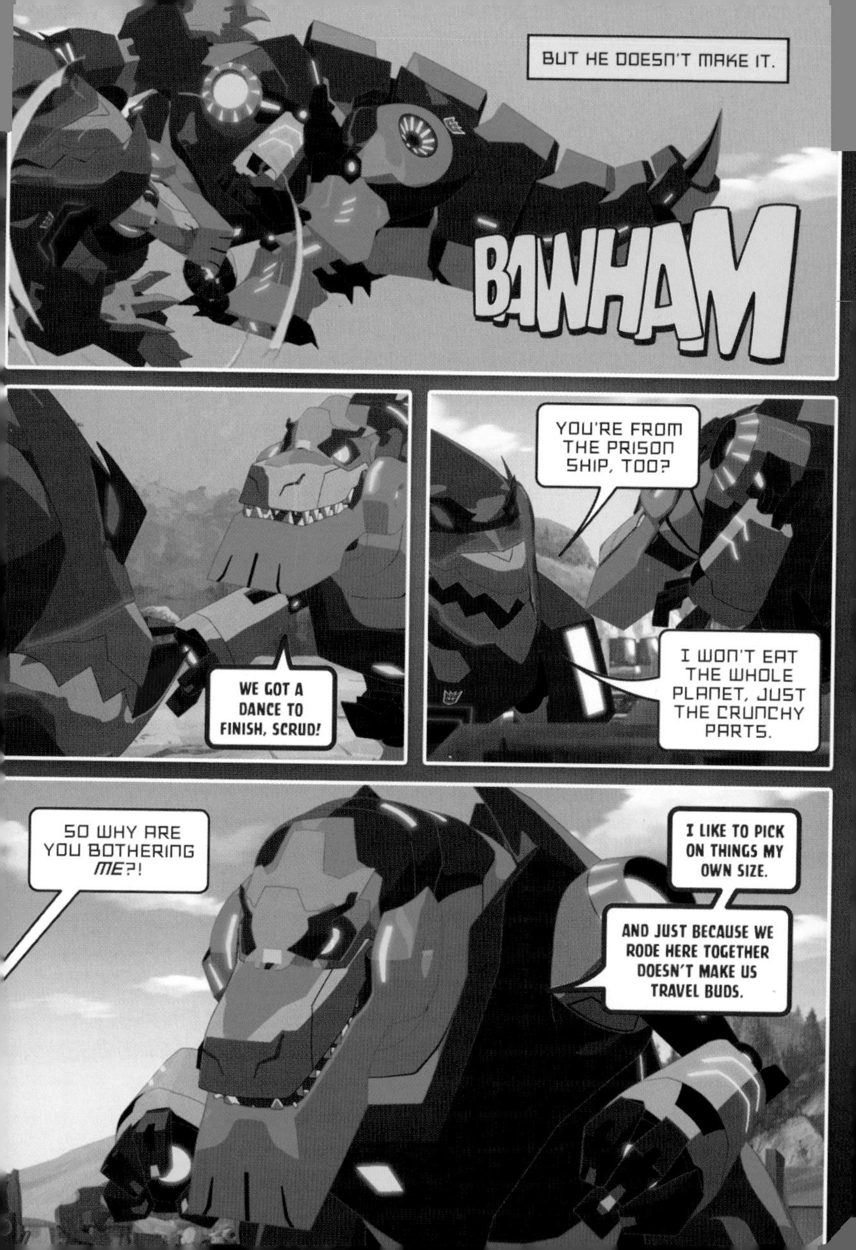
BUT HE DOESN'T MAKE IT.
BAWHAM
WE GOT A DANCE TO FINISH, SCRUD!
YOU'RE FROM THE PRISON SHIP, TOO?
I WON'T EAT THE WHOLE PLANET, JUST THE CRUNCHY PARTS.
SO WHY ARE YOU BOTHERING *ME*?!
I LIKE TO PICK ON THINGS MY OWN SIZE.
AND JUST BECAUSE WE RODE HERE TOGETHER DOESN'T MAKE US TRAVEL BUDS.

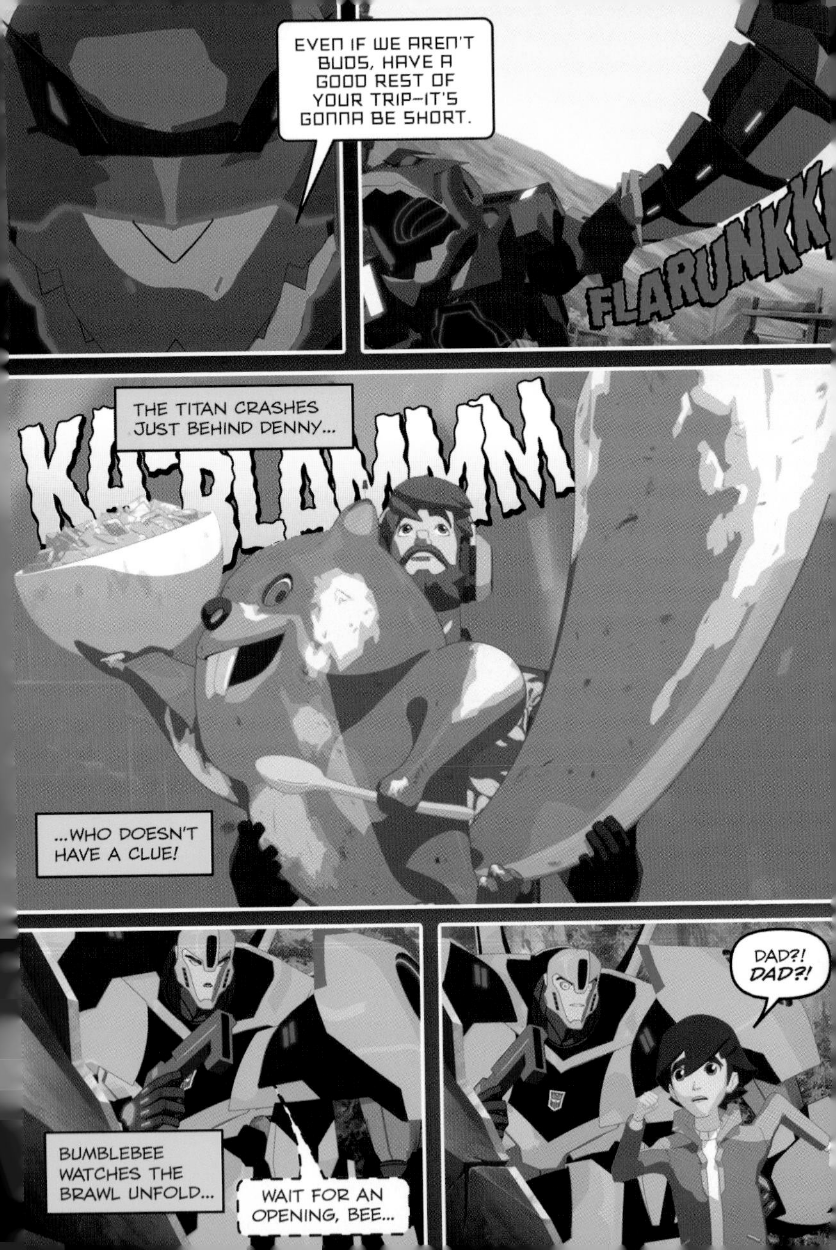

EVEN IF WE AREN'T BUDS, HAVE A GOOD REST OF YOUR TRIP—IT'S GONNA BE SHORT.
FLARUNKK
THE TITAN CRASHES JUST BEHIND DENNY...
KA-BLAMMM
...WHO DOESN'T HAVE A CLUE!
BUMBLEBEE WATCHES THE BRAWL UNFOLD...
WAIT FOR AN OPENING, BEE...
DAD?! DAD?!

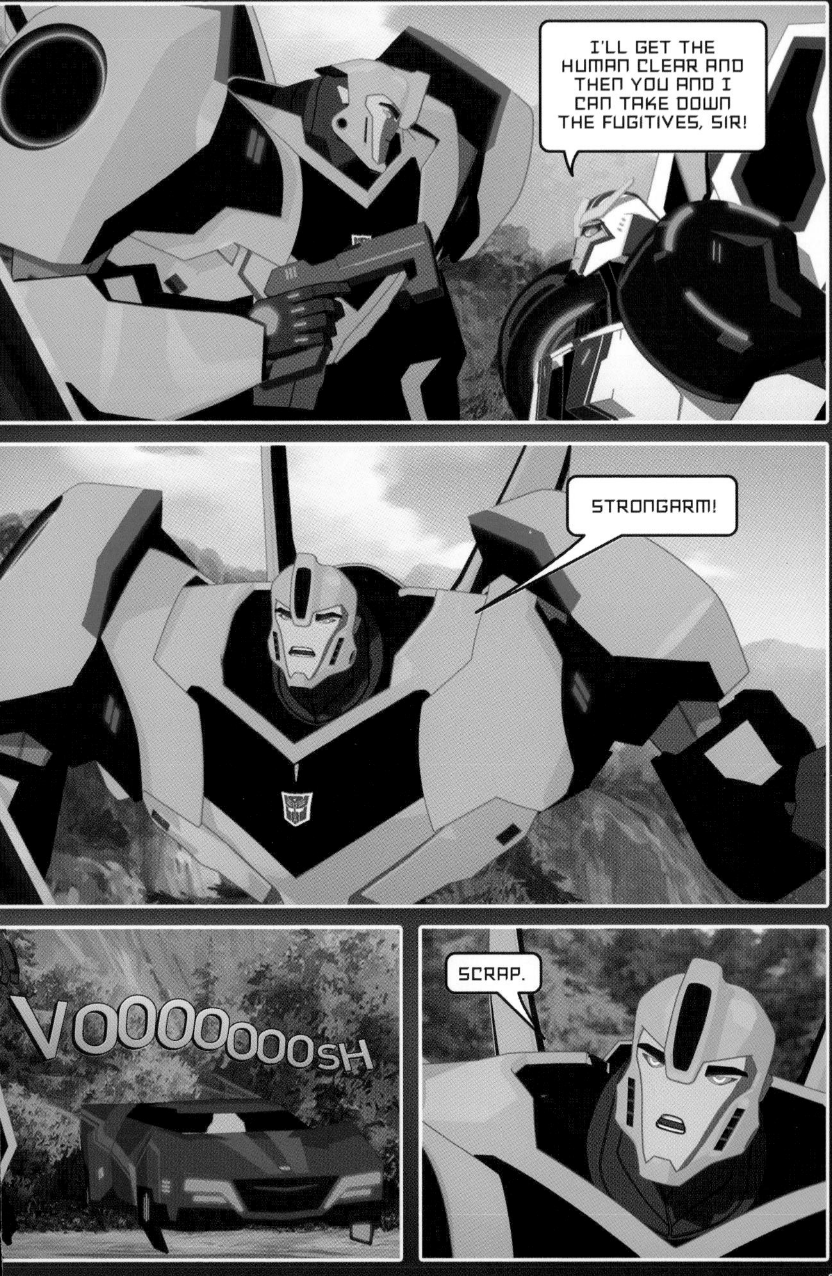

I'LL GET THE HUMAN CLEAR AND THEN YOU AND I CAN TAKE DOWN THE FUGITIVES, SIR!
STRONGARM!
VOOOOOOOSH
SCRAP.

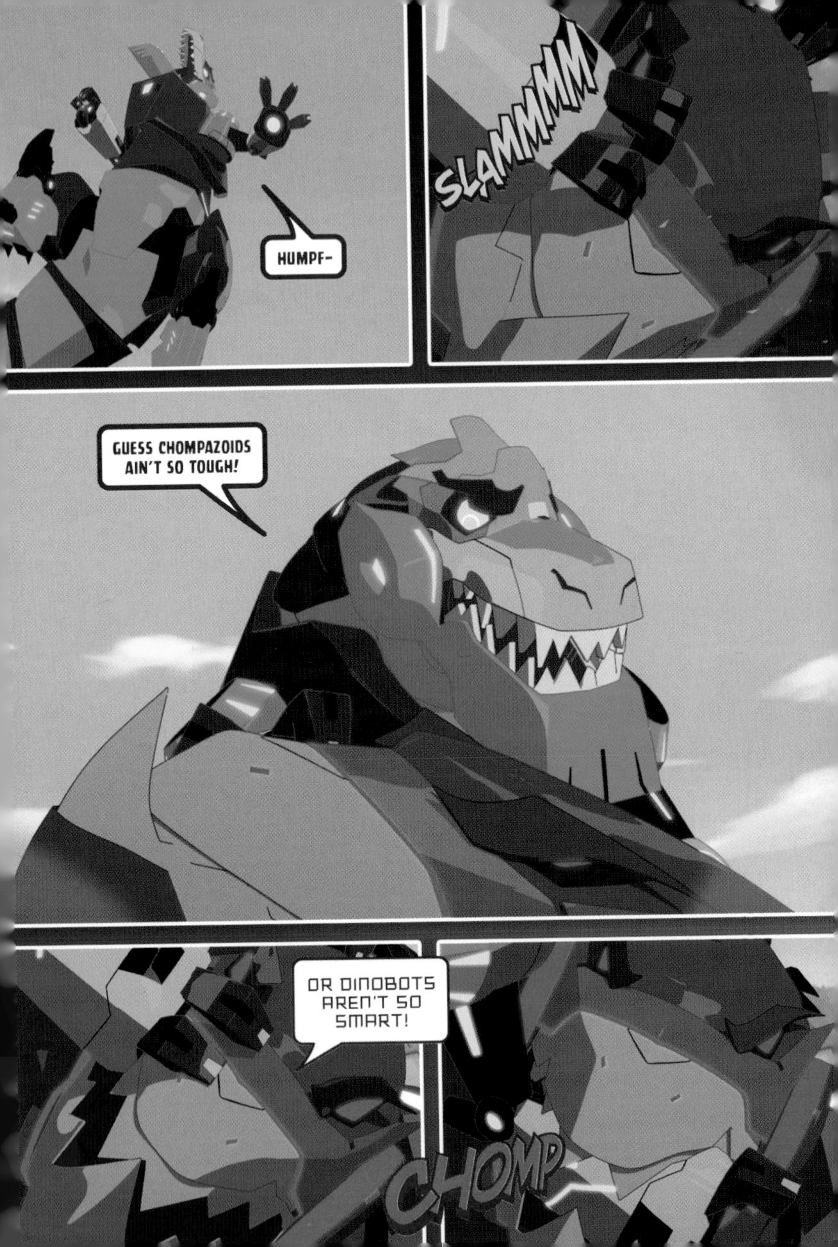
HUMPF-
SLAMMMM
GUESS CHOMPAZOIDS AIN'T SO TOUGH!
OR DINOBOTS AREN'T SO SMART!
CHOMP

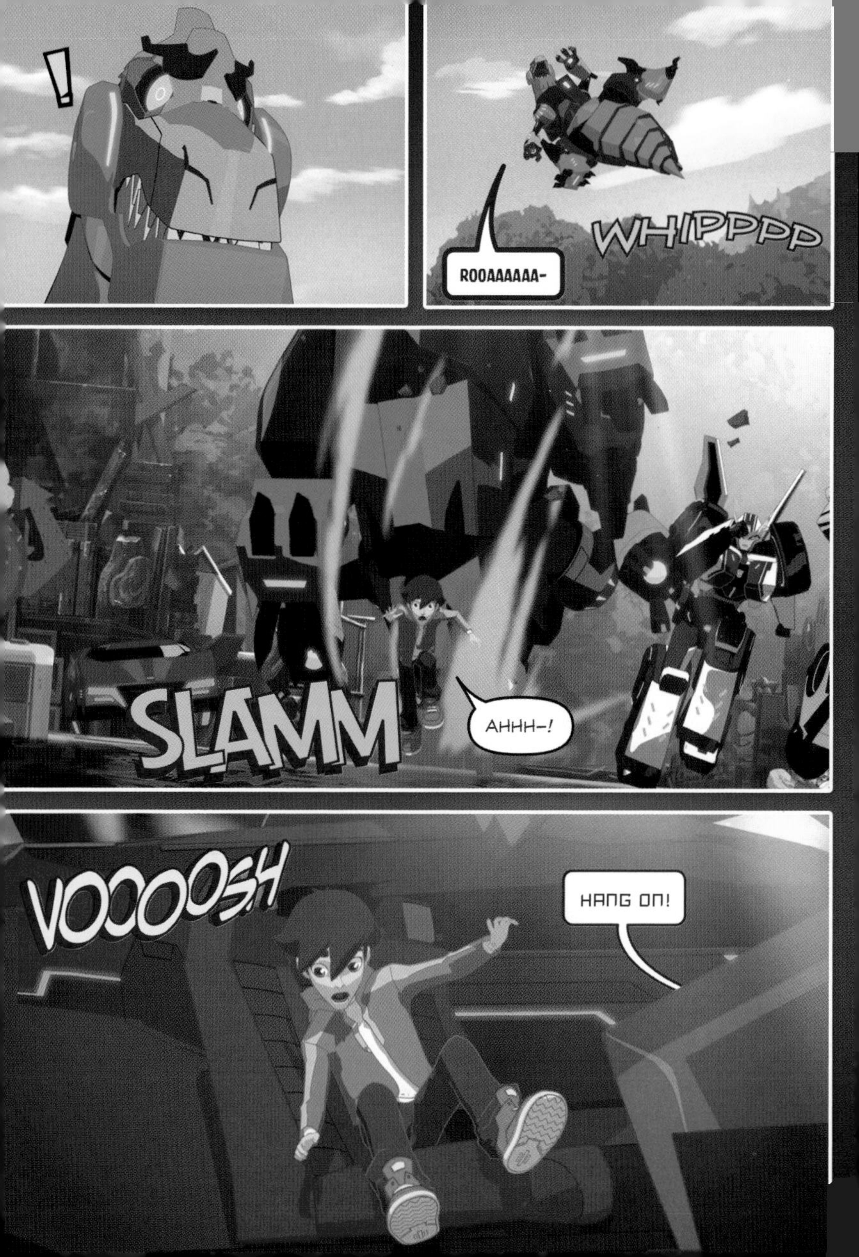
!
ROOAAAAAA-
WHIPPPP
SLAMM
AHHH-!
VOOOOSH
HANG ON!

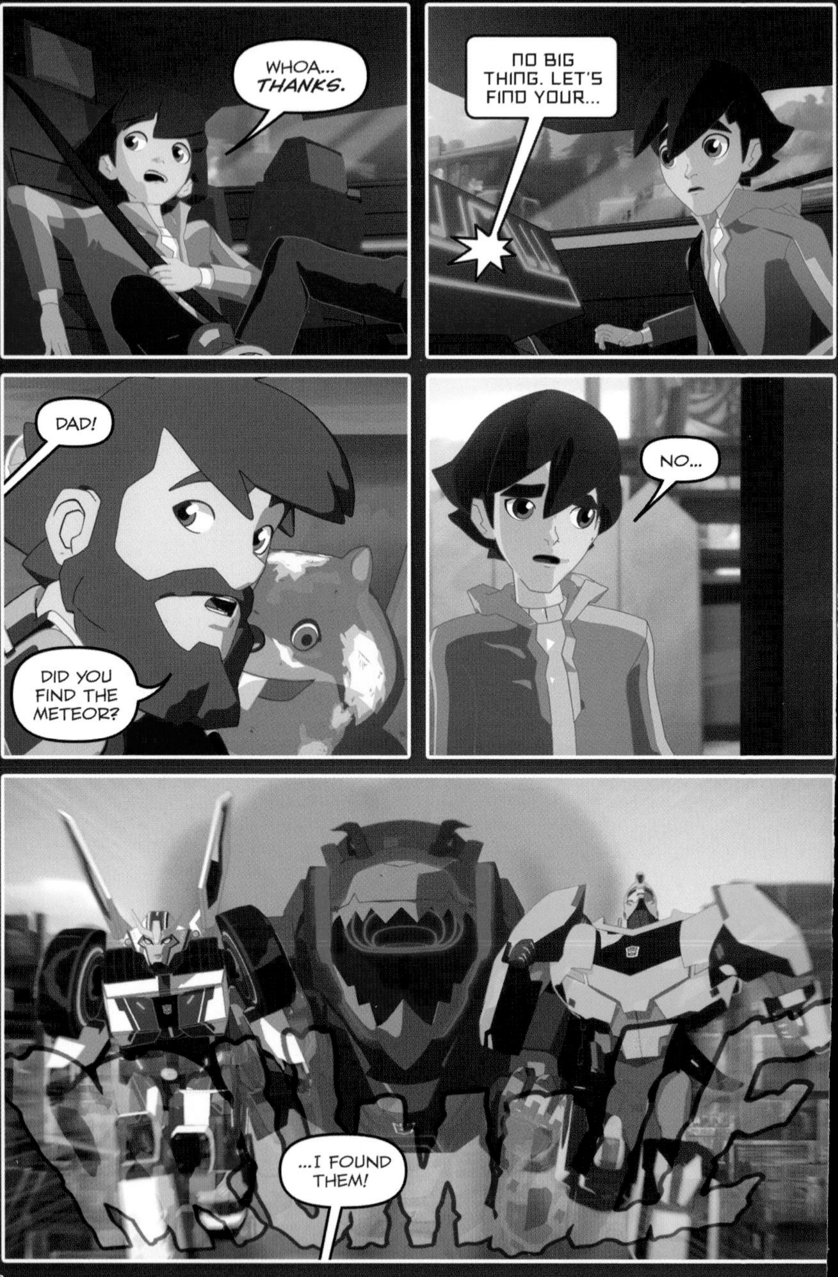
WHOA... THANKS.
NO BIG THING. LET'S FIND YOUR...
DAD!
DID YOU FIND THE METEOR?
NO...
...I FOUND THEM!

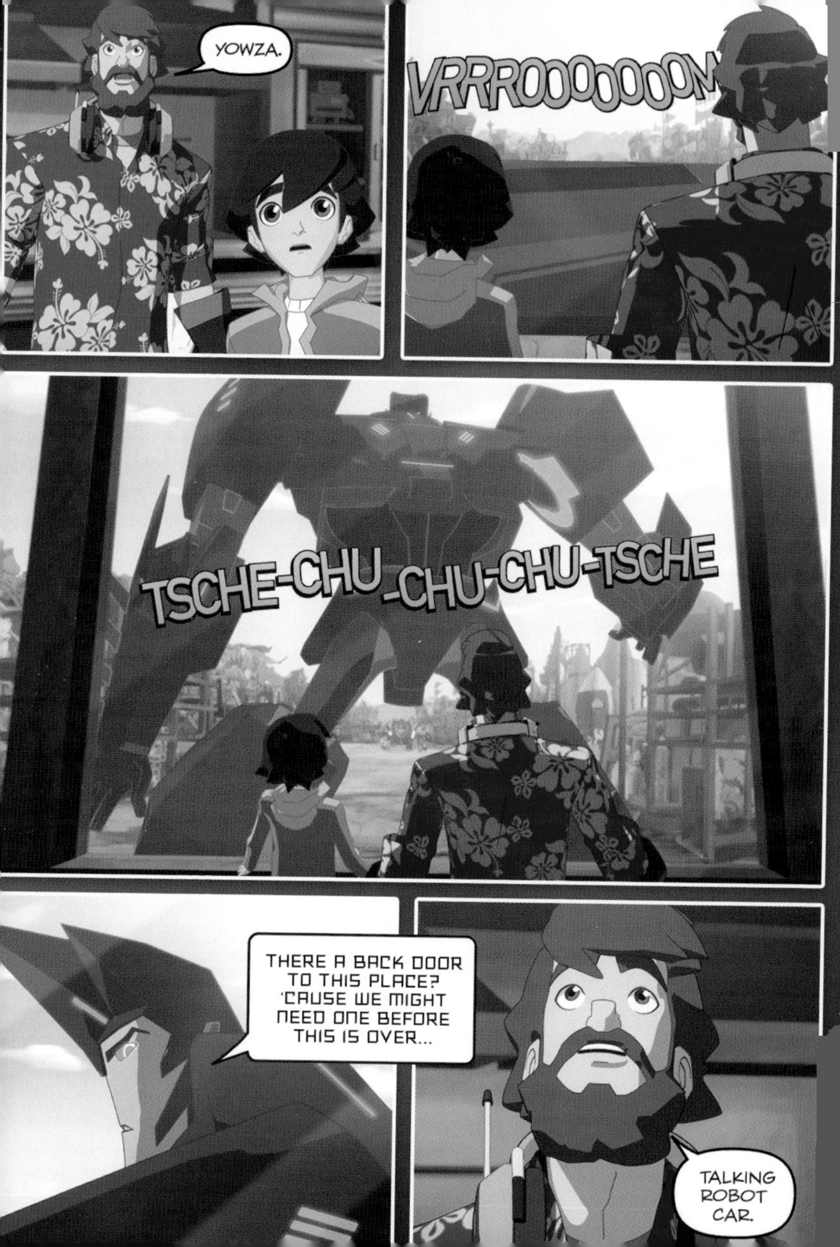
YOWZA.
VRRROOOOOOOOM
TSCHE-CHU-CHU-CHU-TSCHE
THERE A BACK DOOR TO THIS PLACE? 'CAUSE WE MIGHT NEED ONE BEFORE THIS IS OVER...
TALKING ROBOT CAR.

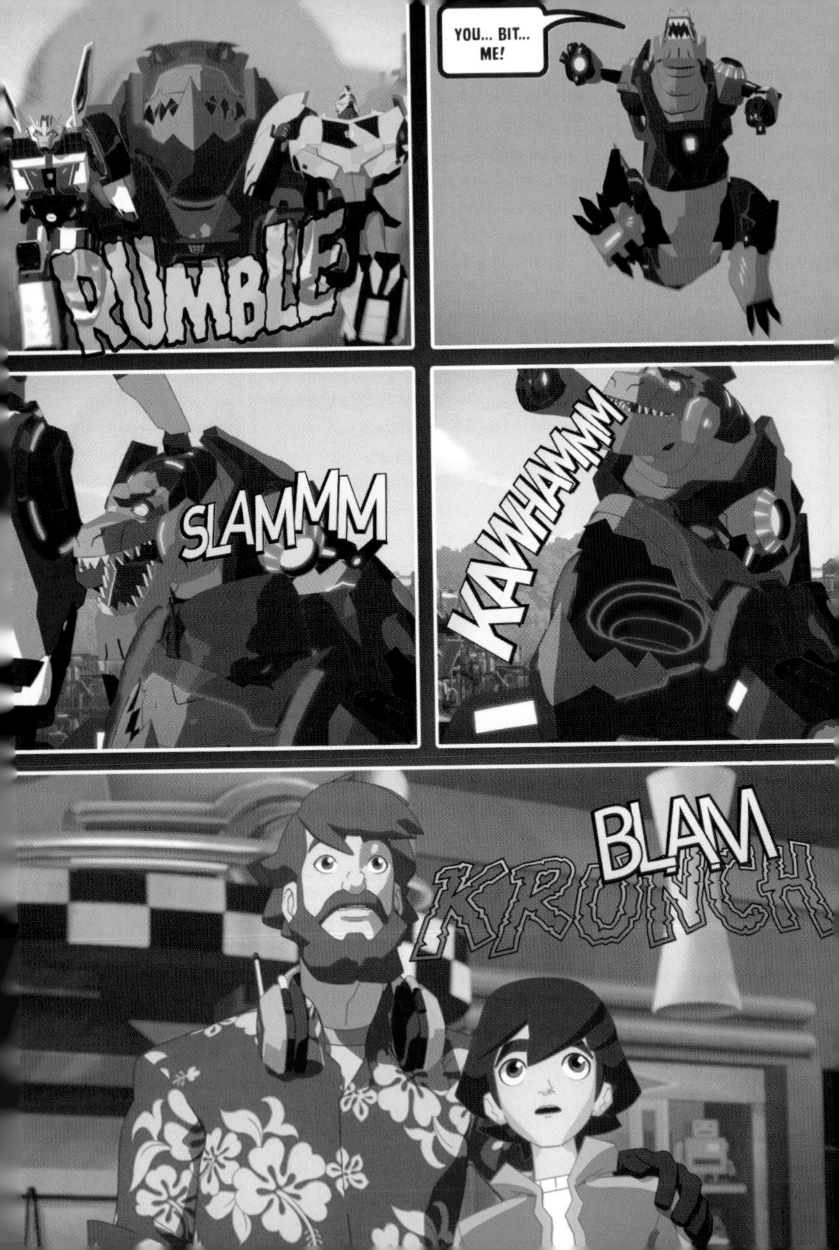
RUMBLE
YOU... BIT... ME!
SLAMMM
KAWHAMMM
BLAM
KRUNCH

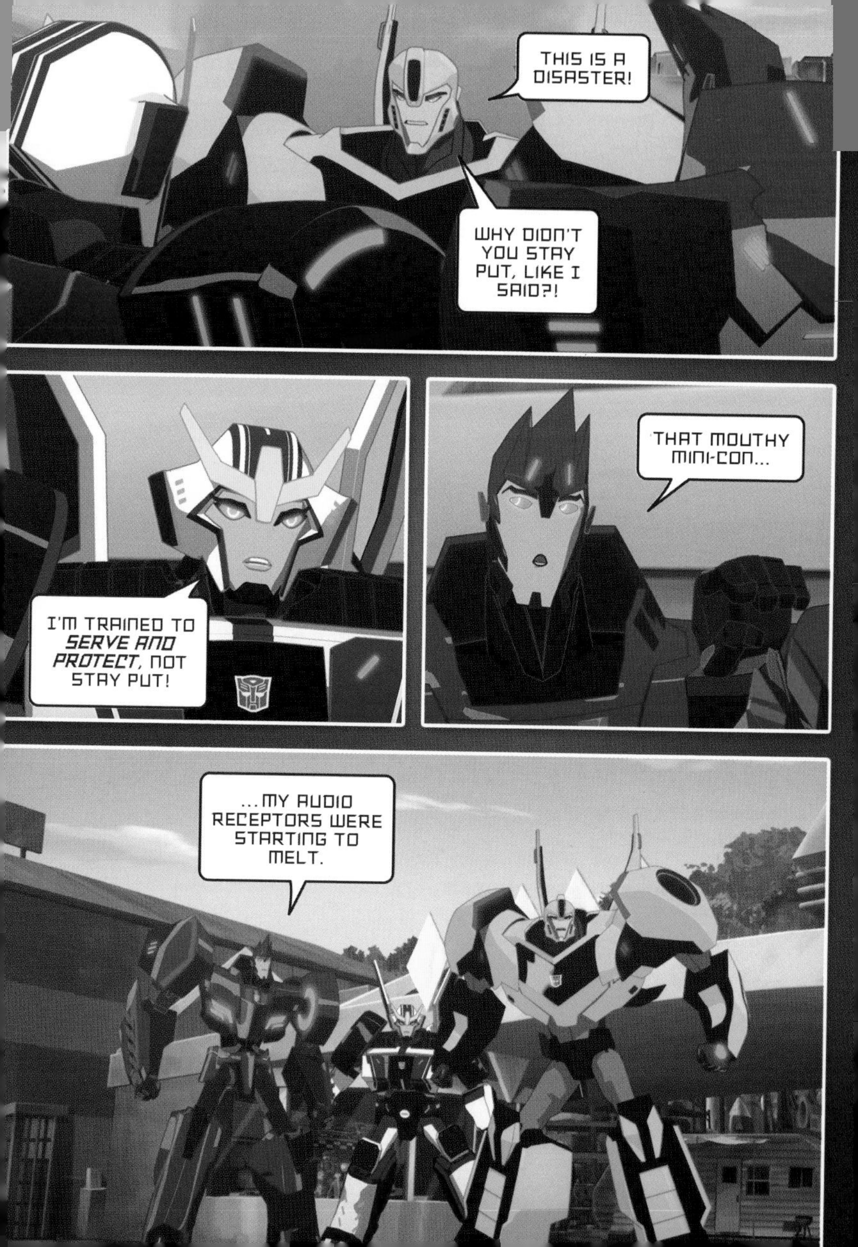
THIS IS A DISASTER!
WHY DIDN'T YOU STAY PUT, LIKE I SAID?!
I'M TRAINED TO *SERVE AND PROTECT*, NOT STAY PUT!
THAT MOUTHY MINI-CON...
...MY AUDIO RECEPTORS WERE STARTING TO MELT.

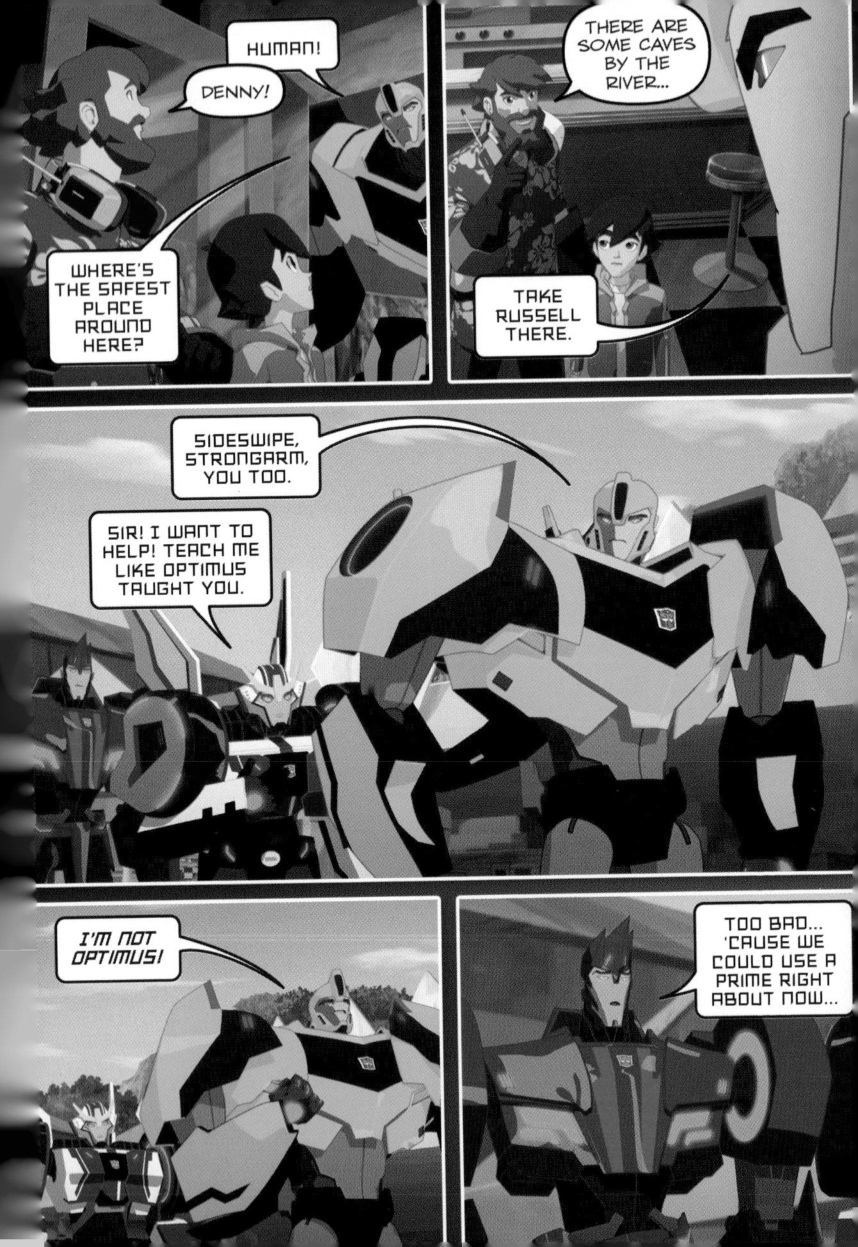

HUMAN!
DENNY!
WHERE'S THE SAFEST PLACE AROUND HERE?
THERE ARE SOME CAVES BY THE RIVER...
TAKE RUSSELL THERE.
SIDESWIPE, STRONGARM, YOU TOO.
SIR! I WANT TO HELP! TEACH ME LIKE OPTIMUS TAUGHT YOU.
I'M NOT OPTIMUS!
TOO BAD... 'CAUSE WE COULD USE A PRIME RIGHT ABOUT NOW...

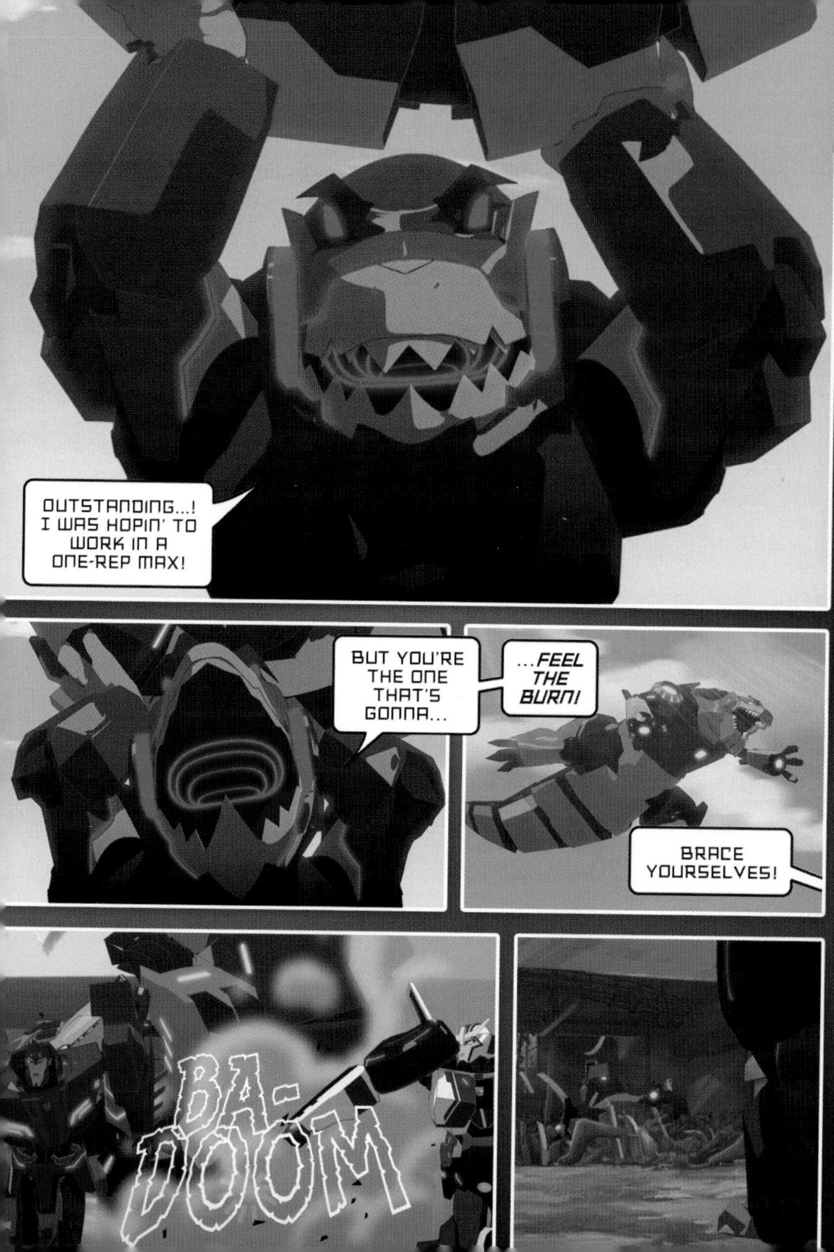

OUTSTANDING...! I WAS HOPIN' TO WORK IN A ONE-REP MAX!
BUT YOU'RE THE ONE THAT'S GONNA...
...FEEL THE BURN!
BRACE YOURSELVES!
BA-DOOM

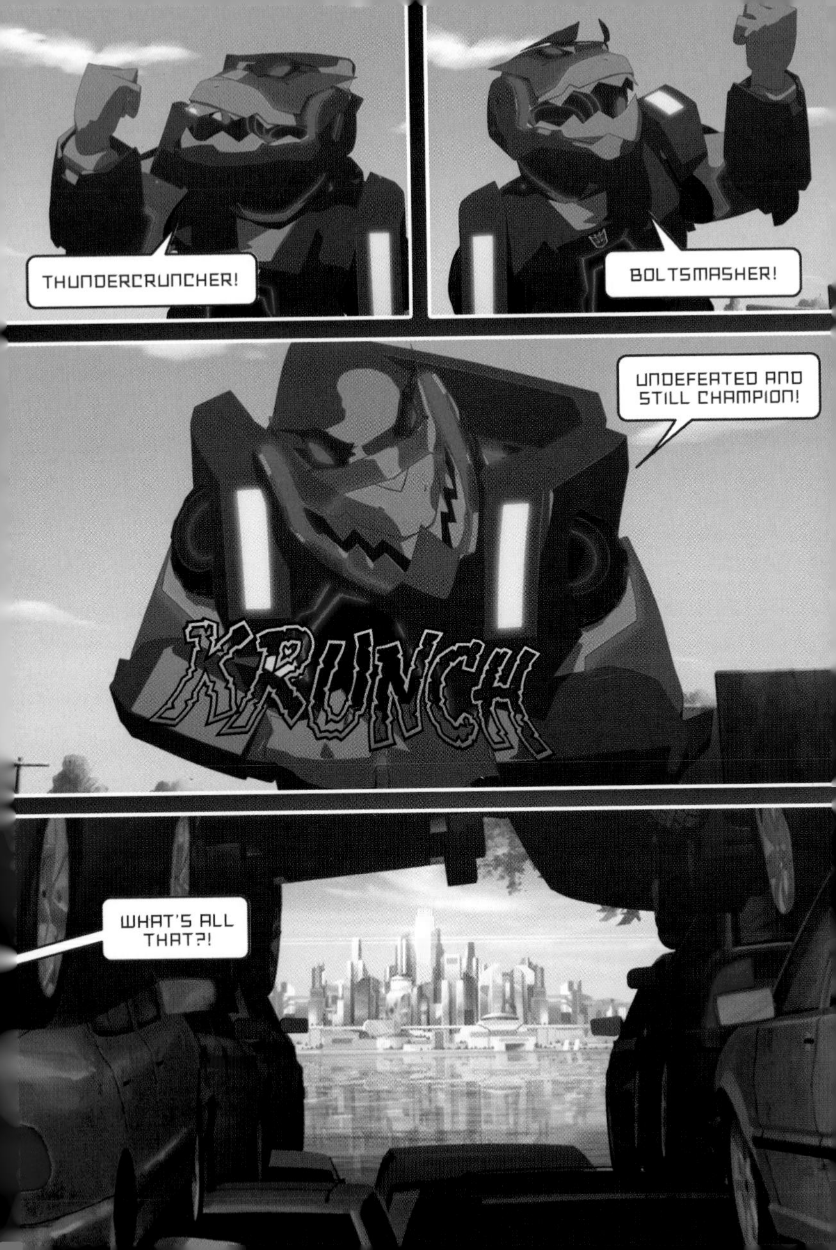
THUNDERCRUNCHER!
BOLTSMASHER!
UNDEFEATED AND STILL CHAMPION!
KRUNCH
WHAT'S ALL THAT?!

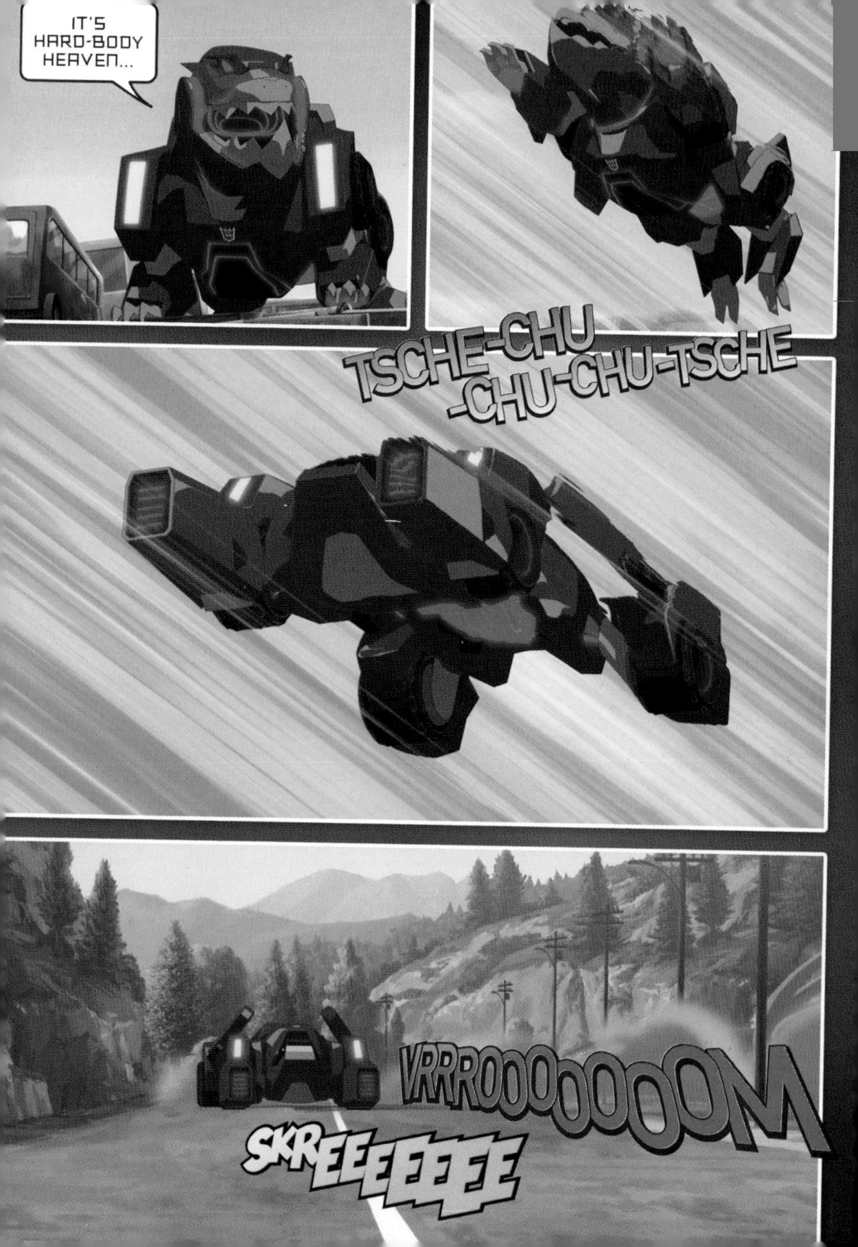
IT'S HARD-BODY HEAVEN...
TSCHE-CHU -CHU-CHU-TSCHE
VRRROOOOOOOOM
SKREEEEEEE

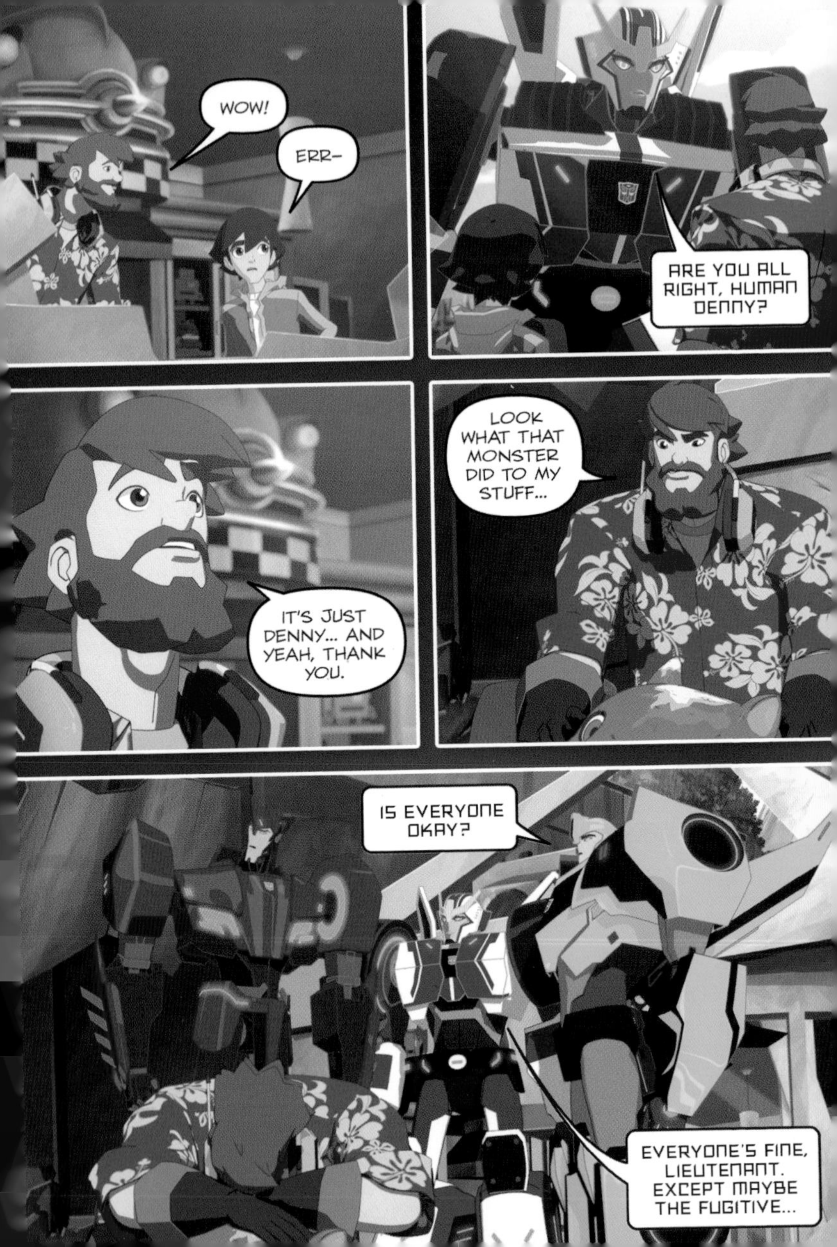
WOW!
ERR-
ARE YOU ALL RIGHT, HUMAN DENNY?
IT'S JUST DENNY... AND YEAH, THANK YOU.
LOOK WHAT THAT MONSTER DID TO MY STUFF...
IS EVERYONE OKAY?
EVERYONE'S FINE, LIEUTENANT. EXCEPT MAYBE THE FUGITIVE...

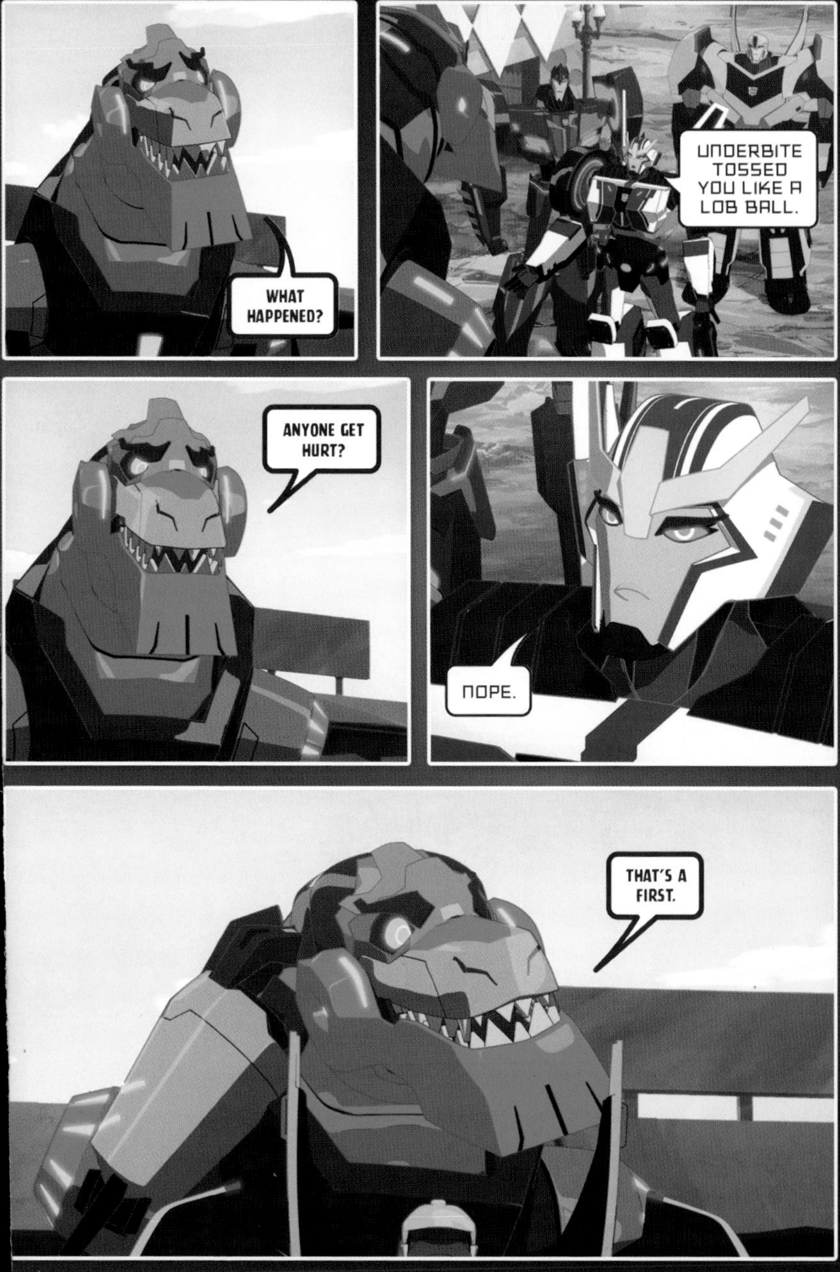
WHAT HAPPENED?
UNDERBITE TOSSED YOU LIKE A LOB BALL.
ANYONE GET HURT?
NOPE.
THAT'S A FIRST.

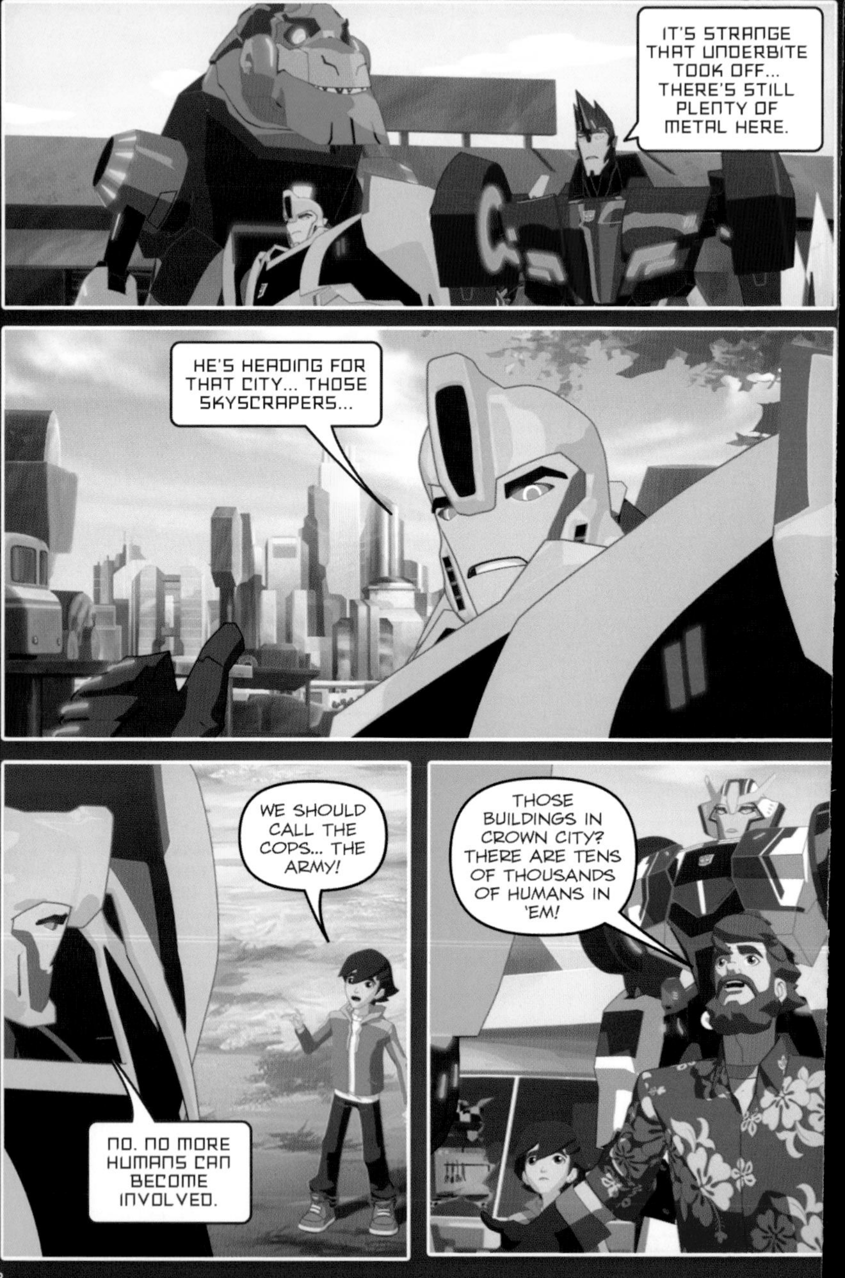
IT'S STRANGE THAT UNDERBITE TOOK OFF... THERE'S STILL PLENTY OF METAL HERE.
HE'S HEADING FOR THAT CITY... THOSE SKYSCRAPERS...
WE SHOULD CALL THE COPS... THE ARMY!
NO. NO MORE HUMANS CAN BECOME INVOLVED.
THOSE BUILDINGS IN CROWN CITY? THERE ARE TENS OF THOUSANDS OF HUMANS IN 'EM!

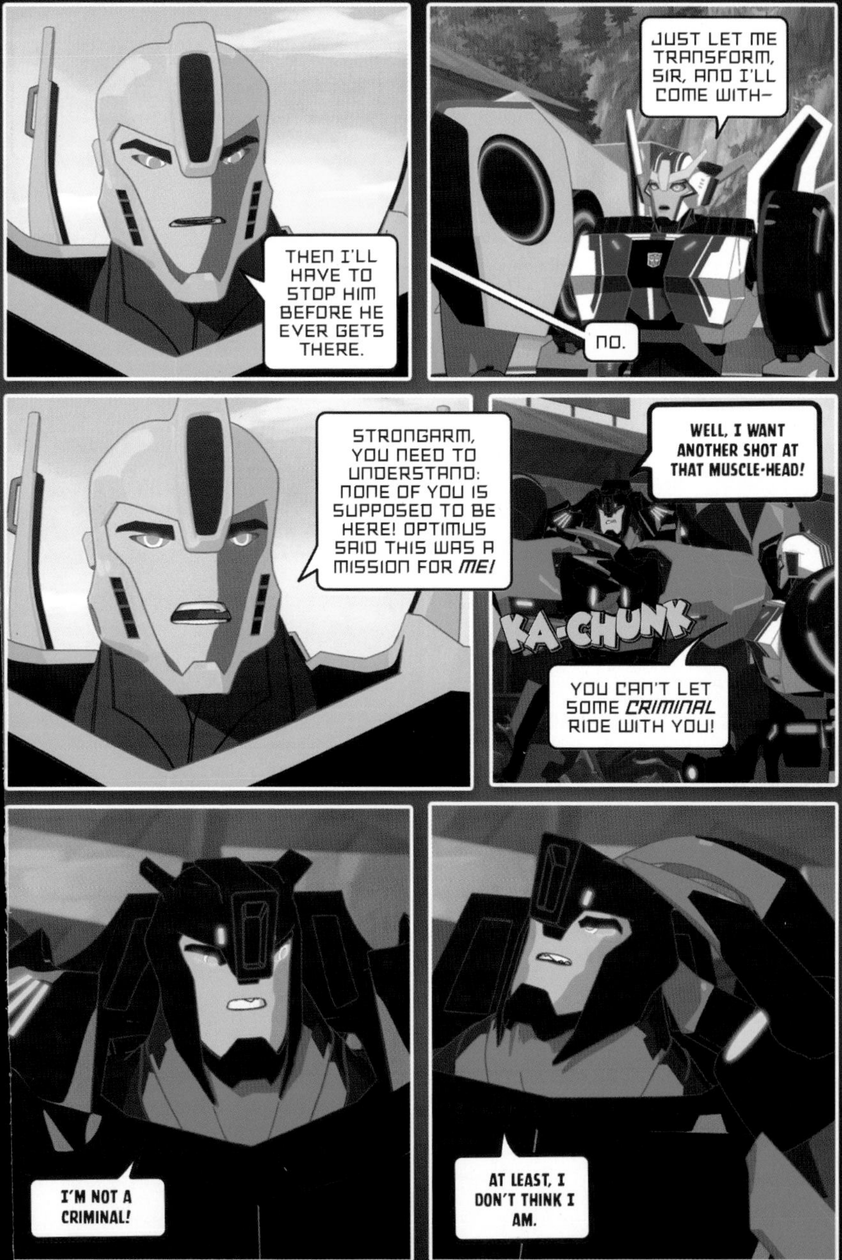
THEN I'LL HAVE TO STOP HIM BEFORE HE EVER GETS THERE.
JUST LET ME TRANSFORM, SIR, AND I'LL COME WITH–
NO.
STRONGARM, YOU NEED TO UNDERSTAND: NONE OF YOU IS SUPPOSED TO BE HERE! OPTIMUS SAID THIS WAS A MISSION FOR *ME!*
WELL, I WANT ANOTHER SHOT AT THAT MUSCLE-HEAD!
KA-CHUNK
YOU CAN'T LET SOME *CRIMINAL* RIDE WITH YOU!
I'M NOT A CRIMINAL!
AT LEAST, I DON'T THINK I AM.

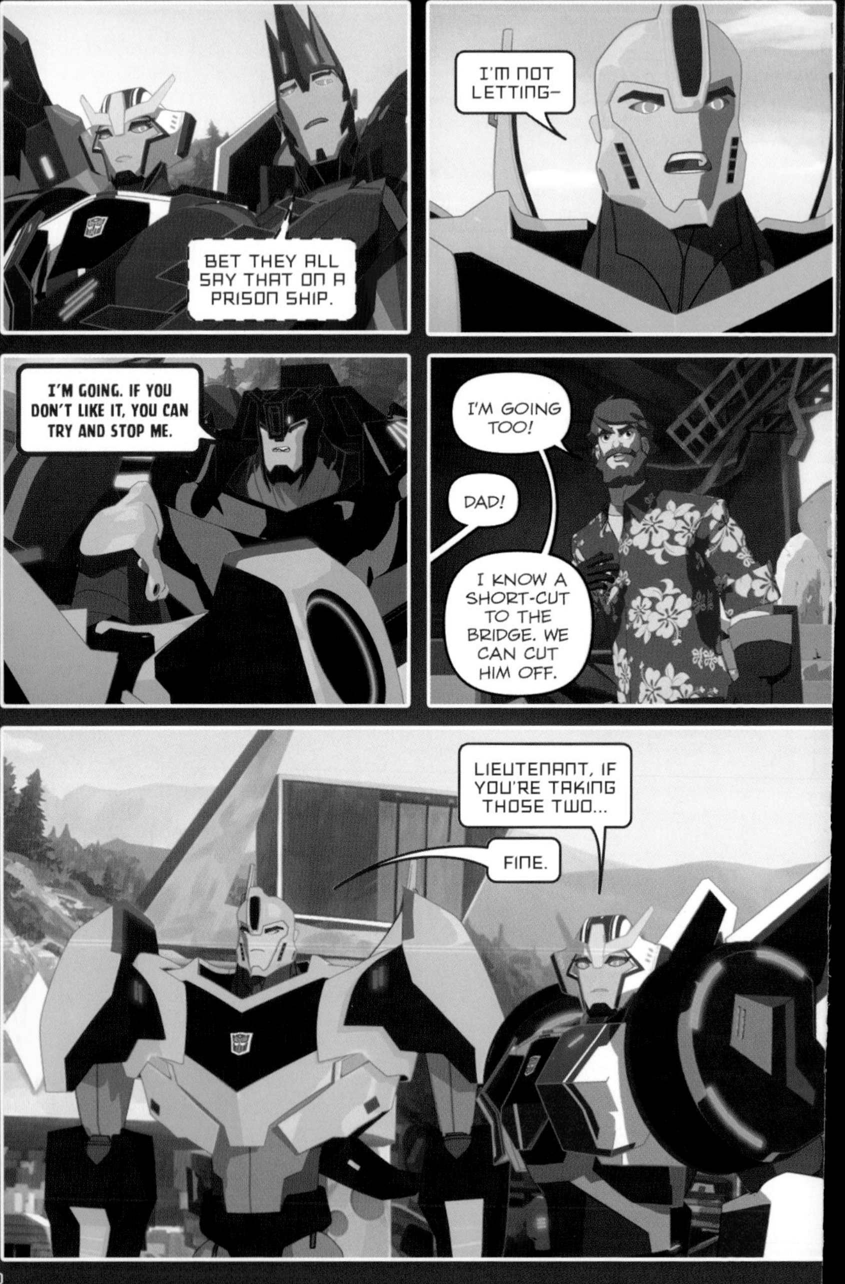
BET THEY ALL SAY THAT ON A PRISON SHIP.
I'M NOT LETTING—
I'M GOING. IF YOU DON'T LIKE IT, YOU CAN TRY AND STOP ME.
I'M GOING TOO!
DAD!
I KNOW A SHORT-CUT TO THE BRIDGE. WE CAN CUT HIM OFF.
LIEUTENANT, IF YOU'RE TAKING THOSE TWO...
FINE.

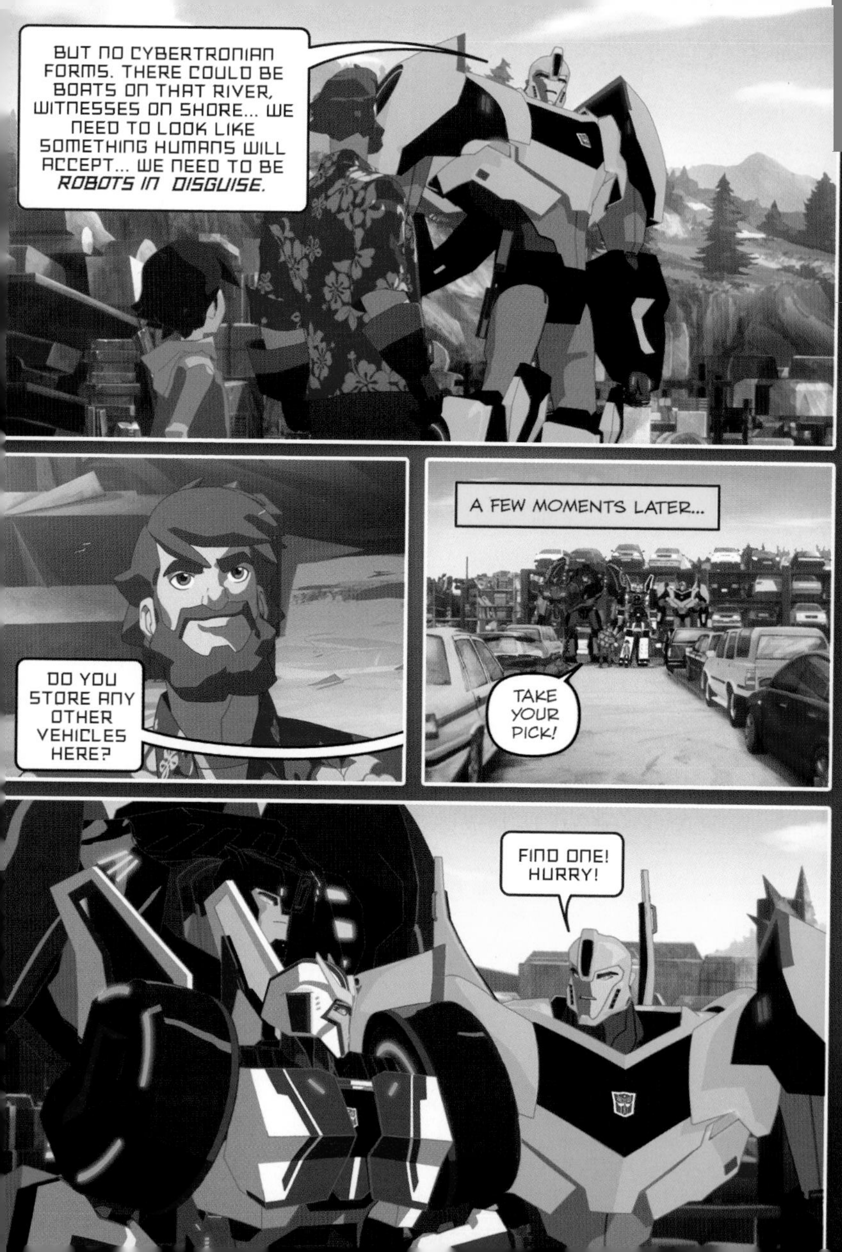

BUT NO CYBERTRONIAN FORMS. THERE COULD BE BOATS ON THAT RIVER, WITNESSES ON SHORE... WE NEED TO LOOK LIKE SOMETHING HUMANS WILL ACCEPT... WE NEED TO BE *ROBOTS IN DISGUISE.*
DO YOU STORE ANY OTHER VEHICLES HERE?
A FEW MOMENTS LATER...
TAKE YOUR PICK!
FIND ONE! HURRY!

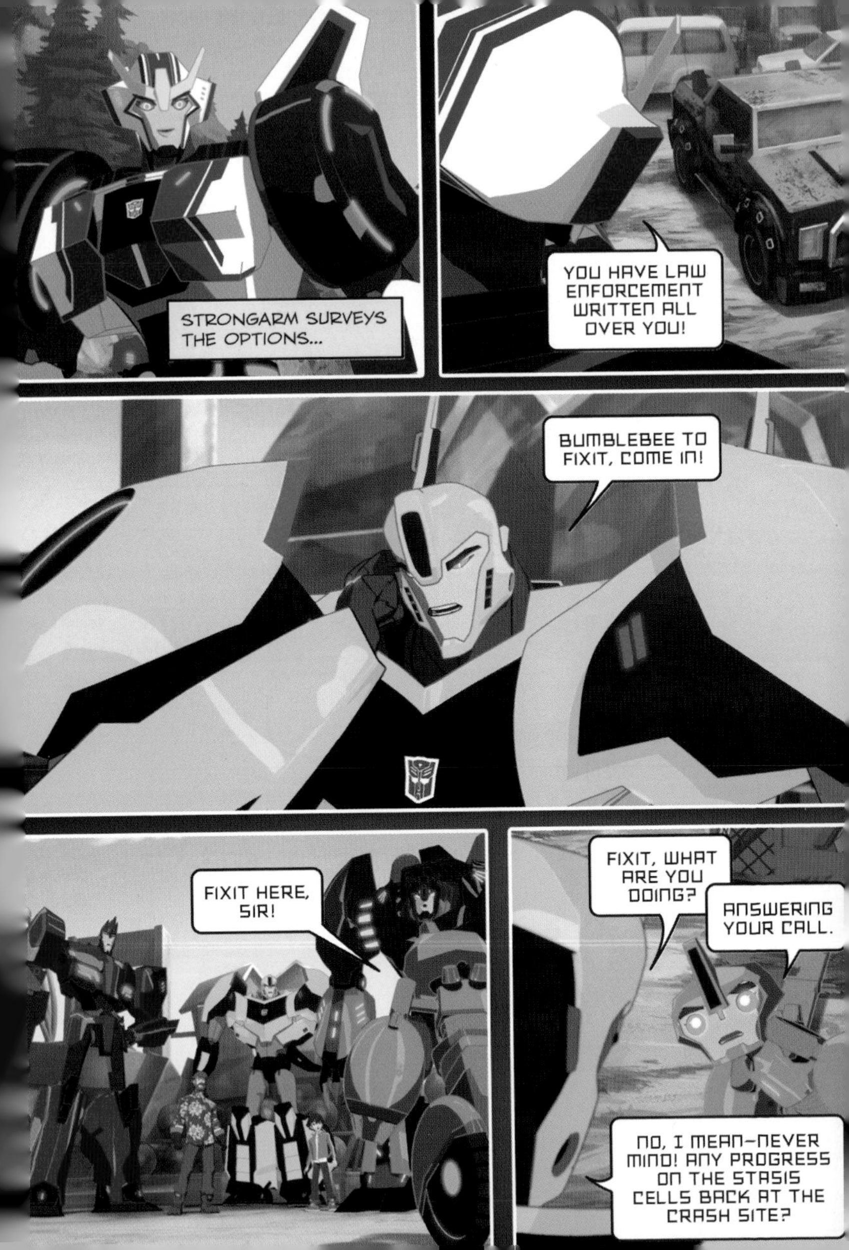
STRONGARM SURVEYS THE OPTIONS...
YOU HAVE LAW ENFORCEMENT WRITTEN ALL OVER YOU!
BUMBLEBEE TO FIXIT, COME IN!
FIXIT HERE, SIR!
FIXIT, WHAT ARE YOU DOING?
ANSWERING YOUR CALL.
NO, I MEAN—NEVER MIND! ANY PROGRESS ON THE STASIS CELLS BACK AT THE CRASH SITE?

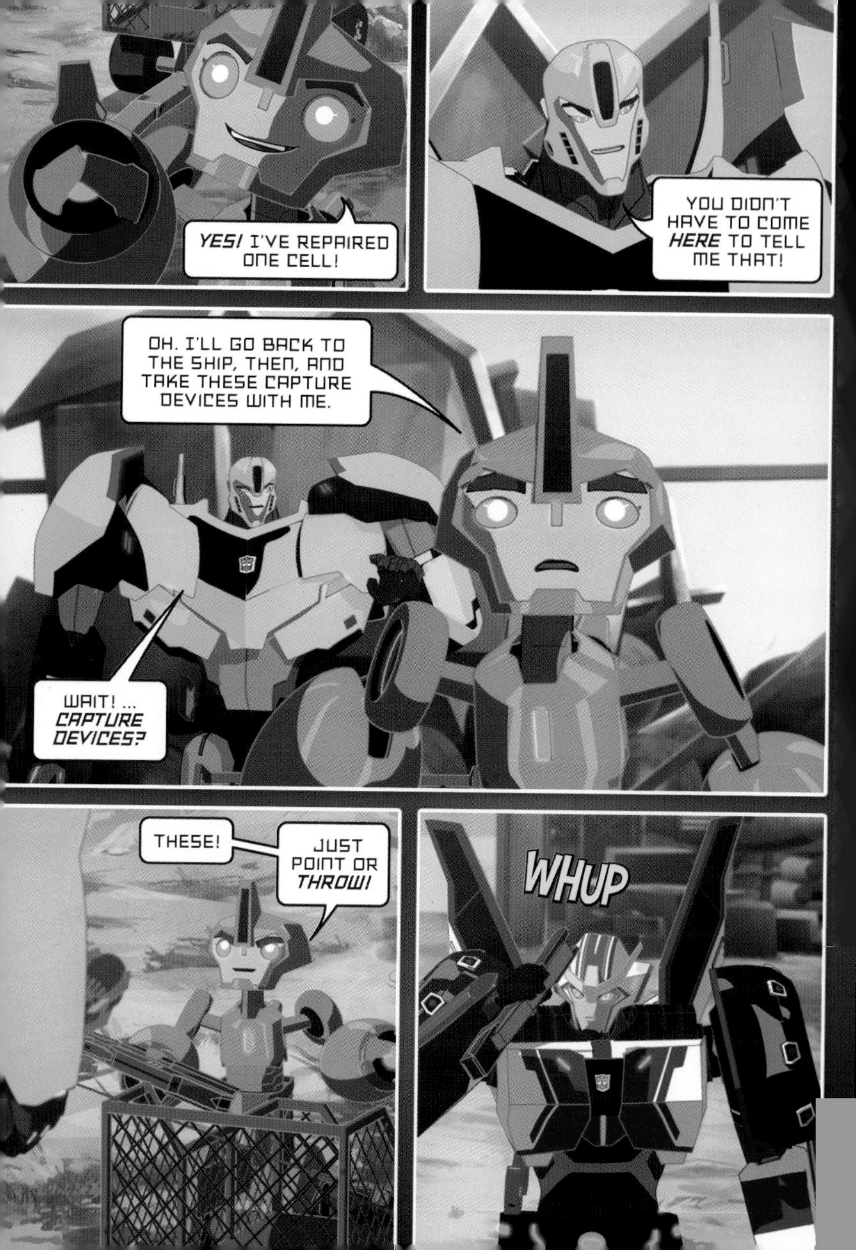

YES! I'VE REPAIRED ONE CELL!
YOU DIDN'T HAVE TO COME HERE TO TELL ME THAT!
OH. I'LL GO BACK TO THE SHIP, THEN, AND TAKE THESE CAPTURE DEVICES WITH ME.
WAIT! ... CAPTURE DEVICES?
THESE!
JUST POINT OR THROW!
WHUP

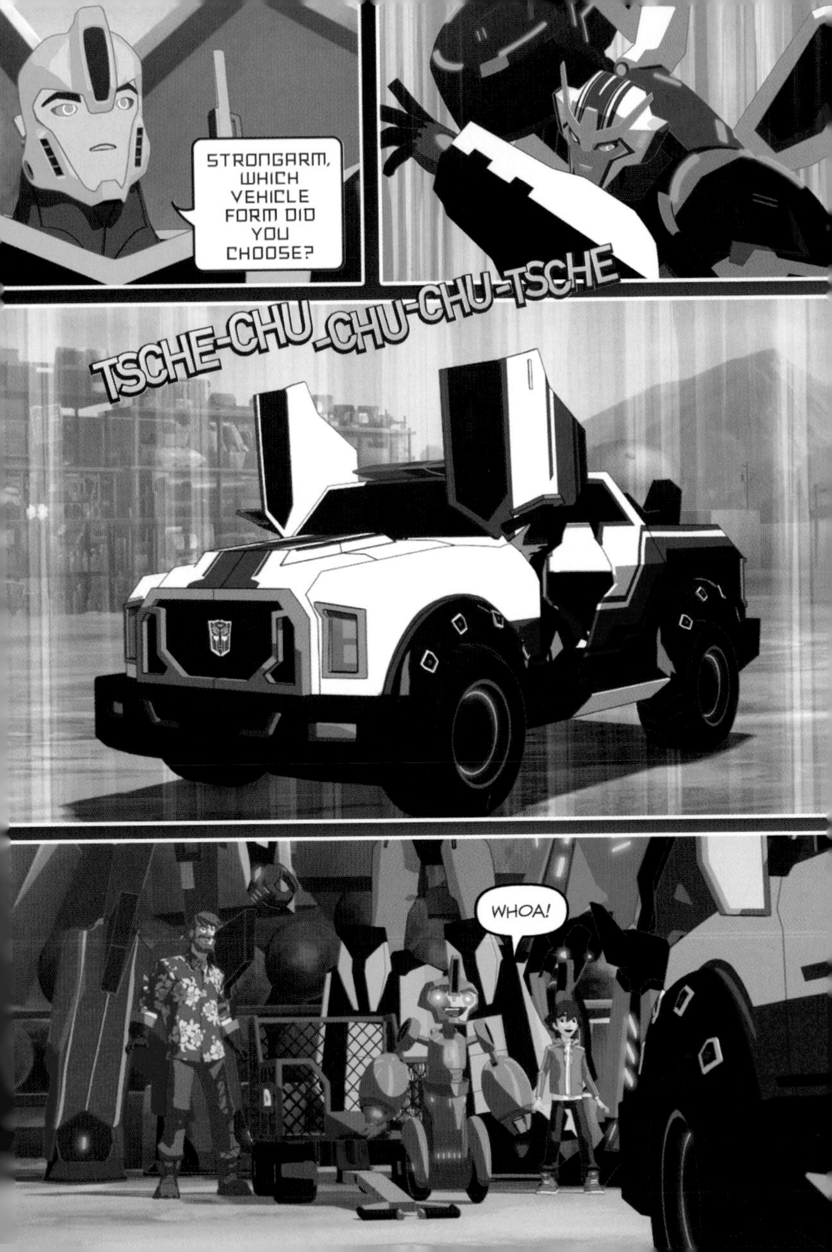
STRONGARM, WHICH VEHICLE FORM DID YOU CHOOSE?
TSCHE-CHU-CHU-CHU-TSCHE
WHOA!

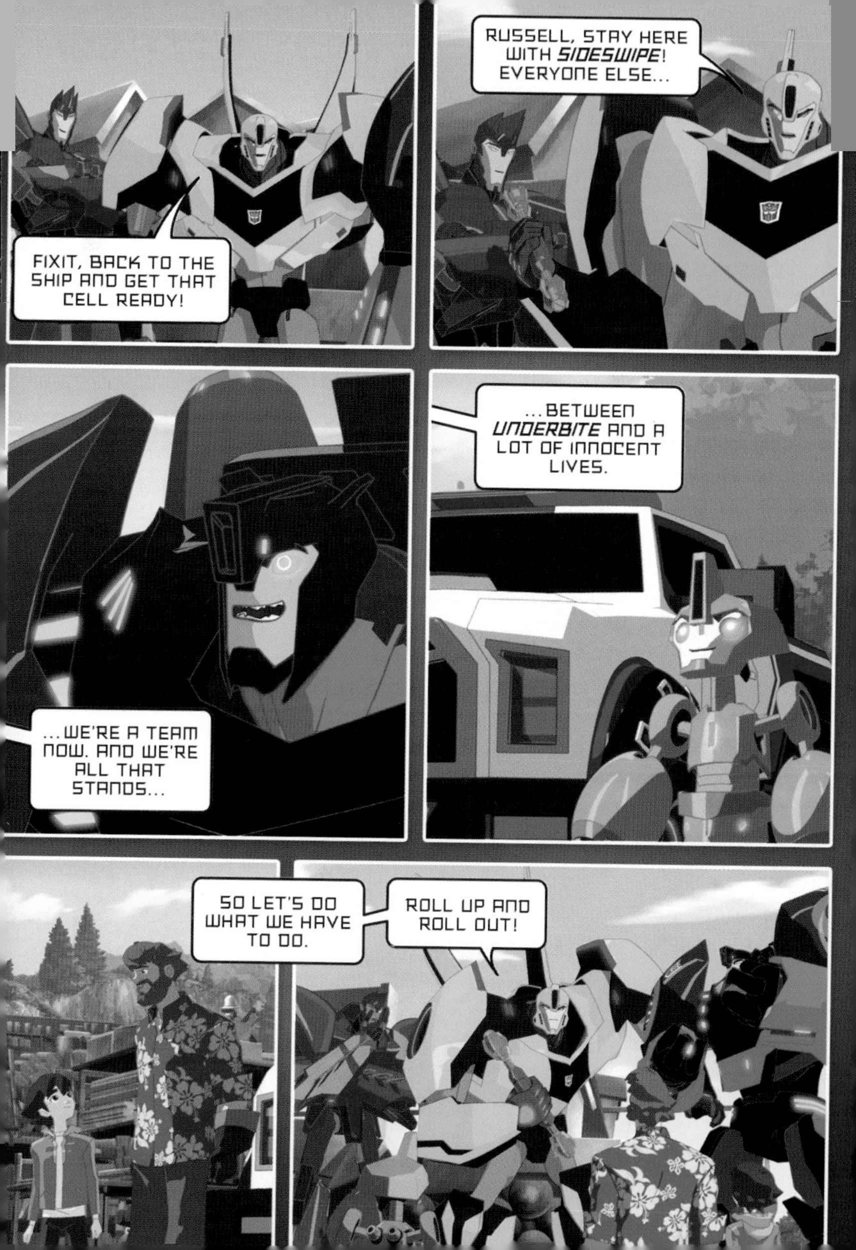

FIXIT, BACK TO THE SHIP AND GET THAT CELL READY!
RUSSELL, STAY HERE WITH *SIDESWIPE*! EVERYONE ELSE...
...WE'RE A TEAM NOW. AND WE'RE ALL THAT STANDS...
...BETWEEN *UNDERBITE* AND A LOT OF INNOCENT LIVES.
SO LET'S DO WHAT WE HAVE TO DO.
ROLL UP AND ROLL OUT!

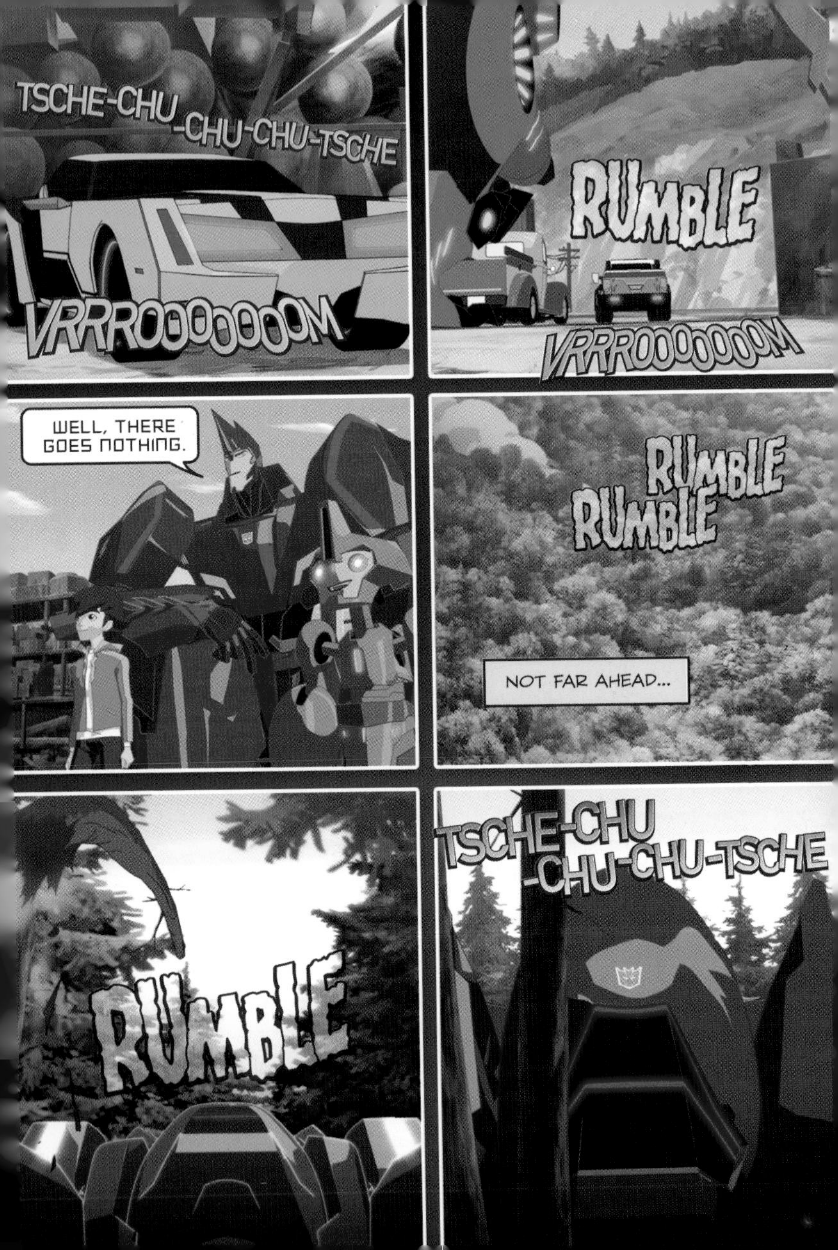
TSCHE-CHU-CHU-CHU-TSCHE
VRRROOOOOOOM
RUMBLE
VRRROOOOOOOM
WELL, THERE GOES NOTHING.
RUMBLE RUMBLE
NOT FAR AHEAD...
RUMBLE
TSCHE-CHU -CHU-CHU-TSCHE

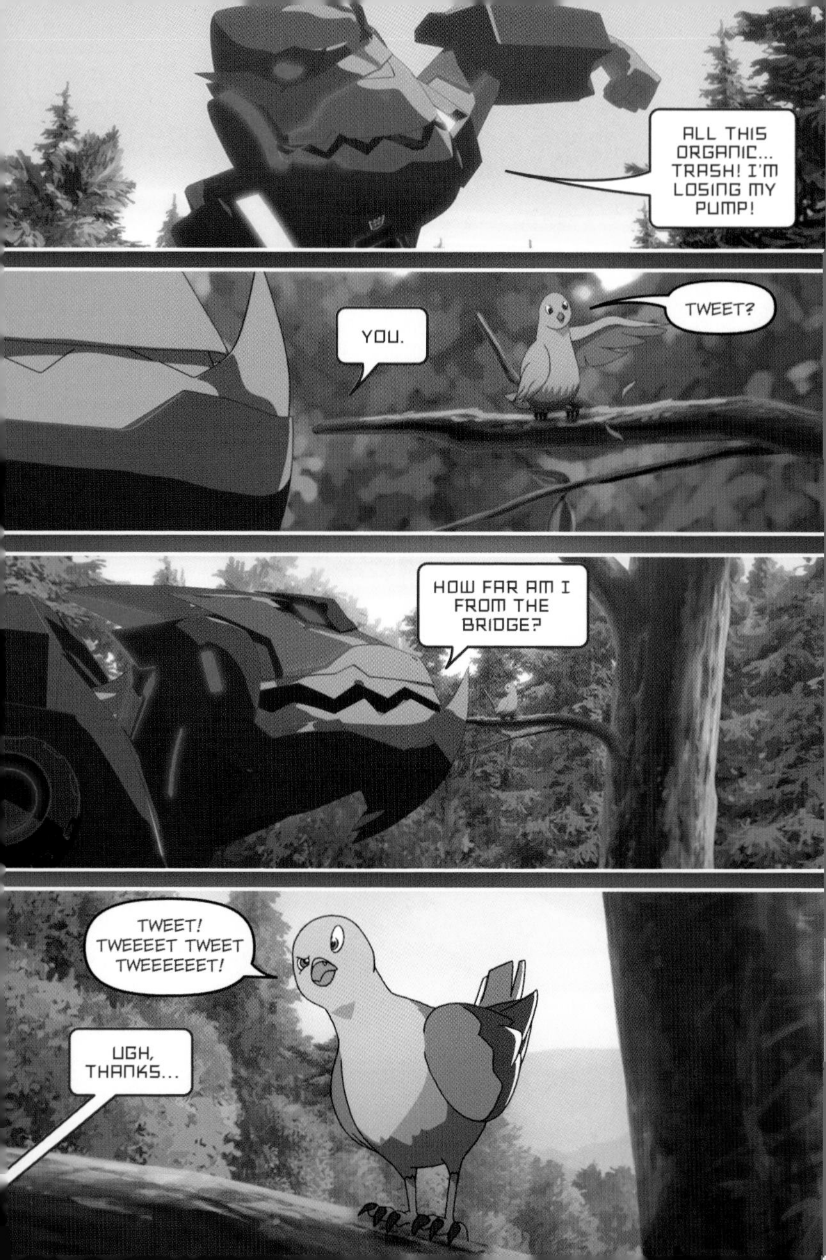
ALL THIS ORGANIC... TRASH! I'M LOSING MY PUMP!
YOU.
TWEET?
HOW FAR AM I FROM THE BRIDGE?
TWEET! TWEEEET TWEET TWEEEEEET!
UGH, THANKS...

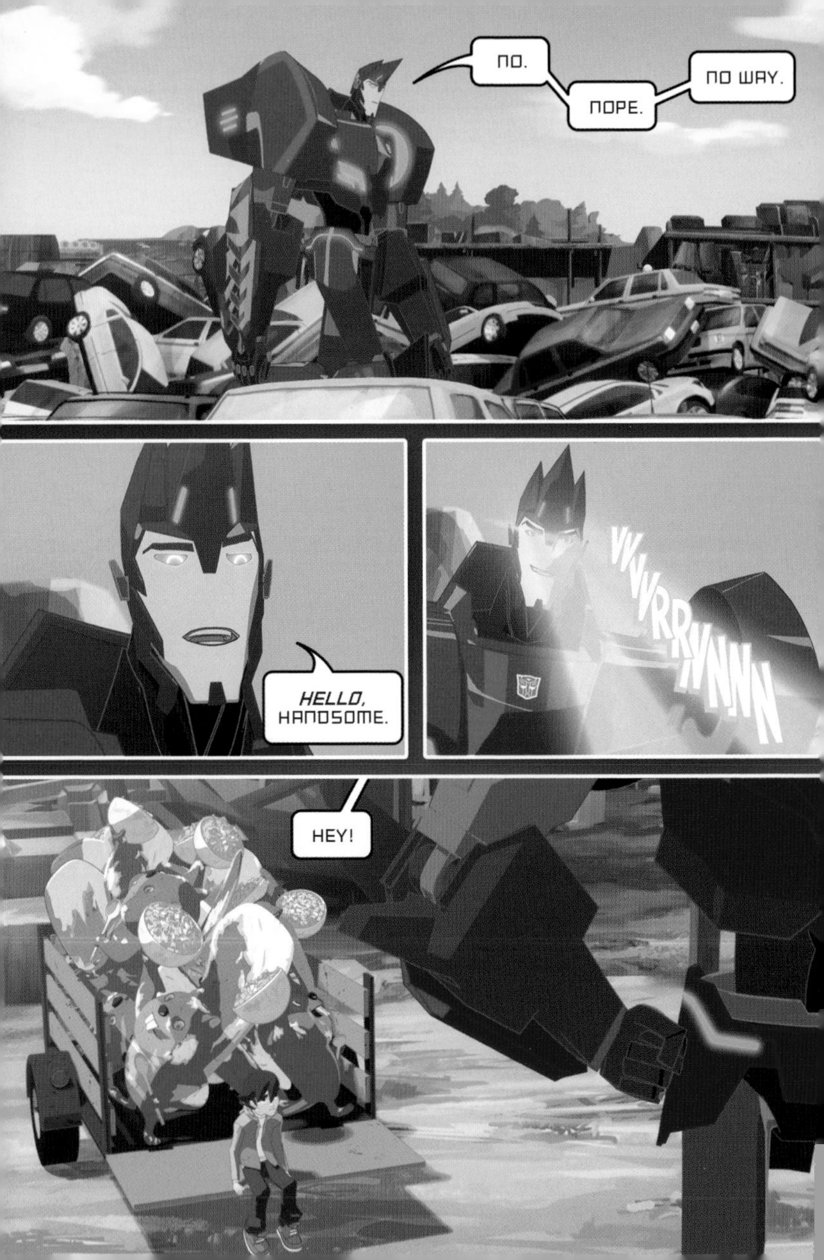
NO.
NOPE.
NO WAY.
HELLO, HANDSOME.
VVVRRRVNNN
HEY!

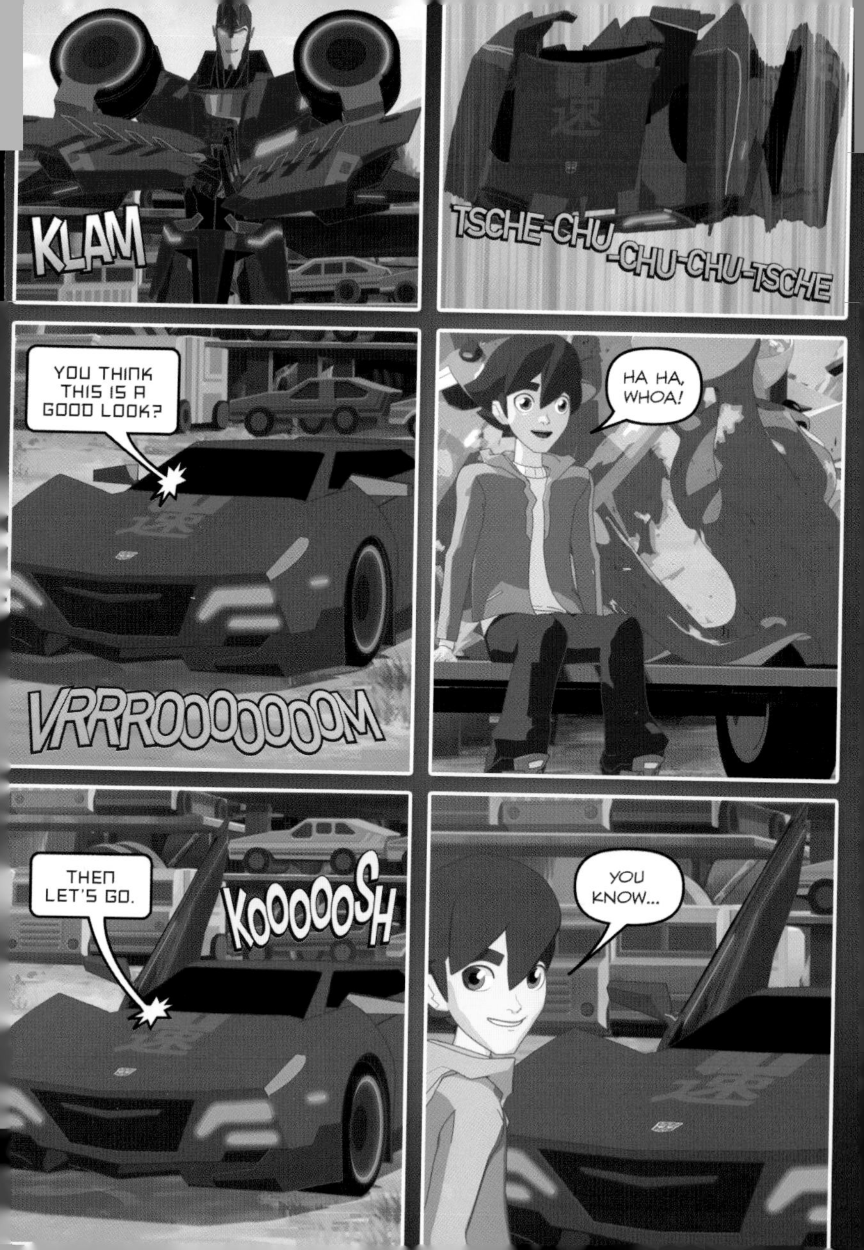
KLAM
TSCHE-CHU_CHU-CHU-TSCHE
YOU THINK THIS IS A GOOD LOOK?
VRRROOOOOOOM
HA HA, WHOA!
THEN LET'S GO.
KOOOOOSH
YOU KNOW...

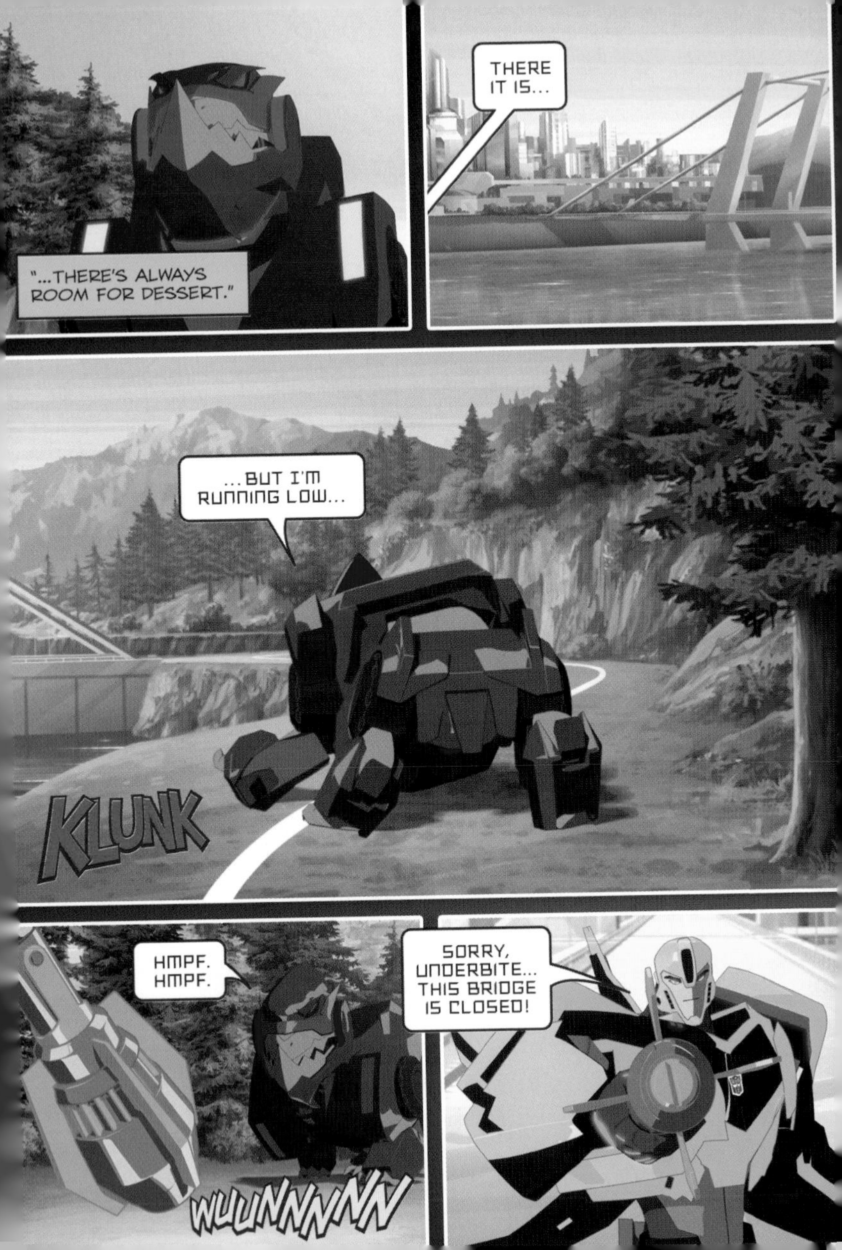
"...THERE'S ALWAYS ROOM FOR DESSERT."
THERE IT IS...
...BUT I'M RUNNING LOW...
KLUNK
HMPF. HMPF.
WUUNNNNNN
SORRY, UNDERBITE... THIS BRIDGE IS CLOSED!

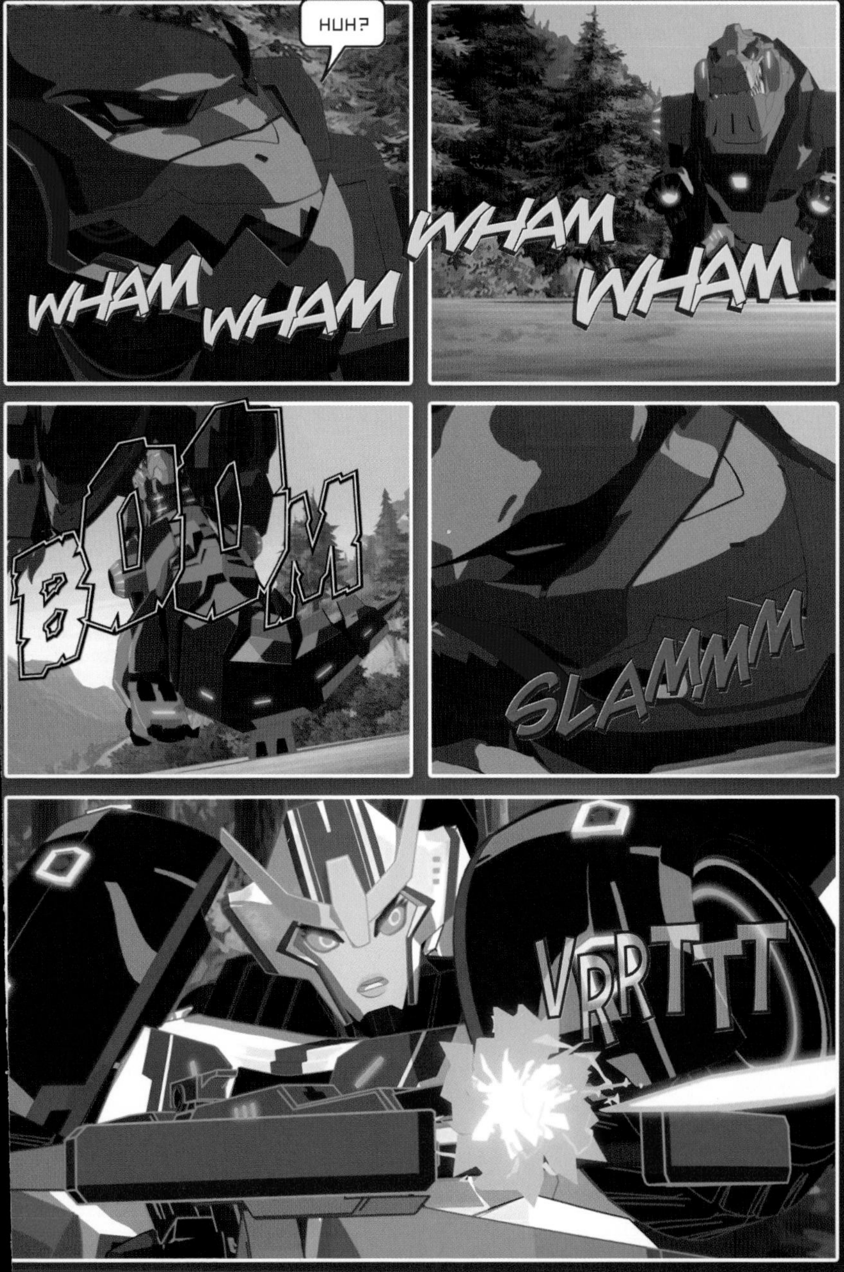
HUH?
WHAM
WHAM
WHAM
WHAM
BOOM
SLAMMM
VRRTTT

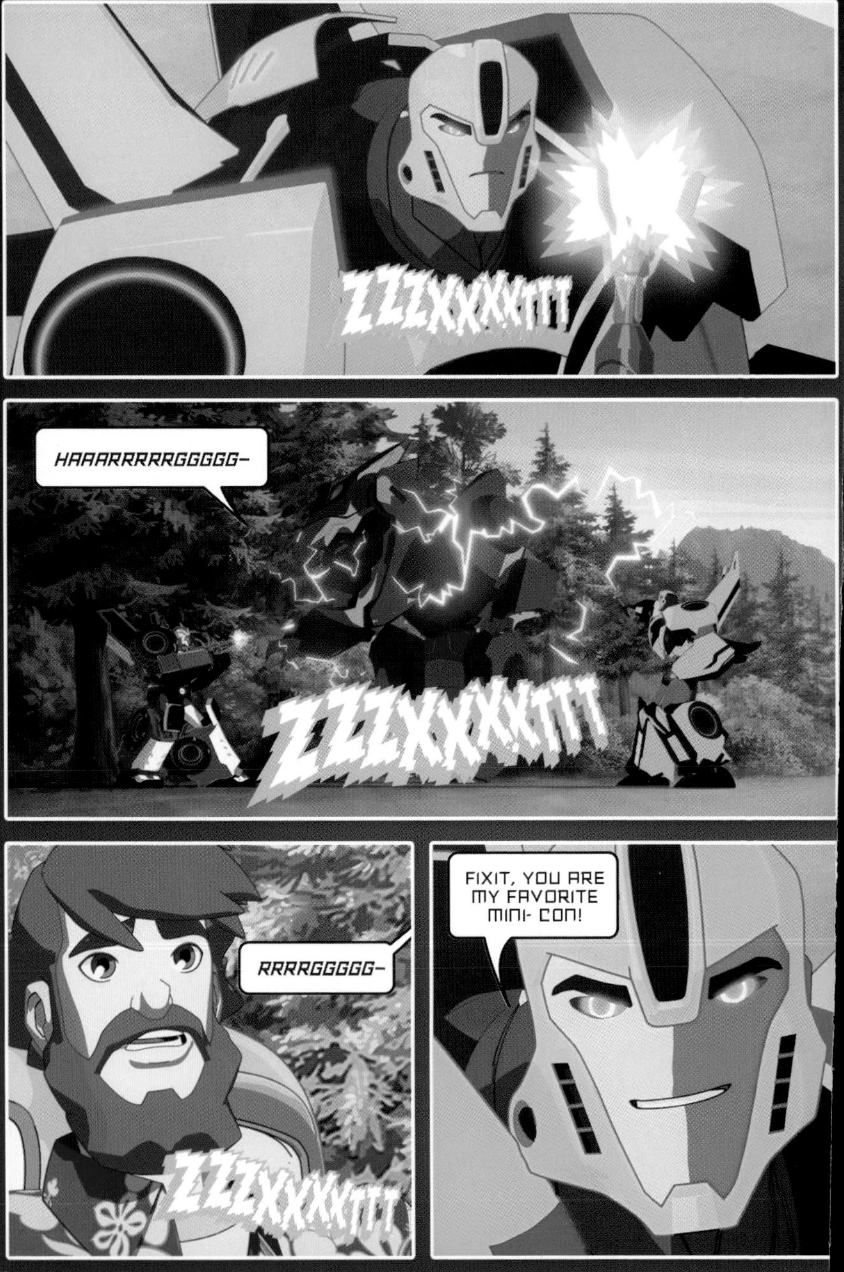
ZZZXXXXTTT
HAAARRRRRGGGGG–
ZZZXXXXTTT
RRRRGGGGG–
ZZZXXXXTTT
FIXIT, YOU ARE MY FAVORITE MINI- CON!

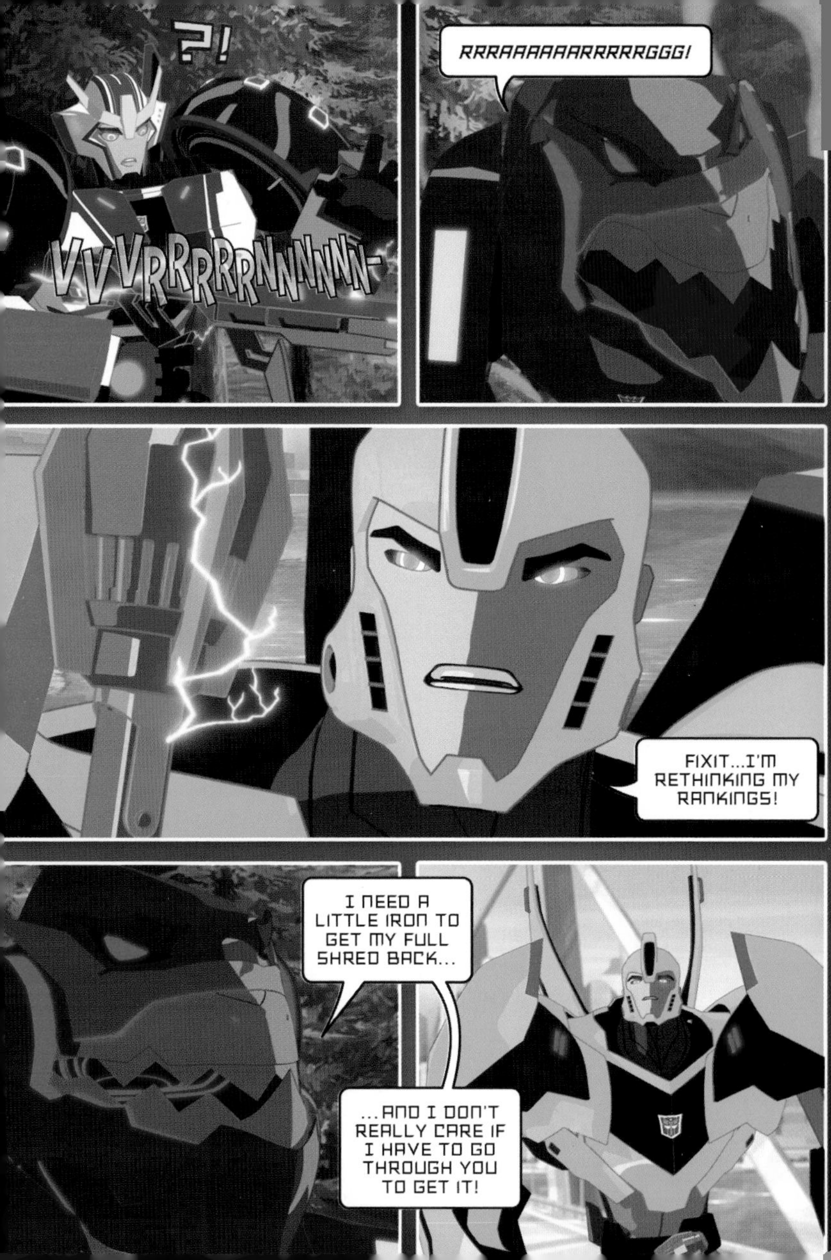
?!
VVVRRRRRNNNNNN-
RRRAAAAAAARRRRRGGG!
FIXIT...I'M RETHINKING MY RANKINGS!
I NEED A LITTLE IRON TO GET MY FULL SHRED BACK...
...AND I DON'T REALLY CARE IF I HAVE TO GO THROUGH YOU TO GET IT!

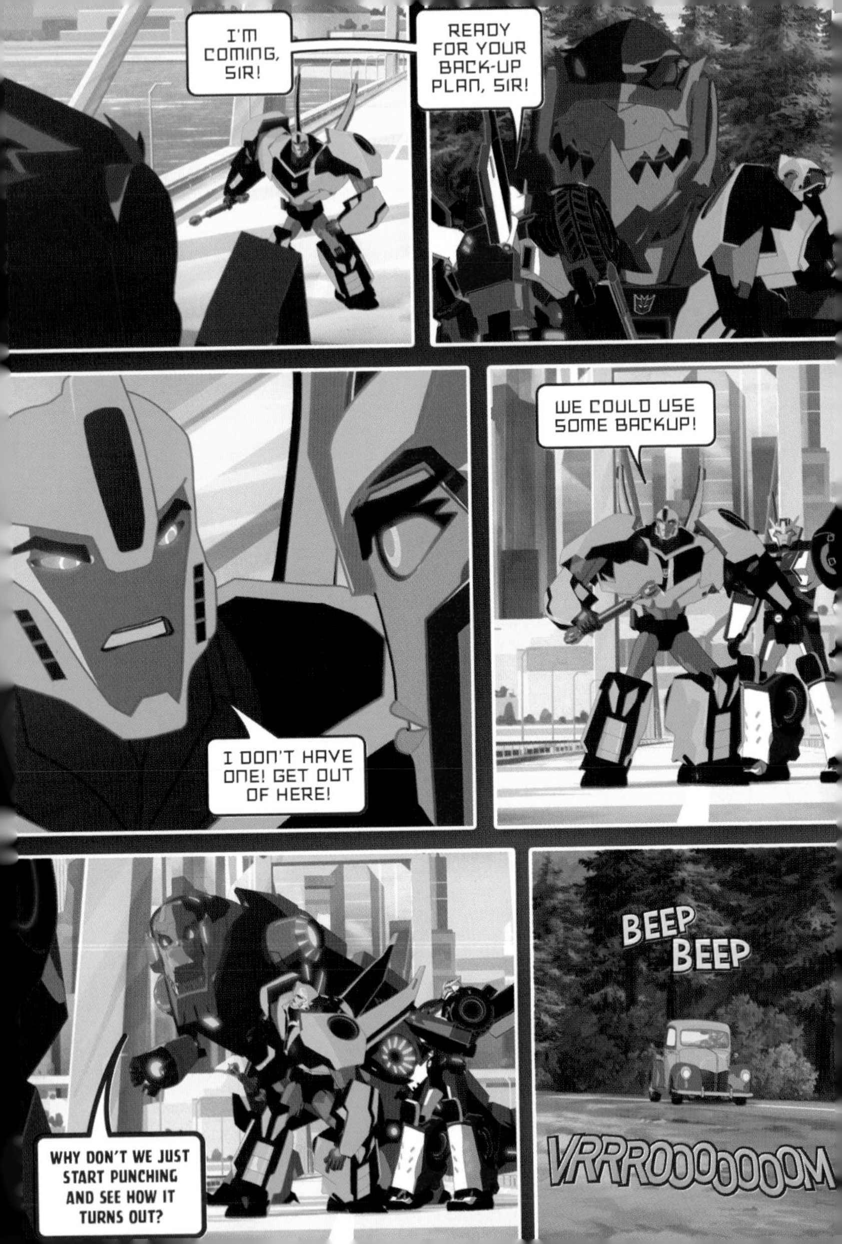
I'M COMING, SIR!
READY FOR YOUR BACK-UP PLAN, SIR!
I DON'T HAVE ONE! GET OUT OF HERE!
WE COULD USE SOME BACKUP!
WHY DON'T WE JUST START PUNCHING AND SEE HOW IT TURNS OUT?
BEEP BEEP
VRRROOOOOOOOM

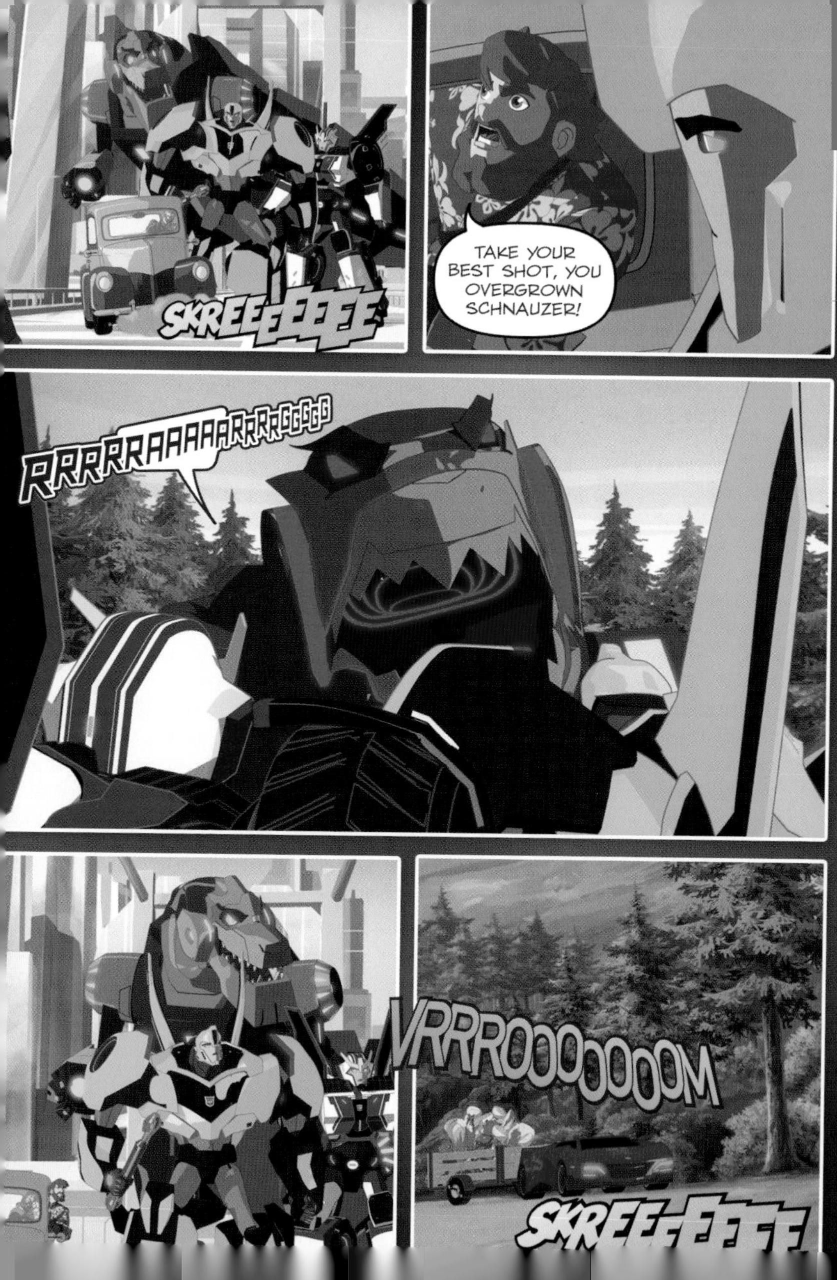
SKREEEEEEE
TAKE YOUR BEST SHOT, YOU OVERGROWN SCHNAUZER!
RRRRRAAAAAARRRRGGGGG
VRRROOOOOOOM
SKREEEEEEE

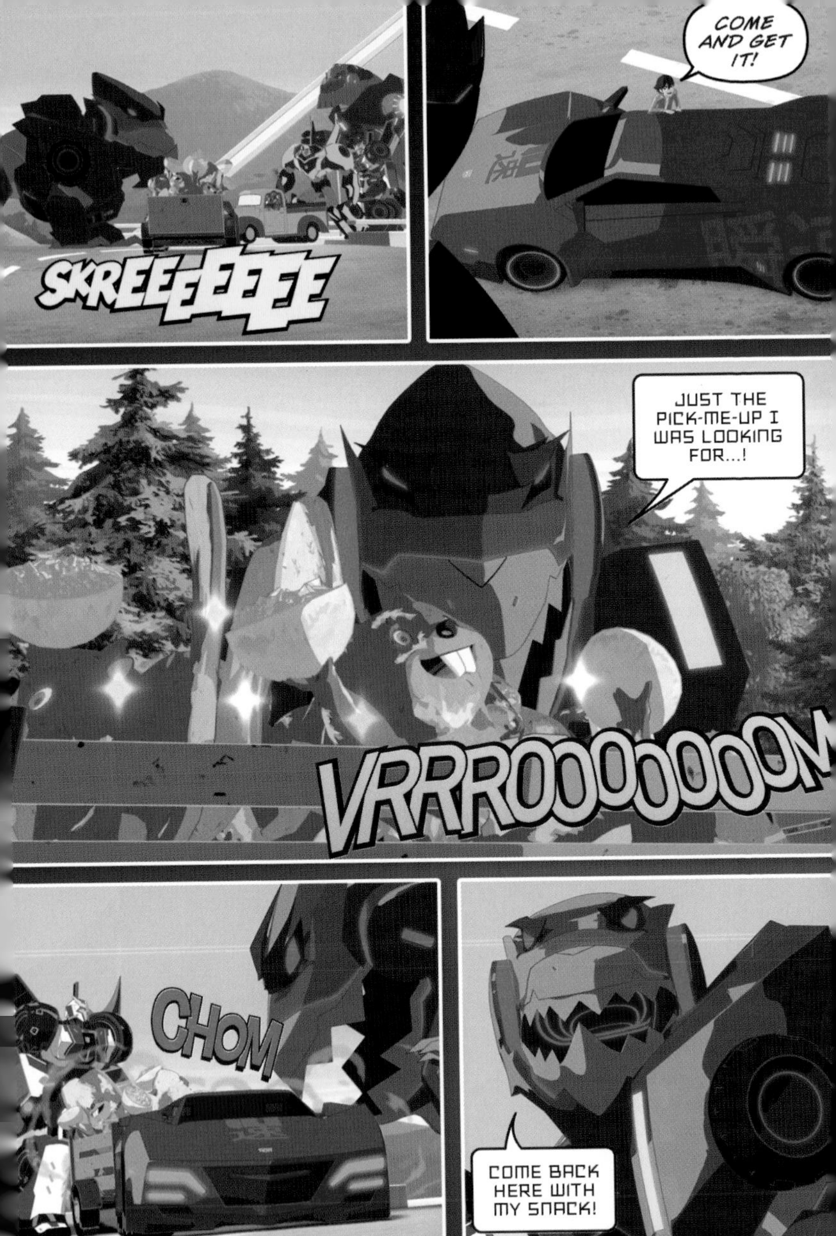
SKREEEEEEEE
COME AND GET IT!
JUST THE PICK-ME-UP I WAS LOOKING FOR...!
VRRROOOOOOOOM
CHOM
COME BACK HERE WITH MY SNACK!

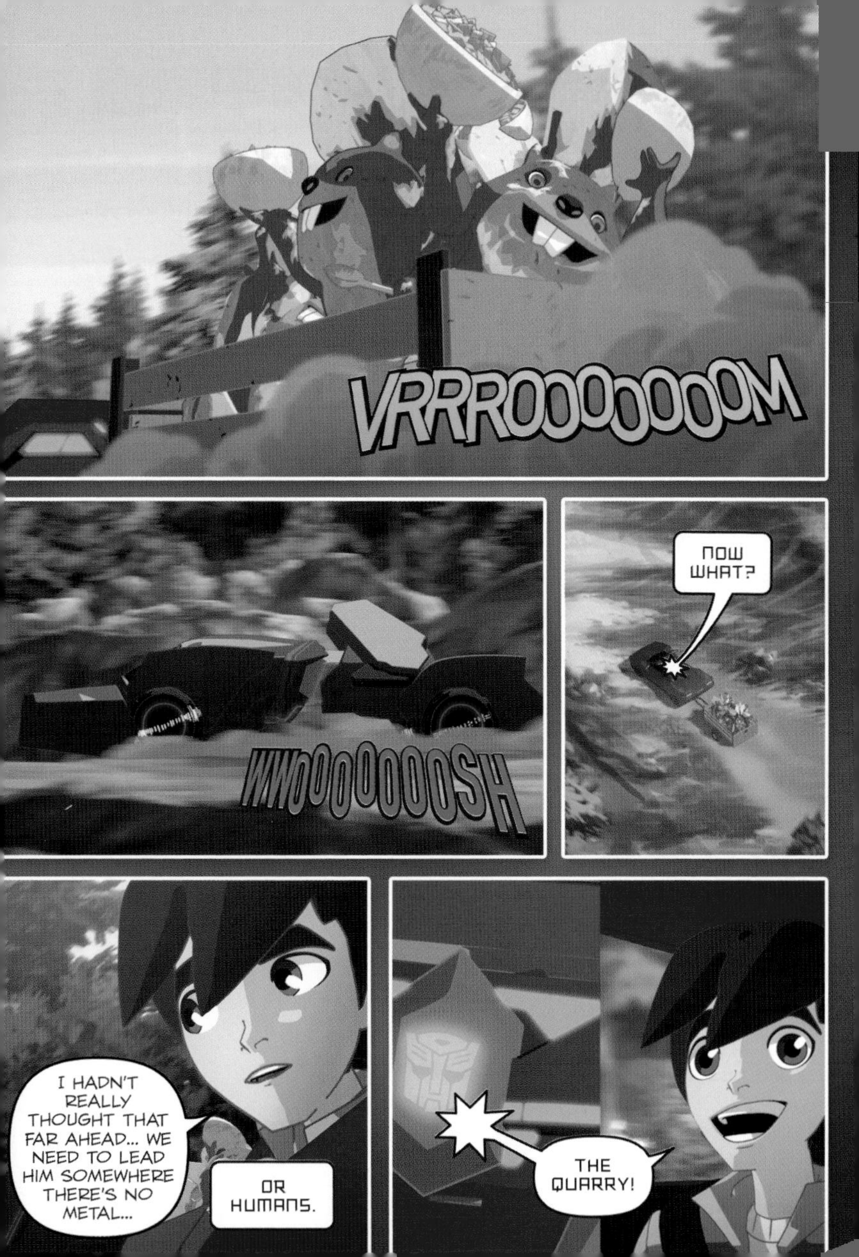
VRRROOOOOOOOM
WWOOOOOOOSH
NOW WHAT?
I HADN'T REALLY THOUGHT THAT FAR AHEAD... WE NEED TO LEAD HIM SOMEWHERE THERE'S NO METAL...
OR HUMANS.
THE QUARRY!

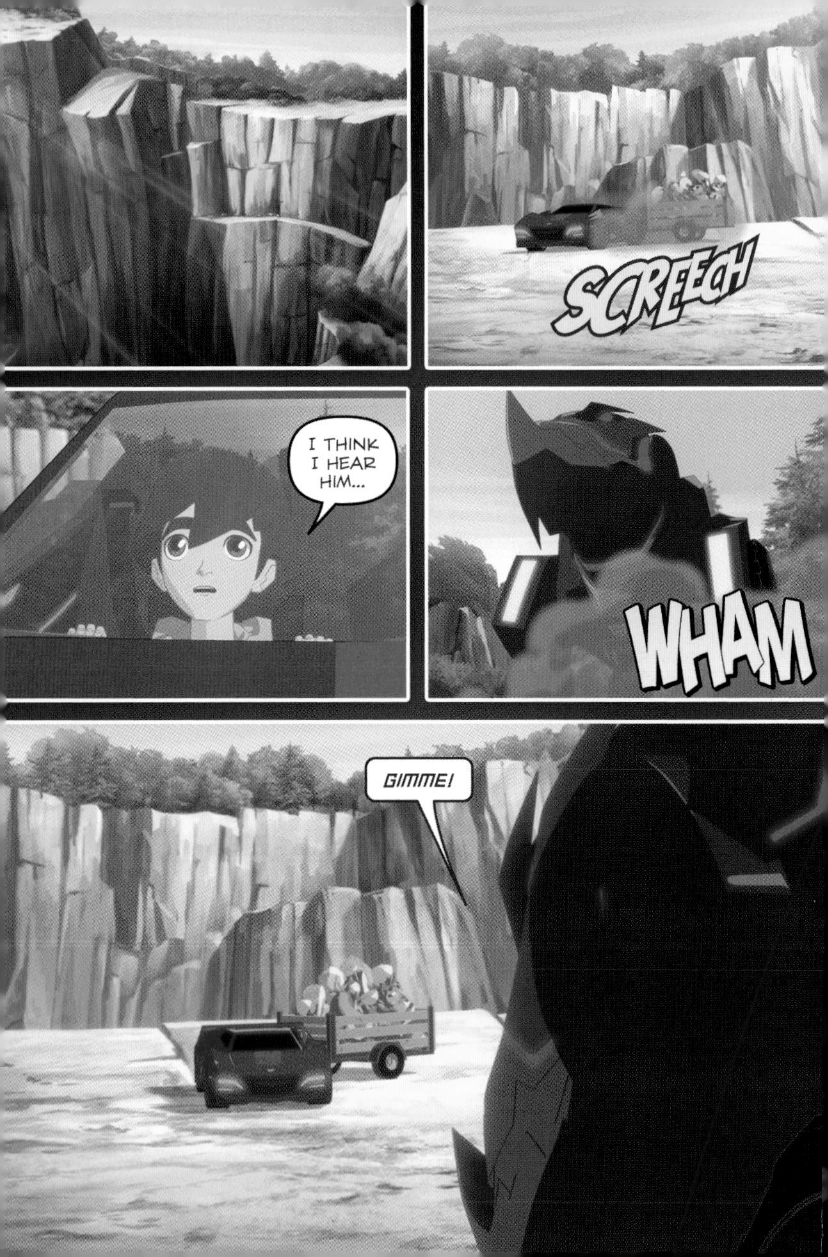
SCREECH
I THINK I HEAR HIM...
WHAM
GIMME!

UNDERBITE LUNGES AT THE TRAILER...

VVVRRROOOOOSH
SLAMMMMM

SQUEECH

...AND SLIDES RIGHT UP TO THE EDGE!

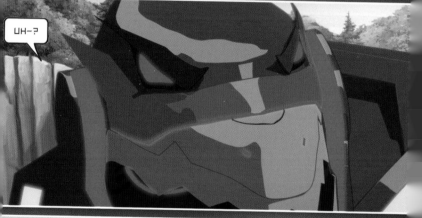

UH-?

VRRROOOOOOOOM

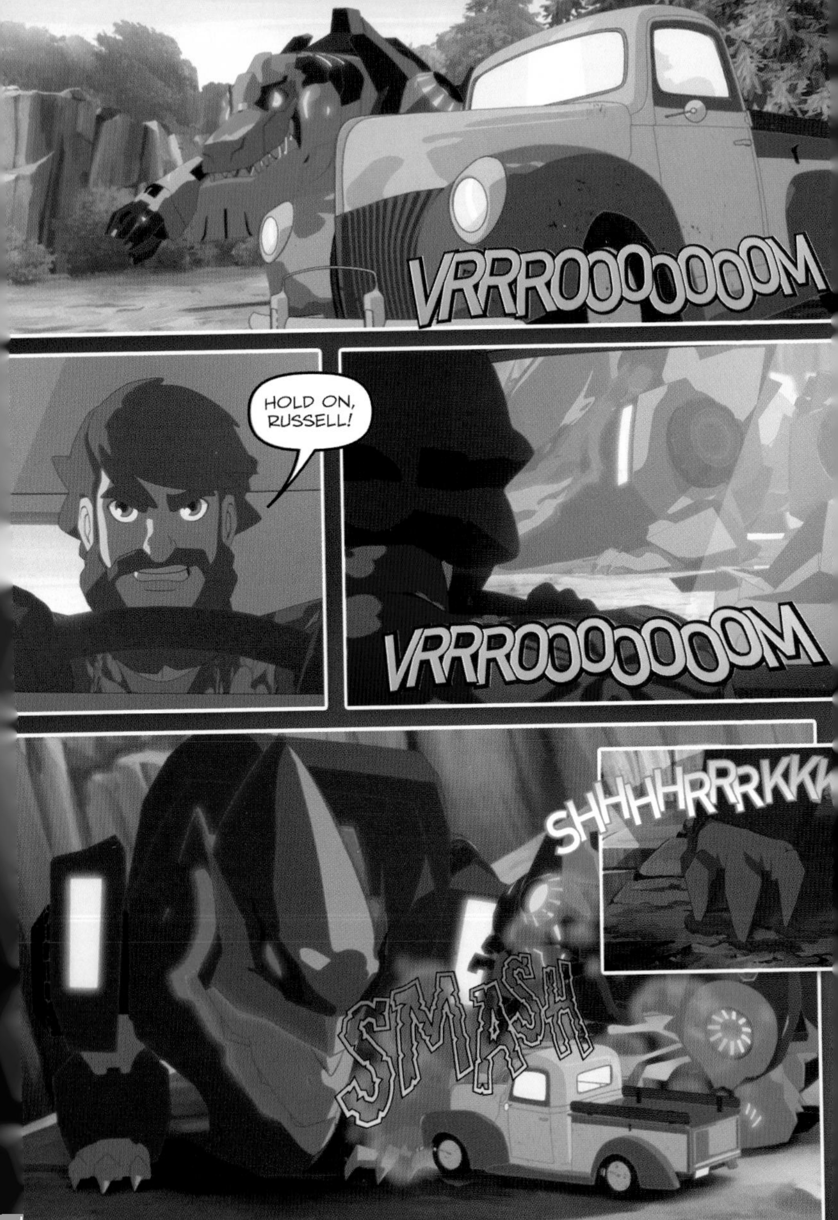
VRRROOOOOOOM
HOLD ON, RUSSELL!
VRRROOOOOOOOM
SHHHRRRKK
SMASH

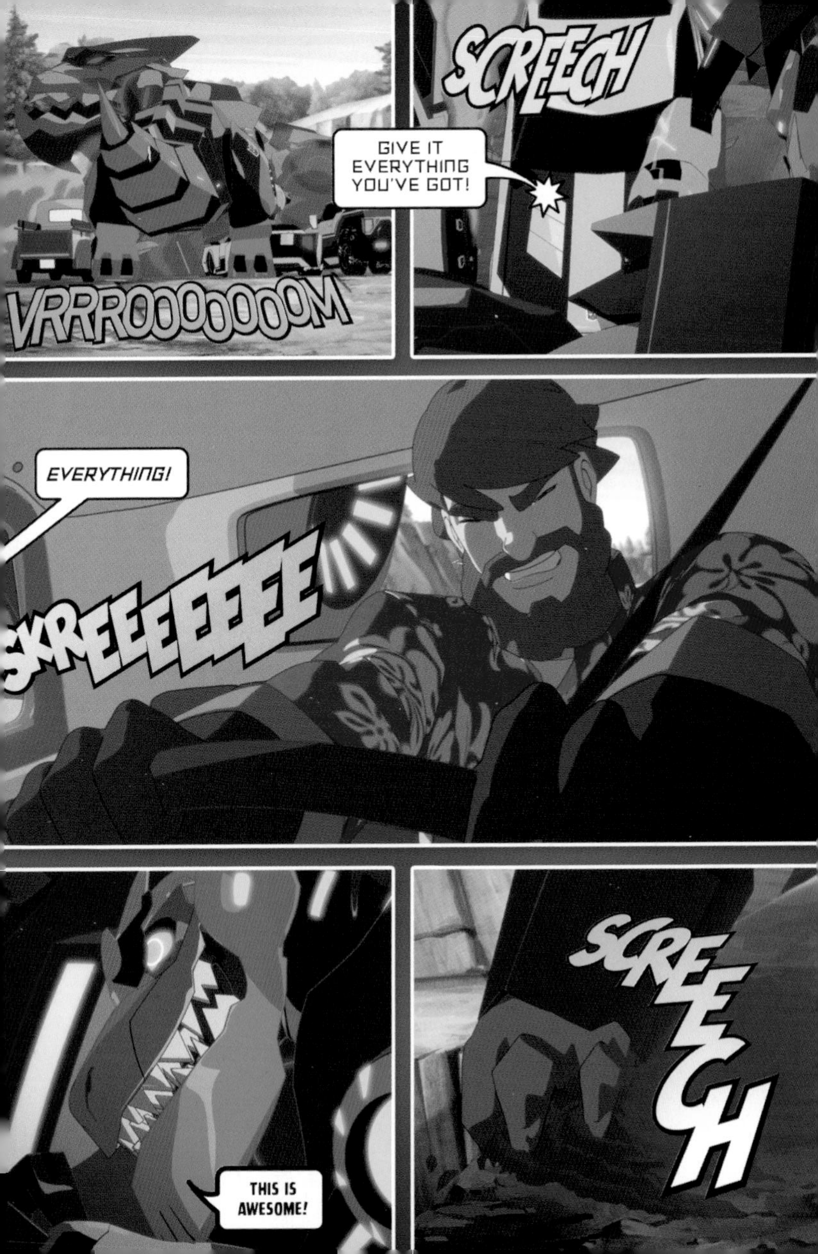
VRRROOOOOOOM
SCREECH
GIVE IT EVERYTHING YOU'VE GOT!
EVERYTHING!
SKREEEEEEE
THIS IS AWESOME!
SCREEECH

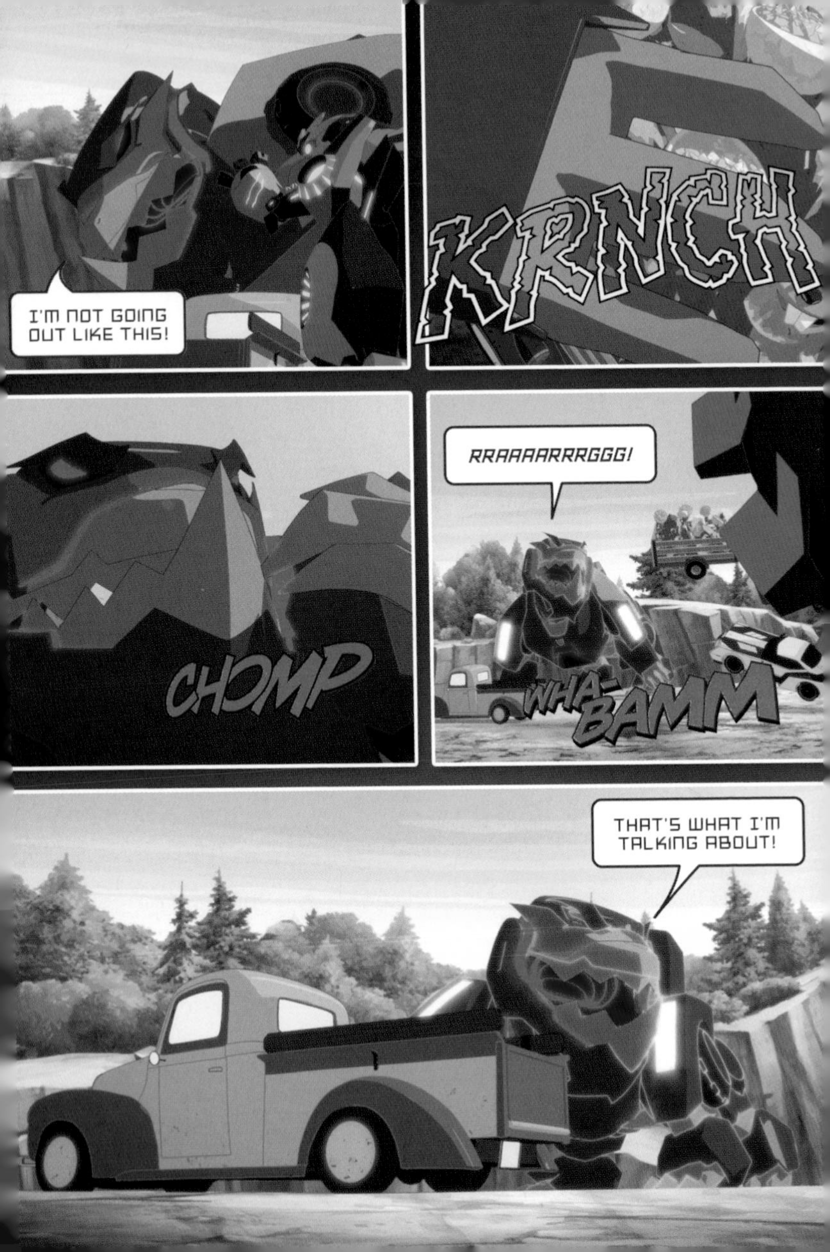

I'M NOT GOING OUT LIKE THIS!
KRNCH
CHOMP
RRAAAARRRGGG!
WHA-BAMM
THAT'S WHAT I'M TALKING ABOUT!

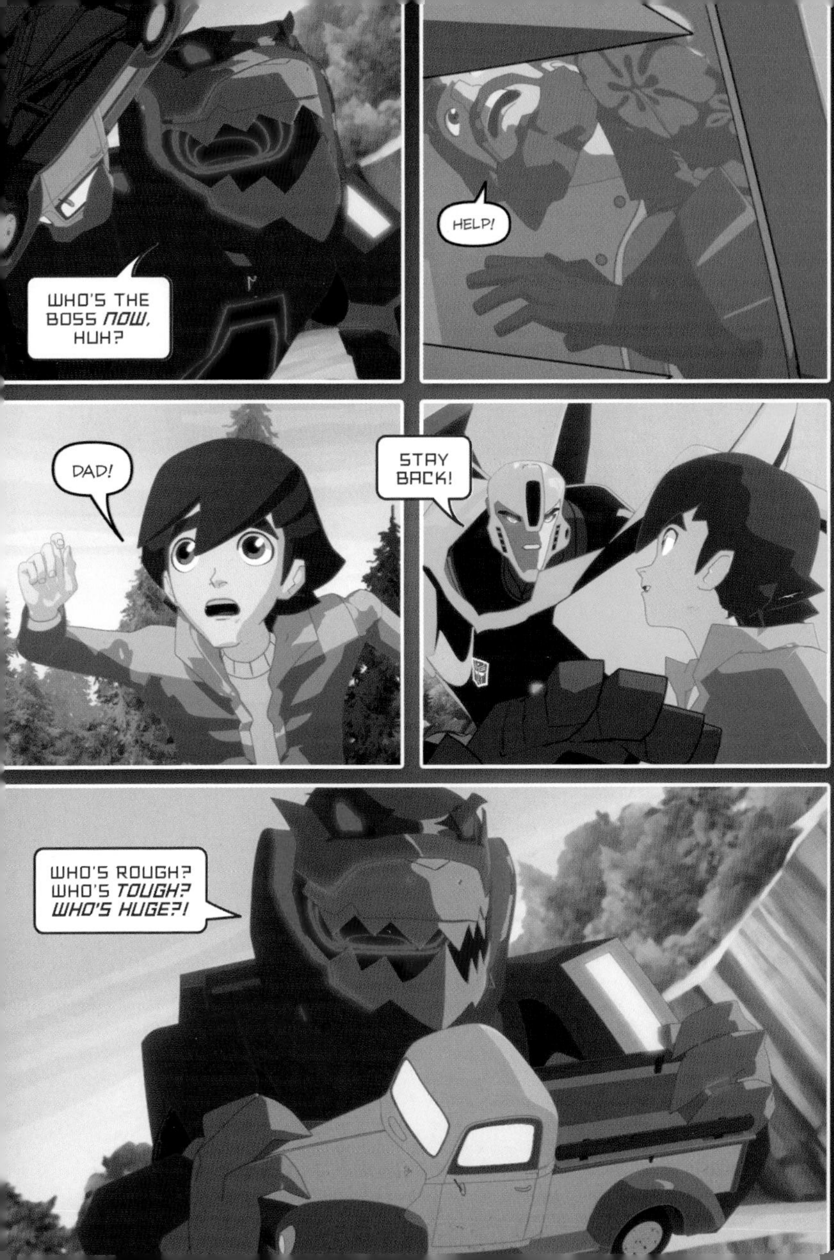
WHO'S THE BOSS *NOW*, HUH?
HELP!
DAD!
STAY BACK!
WHO'S ROUGH? WHO'S *TOUGH?* ***WHO'S HUGE?!***

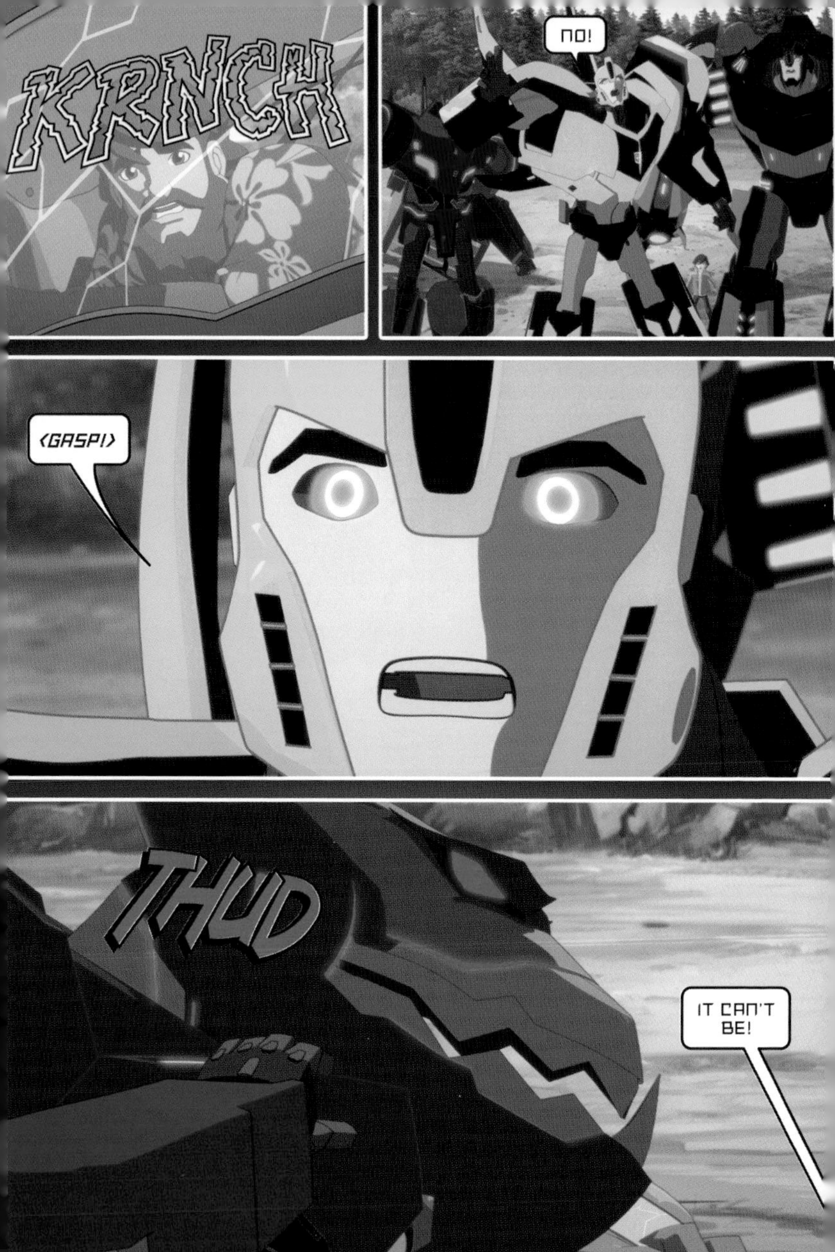
KRNCH
NO!
<GASP!>
THUD
IT CAN'T BE!

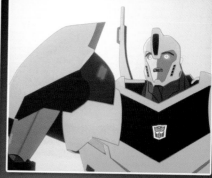

BUT IT IS...

...OPTIMUS PRIME!

WHAMMM

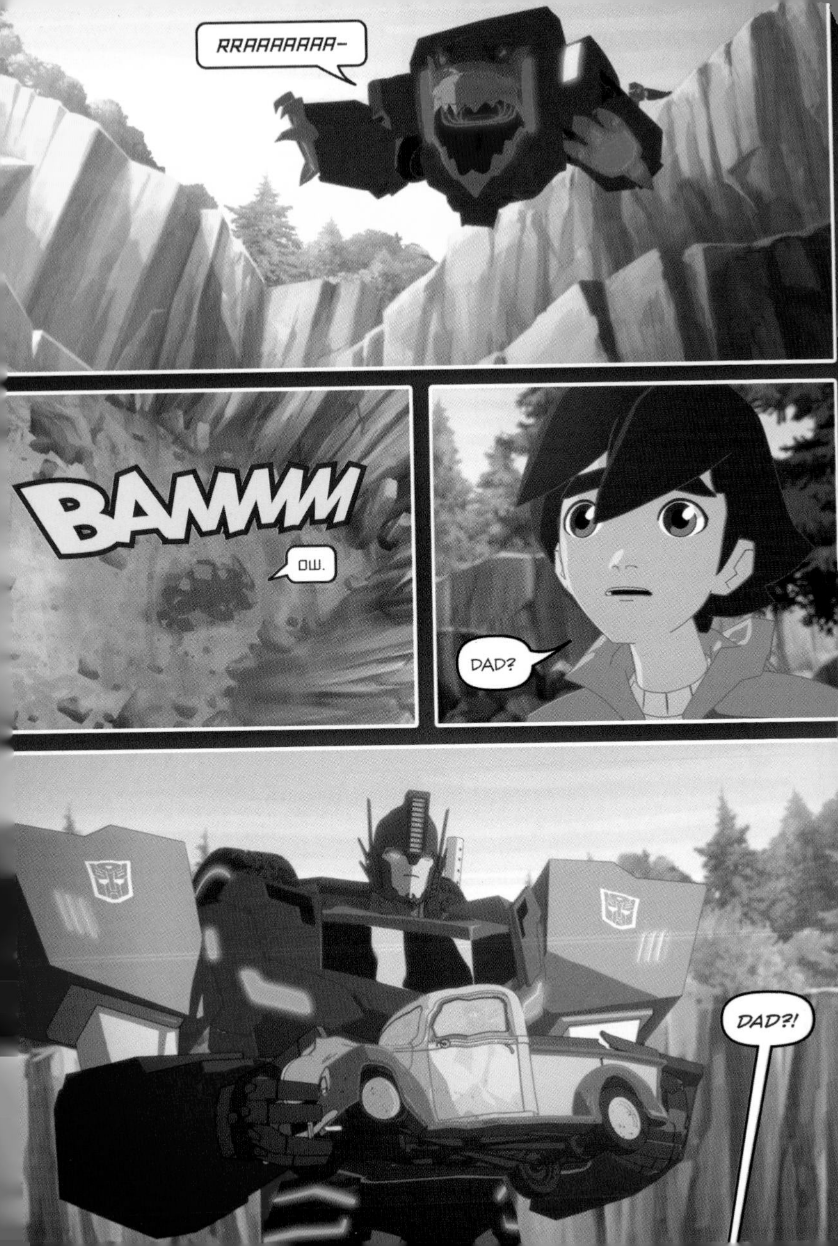
RRAAAAAAAA-
BAMMM
OW.
DAD?
DAD?!

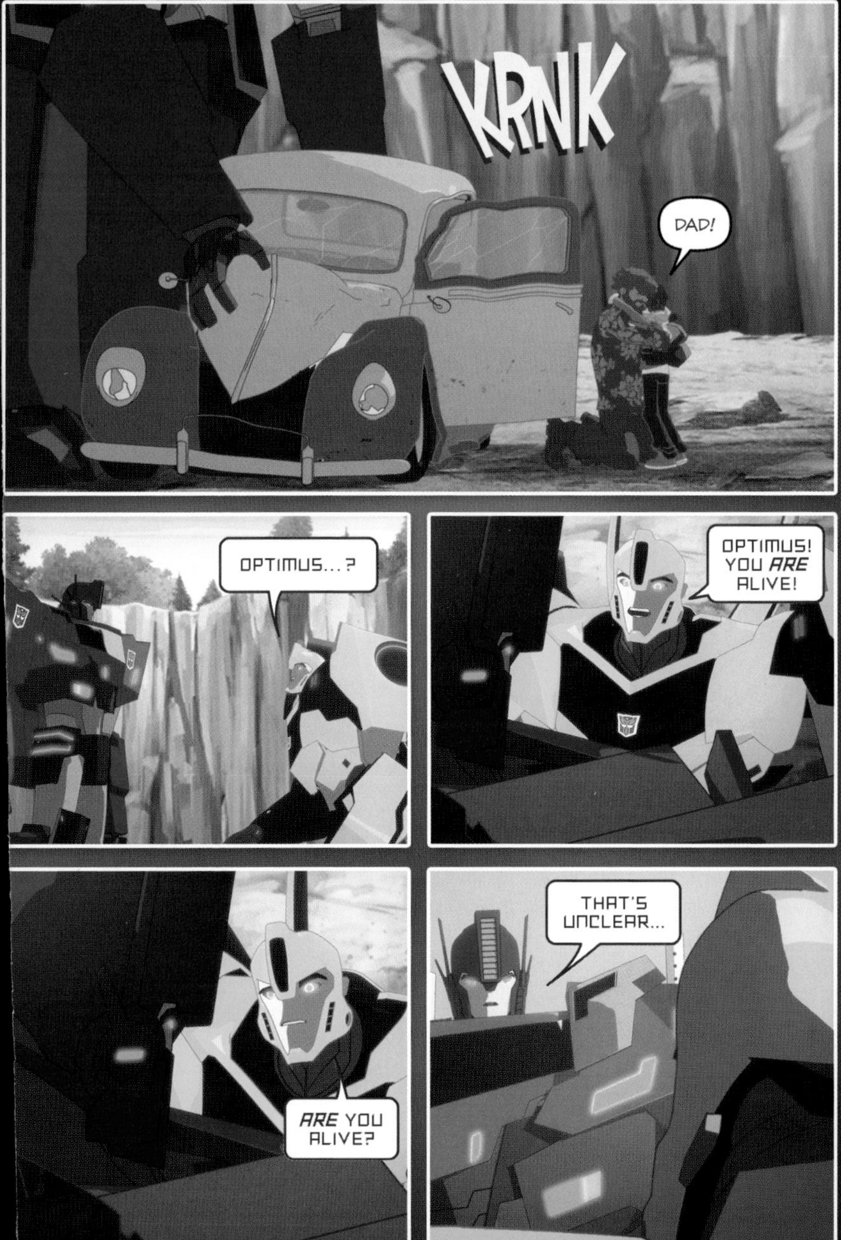
KRNK
DAD!
OPTIMUS...?
OPTIMUS! YOU ARE ALIVE!
ARE YOU ALIVE?
THAT'S UNCLEAR...

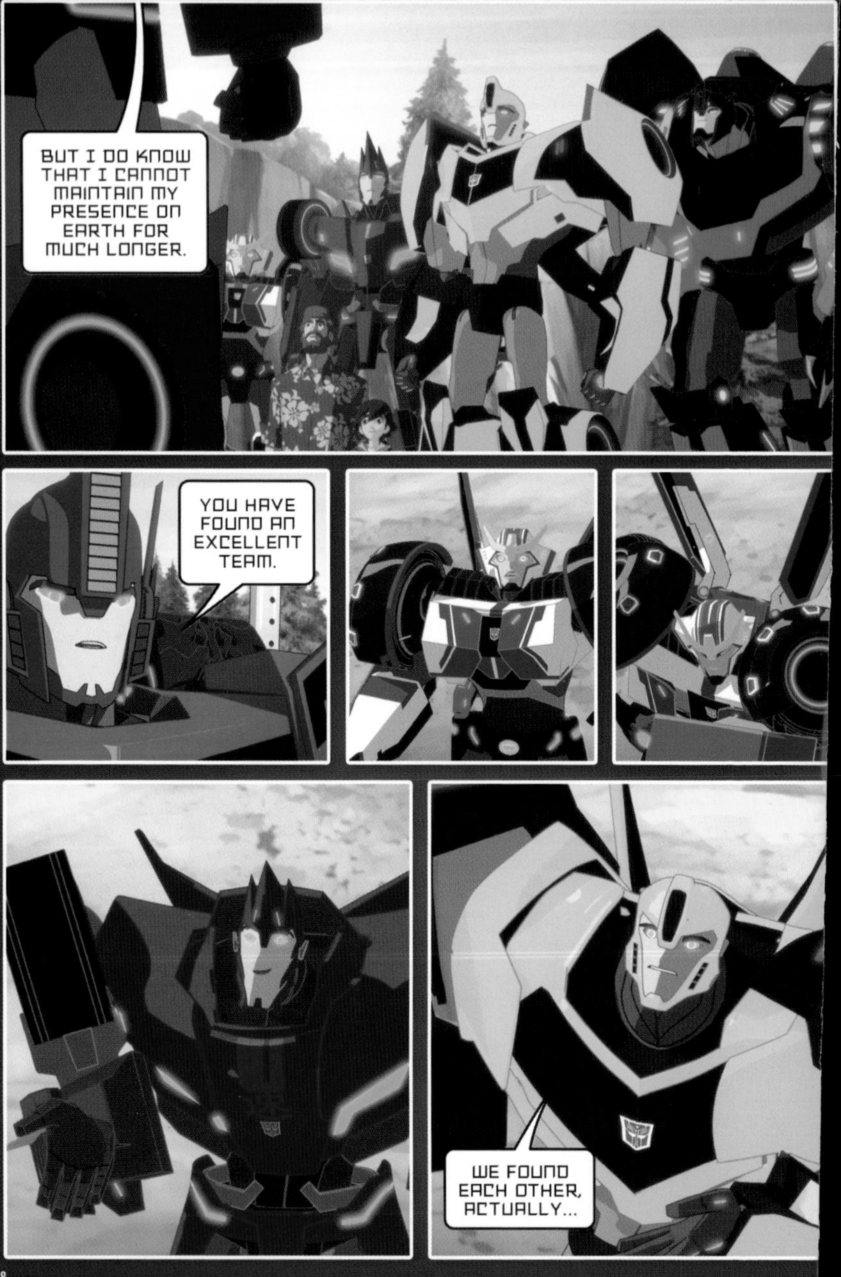
BUT I DO KNOW THAT I CANNOT MAINTAIN MY PRESENCE ON EARTH FOR MUCH LONGER.
YOU HAVE FOUND AN EXCELLENT TEAM.
WE FOUND EACH OTHER, ACTUALLY...

TOGETHER, YOU WILL CONFRONT MANY CHALLENGES. THE FORCES FACING EARTH ARE IMMENSE AND FORMIDABLE.

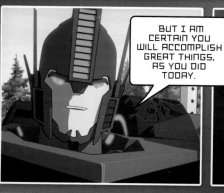

BUT I AM CERTAIN YOU WILL ACCOMPLISH GREAT THINGS, AS YOU DID TODAY.

BUT WE NEEDED YOUR HELP, OPTIMUS... WE'LL ALWAYS NEED YOUR HELP.

YOU *ARE* READY TO LEAD, BUMBLEBEE.

DO NOT DOUBT YOURSELF.

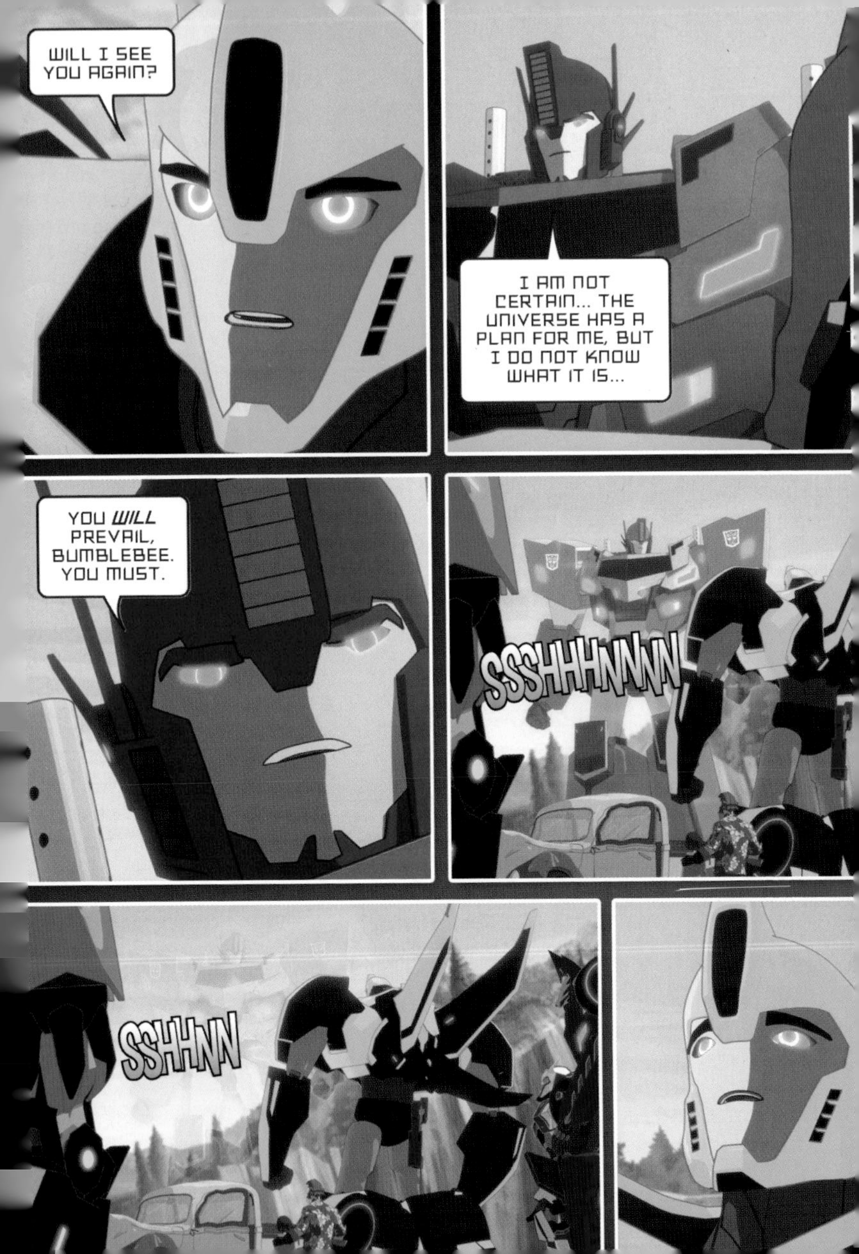

WILL I SEE YOU AGAIN?
I AM NOT CERTAIN... THE UNIVERSE HAS A PLAN FOR ME, BUT I DO NOT KNOW WHAT IT IS...
YOU *WILL* PREVAIL, BUMBLEBEE. YOU MUST.
SSHHHNNNN
SSHHNN

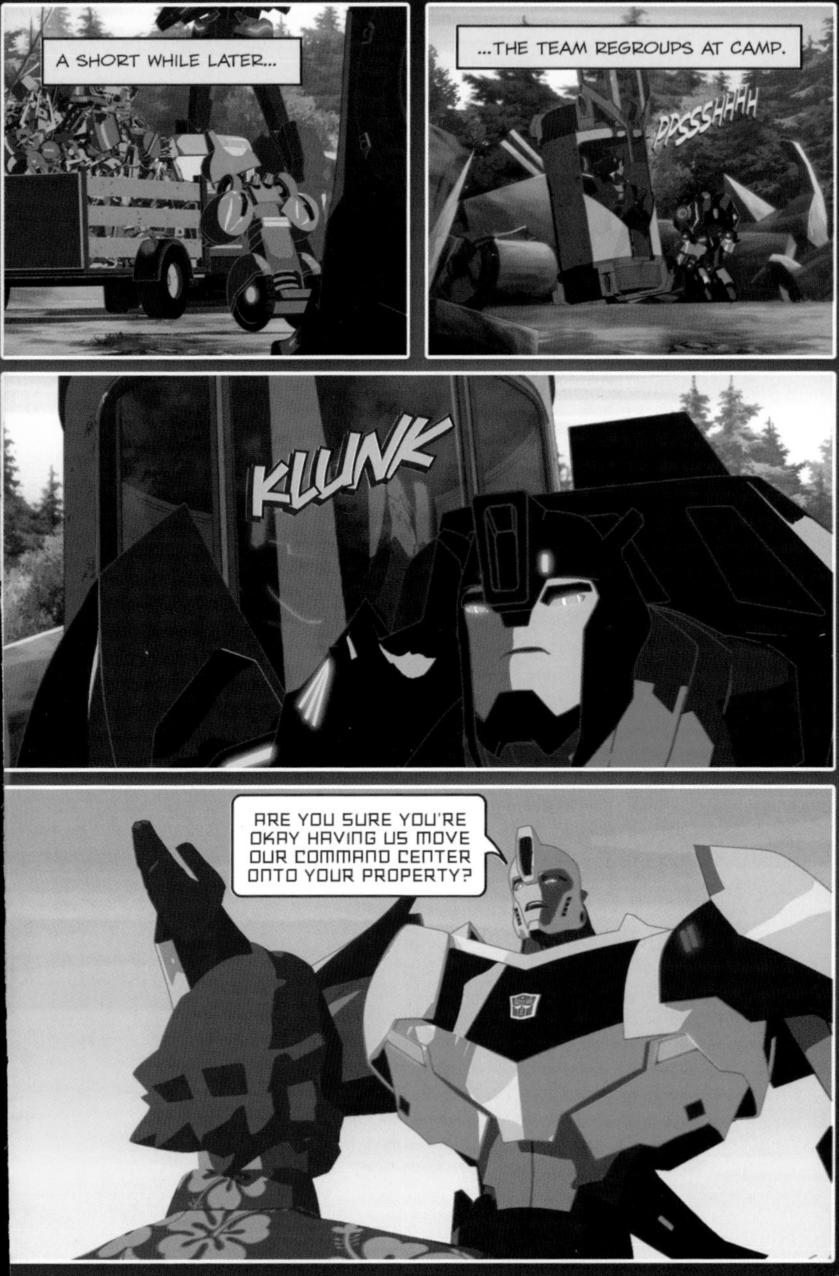
A SHORT WHILE LATER...
...THE TEAM REGROUPS AT CAMP.
PPSSSHHHH
KLUNK
ARE YOU SURE YOU'RE OKAY HAVING US MOVE OUR COMMAND CENTER ONTO YOUR PROPERTY?

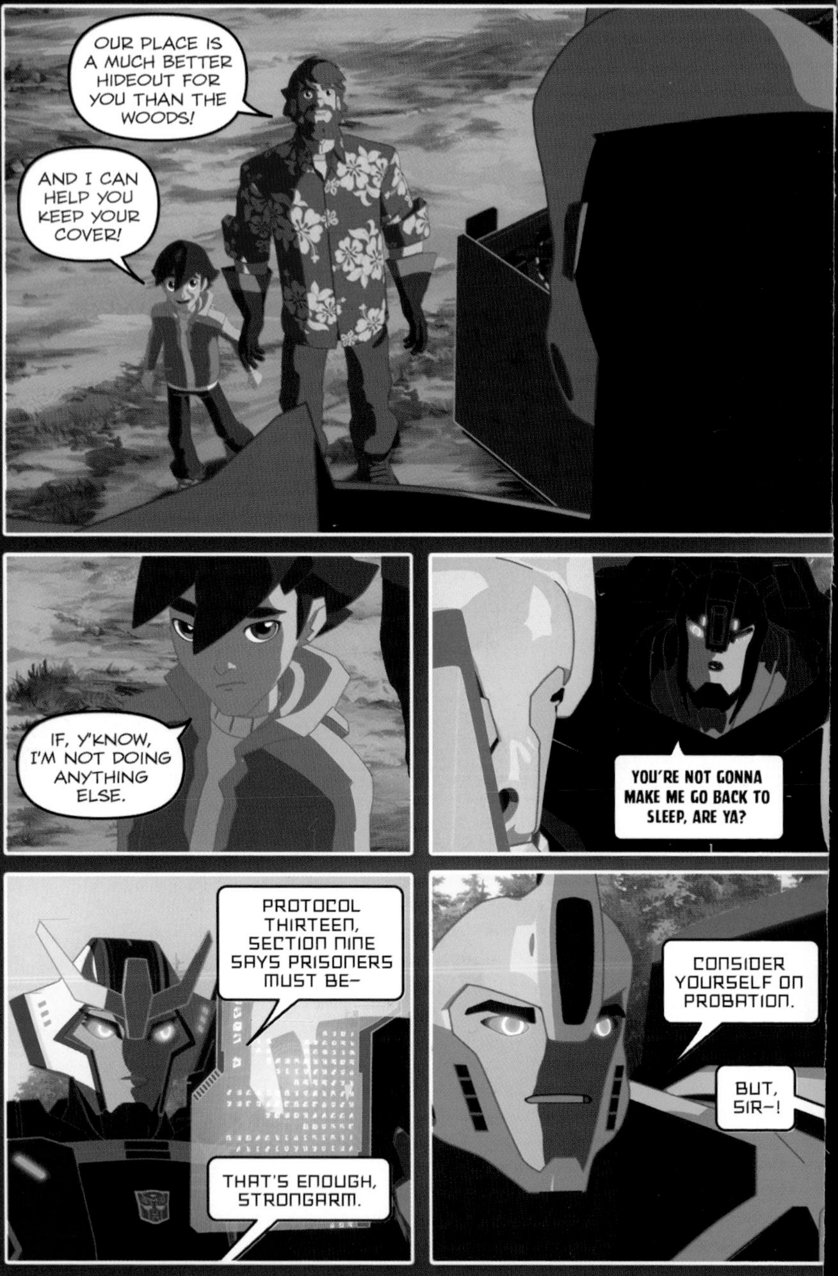
OUR PLACE IS A MUCH BETTER HIDEOUT FOR YOU THAN THE WOODS!
AND I CAN HELP YOU KEEP YOUR COVER!
IF, Y'KNOW, I'M NOT DOING ANYTHING ELSE.
YOU'RE NOT GONNA MAKE ME GO BACK TO SLEEP, ARE YA?
PROTOCOL THIRTEEN, SECTION NINE SAYS PRISONERS MUST BE–
THAT'S ENOUGH, STRONGARM.
CONSIDER YOURSELF ON PROBATION.
BUT, SIR–!

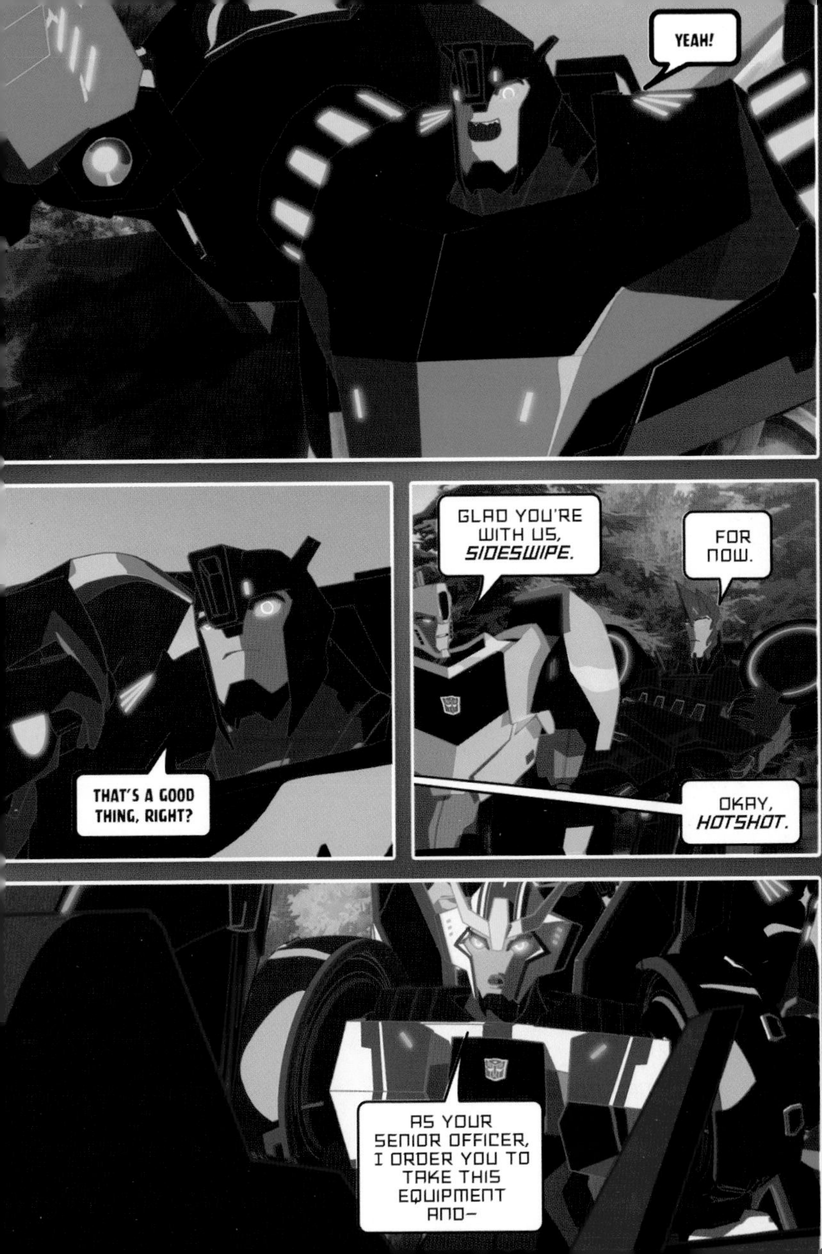
YEAH!
THAT'S A GOOD THING, RIGHT?
GLAD YOU'RE WITH US, *SIDESWIPE*.
FOR NOW.
OKAY, *HOTSHOT*.
AS YOUR SENIOR OFFICER, I ORDER YOU TO TAKE THIS EQUIPMENT AND–

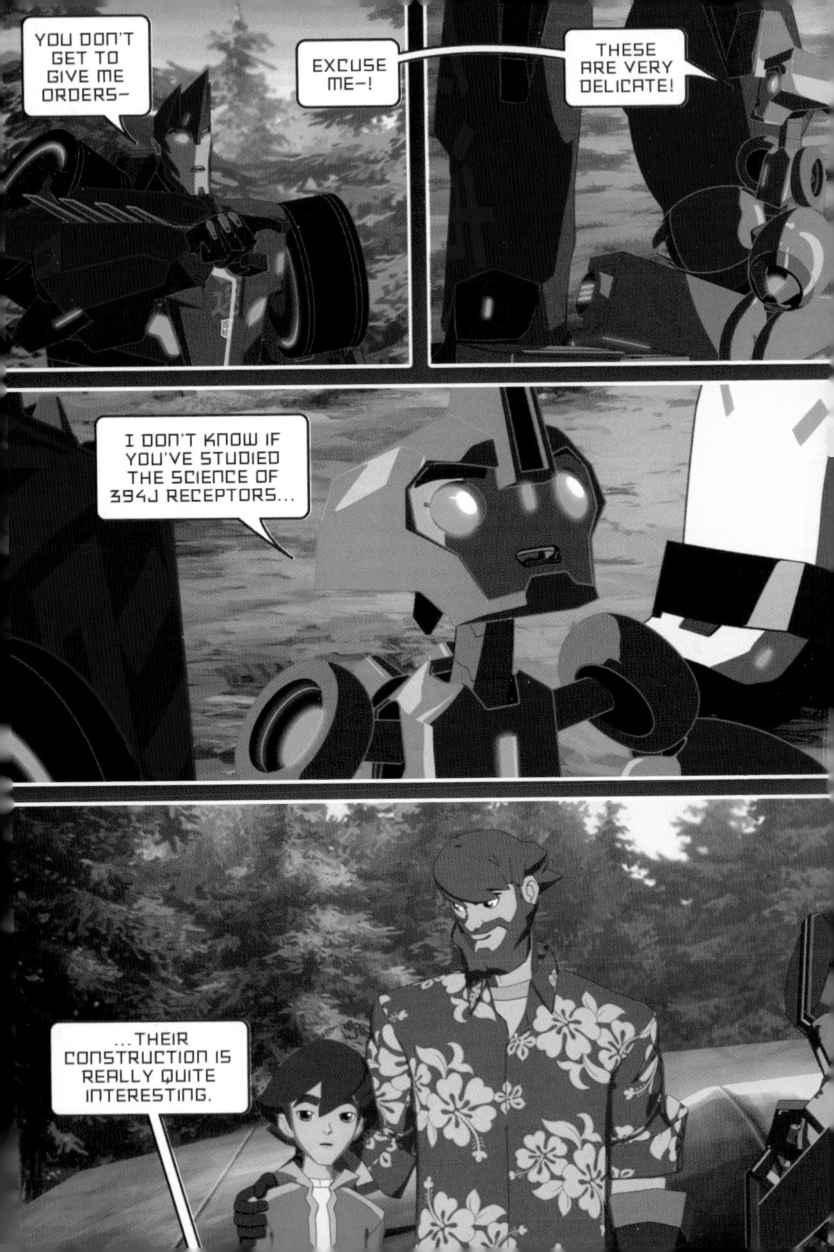
YOU DON'T GET TO GIVE ME ORDERS–
EXCUSE ME–!
THESE ARE VERY DELICATE!
I DON'T KNOW IF YOU'VE STUDIED THE SCIENCE OF 394J RECEPTORS...
...THEIR CONSTRUCTION IS REALLY QUITE INTERESTING.

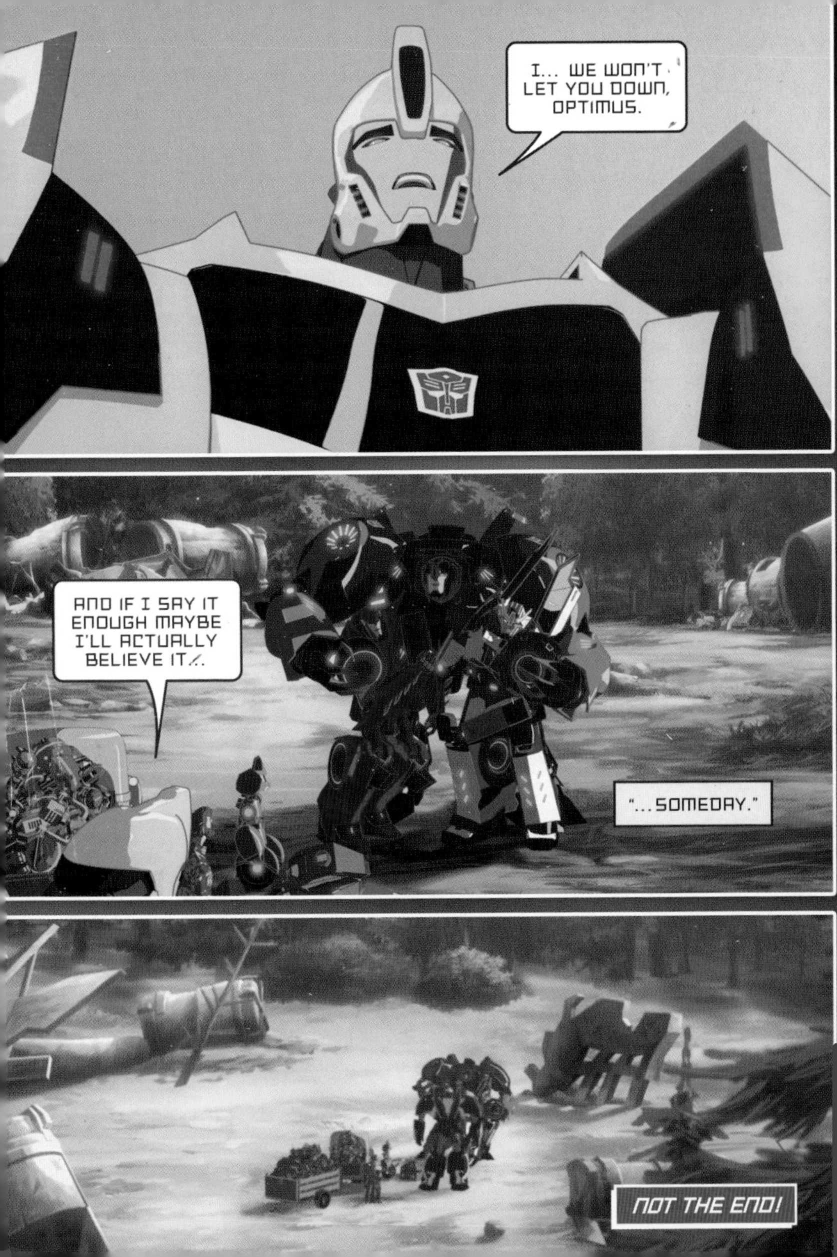
I... WE WON'T LET YOU DOWN, OPTIMUS.
AND IF I SAY IT ENOUGH MAYBE I'LL ACTUALLY BELIEVE IT...
"...SOMEDAY."
NOT THE END!

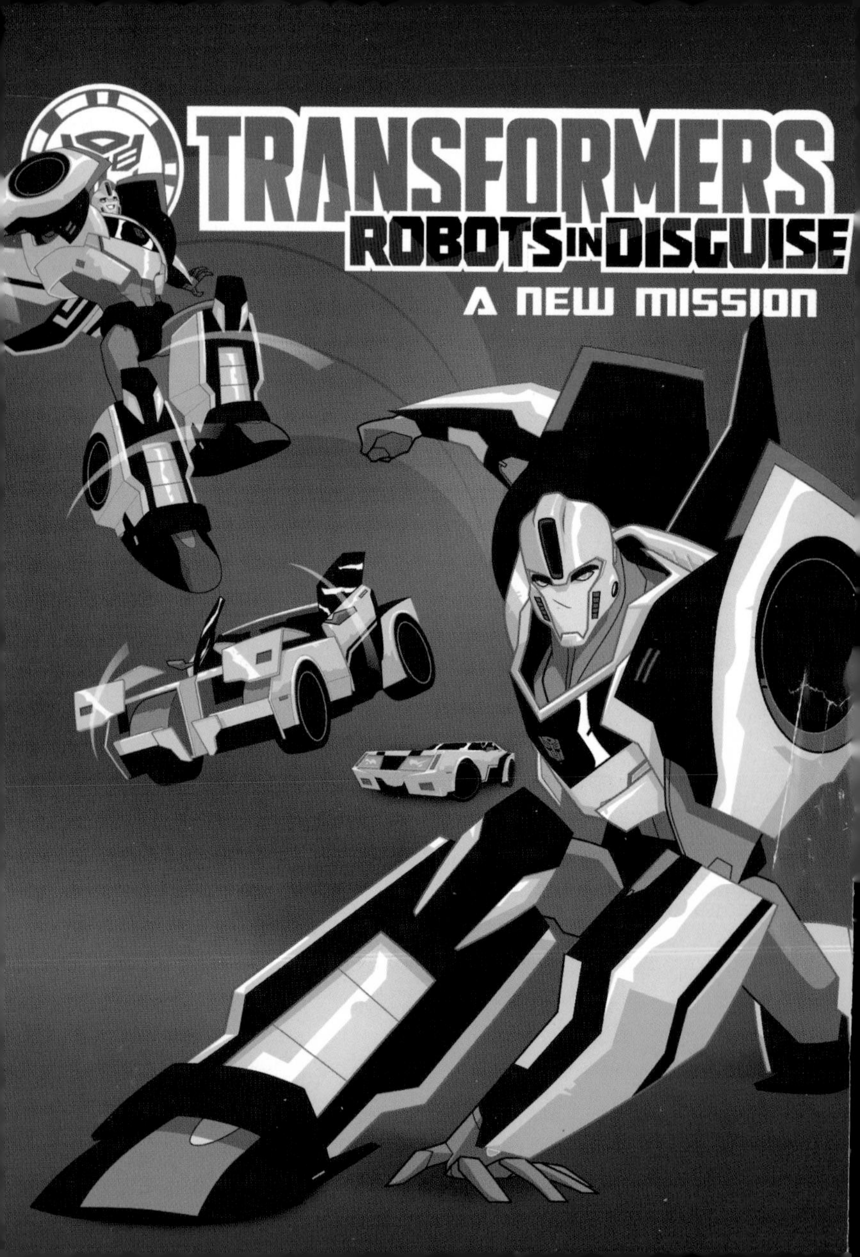
TRANSFORMERS
ROBOTS IN DISGUISE
A NEW MISSION